"The author of the Dragon Prince and Dragon Star trilogies as well as the urban fantasies *Spellbinder* and *Fire Raiser* returns to high fantasy with a captivating tale of magic, theater, politics, and love. She sets her story in a Renaissance-like world, a place recovering from a devastating war that resulted in the stringent regulation of potentially harmful magic. Verdict: Rawn's storytelling mastery, ability to create unforgettable characters, and fresh approaches to world-building and magic theory make this a must-read for an audience that extends well beyond her fans."　　　　—*Library Journal* (starred review)

"With a fully realized world and magical system, as well as a character-driven plot, this will appeal to fans of traditional fantasies like *Warbreaker* by Brandon Sanderson or Michael J. O'Sullivan's Riyria series. Highly recommended."　　　　—*Booklist*

TOR BOOKS BY MELANIE RAWN

Spellbinder
Fire Raiser

THE GLASS THORNS SERIES
Touchstone
Elsewhens
Thornlost

MELANIE RAWN

Thornlost

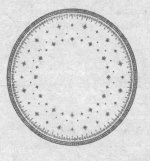

BOOK THREE OF THE GLASS THORNS

A TOM DOHERTY ASSOCIATES BOOK
NEW YORK

This is a work of fiction. All of the characters, organizations, and events portrayed in this novel are either products of the author's imagination or are used fictitiously.

THORNLOST

Copyright © 2014 by Melanie Rawn

All rights reserved.

A Tor Book
Published by Tom Doherty Associates, LLC
175 Fifth Avenue
New York, NY 10010

www.tor-forge.com

Tor® is a registered trademark of Tom Doherty Associates, LLC.

ISBN 978-0-7653-6720-4

Tor books may be purchased for educational, business, or promotional use. For information on bulk purchases, please contact the Macmillan Corporate and Premium Sales Department at 1-800-221-7945, extension 5442, or write to specialmarkets@macmillan.com.

First Edition: April 2014
First Mass Market Edition: February 2015

Printed in the United States of America

0 9 8 7 6 5 4 3 2 1

FOR

Barbara Jean Doty

AND

Jeane Relleve Caveness

Thornlost

One

REALITY INTRUDED ON Cayden's notice in the form of a flaming pig.

Seated in a place of honor in the small courtyard of Number 39, Hilldrop Crescent, he had an excellent view of every marvel of cookery that came out of Mieka Windthistle's kitchen door. Each was placed on a long trestle table for inspection by the guests, many of whom Cade didn't know. Friends and family were in attendance, of course, but there were also neighbors who knew the new residents of Number 39; those who didn't yet know them but were untroubled by the scandalous reputations of theater folk; those who were curious; and those who simply had heard that food and drink were to be had all afternoon and into the evening. Fortunately, Hilldrop wasn't a large village—a central cluster of shops and two small taverns, mayhap forty houses, most with a bit of acreage for grazing, and a tiny Chapel visited every fortnight or so by a Good Brother or Good Sister attending to the spiritual needs of the village. Simple folk they were in Hilldrop, all Human to look at, though with a hint of other races here and there, and Cade had found them friendly enough. They'd no reason not to be. There was music all afternoon, local musicians on flutes and drums thrilled beyond words to be accompanying the famous cousins Alaen and Briuly Blackpath and their lutes. Later there would be dancing round the bonfire. For now there was a parade of culinary wonders, all presented first to Cayden Silversun.

There was also thorn, but that was not offered to other guests.

Cade had been doing quite nicely all afternoon on a combination of very fine ale and one or another of Bri-shen Staindrop's mysterious concoctions of thorn. The latter was responsible for the way he saw the food. First had been a completely feathered purple swan that blinked its glassy green eyes, stretched its wings, and flew off its platter into the lazy spring afternoon. A little while later a blue and red striped lamprey—fully five feet long and glowing like a lantern lit by Wizardfire, coiled in a bed of salad greens—was sliced its entire length by a sharpened snake wielded by Mistress Mirdley. It spewed dozens of tiny yellow butterflies that followed the swan skywards. A pink porpoise was next, arched above frothing cabbage waves that shimmered white and green in the gathering dusk. The poor thing flapped its orange fins in valiant effort, but failed to join the butterflies and the swan.

Some part of Cade knew that none of these things actually happened, and that the swan, lamprey, and porpoise had all been the proper colors and carved up and eaten. Plates had been given to him, loaded with meat and appropriate garnishments. But it suited him to choose to believe in the butterflies.

The pig was different. As the sun dipped below the western hills and vague spring shadows spread through the courtyard, all the lovely prancing colors and blossoming visions dissolved when the pig was brought out on a pair of planks, ablaze from the curl in its tail to the apple in its mouth. He expected it to do something: snort rainbows out its snout, leap upright and dance a jig. (A piggy-jiggy, he told himself, vastly pleased with the rhyme; he'd make of himself a famous poet yet, see if he didn't.) At the very least, the flames ought to turn to glass and, fittingly for Touchstone, shatter.

But the flames were real, and as the rumbullion burned out, the pig did nothing more spectacular than lie there on the planks. Space was made on the table so Mistress Mirdley could carve with a knife that was definitely a knife. As a plate was piled for him, Cade's last hope was that the apple would sprout wings and flutter off to join the butterflies. The apple stayed an apple as the plate was presented to him: his Namingday, after all, and his the honor of the prime slices and garnishments. He smiled past his disappointment that the thorn had faded, and made much of praising the pig that had betrayed him by staying a pig.

With the thought of betrayal, he absolutely avoided looking at Mieka.

Mieka's mother-in-law, who had betrayed Cayden's secret to the Archduke after Mieka had drunkenly burbled it to her daughter, had been sneaking sidelong looks at him since his arrival. He could guess what she was thinking: There must be some sort of mark on him, some significance of face or glance that indicated he was something other than a Master Tregetour newly turned twenty-one years old. That which he truly was, some sign must needs betray.

That word again. With his extensive—nay, exceptional—vocabulary, he ought to be able to think up something else to call it. But a betrayal was a betrayal, just as the pig was a pig, and when Mieka came by to refill his glass, the last lingering bit of thorn mocked him by overlaying the glisker's perfect, quirky Elfen face with a snuffling swinish snout.

He realized he was writing it all in his head, and quite badly, too. For one thing, he was punning—*snout* was local colloquial for someone who betrayed his mates to the constables—and Cayden never punned. Worse, as if that triple *s* of *snuffling* and so forth weren't bad enough, the odd little almost-rhyme of *local colloquial* was just plain awful. He was a Master Tregetour. Before inflicting things like that on anyone, including himself, he ought to rip his own brains out through his nose with a hoof-pick.

It was definitely time to go home. He'd been here since the afternoon, partaking of liquor in public and Mieka's collection of thorn in private. It had been over two hours since the last pricking of mysterious powder, and Mieka hadn't been round to suggest more. Cade could stay drunk, of course. There was alcohol aplenty in the barrels of Auntie Brishen's whiskey and casks of very good locally brewed ale. But with thorn, the pig would not have disappointed him by staying a pig, and he didn't feel like dealing with reality just now. Especially not if reality included listening to another chide from Mieka's wife about polishing up her husband's accent. Sweet and delicate as the renewed entreaty was, Cade heard the impatience behind it. He bent his head over his plate of no-longer-flaming pork and wished somebody would come by with a full bottle just for him.

"Dearling, you have such a beautiful voice, and you're so brilliant in the way you think, but there are some people who won't hear anything you say, because of the way you say it."

"Anybody worth the talkin' to won't be carin' much, now, will they?"

Fundamentally, she was right. The drunker Mieka got, the fewer *g*'s attached to the ends of words and the worse his grammar became. Hadn't Cade worked to smooth out his own accent after it turned sloppy during his years at Sagemaster Emmot's Academy? He saw the adoption of slurrings and slang as a deliberate, if unrealized at the time, taunt to his mother: typical adolescent rebellion. He also understood why he had abandoned those slumping consonants and harsh vowels. Words were important to him. Vital, in fact. Slapdash speech could not but influence the way he used words on paper. Precise; controlled; things Mieka was only onstage (it never looked that way, but he was). Offstage, he was . . . Mieka. No sense trying to change him, to make him other than what he was. If that was his wife's goal, she was doomed to frustration.

"But, Mieka, when there are noble ladies present—"

Among the friends, relations, business associates, and new neighbors in the town of Hilldrop gathered in the little courtyard this night, there was only one noble lady: Cade's mother. The fact that she was here at all was another shard of reality he didn't much care for. Yet Lady Jaspiela seemed content to occupy a chair padded with velvet cushions over there under the rose trellis by the kitchen door, where she could survey the company and yet preserve a suitable aristocratic distance. And keep an eye on Derien, Cade added to himself: Derien, his adored little brother whose idea all this had been. One huge party to combine Cayden's twenty-first Namingday, the Windthistles' much delayed home-cozying, Touchstone's recent triumph with "Treasure," the completion of renovating the barn, and the arrival of Yazz and his new wife, Robel.

Oh, and a belated Namingday party for Mieka's daughter, whom Cade had glimpsed exactly once since her birth.

"If you'd just be a little more heeding—you meet so many important people now, like Her Ladyship, and what if we're invited to—"

"Be puttin' an end to it, lovie," Mieka laughed. "There's me girl!"

Somehow young Mistress Windthistle had missed the fact that Lady Jaspiela had been Mieka's devoted admirer since first they met. The girl didn't seem to be the shiniest withie in the glass baskets. But there was something else that escaped her, something more . . . *profound* wasn't the word he wanted, but he was drunk and it would have to do. There were distinctions of bloodline and social class to which certain members of the nobility clung like drifting spars after a shipwreck. Manner of dress and address, the precise depth of a bow and the particular flourish of a feathered hat . . . Mieka had long since sussed out Lady Jaspiela's rather mundane snobberies. Of course, he knew that Cayden, too, was a snob, and had teased him about it more than once. Cade's haughtiness was of the intellect, and he had scant patience with what he saw as inferior minds. Mieka claimed to be unable to decide which was worse: the innate arrogance of the aristocrat or the learned conceit of the academic.

I am what I was born, Cade told himself, and he'd much rather be born with a mind than with a mindless zeal for his own antecedents. He blessed the Lord and Lady and all the Angels and Old Gods who had given him the capacity to express himself in words, to step back from whatever was going on around him in order to observe and catalog it for possible future use, to keep himself separated from the seethe of events and emotions that he nonetheless gathered up to feed his art. Rather Vampirish, but that was how things were.

If he was what he was—so, too, was Mieka. And again Cayden wondered why he didn't find it extraordinary that he hadn't murdered the Elf for having revealed his secret. He'd even experienced an Elsewhen about it, a few days after their triumph at the Royal wedding celebrations this spring. He took it out now and examined it, allowing himself leisurely enjoyment of Mistress Caitiffer's shock. And her hatred.

{"Make no mistake, woman. I will *finish* you. I know a few things that I'm sure you'd prefer remained unknown in certain quarters."

"You know nothing!"

"Don't I?" He smiled. "You're forgetting what I am, what I can see."

The old woman's lips tightened but then she gave a little shrug. "And to ruin me, you'll offer what you know to the Archduke—"

"Good Gods! Are you truly that stupid? I don't have to offer him anything. What's going to happen . . . well, I've already seen it, you know," he said, lowering his voice as if confessing. "Just as I saw you write the letter to the Archduke that told him what I am. 'Something to His Grace's advantage,' that's how you phrased it. Purple wax to seal it. I saw it all."

"And couldn't prevent it!" she spat. "No more than you could prevent that stupid little Elf from spilling the whole tale one night, or prevent my daughter from telling me after! He was that furious with you, and that drunk, and will be again, and what won't you be able to stop him doing the next time?" Then, as if the question had been feeding on her insides, she demanded, "Why didn't you kill him? You knew what he'd done, that he'd betrayed you. You saw it all, and yet you forgave him. Why didn't you kill him?"

He laughed at her. "Kill the best glisker in the Kingdom? Oh, I don't think so. He does have his uses. And I'm not quite finished with him yet."}

Forgive—there was another interesting word. Some part of him knew that Mieka was Mieka, and would do what he would do; as well blame him for breathing. Why fight it? What Cade *would* fight for, would spend himself to the marrow of his bones fighting for, was that future where Mieka surprised him with a party on his forty-fifth Namingday. He liked taking this Elsewhen out to examine, to see again the grin on Mieka's face and the little diamond sparkling from the tip of one ear. Especially did he like the singing certainty that Touchstone would still be together, would still be wildly successful—and that Mieka would still be alive.

{"You didn't remember, did you?" Mieka challenged.

"Remember? What's all this, then? Remember what?"

Excited as a child, he gave a little bounce of delight that his surprise had turned out a surprise after all. "Happy Namingday, Cayden!"

He was right; it was past midnight, and it was his Namingday. "Forty-five!" Cade groaned. "Holy Gods, Mieka, I'm too old to still be playin' a show five nights out of every nine!"

"Oh, *I* know that," Mieka said with his most impudent grin. "But try telling it to the two thousand people out there tonight who kept screaming for more!"}

That was the Mieka he wanted to see. Which of Cade's own decisions led to that Elsewhen, he couldn't know. Not yet. Maybe not ever. He had to trust in himself, and in Mieka, to make the right choices. But that was the future he wanted, the one he would fight for.

As of tonight, he had exactly twenty-four years to wait.

Ah, but mayhap it hadn't been an Elsewhen at all, only something concocted by thorn. If that one wasn't really a possible future, then the other one, the terrifying one, couldn't be real, either.

{He stared at the words so hastily scrawled by Kearney Fairwalk, read them once, and again.

Mieka died a few minutes after midnight.

The horror was cold and raw and completely sobering. Into the huge silence his own voice said, "But I'm still here."}

The magnificent self-importance of it, the colossal arrogance: he, Cayden Silversun, was the only person who truly mattered.

Both visions had come to him while deep in thorn-induced dreams. They weren't the regular sort of Elsewhen. He couldn't decide if they had been prompted or merely enhanced by thorn. But he knew that he must accept both, or reject both. Each must be real and possible, or neither must be. He couldn't pick the one he wanted to believe and choose to ignore the other.

Someone had gone round to light torches throughout the little courtyard, and someone else had come by to refill Cade's glass when he wasn't looking. A nice courtyard, it was, and a tidy house, and the newly refurbished barn was as he remembered it from the Elsewhen that had come to him on the day Mieka bought the place. Well, as it had been—would be—before Mieka blew it up with cannon powder.

Cade drank a private toast to the absolute certainty that this vision was truly an Elsewhen, unprompted by thorn, and he wouldn't have to wait twenty-four years for it. Until it happened, he'd enjoy the prettiness of the thatched-roof cottage and its courtyard and barn, all lit up and filled with food, drink, a bonfire, garlands of beribboned flowers, laughter, music, every charming thing that celebrated a young man's coming of age.

But no gifts. Not yet, anyway. As the day had progressed into evening—lurching or flowing, depending on whether he was just drinking or whether he and Mieka had sneaked off for another sampling of thorn— he'd begun to wonder if the party itself wasn't his gift. No, there was always something special to commemorate a man's twenty-first. In that future-to-be, when he'd turn forty-five, Mieka had given him a pair of crystal wineglasses. One day he'd have to open that Elsewhen inside his head just to take a closer look at them. Blye's work, they must have been. And Blye on the sly (ah, there he was, rhyming again!), because without an official hallmark bestowed by the Glasscrafters Guild, she wasn't allowed to make anything hollow. On the other hand, in twenty-four years, things might have changed. He liked that thought, and tucked it away for further contemplation at a time when he wasn't owl-eyed.

One day he'd make the choice that led to that future of the wineglasses and the diamond earring. It was all his to decide. He wouldn't have foreseen it, otherwise, because every Elsewhen he experienced was a direct result of his own actions. The futures that he could not affect, those were the ones he never saw in advance.

The visions had changed over the years—not just their content, but the manner of their occurrence. It used to be that he'd hear a few words, glimpse a scene. As he'd got older, some of the Elsewhens became longer, more elaborate, with greater detail. The turn he'd reviewed just a little while ago, for instance: at fifteen or sixteen, there would have been just the woman and her nasty laughter. Sagemaster Emmot had told him that as the years passed and his brain matured, the visions would mature as well.

"When first this began, your mind didn't quite know what to do with it. As age and experience increase, your mind will recognize that it needs to respond in certain ways. The first time someone who will become a musician hears music, his brain hasn't yet learned how to organize the sounds, much less reproduce them. Eventually there is enough music stored in his mind that the response becomes intuitive—but it also requires the application of learned knowledge in order to manage the sounds, arrange them into comprehensible patterns. By the twenty-third year, or thereabouts, the brain has matured through a combination of instinct, experience, and education. When the visions come, you'll know precisely what they are, how to view them, how to understand them. It may even be that you will be able to control the timing of these visions."

Gods, how he hoped so. He'd almost stopped being afraid that a turn would take him when he was someplace dangerous—on the stairs, on horseback—because there seemed to be a portion of his brain that took care of his body in the here and now while the Elsewhens were sending his thoughts into the someplace and whenever. Again, the example was the way the vision of Mistress Caitiffer had first taken him: during the time it took to unfold inside his mind, he'd walked from the back door of his parents' house almost to Blye's glassworks on Criddow Close. He supposed it was a bit like Mieka's ability to comport himself with near-perfect normalcy even though the look in those eyes proclaimed that he was thorned to the tips of his delicately pointed ears.

To be sure, in the scant weeks since Touchstone's first performance of "Treasure," there had been more Elsewhens than just the one featuring Mieka's mother-in-law. But that one had been the most satisfying. He'd smiled as he made his threat, and although he wasn't sure what knowledge he had of her—or would have—that frightened her into compliance, that smile had felt very good. One of the frustrating things about an Elsewhen was that when they occurred he rarely knew what he would know in the future. During the one about his forty-fifth Namingday, for instance, there hadn't been a thought in his head about why he and Mieka shared a house. He knew that portions of it were his, and portions of it were Mieka's, but how this had come about was a mystery. Cade had gone over that one several times, trying to glean a hint or two, but he no more understood the reasons for their living arrangement than he knew what Mieka's upstairs "studio" was for. He knew it existed, because the word had been in his mind, but—would Mieka take up painting? Sculpting? Music? *Studio* implied *art,* but if the Elf had any talent other than glisking, Cade had never seen any sign of it. An odd little mystery, and one he looked forward to solving.

The various thorn he'd indulged in during the afternoon had all faded by now. The feasting was over, the dancing had begun, and Cade laughed quietly into his glass as his little brother, Derien, partnered two girls at a time: Cilka and Petrinka Windthistle. He was almost nine, the twins were almost fourteen, and he was already taller than they, already growing the long bones that were his Wizardly heritage. Just as there was the promise of a tall and elegant body in him, there was also the promise of a handsome face, with a singular sweetness about his clear brown eyes. He bowed and flourished in all the right places, and stepped lively around the two laughing white-blond Elfen girls in the movements of the dance, but didn't dare what their elder brother Jedris did. Cade nearly spluttered his drink as Jed tossed his wife in the air and caught her in strong arms, holding her high off the ground. Blye shrieked and pretended to box his ears. This party was for her, as well; five days ago she, too, had turned twenty-one. She and Jed had celebrated quietly in their home above the glassworks on Criddow Close, enjoying a scrumptious feast sent by Touchstone. Blye was growing truly pretty, Cade decided with a fond smile. Marriage agreed with her. She looked so happy, swinging high in her adoring husband's arms.

But then she was yelling in earnest, in astonishment, and pointed to the main road.

That was how Cayden discovered his Namingday present.

Not strictly just his, of course. It was for all four of them, for Touchstone.

The wagon came rumbling down the lane, pulled by two huge dun-colored horses, driven by Yazz with Robel at his side. It was a beauty. (And so, he noted, was Robel: masses of flaming red hair piled atop her head to make her even taller, a face as sternly perfect as the faces of archaic queens on well-worn coins, and a body made of just the right proportions of sturdy bones, supple muscles, and firmly rounded flesh. Scant wonder Yazz had trudged multiple times through heavy snows to win her.)

All excitement centered on the massive white wagon as it looped round the bonfire and pulled to a stop in the cobbled courtyard. Kearney Fairwalk had promised the absolute latest by way of springs and wheels and lanterns and interior comforts, and Cade supposed that all those things and more were present in abundance, but what made his heart swell to bursting was the way it had been painted. Although the bold red TOUCHSTONE on either side, down below the windows, was good advertising and a point of pride, and the symbols in black below each window made him smile (a spider, a drawn bow, a thistle, and a hawk), it was the painting between the two windows that made his jaw clench and his fists tighten. He knew who had worked it. A map of the Kingdom of Albeyn: green land, brown delineating the main highways, blue for the lakes and rivers and surrounding Ocean Sea, purple jags for the Pennynine Mountains, tiny red dots for all the stops on the Circuits, and gold for Gallantrybanks. Way down at the bottom corner was a little silver hawk with arching wings. The maker's mark.

"Do you like it? Do you?"

He looked down at his little brother's flushed, eager face. "It's—yes." He swallowed hard, and bit his lip, and smiled. "Yes, I like it."

All at once the back door opened, stairs unfolded, and Lord Fairwalk stepped cautiously down. After him, less decorous—or perhaps thirstier—leaped Vered Goldbraider and Chattim Czillag. Cade had wondered sporadically through the afternoon whether any of the Shadowshapers would accept the invitation, eventually deciding that they felt it was too much of a drive from Gallantrybanks. Well, evidently not, when Auntie Brishen's whiskey was on offer.

Cade greeted his friends, accepted their good wishes and the apologies relayed from Rauel Kevelock and Sakary Grainer, saw them provided with brimming cups of whiskey, and prepared to hear all about the marvels of the wagon. He was a trifle miffed that Touchstone wouldn't be the first to ride in it.

"Well? Waiting for an invite, are you?" Vered demanded. "Go in, have a look!"

Mieka and Jeschenar had already swarmed past and were laughing their delight. Rafcadion ambled over to make a slow, contemplative tour around the wagon while Yazz unhitched the horses. Cade could only stand there, his drink in his hand, still staring at the map.

He knew, in the abstract, that he'd been to all those places and more besides. There was the strange old mansion outside New Halt, for instance, where they'd twice played to an audience of one, and been spectacularly well paid for it. Neither was Lord Rolon Piercehand's residence, Castle Eyot, picked out on the map, the place where each group on the Royal, Ducal, and Winterly had a few days of rest between the northern and southern portions of the Circuits. It occurred to him that from now on they'd know exactly where they were at all times. What was it Mieka had said once? Something about not always being sure he knew where he was or where he was going, but nice to know where he'd been. With this map, they'd always know the place they'd just been, the place they were at, and the place they soon would be. He wasn't entirely sure how he felt about that, and couldn't have explained why. Mayhap it was because one could never tell what might happen in between.

"I agree," Chat's voice said at his side, and for a moment he wondered if he'd spoken aloud. The Shadowshapers' glisker went on, "Better to have a look inside after everyone else has poked through it. A marvel and a wonder it is, no doubt. But me, I'd like a peek at the baby."

Cade glanced round for someone to act as escort, and decided he himself would do. The crowd thinned considerably ten steps from the wagon, and it was almost quiet when they went into the house by the kitchen door. Mistress Mirdley was there, tidying up by means of an Affinity spell. Once the first plate had been cleared by hand into a rubbish bucket, the others were easy. Dirty plates were held up one by one, and what food remained on them slipped smartly off to join meat, veg, and bread already binned. The trick was to focus the spell narrowly enough so that the usable leftovers on the table and counters didn't whisk themselves into the bucket as well.

Chat greeted the Trollwife with a bow and a smile, reported that his wife and family were all well, and begged to be allowed a glimpse of the newest Windthistle. Mistress Mirdley gestured towards the hearth, where a large and ornately painted cradle stood just far enough back to provide the baby with warmth but not heat. Leaving the last few plates on the sink counter, she shuffled over to the cradle and twitched back the coverlet.

Jindra had her father's hands, with the ring and smallest fingers almost the same length, his elegant Elfen ears—and his thick black eyebrows, poor little thing, Cade thought, peering into the cradle. She had been born at Wintering. After Touchstone's return from the Winterly Circuit, he'd done the polite thing by calling at Wistly Hall with a squashy stuffed toy for the baby and flowers for her mother, but both had been sleeping, so the irises had gone into a vase and the pink bunny had gone into a basket full of other presents. Cade had had a brief glimpse of Jindra's face: closed long-lashed eyelids, a wisp of black hair straying from beneath a knitted cap—then went into the parlor for a drink, and then departed. In the intervening weeks, there had been rehearsals and performances, and once Mieka had reclaimed his house and moved his family, there'd been no convenient opportunity to come out to Hilldrop for a visit. Nice, reasonable excuses for what Cade admitted to no one but himself: that he avoided Mieka's wife with the devotion of a Nominative Brother to study of *The Consecreations*.

"Lovely!" said Chat. "A real heartbreaker!"

There was very little of her mother to be seen in Jindra's face. The nose, perhaps, and the fullness of the pursed lips, but that was all. Any doubts anyone might have had—well, that Cayden had, and never spoke about—regarding the child's paternity were obviously ludicrous. Jindra was Mieka's daughter right enough. She even had those eyes, Cade thought helplessly, as for the very first time in his presence the baby opened her eyes and looked directly at him. Big, bright, changeable eyes, blue-green-brown-gray all at once—but surely it was only imagination that made him see the same sparkle of mischief, the same golden glint of laughter.

What happened then was a thing he had heard about from besotted fathers and read about in sappy poems and seen enacted in sentimental plays. Nonsense, he'd always reckoned it, to think that there could be any sort of fundamental contact between a full-grown adult and a months-old baby.

He'd reckoned wrongly.

Mistress Mirdley stood beside him, nudged him with a shoulder. "You can touch her, you know. She won't break."

He saw his own hand reach towards Jindra's, saw her fist close around one of his fingers. She was still staring up at him. She cooed.

He'd seen her eyes before, of course. He'd seen her, snarling at her own daughter. He didn't want to remember it, but remember it he did.

{"Your grandsir was a selfish, spoiled, heartless bastard who cared about drinking, fucking, and thorn. He never gave a damn about your grandmother nor me. He did whatever he pleased with whomever it pleased him to do it with, without a thought to anyone else—"}

Jindra grasped his finger and blinked her extravagant lashes at him. Mistress Mirdley said, "Prettiest little thing, isn't she? Scant wonder, her parents being such beauties."

{The little girl watched with solemn eyes as her father staggered into the house, clutching a huge stuffed toy under one arm. He caught sight of her, laughed, tossed the brown velvet puppy at her. "F'r you, sweetest sweeting!" She made no move towards it, mistrusting of his uncertain limbs. His grin became a scowl. "Well, then? G'on! It's yours, you silly girl!" When she stayed where she was, warily silent, he kicked the toy into a corner on his way to the bottles on the sideboard and muttered, "A bitch for a bitch — just like y'r mum!"

The turn didn't surprise him, exactly. But something else followed instantly; something happened to him that was really very simple. He would do anything to keep this baby from becoming that mute, mistrustful little girl, that damaged woman. He would fight for her. Protect her. Keep her safe.

Jindra latched on to his thumb with her other fist. She smiled at him, all toothless pink gums and rosebud mouth, plump cheeks and beguiling eyes. He tried to tell himself that everybody went all gooey about babies. Hardened criminals became mush at the sight of helpless infants. Babies were tiny and fragile and defenseless and vulnerable and—and good Gods, she wasn't even *his*.

"Cade! They accepted me, I'm in!"

"Of course you are." He set aside his book and looked over the rims of his spectacles, smiling at the whirlwind of long black hair and colorful fringed shawls that danced through the drawing room. "Your father and I always said you'd be accepted, didn't we?"

"Oh, but Fa is forever telling me I can do anything—"

"—and do it perfectly the first time you try it, yes, I know." He pretended a dramatic sigh. "The regrettable incident with the carriage proves he's not completely objective about these things. But when are you going to learn that *I* am *always* right?"

And he would have to be, wouldn't he? As the second

turn vanished and he again felt Jindra's hands clinging to him, he realized he would have to make the right decision every single time.

The reminder was like a last lingering tweak of thorn in his veins: she wasn't even *his*. And, like thorn, it mocked reality.

But he knew the difference between what he dreamed and what was real. Jindra was real. All else was might-be or could-be or must-never-be.

She was one more thing to fight for, was Jindra Windthistle.

Two

"Oy!" yelled Mieka from the kitchen doorway, disturbing the touching little scene by the cradle. "C'mon out here, Cade, you'll miss it!"

The baby began to cry. Mieka was astonished when Cade rounded on him furiously, looking ready to throttle him. "Now see what you've done!"

"Mistress Mirdley will take care of her," Mieka replied with a shrug. Somebody always took care of the baby. That was what wives and sisters and mothers-in-law and all suchlike family were for. He never worried his head about it. "Hurry! Vered says—"

Chat swore and pushed past him. Mieka grabbed Cade's elbow and hauled him out into the torchlit courtyard.

"And here he is! Cayden Silversun!" bellowed Vered with a bow and a flourish. He stood on the top step of the wagon, smoothly in command of all attention. "Somebody sit him down—yeh, right there will do—" He pointed, and Mieka dragged Cade to a bench near the horse trough. "And here we all are, celebrating his twenty-first Namingday—though it's to be doubted, make no mistake. I never question a lady's word, of course, so I must accept that the lady over there is indeed his mother.

But judging by the looks of her, if she truly is his mother, Cade can't be older than thirteen!"

Mieka sniggered under his breath. Lady Jaspiela had condescended to attend the festivities as a dutiful mother ought on a son's twenty-first, but only after Mieka begged his very prettiest. Zekien Silversun's duties at the Palace took precedence over any duty to his elder son; no surprises there. Mieka had never even met the man, and had often wondered if he felt anything for Cade or Derien at all. Lady Jaspiela looked torn between pleasure at the compliment and the indignity of being singled out in this distinctly downmarket crowd. Her expression became one of frozen graciousness. Mieka held his breath, waiting for the tregetour's infamously sharp tongue to slice her to ribbons. But Vered was on his best behavior tonight. When he wished, he could charm the scales off a wyvern and have the beast begging him to take its teeth and talons, too.

"Be that as being may be," Vered went on, "me and me mates, we puzzled long and longer still how to celebrate this important occasion." He conjured a withie from one vermilion velvet sleeve. "Something appropriate, we decided." A second withie appeared from the other sleeve. "In keeping with our mutual profession, as it were." He paused, made a shocked face, and looked down at himself. His body twitched, first the shoulders, then the hips, and finally he kicked out a leg and shook a third glass twig from his trousers. Chat, below him on the bottom step, caught it as it fell and handed it up to him with an eloquent rolling of his eyes.

"Is that all he keeps in there?" a woman's voice called out, and with a cheerful leer Vered yelled back, "Wouldn't you like to find out, sweet cheeks?"

"Get on with it!" Chat admonished.

Vered bowed, then leaped from the steps and tossed

him a withie. Chat had barely sent it back to him when
Vered threw another one. The new wagon had been
placed almost in the middle of the little courtyard, and
as the pair juggled the glass back and forth, they gradually positioned themselves on either side of it until they
could no longer see each other. With each throw, the withies flew high over the wagon, caught and sent back with
a skill that had the crowd gasping, until all three were
in the air at the same time. Chat pulled a fourth withie
from his jacket, and then a fifth. He and Vered flung them
so fast now that they looked a single glittering arch over
the wagon, shattering all at once into a million shards
that brought a few screams from the audience, especially
when all the splinters caught fire.

That would have been quite enough of a show, Mieka
thought, impressed in spite of himself. But Chat and Vered
weren't finished. The arc of flames turned silver and began to writhe, scrawling two words between the courtyard and the stars: HAPPY NAMINGDAY.

Tregetour and glisker met at the wagon steps again to
accept the applause, looking thoroughly pleased with
themselves. Mieka understood the feeling. This was how
magic was supposed to be done: with joy and skill, with
easy grace, with suppleness and creativity. Some people
(Cade, for one) treated theater so seriously, so earnestly,
that the joy of the magic could go missing. Not tonight.
There was indeed a reason they called it a *play*.

Mieka poured out a pair of whiskeys and approached
his friends, clinking the pewter tankards as a substitute
for clapping his hands.

"Beholden, mate," Chat said, and drank deeply. He
wiped his mouth and his forehead, giving a gusting sigh.
"Bit tricky, that last thing. Vered can't spell, y'see."

His tregetour made a face at him and grabbed the other
tankard. "It innit that so much as the right amount of

magic for the fire and the letters. Been trying it out with shorter stuff—"

"Just think," Chat interrupted, "only three days ago, 'Sod off' was his limit!"

"—but I've got it now so I can do 'Shadowshapers' in any color I please." He took a pull at his drink. "Now all I need do is figure out how not to set the stage curtains afire."

"It was brilliant," Cade said from nearby. "If you ever lose your place on the Royal, you can hire yourselves out as advert specialists." He grinned and toasted them with his drink. "'Haymaker's Helpful Housewares' and the like."

Mieka shook his head. "Too many letters."

Vered patted his pockets. "Must be another withie around someplace—with enough left in it for a 'Fuck you'!"

After this culminating spectacle—better than fireworks at a Royal Namingday, Mieka heard somebody say— the party began to break up, and not an instant too soon, as far as he was concerned. He'd exhausted his capacity for charming the villagers about three hours ago. His wife and her mother had resisted the notion of inviting the neighbors, but experience had taught Mieka that no one sent to the constables about any ruckus if they were partaking in the ruckus themselves. (Not that this had been a wild party by anyone's standards, especially Mieka's.) It would be nice to relax with only his friends and family about the place. Last chance of it, he reminded himself, before Trials, after which everyone knew that Touchstone would be off on the Royal Circuit for the summer. He loved having a home of his own, but too often it was so quiet out here in the country that he could hear the clicking and whirring of his own thoughts. Or that poxy windmill up the road—now, *that* was clicking and whirring to drive a man mad. He was fully aware of the irony: lack of the constant background noise of the city ought to soothe his sensitive Elfen ears. But a lifetime as a Gallybanker had trained him to hear what was important and ignore everything else. In Hilldrop, there was little to compete with the baby's crying except the occasional whimpers of the pet foxling his wife had rescued from the woods, and his mother-in-law's complaints. He hadn't yet invited her to feel free to resume her city employment as a seamstress if she didn't like it here, but . . . a good thing he'd be gone soon.

He played the gracious host, standing with his wife at the gate to bid farewell to their local guests, making sure that each departing group had a candle to light the way home. Tallow candles—he wasn't about to pay for wax—and lighted with real fire, not the kind made by Wizards or Elves or Goblins. He'd seen furtive glances directed at the more obviously Elfen Windthistles, at Alaen and Briuly, and especially at Mistress Mirdley, and when Yazz and Robel arrived, there had been a collective jolt of shock. Mieka rightly judged this to be the sort of place that tolerated magical folk but didn't particularly embrace them with glad arms. He did note, though, that many of the women were friendly enough so that he needn't worry about his wife's being too lonely while he was away. She'd have her mother for company, of course, but a young woman needed companions of her own age just as a young man did.

The looks the local men gave her weren't as pleasing to him. Well, they *were,* but they really weren't. He tightened his arm around her shoulders, and she leaned trustingly into his body. There was fierce pride in knowing that the most beautiful girl in the Kingdom of Albeyn belonged to him. Every man who gave her a look envied him. But they had no business giving her a look or anything else. She belonged to *him*.

At last they were all gone and he was free to supply himself with a fresh glass of Auntie Brishen's finest. He dragged a chair near the bonfire and sprawled, listening as the house and courtyard quieted down. The Blackpath cousins had taken a hire-hack back to town. Mieka's parents and siblings would be staying the night and taking the public coach in the morning. He was hoping Cade would linger as well, but suspected Lady Jaspiela would require him to escort her and Derien home to Redpebble Square. He missed talking with Quill. Plenty of time to catch each other up at Trials and then on the Royal, he reminded himself. Unless they spent the whole time rehearsing some new playlet, which was entirely likely. Never one to bask in accolades more than a fortnight old, Cade would have some new idea to share with Touchstone, something to work on and argue over until they were ready to go for each other's throats before Mieka laughed them out of it. He grinned happily to himself. Gods, how he loved being a player!

"Did I hear that Alaen keeps stopping by?"

He glanced up at Chat and nodded. "Just the once. Se'ennight ago, thereabouts. Drunk, thorned to the eyeballs—"

"Let me guess—crying over Chirene," Vered interrupted, seating himself on a milking stool. Jed and Jez had found some odd things lying about in dozens of pieces when they worked on the barn, including the carved and painted wooden cradle Jindra slept in.

"Moaning like a cat about to yark," Mieka confirmed. "Thought she and Sakary were still living here, didn't he."

"Silly git." Chat hauled another chair over and straddled it, arms folded atop the ladderback. "He's taken to lurking round our rehearsals, befriending Sakary. Every once in a while they go home together for tea."

"You mean he doesn't *know*?"

Vered shrugged. "I think he thinks on it as her due. Beautiful women attract admirers—like a fine horse, or a hunting dog. Increases their value."

"She'd never throw him over for a skint musician," Chat stated. "And everybody knows it."

"Everybody except Alaen, of course." Cade joined them and stole Mieka's whiskey. After taking a healthy swig, he passed it back and went on, "He might not always be broke, y'know."

"Now that the Oakapples have been polished up again?" Vered snorted. "Welcomed all his kin with cuddles and kisses, has His Lordship? Everyone with half a claim rushing to his door, ready at last to admit to the family name for a share in the family wealth!"

Mieka alone knew what Cade had really alluded to: the true location of the Treasure. Touchstone knew where it was. The Rights of the Fae were there for the taking, a necklace and a crown—and what wouldn't King Meredan pay to get his hands on what one of his ancestors had been denied? Cade's opinion was that the Rights were mostly meaningless nowadays, mere historical curiosities, for the Fae had disdained the Kingdom these many centuries now for their own lands, only occasionally venturing into the world everyone else lived in. It wasn't as if they'd accept just anyone who wore the crown as their king. Rafe, however, wasn't so certain about the simple heirloom value. What if, he proposed, the Rights could bring the Fae to heel? Meredan could crown himself King of the Fae, and they'd have to come out of the Brightlands and bring with them all the magic they'd taken with them. Would that magic then be at Meredan's service? If so, what would he do with it?

Cade had looked startled by these notions, then shrugged. From what he'd seen of his great-great-whatever-grandmother, who'd told him the real story of how the Rights had come to be hidden, the Fae served no one but the Fae themselves.

Cade believed, and Mieka agreed with him, that the symbolism was all that remained. But to gain that symbolism, the King might pay a truly obscene amount of money. It could be Alaen's if he was of a mind to go find the Rights, which hinged on how much attention he'd paid to Touchstone's performance, whether he'd connect the old family stories he and his cousin Briuly had heard with what he'd seen, and the chances of his being distracted from hopeless yearning after Chirene. Mieka wondered if the prospect of all that coin piled up in a bank would tempt the lady from her husband and children. He didn't know her well enough to judge, but the possibility might goad Alaen into action.

Cade was determined that the staggeringly rich Lord Oakapple should not benefit by the finding of the Rights. He had his good name back, and that ought to be enough for him. Mieka didn't much care one way or the other who ended up with the stuff, except that he'd like to see the things for real. Just to make sure he'd got them right onstage. Cade had described them intricately from his glimpse in the Elsewhen, but—

"Very clever of you," Vered was saying, "to work it all out, no doubting. But it wasn't Alaen or Briuly or any of the other Blackpaths or whichever relations did it, 'twas Cade. If anyone's to be rewarded—" As Cade gave him an innocent smile, Vered whistled between his teeth. "How much?"

"Why, what a very ill-bred question, Master Goldbraider!"

"It was a commission, remember," Mieka put in help-fully. "We did the job of it, he had to pay us."

And quite handsomely, too. Cade had got extra, of course, but the rest of Touchstone had profited as well. Mieka's gaze strayed to the remodeled barn that was the direct result of the heavy purses Lord Oakapple—weeping with gratitude—had presented to them. Jeska had used his to rent very nice lodgings in a very nice part of Gallantrybanks. Rafe's had gone into his savings. He and Crisiant were perfectly comfortable for now with their rooms above the Threadchaser bakery, but eventually they'd have children and Rafe would buy a house. Mieka still didn't know what Cade planned to do with his earnings. He knew that the height of Cade's ambition was to move out of Redpebble Square and into his own flat, but had heard nothing to indicate he'd even begun looking for a place yet.

Now that he was twenty-one, of course, Cade would be coming into the money his grandsir had left him. That explained it, Mieka told himself. Cade had been waiting for the whole pile, at which point he'd buy himself a grand mansion and one would need a signed-sealed-and-beribboned invitation to get past the foot-man. Foot*men*, he amended, to fetch and carry, and lots of pretty maidservants to clean up the clutter, a librarian to put all the books back in order after a research binge, a coachman to drive a shiny new carriage, and a groom for the horses—and please all the Gods that Quill wouldn't pester him again about learning how to ride—

"Mieka? Mieka!"

He started, nearly dropped his drink. "Yeh? What?"

"Look at that!" Chat sniggered. "Answers to his name! Good puppy!"

"Is he lead-trained yet, for walkies?" Vered asked.

"Not even fully house-trained," Cade told them. When Mieka opened his mouth to complain, Cade pointed a finger at him. "Shut it, or I'll show them that rug you brought back from the Continent last year and tell them why it needed cleaning. Mieka, our colleagues have made the observation that the old version of 'Treasure' will need some rewriting before anyone else can do it at Trials from now on. Shall we distribute our script and performance notes?"

Mieka sucked in an outraged breath as Chat said very earnestly, "Think of the rest of us poor sods, floundering about the Fliting Hall stage, trying to remember the fine distinctions Touchstone gave to the piece—"

"Lacking the specifics," agreed Vered, "we'd all make fools of ourselves. And it's only right and proper for you to share. You're the ones ruined the damned thing for the rest of us. We can never do the old version again."

Mieka struggled not to snarl. No player ever shared his folio. No glisker ever revealed his color coding for the glass baskets and withies, no masquer ever disclosed his performance notes, no fettler ever gave away his written annotations on the scripts. And most especially no tregetour ever distributed free copies of a play for all the world to see.

"Of all the bloody cheek!" Then he saw that Cade was barely keeping laughter in check, and knew he was being teased. He swallowed hard, then managed, "Well, can't see the harm in it. It ain't as if anybody could do it the way we do it, right? But you're welcome to try!"

"What I'm thinking," said Rafe from just beyond the firelight, "is that they ought to retire the thing."

Jeska had wandered up, and was nodding. "Or have no one but us do it at Trials from now on. No more sweats over mayhap drawing something horrible. Guaranteed Royal Circuit for us, every time."

"What *I'm* thinking," Vered mused, "is that it's nonsense to base Trials on the old plays at all. How often do we do any of them on the circuits? Never! Or almost," he amended. "We play what sells, and what we make on our own, and none of the Thirteen has much to do with anything anymore—except at Trials."

"The Stewards would have a collective seizure," Cade remarked, but there was that in his eyes which meant he was already envisioning it, and liking what he saw.

Evidently Rafe wasn't so sure. "If we all did what we liked at Trials, how would they judge? At least the Thirteen give a benchmark of sorts—"

"They'd have to judge us on our best," Chat said. "Not on whether we can make something good out of what everybody knows isn't much more than warmed-over crap."

Touchstone's initial reputation had come from making something spectacular out of "The Dragon," and they had just done the same with "Treasure." But the idea of tossing out all those others was intoxicating. Never having to rehearse the deathly boring Second Peril again—

"This notion of judging, and ranks on the circuits," said Vered, shaking his head. "I'm not much liking it anymore, anyways." Then he tossed back the rest of his drink and bounded to his feet, swaying a little. "Miek, old son, would you happen to have a blanket or three and a spare pile of hay? I've a sudden longing to relive the simple rustic joys of our early years as destitute traveling players."

A little gasp made Mieka turn. His wife stood there with a tray of fresh drinks, scarlet-faced and scandalized. "Oh, no! We've beds to spare! We never would have invited—I mean, we'd never ask people like *you* to our house without—"

"Soothe yourself, girl." Mieka grinned. "If they're pining for the memories, who are we to deny them?"

"Talking of beds," Cade said, "I heard the Minster chime not long ago, and it's time I escorted my mother and brother and Mistress Mirdley to their own beds in Gallybanks." He rose and bowed—perfectly steady, even with the quantities of alcohol and thorn he'd imbibed today. Mieka was impressed. "I'm forever beholden to you, Mistress Windthistle, for my wonderful Namingday party."

"But I thought you'd stay here!" Mieka whined. "I'd planned for us four to sleep in the new wagon!"

"Plenty of time for that," Vered reminded him. "In fact, Chat and I will be glad to try out the beds for you—no, Mistress, don't worry your lovely head for an instant. It's our duty to our fellow players, to make sure their wagon is at least half as comfortable as our own."

His wife's flawless forehead wrinkled in a frown. Not really seeing the problem, Mieka was further confused when Cade joined her in looking dissatisfied.

"We'll be entirely happy in the wagon," seconded Chat. "Please don't trouble yourself."

"All settled, then?" Vered tossed back his shaggy fair hair, beamed a smile at them, snagged his glisker's elbow, and made for the house. "Getting a smidgeon chill out here—time for the hearth within the home for a last few rounds. G'night, Cade!"

"He'll be useless tomorrow," Cade predicted, watching them go.

"He always is," agreed Mieka, "after more than two cups of anything stronger than wine. Are you sure you won't stay?"

"Beholden, but no. Again, Mistress, I'm in your debt. It was an excellent day." When Mieka pouted, Cade sighed with exaggerated patience. "Kearney was kind enough to bring my mother in his carriage, but he lives across town from Redpebble and even if we leave right now, it'll be past midnight before his horses get home and stabled."

Mieka followed him into the house to collect Derien, Lady Jaspiela, and Mistress Mirdley. Vered was right: The spring evening had cooled considerably, and there was a fire going in the drawing room hearth, with much of his family grouped round it. He cheered up at the sight. This was what a home ought to be: warmed by liquor and firelight, noisy with the laughter of guests he enjoyed. If only he could've persuaded Cayden to linger, it would all have been perfect.

The change in temperature from outside to inside reminded him—finally—of his Namingday gift for Cade. Weaving his way through the crowd, he scurried down the hall to his bedchamber and rummaged about in the tall oaken cupboard that had been a wedding present from Jed and Blye. Moments later he had wrestled the big muslin-wrapped package from its hiding place.

Anticipating Cade's move into his own digs, Mieka had designed, and his wife and her mother had made, a counterpane. Well, *designed* probably wasn't the right word; he'd told them his idea, and they'd executed it. The quilted coverlet was thickly embroidered with a pattern of white goose-feather quills on a dark blue background. The border featured little bottles of ink in every color imaginable, with comical splotches here and there to show it had been spilled. And at the writing end of one feather was a tiny silver teardrop charm to symbolize the magic Cayden created with his words. How anyone, even accomplished needlewomen like his wife and her mother, could take silks and threads and craft something so wonderful was beyond his understanding. But probably people said the same thing about what his father did when making a lute, or what Mieka himself did with the magic Cade gave him in the withies.

The carriage had pulled round in front of the house, and everyone but Cade had climbed into it. Mieka's mother, with the three-year-olds Jorie and Tavier drowsing in her arms, one on each hip, was supervising the loading of a hamper, but doing it quietly. Mistress Mirdley had helped with the cooking, and in all fairness should take some of it home with her. Besides, more food remained than even the tribe of Windthistles could eat, and it was only sensible to make sure none of it went to waste. Mieka knew that these considerations were neither here nor there nor anywhere else to Lady Jaspiela's way of thinking. She would take offense at any implication that other people's leftovers were needed to feed her household. So Mieka had had a brief word with his mother earlier, and she had nodded understanding.

"A proud woman, she is," Mishia Windthistle had sighed. "One could wish she'd unbend enough to say how proud she is of Cayden . . . oh, she is, and no mistaking it," she'd added when Mieka stared at her. "How could any mother not be priding herself on a son like that?"

There were mothers, and then there were mothers, as Mieka knew very well. But he didn't belabor the point. Now, as Jeska and Rafe hugged their tregetour farewell for the night, and Lady Jaspiela raised her noble voice impatiently, Mieka sighed a sigh of his own. One day the woman might admit she was proud of her elder son. He didn't plan to sit up nights waiting for it.

"Quill!" He saw his friend turn towards him, and heaved the package. Cade barely caught it. "For if you get cold," Mieka told him.

Rafe pretended amazement. "There's a *girl* tied up in there?"

Crisiant gave her husband a thoughtful glance. "Cade has always liked them pocket-sized, hasn't he?"

Cade made a face at her and undid the ribbon. The counterpane unwrapped itself. Mieka doubled over laughing as Cade struggled to keep it off the ground. Jeska cowered back in mock horror, yelling, "It's alive!"

"A sword!" Rafe called out. "A knife! A toasting fork! Anything to stab it before it eats my tregetour!"

"Don't be so bleedin' silly!" Mieka chided. "Not enough meat on him to tempt a starving cat."

Cade eventually wrestled most of the slippery silk into his arms. He wore a look of comical helplessness—quite deliberate, Mieka knew. Quite the entertainer himself at times, was Cayden Silversun.

Mieka clucked his tongue against his teeth as he tucked up a few loose folds. "Clumperton. It's a miracle, it is, that you can put one foot in front of the other and not fall over. Go on, get in and spread that over your mother and brother before they freeze. Happy Namingday, Quill!"

The gray eyes glinted merrily at him. "And to think I've a whole year and more to think up something for *your* twenty-first!"

"I tremble in terror, O Great Tregetour," Mieka assured him.

"You'd damned well better!"

A few minutes later the counterpane had been duly deployed to keep the carriage's occupants warm. Kearney was full of praise for its beauty and the skill of its makers. Lady Jaspiela unbent enough to finger the de-

sign of feathers and nod approval. Derien was already
asleep on Mistress Mirdley's lap. Mieka waved them
onto the road, then returned to the courtyard.

It was a rather abrupt end to the party. Yazz had
doused the bonfire. Robel was stacking chairs, and
Mieka spent a minute or two admiring the swish and
rustle of her skirts and the luscious figure beneath them.
Jezael was consolidating the remains of three barrels
of ale into one, and Mieka offered to help by draining
one of them down his own throat. His elder brother
snorted.

"Help me with these or I'll drown you in one of them—
the way Mum should've done to you at birth."

"That I was born at all is your fault, yours and Jed's,"
he retorted, and helped Jez heft a barrel. "You turned
out so revoltingly adorable that she wanted more. How
was poor Mum to know she'd get me and Jinsie instead?"

"It's a wonderment to me that Cilka and Petrinka
and then Tavier and Jorie came along, then. And I've no
idea in the world why your little Jindra is such a darling, with you for a sire. Are you planning on more? Or
are you scared you might get something like *you* next
time?"

The barrel safely drained, Mieka pushed it into his
brother's massive chest. It made no impression, other
than to make him grunt. Jez let it fall, then reached over
and snagged Mieka by his collar, lifting him effortlessly
a few inches off the ground.

"Now, what was that you were trying to say, little
brother? Something along the lines of 'I'm sorry, Jez'
and 'You're always right, Jez'?"

He barely had time to kick and flail a bit, as had been
usual with this game since they were children, when Jez
abruptly released him. He landed on his bum on the

cobblestones, and glared up—way up—at his brother. "Is this any way to treat a famous Master Glisker who's celebrated and praised the length and width of Albeyn?"

But Jezael wasn't looking at him. He was smiling in the direction of the house as he murmured, "I'll finish you off later, Your Lordship." Then, more loudly: "Time to put your husband to bed, I think—he's falling-down drunk!"

"I only fell down because you dropped me!" He scrambled to his feet and brushed himself off, then seized his wife around the waist and kissed her. She resisted, so he kissed her harder. When she yielded, he relented, and hugged her. "You should've come with me to see the Silversuns off."

"I couldn't. Oh, Mieka, I just couldn't, not after what was said." He racked his memory for some unseemliness, but she spared him the trouble by rushing on. "It's just not done, to invite someone to a celebration so far from the city and then—and then someone implying we've not enough beds for them—"

"Oh, that." He shook his head. "Don't anguish yourself about it, girl."

"But I so much wanted Lady Jaspiela to like us—"

"Lady Jaspiela likes us fine. Would she have come today if she didn't?"

"But, Mieka—"

"Enough." He knew where this conversation was headed. She wanted Lady Jaspiela to like them enough to invite them to Redpebble Square, preferably when there were other highborns about. As if there were any fun to be had in a swarm of nobles—except to scandalize them. Still, because he knew it was important to her, he added, "While we're at Trials, why don't you visit at Wistly for a few days? You could go see Blye and Jed, and just happen to drop in on Lady Jaspiela, and—"

"Without an invitation? It's not done, Mieka, it just is not *done*!"

Annoyed, he shrugged and let her go. "Just as you fancy. Let's get some mulled ale going in the drawing room, shall we? The night's gone chill."

Three

GALLANTRYBANKS WAS A long drive from Hilldrop.
A *very* long drive.

The trip wouldn't have been half so tedious if Derien
had been awake. Circumspect and manners-minding as
the brothers usually were around their mother, still there
would have been interesting conversation. As it was, the
boy slept in Mistress Mirdley's lap, only his tousled dark
hair visible amid the billowing counterpane. It fell therefore to Cade to make polite social mouthings from time
to time.

Kearney Fairwalk was no help. When it came to His
Lordship, Lady Jaspiela swung between two extremes:
respect for his ancient name and title, and total incom-
prehension of why he had chosen to amuse his noble
self by managing a theater group. Depending on which
attitude she exhibited at any given time, Kearney either
obliged her with Court gossip or shut up completely. Tonight was one of the silent times. He had, after all, just
delivered the wagon in which her elder son would be
traipsing across Albeyn making an exhibition of himself.
After apologizing for any discomfort she might experience on the drive back to Gallantrybanks, he subsided

into the carriage's farthest corner and to all appearances went to sleep.

So, after a few miles, it was up to Cade to start a conversation. He expressed his appreciation that his mother had taken the trouble to come all this way for his Namingday party. She answered that it had indeed been tiring. A few minutes later he remarked on how nice Mieka's neighbors seemed to be. She replied that she hadn't spoken to any of them. Another mile or two went by before he mentioned that Mieka's little daughter was a very pretty child.

Lady Jaspiela shrugged, a rustling of silk in the darkness of the carriage. "They had best hope that she grows up prettily enough to compensate for her circumstances. One can scarcely expect a worthwhile marriage for the daughter of a theater player and a seamstress."

"Windthistle is one of the oldest Elfen names there is."

"A meaningless consideration, after this descent into the working classes."

Though he couldn't see her face, he knew precisely which of her many condescending expressions she would be wearing. "*I'm* a theater player," he said. Then, most unwisely: "*I'm* working class."

"No, you are not. There is a difference, Cayden, between how a gentleman amuses himself in his youth and what a person must do to keep a roof over his head."

A slight, involuntary movement of Kearney's shoulders told Cade that he was faking sleep. The grunt and sigh that followed signaled that he intended to go on faking; no gentleman would make such boorish noises while conscious, and therefore His Lordship *must* be asleep. Cade rather admired the shrewdness of the deception, and for the rest of the drive kept his mouth shut.

At some point along the rest of the silent way home

he realized that his mother had given him the first hint of what was to come. And it came only minutes after leaving the elegant confines of Lord Fairwalk's carriage for the vestibule of Number Eight, Redpebble Square. Lady Jaspiela told Mistress Mirdley to take Derien up to bed, then turned to Cade.

"A few moments of your time, please, Cayden."

He knew what she wanted to talk about. Money. More to the point, *his* money, the inheritance from his father's father, who'd been a Master Fettler back in the day. She was about to tell Cayden that because he was now financially independent, he need not continue in the theater. She would mention the advantages of his acquaintance with Princess Miriuzca, Prince Ashgar's bride. She would remind him of his father's position at Court and of her own noble antecedents, and end with the observation that whereas he'd enjoyed a certain amount of success, it was time he settled to a profession worthier of his ancestors than that of Master Tregetour.

He was right about the money, but wrong about everything else.

She led him into the drawing room. One of the footmen had made up a nice little fire against the spring evening's chill, and left a long-necked bottle of Colvado brandy and a pair of snifters on a side table. This told him she had been planning this discussion and had left orders for her comfort. Cade poured liquor into each glass, presented her with one, and waited while she seated herself with an instinctively well-designed arrangement of skirts. Some portion of his mind made note of the precision of the drapery for use onstage; the little details of a performance always meant so much.

"It's late, so I will be brief," she said. "At this point in your life, your father and I had expected that you would be decently established in a profession, perhaps even advantageously married to a young woman of rank and distinction. We—"

"I hadn't expected to still be living at home, either."

"You will have the courtesy to let me finish, Cayden. We had thought that by this time we would be turning our entire efforts to Derien, to his education and future prospects. As it happens, he has developed a curiosity about foreign lands—very much due to your travels last year, and I am grateful to you for sparking this interest. The favor shown you by the Princess is another thing I had not expected, but is also gratifying. And you have made other contacts among the nobility which I know *you* do not care to use, but which will be essential to your brother. With the proper training and connections, Derien may well become a Royal envoy. But such things come expensive." She sipped at her brandy and set the glass aside. "He will be nine years old this summer. By this autumn I hope to see him enrolled in the King's College rather than the littleschool he now attends. There, he will receive the best education, and make the friends necessary for his advancement." She paused again. "We must wait, of course, for the particular style of his magic to appear. But in anticipation of that day, your father and I wish to see him placed as favorably as possible."

He drank brandy and waited for her to go on.

"Your father's father was under the impression, as was I, that you would be my only offspring. Cadriel Silversun died years before Derien was born. Thus no provision was made for another son or daughter. The whole of his legacy, while not vast by certain standards, is now yours." She looked him directly in the eyes. Hers were dark and determined, and he saw that there were a few tiny dry lines at their corners. "I am certain you understand what I am asking of you now."

He had the irrelevant thought that Derien was lucky to have been born a boy. What their mother would have done with a daughter didn't bear contemplating. Married off as young as decently possible to some rich, well-connected lord—if she turned out "prettily enough." If not . . . if he'd had a sister who looked like *him* . . .

"Cayden. I desire to know what you intend to do."

She wanted something from him. Something only he could give her. She was actually *asking* him rather than demanding, ordering, insisting, informing him of a decision already made. This was unprecedented. He wished he weren't so tired; he could have enjoyed it more. He finished off his brandy in one gulp—disgraceful, not to savor a fine liquor, but he wanted to get this over with.

"Share the money with Derien? Of course. On one condition."

He watched triumph blaze in her eyes, and the quick flare of angry outrage that followed it. Interesting, to see her struggle between elation that he would do as she wanted, and fury that he dared demand anything in return.

"Once the paperwork is done and the money is officially mine, it goes into a fund with two names on it, and two names only: mine and Lord Fairwalk's."

The implication sent an ugly flush into her cheeks. Once more she fought rage, and the effort shook her voice. "That is unworthy of you."

"But prudent. Be as insulted as you please, Mother. You've got what you wanted—for Derien, for his education and support." He laid a light emphasis on the name. "And as for still living here, I'll be gone at Trials soon, and then on the Ducal or Royal Circuit all summer and into the autumn, and then I'll be gone for good."

"You've found rooms?"

"Not yet." And he would have to make drastic alterations in his searchings, now that he wouldn't have his grandfather's money to spend. Lord Oakapple's purse would go only so far. Touchstone was still owed for the trip to the Continent last year, there being some contention regarding a shattered row of windows at the Princess's father's palace, but Kearney was working on that. In any event, the rooms he'd end up with would no doubt horrify her if she ever saw them, which he had every confidence she never would. "After I come back from the Circuit. Then you and Father can concentrate *every* effort on Dery." He started for the door, then swung back round. "One other stipulation. He never knows where the money came from. As far as he's concerned, you've spent years scrimping for this. Agreed?"

Through rigid lips she said, "Agreed."

With a nod, he left her and climbed the wrought-iron stairs up to the fifth floor. His bedchamber was despicably tidy. He had the urge to rip everything to shreds, smash the windows, splinter the furniture. Instead, he undressed, and before he crawled into bed gave himself a Namingday present: a night's dreamless sleep with the application of a thornful of blockweed.

* * *

"AMAZING, WASN'T IT?" Blye remarked the next afternoon. She had returned that rainy morning to Gallantrybanks with her in-laws, though Jed had stayed behind in Hilldrop to supervise the final fittings on Mieka's refurbished barn. "Lady Jaspiela Highcollar, mixing with the common folk at a country party!"

"Did she 'mix'? I never saw her 'mixing'—in fact, she told me flat out that she hadn't even spoken to any of Mieka's neighbors."

Cade handed her another glass plate from the set she was preparing for display. Forbidden by Guild rules to make anything hollow, Blye satisfied the inspectors who came round by having all manner of acceptable things for sale in the shop. Plates and platters, candleflats and windowpanes, anything that would legally justify her prosperity. Her real money was in making withies for Touchstone and the Shadowshapers—but the glass twigs were hollow, and thus officially prohibited to her. So these she made in secret. Usually Rikka Ashbottle, Blye's not-apprentice—because of course only a master crafter could have an apprentice—would be doing this polishing work, but Rikka was out running errands.

"I imagine Mieka's neighbors were too overawed to talk to Her Ladyship, but she was there, wasn't she?" Blye slanted him a smile, dark eyes gleaming beneath a fringe of white-blond hair. She held the plate over a little device made long ago by her father: a glass beaker with a cork to stopper the place where one poured in the water and a thin spout for steam to escape. She could just as easily have used a teakettle, but the beaker was prettier, all swirled about with orange and yellow. Cade had obliged her by calling up a bit of Wizardfire beneath the beaker where it rested atop a steel ring. The steam fogged the glass plate, which she handed to Cade for polishing. This worked on wineglasses, too, but of course she wasn't allowed to make those. Not officially, anyway.

"It was a real treat," Blye continued, "seeing her amongst farmers, blacksmiths, brewers, and such in their go-to-Chapel best."

"The working class. It's escaped her notice that *I'm* working class."

She made big, mocking eyes at him. "With all Touchstone's acclaim? Lord Oakapple's patronage? Lord Fairwalk? Talks with the Princess? The Highcollar and Blackswan and Mistbind in your blood?"

"We're all of us just ordinary working-class gits, Touchstone," he stated firmly. "Common everyday Gallybankers. What we have is what we earned, not what we inherited."

Which had made it remarkably painless to share the inheritance from his grandfather. And that was odd, because he'd been looking forward to it, counting on it, ever since he found out about it years and years ago. Yet here he was, keeping the bulk of it in the bank to provide for his little brother. That it was for Derien made it easy, but while thinking about it this morning, he'd realized that he felt *free*. This was even odder. Wasn't it supposed to be the other way round? *Money* was supposed to be liberating. Not having to worry about how to pay for this and that, being able to afford a fine place to live, servants, good food and excellent drink—wasn't that supposed to free up one's time and mind for nobler things? But it also would have set him apart from his partners. And he couldn't really think of that money as his, no matter what his grandfather had intended. No, better to live off what he made through his own work.

He opened his mouth to say something of the sort to Blye—not about transferring the inheritance to Dery, for only he and his mother and Kearney, and possibly his father, would ever know about that—but whatever he'd meant to say vanished when he saw she was scowling at him.

"*Ordinary?* When have you ever been *ordinary*?"

Cade had no idea what had prompted the scowl or the sharp tone of voice. "I just meant—"

"I know what you meant. D'you think that what you are and what you can do is *ordinary*? I just wish to all

the Gods that you'd stop wasting your time telling yourself and everybody else that *ordinary* is what you ought
to be or want to be. Pretending you want it is even worse,
because you don't." She set down a plate and folded her
arms, glaring up at him.

"How would you know?" he flared. "Why can't I—"
He broke off as Blye's cat, Bompstable, reacting to their
raised voices, leaped onto the counter and began pacing
between them as if on guard duty, ready to come to
Blye's defense if needed. Cade dragged his gaze from
the cat's narrowed green eyes and in a calmer tone asked,
"Why can't I have a regular kind of life? Rafe does.
And Mieka—"

"Oh, yeh, his home is just a dream come true, innit?
With that Harpy of a mother-in-law nagging him to
give up theater and find a place at Court because the new
Princess is *so* fond of Touchstone and she'd be just the
person to get him a cushy living and maybe even some
kind of title—"

"*What?*"

"You didn't know? Jez overheard her one afternoon
while he was out there working on the barn. And very
eloquent she was, too!"

Mieka Windthistle, Court flunky. If it hadn't be so
horrifying—and so close to what his mother had always
wanted for *him*—he would have laughed.

Blye was still scowling, but not so fiercely. She
stroked Bompstable, who had settled down in a furry
white lump beside her to purr. "Rafe and Crisiant are
happy, but that's because she *knows*. She understands it
all because she grew up with him, she knows what's
inside him and that if she tried to change it, he'd be less
than what he ought to be. You don't think Mieka's wife
knows him the way Crisiant knows Rafe, do you? She
hasn't the first notion of why or how he does what

he does, leave alone that he *has* to do it or become a splintered shard of himself. She loves him, that's not in question. But she wants to change him, make him into what she thinks he ought to be. She's pulling him in one direction and Touchstone is yanking him in another, and one of these days he's going to come apart and it won't be pretty to watch. He isn't *ordinary* any more than you are."

It took him a few moments to recover from all that. At length, he said, "Do you know how Jed figures out what needs doing to a building and puts it to rights? Does Mishia Windthistle understand how Hadden makes a lute?" He snorted a bitter laugh. "Does my mother know what my father's work for Prince Ashgar really is? And if she does, does she care?"

"Oh, please!" She rolled her big brown eyes. "That's not what I'm saying and you know it. How do you put your magic inside the withies? I couldn't tell you, and I *make* the damned things! But I know *you,* Cayden, how you think and what you're like inside. I know Mieka, too. And it's been obvious from the start that his wife doesn't have the slightest idea who he really is or what he needs."

"They're happy," he observed. Eventually they wouldn't be, but for now . . .

"Are they?" She gave an irritated shrug of one shoulder and pulled Bompstable into her lap. "Rafe and Crisiant are a success because she knows him down to his marrow. She understands. It's the same with Jed and me. I don't have to work anymore, did you know that? He and Jez are making enough to keep us very nicely. But I still work."

"Because you want to."

"I *need* to," she corrected. "And if that makes me a freak, so be it. I married a man who understands that I love what I do. And that I wouldn't be who I am, who he loves, if I didn't have work that I need to do. Mostly we get defined by words like daughter, sister, wife, niece—all of them words that depend on other people. It's how we define *ourselves* that's the truth of what we are. Mieka is Mishia and Hadden's son, Jindra's father, his wife's husband, and brother to that whole tribe of Windthistles, but what he truly is—that's a glisker, a player. Part of Touchstone."

"Part of something worth being part of," Cade murmured. "He's said that." And hadn't Cade himself realized last summer that Mieka truly *needed* to be onstage, performing for hundreds of people—and eventually thousands, if his Elsewhen was to be trusted?

"If he wasn't Touchstone's glisker, he'd be with some other group. Just the way you'd be writing plays and priming withies whether it's with Touchstone or somebody else. It's the way you define yourself. Through your work." She smiled a little. "What you earned, not what you inherited."

"I don't know why you think Mieka isn't happy," said Cade, frowning. "The girl is everything a man could want." He heard himself saying it and couldn't believe the words were coming out of his mouth. "Beautiful, sweet, modest—she didn't bring any money to the marriage, but who cares when a girl's that lovely?" It was all true, though, wasn't it? "She adores him, a blind man could see that. She's made a perfect home for him, given him a child—"

He broke off as Blye's face went blank as a pane of glass. Oh Gods, was that it? The one word she hadn't mentioned in her definitions was *mother*. He knew she and Jedris had been trying, thus far without success. It happened that way sometimes: the mix of races was too complex, and there'd be too much of one thing and not enough of another to make pregnancy possible. Blye was mostly Goblin, though with enough Human so she didn't look it. The Windthistles were mostly Elfen, with dollops of Piksey, Human, Wizard, Sprite, and possibly Fae. Cade had never even considered that conceiving and bearing a child might not be possible for her and Jed.

"You shouldn't worry too much about it," he said on impulse. "You haven't been married all that long, and sometimes it takes awhile—"

"I don't have any idea what you're talking about." Her tone warned him that he'd better not have any idea what he was talking about, either. He reached over to her, wanting to comfort. She shook him off and wouldn't look at him. "I think these are done," she said, pointing to the stacked and polished plates. "Rikka can arrange them when she comes in. Beholden for the help."

"Blye—"

"Go home, Cayden. Just—go home."

He gazed down at her bent fair head. Then he went home.

A slow, steady rain had dampened his shoulders and hair before he reached the back door of Number Eight. On the lowest of the three short steps was Mistress Mirdley, sheltered under the awning as she waited for the rain to fill an iron cauldron usually kept in her stillroom. Folded atop a stool on the step was the counterpane Mieka had given Cade last night.

She didn't glance up as he approached. "You'll be wondering why it already wants a wash," she said. "You didn't feel it, did you? Not any of it."

"Any of what? I was supposed to feel something?" He brushed rain off his clothes and jumped up to the top step, out of the wet.

"Wizard," she accused cryptically. From a pocket of

her apron she tugged a blue glass bottle, then a green one, then a brown one, then a clear one. "Never sense any magic but your own, do you?" she went on as she measured out careful droplets from each bottle into the virgin rainwater. Scents wafted from each: anise, bay, lavender, sage. "You'll not be remembering much from what I taught you of hedge-witchery when you were little—"

"I remember enough," he said brusquely. "I know that's not just washing water, it's for purifying."

She tucked the bottles back in her pocket and took out several more, these of silver stoppered with cork. The contents were trickled by turns into the cauldron. "Your nose reminds you. Good."

"The sense of smell is probably the most evocative," he said, quoting Sagemaster Emmot, taking refuge in rote learning just as earlier, with Blye, he had taken refuge in societal cant. "It goes directly to the brain, bypassing what you use to analyze and define what you see or hear or touch. It calls up memories—" Aware that he was babbling, he compressed his lips for a moment, then asked, "Why the clove?"

She ignored the question. "You recognize some of these from what I put into your satchel when you're off gallivanting about. Ever taken an itch from nasty sheets in those upstairs tavern rooms? Of course not. What's washed into your nightshirts protects you. Now, these others, they're things you've not been needing until now."

"Clove?" he repeated.

"Recall it from toothaches, I'd imagine," she said grimly. After stashing the silver vials, she produced a wooden spoon and crouched to stir the mix. Widdershins, he noted absently. "More to it than that, or so my old granny avowed. What you'll not have recognized is mulberry. Betony. One or two others." She looked up at him and he took an involuntary step back, his spine against the door. "It's purifying that's needed here as well as protection, and banishment, and a reverse of spells to send them back to the one who cast them."

"Spells!"

"Here." She gave him the spoon. "Keep stirring that."

Bewildered, and not knowing whether to be scornful or scared, he crouched down and circled the spoon left-wise round and round the cauldron. He knew who had made the counterpane, cut and pieced the material, embroidered all the feathers, stitched every stitch. It was ludicrous to think that there might be something dangerous about it.

A sudden glimpse of a remembered Elsewhen: slender fingers taking tiny, quick stitches in silk the color of irises, and unintelligible words chanted low and fierce as the girl worked on a gift for the Elf she so deeply desired. And then a memory: he and she in an alleyway, the gloat of triumph in her eyes that told him she was winning and knew that eventually she'd win.

No. She wouldn't dare.

Rain dripped onto his head from a hole in the awning. He cursed under his breath and shifted position, still stirring, his shirtsleeve wet to the shoulder.

But hadn't Jinsie said last year that there was magic about, some sort of spellcasting being used on Mieka—

She wouldn't *dare*.

And even if she dared, even if there was some unrightness about the counterpane, why hadn't Mistress Mirdley refused to be anywhere near it last night in the carriage?

But then he remembered that she'd gathered it around Derien and Lady Jaspiela, and not a bit of it had touched Cayden at all.

A little shower of sea salt went into the cauldron, startling him. Sprigs of mint, marjoram, rosemary tied together with black silk thread were tossed in. At last the counterpane itself was squashed into the water, the rain still drizzling down.

"Why?" he managed.

"Why did they do it, or why is this necessary?" She took the spoon from his hand and jabbed at the counterpane, shoving all of it underwater. "You don't know what they are, those two," she muttered. "*Caitiffer* they call themselves, as if no one remembers the word."

Cade was possessed of a vocabulary rather larger than the usual, even for a tregetour, and he'd never heard the term in any context other than this particular surname. He said as much, tentatively.

"And a good reason for it, you'll be thinking once you know!"

"Tell me?"

"Not here. Not where anyone could walk by and listen."

So it was in silence that he helped her wring out the soaked counterpane, wondering the whole while why she didn't use an Affinity spell to return the water in the material to the water in the cauldron, the way she did with all the other washing. He made as if to tip the cauldron over so the remains could spill down the little slope to the runnel in the middle of Criddow Close and thence to the sewers.

"Leave that be!" snapped Mistress Mirdley. "There's other uses for an unbemoiling! Come inside out of the wet."

In the stillroom, chairs were arranged and the material was draped over it. He was relieved to see that none of the colors had run, but when he saw that the little charm was missing, he finally broke the silence.

"Where's that droplet thing of silver that was at the tip of that feather?"

"*That* I took care of last night, and melted in Blye's kiln this morning before you were even awake."

"You can't mean—"

"I do mean. Methinks Blye sensed a bit of a something about it, but I had it in the fire before she could be sure. Silver? Huh! Naught but polished steel—and all the more powerful because of it."

He knew about steel. His other grandfather, Lord Isshak Highcollar, had worn a steel ring on each thumb. They were not just tokens of his submission to the King or reminders of the King's mercy in not lopping those thumbs off, as had been done to Sagemaster Emmot. Expertly bespelled, the steel rings—or, more accurately, the iron used to make them—prevented a Wizard from using his magic.

Settling herself on a wooden stool at the stillroom workbench, Mistress Mirdley dried her hands on her apron. "Now. Heed me smartly, Cayden. When first I saw those two, I gave them the benefit of kindness. It would be as if people judged you by your grandmother Lady Kiritin. And that wouldn't be fair."

He shrugged. The devastations caused by his grandmother's idea about using withies as exploding spells that maimed or killed had resulted in laws forbidding glasscrafting to all Wizards. He'd broken those laws on several occasions.

"But to keep that name . . ." Mistress Mirdley shook her head. "Thought it would be taken for a married name, I suppose, come from the male line and not the female."

Before he could ask why this made a difference, she opened a little jar of salve and began rubbing it into her hands as she talked.

"What it first meant was 'slave.' Generations ago,

with the First Escaping—you'll have heard of that in school, I hope?"

He nodded. Magical folk had at various times through the centuries departed the Continent, unwelcome at best and persecuted at worst. They had found refuge in Albeyn because the Royal Family had a few Wizardly bloodlines, and mayhap other things besides.

But what Mistress Mirdley told him that morning was something he'd never heard before. Not in little-school, not at Sagemaster Emmot's Academy, not in rumors or gossip or even a hint in a very old play. Wizards and Elves, Goblins and Gnomes, and all other magical folk had been allowed to leave the Continent freely— though freed of most of their possessions. But the Caitiffs, Mistress Mirdley told him, had been sold. What they called themselves was unknown. They were given a name that meant "slave" and sent to the Durkah Isle. On maps it was indicated by a ragged outline, a name, and symbols that designated nothing but mountains of ice.

"Some tried to slip away, but almost all were caught. Or so it was said. All of them women, by the bye, for their magic doesn't pass to their men."

A test was performed on those suspected of being Caitiff. Taken to the nearest Trollbridge, the prisoner was stripped naked and inspected by the presiding Troll for certain signs. If these were present, the woman was cast into the water.

"The testing was always done the day after a good strong rain, so that the water was new. Pure water won't tolerate a Caitiff." She paused. "It's said to be agony beyond any agony for them."

Pure water; new water; rainwater—did young Mistress Windthistle and her mother ever go for walks in the rain? If caught outside in a sudden shower, did they bundle up in hooded cloaks and gloves, and hurry indoors as soon as may be? He pushed the thoughts away and asked, "Did you ever—? I mean—"

"I'm not *that* old, boy! My mam, though, she was brought a few for testing in her time. Told me what to look for in a Caitiff, and how to clean up after one." She nodded to the counterpane spread across chairs. "Mayhap she glossed over a mark now and then, because she knew the woman and knew her not to be what she was accused of being—it's a rare skin without a blotch or blemish someplace. But—"

"The Princess!" he blurted. "Lady Vren—someone told me that her mother came from a distant land to the east, and when she arrived for the wedding, they stripped her starkers and *inspected* her! Was that what they were looking for?"

"It's been so long a while that I doubt they knew the why of it, but by the sound of it . . . yes."

"How does it show? I mean, is there a specific—?"

"That's Troll-lore, boy."

"Umm . . . all right," he mumbled, chastened. "Was the Caitiff allowed to drown?"

"Fished out, dried off, and sent to the Durkah Isle with the rest of her kin. We're not barbarians. And before you ask, iron and steel have no effect on them."

"How many of them were here?"

"A few hundreds." Her muscular shoulders twitched. "Best to be rid of them. They look like anyone else, but they bring a taint to a bloodline."

Instantly indignant, thinking of innocent little Jindra in her painted cradle, he said, "There are people who say that about Gnomes and Goblins too. *And* Trolls."

She nodded, unoffended. "About *everyone*, at some

time or another." Once more she pointed to the counterpane. "Stitching is their specialty. A harmless, womanly occupation, anyone would say—"

Feeling contrary, and wondering why once again he was defending a woman he loathed, he said, "I trust that you know what you're about, but I've seen no proof."

"If it's your thinking that I ought to've waited and let you come out all over in hives, or lose the use of your fingers, or—"

"Would I?" he challenged. "Is that what was becast into that cloth? I touched it last night, when I unwrapped it. I didn't sense anything."

"Wizard," she repeated.

"You knew it was from them and yet you let Dery sleep all wrapped up in it."

"Gracious Gods, boy, what a thorough-thinking brain you've got between your ears! The thing was made for *you*. To sleep beneath. Huddled around you for hours at a time. Seeping into your dreams, mayhap. Who could know what was intended?"

"So you don't really know, either."

"Would you rather I'd waited to make sure?" she snarled. "Three more things I'll tell you, and then we'll talk of it no more. Clothwork is their specialty on the Durkah Isle. Trolls inspect *everything*, and the slightest breath of magic means the whole shipment is destroyed."

"Why is it that Trolls have so much to do with keeping watch over Caitiffs?"

Her only answer was a shrug. "The second thing is this. There's one sort of magical folk on the Durkah Isle, and one only. When enough of them had been exiled to the island, they set themselves to ridding the place of all other races except Human. Wizards, Goblins, Elves, Gnomes—

though not Pikseys or Sprites. They stick to their forests in Albeyn and have never been seen on the Durkah Isle."

"What of the Fae?"

"I can't see even a White Winterchill Fae liking a life in almost year-round snow, can you?"

He had no way of knowing. His own heritage was, apparently, Green Summer Fae; his many-times-great-grandmother had said so.

"Everyone else disappeared." She growled softly. "Illness or accident, that's what they said for years, a climate and a land no one but the toughest Humans and the exiled Caitiffs could tolerate, until no one went there anymore except for the cloth trade. There's but the one port, free of ice only one month a year. And on that island are Caitiff and Human, and during that month the few Trolls who inspect the cloth. And thus it's been for hundreds upon hundreds upon hundreds of years."

"But wouldn't their bloodlines have thinned out by now? Look at Albeyn. With every generation, the mix of races loses a bit of magic—"

"Who told you that? That 'Sagemaster' of yours? I never did like him."

"You didn't? Why?"

Once more she ignored the questions. "There's no Troll would touch a Caitiff woman. The enmity goes too deep."

Knowing she wouldn't tell him the why of that, either, he said, "Even so, after all that time, with only Human and Caitiff bloodlines—"

She capped the pot of salve and began extracting the bottles and vials from her pockets, replacing them on the shelves. "If this is a bit of Elf, and that's Piksey, and the others are Wizard and Gnome and Goblin and Troll, and mayhap a bit of Fae—you mix them all together in proportions nobody can foresee, and you never know what will happen."

Like with him. What particular combination within him had worked with his Fae heritage to cause his Else-whens?

"Mayhap you get nothing more powerful than a weath-ering witch," she went on. "Mayhap a Master Tregetour. Or mayhap nothing at all. But with just the two blood-lines, and mixed together who knows how, with only the women inheriting the magic—the plain fact of it is that even after all this time, every stitch coming from the Durkah Isle is inspected by a Troll."

"Fortyer!" he blurted. "Is that where it comes from?"

"Oh, it's a right bright lad after all, isn't it?" She turned from sorting bottles and regarded him with her fierce little eyes. " 'Tis not the fear of plague that sets apart each Durkah ship for forty days in every Albeyni port. 'Tis the danger of their weavings and sewings. It's one turn of the moon they last, but the inspectors wait an-other ten days just to be safe."

"But the spells can be renewed? Of course," he said, answering his own question this time. "Still—why would the Caitiffs bother? If they know about the fortyer, then why—?"

"What might happen after a month sleeping under that?" She pointed to the counterpane. She bit her lips together, then went on in a low, furious tone, "The third thing is this. My sister's only son commanded the inspections for thirty years before they killed him with a thread mixed in with the salad greens. Sickened the in-stant he swallowed, vomited it all up—but the working was done and the yellow thread was there as evidence after he died." She reached over to test the counterpane for moisture, her thick strong fingers squeezing a corner. A few drops of water plunked to the floor. "A single thread! So you'll forgive me, Your Lordship," she finished bitterly, "if I take precautions when it comes to gifts from Caitiffs!"

Four

EVERYONE KNEW THERE would be no surprises at Trials this year. Touchstone would move up from the Winterly to the Royal, bypassing the Ducal Circuit entirely. But, as Mieka discovered on the journey to Seekhaven, *everyone* did not seem to include Cayden. Snug in their new wagon with Dery's map on one side and TOUCHSTONE on both, the tregetour anguished himself at irregular intervals over what they'd draw at Trials and what they'd play at performances for the ladies and the Court—or if they'd receive invitations for those performances at all.

After a while, the rest of Touchstone began to find Cade's frets annoying. Mieka was all for tying him up and stuffing a gag down his throat. Jeska wanted to banish him topside to the coachman's bench so he could fuss to his heart's content without bothering anybody except Yazz. Mieka agreed to this plan, but only if he was tied up and with a gag stuffed down his throat, because why should poor Yazz suffer? All Rafe did was look up from the book he was reading, fix Cade with a humorless glare, and say, "Shut it or get out and walk."

After this Cade sulked. He did it in silence, praise be

to all the Old Gods. Still, Mieka had learned on their very first Winterly Circuit that Cade had a way of sulking that cast a murk over everyone within pissing distance. Of course, on that very first Winterly, they'd been cramped into one of the King's coaches, not their own luxurious new wagon, but Mieka was discovering that the increase in space and comfort didn't necessarily mean a decrease in the gloom.

It was a lovely wagon, withal. Because it had been delivered to his house, Mieka had been able to explore its every nook and cranny. Yazz, who had driven Auntie Brishen's whiskey wagons for years, was ecstatic about the springs, the ease of harnessing and unharnessing the horses, and all sorts of other things that Mieka neither understood nor cared about. Well, except that however the springs worked, it made for an exquisitely comfortable ride. Personally, he didn't like being within tooth range of any horse, leave alone these huge white monsters leased from the Shadowshapers.

Though he loved the prideful strut of TOUCHSTONE scrawled on the outside, it was the interior that charmed him most. Instead of bunk beds along each side, there were hammocks that tucked away when not in use. This allowed for more open space and decreased the wagon's weight. Woven of stout blue cording, cozied with thin feather-filled mattresses that rolled up into a cupboard, the hammocks swayed gently with the motion of travel. There were cleverly collapsible chairs, and a fold-down table and a little bench where they could play cards or chess on a board painted onto the wood, or eat a meal like civilized persons instead of balancing plates—the same ones Blye had made for them before their very first Trials—on their knees. Mieka's wife had stitched a green velvet cushion for his chair, and had promised to have more ready by the time they returned from Trials. She worried about the plainness of the interior—no carvings, unadorned blankets, simple glass handles on the cabinets and drawers, no paint on the wood. It wanted some color, she'd decided. She was good at that sort of thing, his darling was; his house featured new splashes of curtains and coverlets and suchlike almost weekly, and her mother was working on a tapestry for the drawing room. Their scheme of blue and violet and gray, built around the blue tassels he'd given her, ruled out use of the rug he'd brought home from the Continent. Its wheat-and-green wool, cleaned to perfection by Mistress Mirdley after Cade told her what Mieka had done to it and why, graced the floor of the wagon instead.

At the front were built-in shelves and drawers on either side of a mirror and green glass basin that nestled into the wood, perfect for shaving and washing. Jed and Jez had made the cabinetry for their clothes and gear; Blye had made the mirror and the basin. There were glass-shaded lamps, a niche for a firepocket, specially made compartments for their glass baskets and withies, and two windows on each side. Best of all for Cade and Rafe, the ceiling in the middle was high enough for them to stand up straight without bumping their heads. Yazz had worried that six and a half feet was an unwieldy height and could play merry Hells with the wagon's balance in a stiff wind, but Kearney Fairwalk had assured him that this had been taken into consideration when the wagon was designed and should present no problems. Yazz had grunted the Giant equivalent of *We'll see about that, won't we?* before being distracted by the glories of his coachman's bench: thickly padded leather seat and armrests, two lanterns on each side, brakes at his fingertips, and a tiny firepocket to keep his feet warm. That last wouldn't be necessary, Mieka reflected with satisfaction, because from now on, they'd be traveling in summer, on the Royal Circuit. No more freezing beneath inadequate blankets during the day. No more slogging through the snowy slush of an inny-ard at night. No more shivering in beds with stale sheets rife with small crawly things. They'd travel in summer and autumn from now on, and spend winters in their own warm beds at home.

Aware that any thought of who would be in his own warm bed at home was dangerous when it would be a fortnight before he saw her again, he scooted his chair closer to the fold-down table and rummaged in a drawer for a deck of cards. Cocking a hopeful eyebrow at Jeska, he riffled the cards—just as a wheel bumped over a particularly emphatic rut in the road. The cards went flying all over the wagon.

"Oh, well done!" Cade snapped.

"It wasn't my fault!"

"It never is."

"What's *that* s'posed to mean?"

"You figure it out!"

"I'm the stupid one, remember? You're the smart one, with all the books and writing and deep profound thoughts and Elsewhens and—"

Rafe growled. Mieka reached over to the little glass knob hanging from a wire and pulled it, alerting Yazz with the tinkling of a bell that they wanted to stop.

A roar came through the wooden walls. "Five miles!"

Mieka rang the bell again, more insistently this time.

"Use yer pisspot!" Yazz bellowed.

"Love to," Cade snarled at Mieka. "Right over your head!"

"Fuck you!" Mieka slid from behind the table, flung open the back door, and scrambled up the side ladder to the roof, ignoring alarmed shouts and the frantic ringing of the little bell. It was a slow crawl to the coachman's bench, windy but not especially dangerous if he was careful with the railings to which baggage could be secured for long journeys. He settled beside the un-startled Yazz, folded his arms across his chest, and glowered at the splendid spring afternoon.

A mile or so passed in silence. At last Yazz cleared his throat with a sound like a landslide. "Temperish, eh?"

"He's always like that."

"Not hisself, Miek. You."

"Me!"

Yazz nodded his massive head. Mieka leaned back and tilted his face up to get a look at the Giant. Craning his neck was the only way he ever saw his friend's expression; standing, his eyes were about on a level with Yazz's elbow. The amused tolerance quirking that wide mouth briefly irritated him. But then he sighed and relented.

"He and me, we always know just the wrong thing to say to each other."

"Happens thatwise."

"But it's kind of the only time I can be sure what he's feeling, y'know? Every other while, he's a step or two back from everything and everybody." He raked the hair from his face, enjoying the breeze. "It was more fun last year, and the year before, traveling to Trials with the Shadowshapers. At least around that lot, he talks and laughs and all that."

"Good friends, them."

"The best, outside the four of us." Traveling together had been pleasanter for the Shadowshapers, too, because Vered and Rauel rarely sniped at each other when other people were present. Best, though, was that Cade exerted himself to actual conversation. "There's times when I think we know each other too well, him and me, but—it's like, I can always tell when he's lying, but as for the rest—"

Yazz ruminated on this for a time. Then, with another nod, he asked, "Black Lightning's show at Trials?"

It took a moment to work out what Yazz meant. Then he gave a bark of laughter. "I'll give it a try, shall I? Tell him we ought to go, find out what the competition's doing these days. Get an honest reaction from him, at least."

"Competition," Yazz echoed in a musing tone that told Mieka he'd understood the Giant's implication correctly. "Won't like that much, hisself won't."

Not by half, Mieka agreed silently. Not that anybody but the Shadowshapers could be considered competition for Touchstone. But irritation would at least get Cayden to the theater. Not that it would make any difference, he reflected sourly. The more relentlessly Black fucking Lightning bludgeoned with sensation and emotion, the more unyielding Cade's resistance to it would become. Blye had once advised Mieka to be both clever and mad when it came to dealing with the tregetour's sulks and snits; laugh him out of it. He began to wish for a list of Rules like the one posted in the King's coaches, those seven Rules in particular he had taken such gleeful delight in breaking—without consequences—on their first Winterly. And this got him to thinking, and eventually to grinning.

To no one's surprise (although everyone managed to make the proper exclamations of astonishment), the Trials draw gave Touchstone the same play as last year. The Tenth Peril. The one about the Treasure. On the way out of the castle, Mieka heard somebody mutter, "Always knew the whole thing was rigged." He suddenly had his suspicions that last year had been a swindle as well. At their first Trials, Touchstone's Dragon had been a spectacular success; the next, Black Lightning had somehow got the Dragon and Mieka now reckoned it was apurpose, to show they could outdo Touchstone. And it had worked, damn it to all Hells, because last year Touchstone had drawn one of the most deadly dull of all the Thirteen, and he still hadn't quite forgiven Cade for making them do the tame old version of "Treasure" that had landed them for a second time on the Winterly while Black fucking Lightning got the Ducal. This year, much as the Stewards were muttering that it was near sacrilege to muck about with one of the Perils—Vered had been right about that—it was obvious that somebody had ordered that Touchstone would be performing it.

Their inn assignment had been fixed, as well, but Mieka had nary a complaint. There were better places to stay, or so he'd heard, with nicer rooms and sweeping views of the river, but nowhere could better food and drink be found. By now they were looked upon as "our boys" by the innkeeper, his wife, and their Trollwife, Mistress Luta. They'd been welcomed with all honors and huge flagons of excellent ale. In principle, each group was randomly allocated lodgings at Seekhaven's various inns, and nobody knew who would be where until they arrived at the gates and were given their vouchers. Obviously, this was no more the case than the "random" draw for the Thirteen Perils.

After the draw at the castle, ale and snacks were waiting for them in the inn's back garden. Less than half an hour later, the Shadowshapers showed up. A little while after that, the Crystal Sparks arrived. With them were two young players, maybe Mieka's age and maybe not, whose names he didn't catch, and who hung on every word the collected tregetours spoke. As there were four of them present—Cayden, Vered, Rauel, and Mirko

Challender of the Sparks—that was a whole lot of words.

Mieka woke the next morning unsure of when or how he'd got to bed the night before, or indeed if the bed he was in was his. It turned out that it was; Cade was lounging in the other one, making notes in his folio.

"Good party," Mieka ventured.

"Mm. But that table will never be the same."

"What table?"

"Nor the tabledrape. Good thing it was only bleached linen, and not Mistress Luta's best Frannitch lace."

"Quill!"

An arched brow, a quick sparkle of gray eyes. "You were showing us the latest in dances from the Continent."

"I was?"

"You was. Although personally I never noticed anybody in Gref Jyziero use a tabledrape as a veil while dancing. Atop the table. Starkers." He paused for effect. "With a rose between your teeth."

"I did not!" He hesitated. "Did I?"

Cade looked despicably innocent. "You don't remember?"

He cast frantically through his mind for memory of anything that had happened after the fourth or fifth round of ale. There'd been dinner, although he couldn't have said what, and singing, and more ale, and a lot of talk, and then they'd held a hunt to catch fireflies in the garden bushes—

"Mistress Luta doesn't grow roses!" he blurted.

Cade fell over laughing. Mieka grabbed the nearest pillow and pummeled him with it.

Just like old times.

Better. Wherever they went now in Seekhaven, they were recognized. Lord Fairwalk had ordered new placards made, and their own faces greeted them from shop windows and lampposts. TOUCHSTONE, the text read, and that was all. A master of understatement, Kearney Fairwalk had turned out to be.

"Romuald Needler, now," His Lordship had said, vastly pleased with himself, "had *he* been in charge, he would have put a dragon up top and a crown and necklet below, just to make certain, don't you see. Shocking lack of subtlety."

Needler was to the Shadowshapers what Fairwalk was to Touchstone: manager of their bookings, their travels, their publicity, and their money. That last was getting to be rather a sore point with Mieka. After the trip to the Continent last year and their triumph with "Treasure," he ought to be wallowing in coin. He'd really no idea where it all went. True, his house had been pricey, and the wagon had cost a small fortune, and hire of the horses to haul it would be a drain until Needler could be persuaded to sell a few of his special breed. And that wasn't to forget those windows he and Rafe had shattered while performing for the Princess's father's court. Fairwalk was still trying to resolve that little problem, and bully their full fee from the Crown for the journey abroad. One of the best things about being sure of the Royal Circuit this year was that they'd not be hanging about Gallantrybanks this summer working six nights out of eight to keep themselves from going skint until the Winterly began.

Adding to the lack of surprises was the approach made by one of the Stewards just before their performance of "Treasure" on the Fliting Hall stage. While Touchstone stood about in a back hallway, waiting to go on, a grim old man whose straggly gray beard kept catching on his gold chain of office tapped a finger on one of Cade's glass baskets to get his attention. What he got was a growl and a glare.

"Word to the wise," the Steward muttered. "One or two changes. Just a few lines. Nothing major. Better for all concerned."

Before Cade could explode, Rafe made wide eyes at the man. "Really? What lines might those be?"

Jeska piped up with, "Oh, I think he means the speech at the end—you know, the one that's the same as was said to the Archduke—I mean, the Archduke's *father*—before they executed him? That one?"

"That one," the man echoed stiffly.

"Oh no!" Jeska protested. "Memorized me lines, I have, and if he changes even one word—"

"Stickler for precision, that's our masquer," Mieka contributed.

"It's the poetry of the thing," Rafe agreed. "Rhythm and meter, all the syllables in the right places—"

Mieka nodded emphasis. "But as a Steward, you'd know all about that. Part of the judging, innit?"

"And Master Silversun works so very hard to get it all absolutely completely right," finished Rafe. Then, helpful enough to make his mother proud, he delicately plucked straying strands of gray beard from the gold chain and smoothed them down onto the man's chest. "How long did it take you to knit this?"

"Rafcadion!" Jeska exclaimed, shocked. "His *wife* knitted it!"

Mieka giggled as the defeated Steward jerked away and huffed himself off. "She knitted *him*!"

Rafe lost his smile. "They'll try again, be sure of it, once we're on the road. All those people hearing the real version for the first time—" He shook his head.

"They'll have no luck getting us to change it!" Mieka vowed. "It's brilliant and everybody knows it!"

"That's as may be," Cade said with a shrug. "But there's something else. Tobalt Fluter wrote it all up in *The*

Nayword, didn't he? A nice long review, with all the details. So our version is what they'll be expecting, out on the road. If we don't give it to them, somebody'll have to explain why."

Rafe was shaking his head again. "The 'why' I'm interested in is a Steward asking us to change it now, for Trials. Somebody in the audience we might offend?"

"The Archduke will be here," Mieka suggested.

"The Archduke has already seen it," Jeska reminded him.

Cade snorted. "Who'll take the bet that he didn't care for it much?"

As expected, Touchstone's performance of "Treasure"— rewritten by Cade with help from his Fae ancestress, though nobody but Touchstone knew that—won them Second Flight on the Royal. Mieka was so elated that he didn't even scowl when, on the walk back to their lodgings to celebrate, Cayden muttered, "It isn't as if we could've *lost,* is it?"

"Last year we did," Mieka reminded him.

"The swizz was on then, too." He kicked at a curbstone. "The first Trials, we got that on merit. Last year was rigged for Black Lightning. This year, for us."

Mieka rolled his eyes at Rafe, who shrugged by way of reply. Neither of them mentioned that Cayden had spent the entire journey from Gallantrybanks fretting over whether they'd make the Royal Circuit at all. Instead, Mieka told him, "Well, then, we'll just have to wait for next year, won't we, and blast them and the Shadowshapers and everybody else right off the stage and into the river!"

Cade thought about this and then laughed, and in the way Mieka intended him to. Not with sarcasm, or with bitterness, or with skepticism, but with real anticipation. *That's me Quill,* he reflected, much satisfied: show him someone or something to slam his head against, and he was happy as a Sprite on a springtime spree.

Trials had thus far been lacking in surprises, but one was waiting for them when they got back to their inn. Mistress Luta had planted her considerable bowlegged self in the vestibule, the handles of the inn's largest silver platter gripped in her fists. On the platter was a letter: finest parchment, sealed with brown wax and sporting pale blue ribbons. Mieka thought the letter looked a little lonely, right in the middle of all that shining silver. The Trollwife's eyes were glowing with excitement as she proffered the platter with a deep nod of her head.

"We got Second Flight on the Royal!" Jeska told her, and, lacking a convenient wrist to kiss, leaned over to peck at her cheek.

"Naught it be to *this,*" she growled, blushing.

Cade opened the letter, scanned it, and grinned. "Naught, indeed! We are hereby bidden to lunching at the castle on the morrow."

"Who with?" Mieka demanded.

"'With whom?' is the correct form," Cade chastened, "you illiterate blatteroon." He waved the letter in front of Mieka, ribbons fluttering. "Whose eyes does this color remind you of?"

Snatching the parchment from Cade's hand, Mieka ignored all the words except for the signature at the bottom. He was disappointed not to see Lady Vrennerie's name there. "*Whom,*" he asked deliberately, "is this 'Lady Dylas Clickpine' when she's at home, then?"

"Lady-in-waiting to the Princess. Says right there at the bottom. And it's 'who,' not 'whom.'"

Rafe made big eyes at him and drawled, "Amazing, innit? What a drop or three of noble blood will do for one's understanding of proper grammar."

Cade shrugged. "You went to the same littleschool I

did. Not my fault if you never paid attention. If we're all four of us to go to lunching, three's the limit tonight. Can't go see the Princess all surly with a hangover."

Mieka whined because he was expected to, but privately he considered this wise advice. His mother would throttle him if he disgraced himself in front of Royalty.

Once again the Shadowshapers turned up at their inn—no astonishment, as the drinks were the best in Seekhaven. Jeska, it seemed, now had competition for Mistress Luta's affections: the Trollwife actually blushed when Chat bowed to her. Mieka watched the spread of brick-red color up her cheeks and down her neck, wondering what it was about Chat's uncomely, comically uneven features that could provoke such a reaction. Rauel was the boyish beauty of the group, though Vered with his nut-brown skin and white-blond hair was the most striking; Sakary's looks were remarkable only for the deep red of his curling hair and the intensity of his gaze. Touchstone, Mieka decided with a smirk, was much the handsomer collection of players—despite Quill's frets about the heft of his nose. Silly attitude, Mieka had always thought. He'd grown right fond of that nose, so much more impressive than the mushroomy buttons or halfhearted wedges that decorated most people's faces.

"Second Flight!" was Rauel's greeting. "Right behind us!"

"Just like always!" Vered tossed in as they all made for the bar.

Mieka laughed at them. The edge to their voices was as rewarding as the invitation from Princess Miriuzca. Touchstone's acclaim had to rankle. The Shadowshapers were accustomed to being the absolute best in the Kingdom. Now they had a rival—or, rather, now they *knew* they had a rival, and so did everybody else. Two years ago, Black Lightning had made the Winterly without having gone through Trials (talk of a thing being rigged!), but no group had ever jumped from Winterly to Royal before without playing Ducal in between.

Jeska, with his most Angelic smile, said to the Shadowshapers, "Good of you to be our opening act for the whole summer!"

"Prime them all up," Rafe contributed, "so they're ready for some *real* theater."

This led to growls and laughter and some playful threatened punches. Mieka, dancing lightly out of range of Chat's fist, took it the next logical step, saying, "And prime up the girls, too, so they're ready for some *real*—"

"I've a wife!" Chat exclaimed. "And so do you, lad."

"When did that stop any man worthy of the name, style, and title?" Mieka scoffed.

Not that he'd ever flaunt other girls in front of his wife. That was tasteless. Yet it had turned out convenient, that house outside Gallybanks. He could come into town and sleep at Wistly while Touchstone worked, then go back to Hilldrop for a few days. He did as pleased him with whoever caught his fancy. As long as a man didn't bring home a pox, what business was it of his wife's what he did while he was away from her? It wasn't as if such dalliances actually meant anything.

The first round of drinks was on the house. And the second. When the third came with dinner, Rafe reminded his partners that there was a limit tonight, which led to an explanation of why, which led to more teasing—and more jealousy.

"Ooh, quite the sensation, aren't we?" Vered mocked. "Lunching frivols with Her Royal Selfness, special attention from the Stewards—"

Cade glanced up from layered slices of ham and

chicken under a savory fruit sauce. "Attention?" he asked sharply.

" 'Twas all over Fliting Hall," Rauel told him. "You didn't hear?"

"Him? Before a performance?" Mieka snorted. "Only hears the natter of the anguishings inside his own head!"

"What were they saying?" Cade demanded.

Chat spoke to the chunk of grilled carrot on his fork. "Somebody was fussing over offense to the Archduke. Trying to earn some points of his own, like, though not on the stage."

"I thought it might be something like that." Rafe passed his plate to Sakary, who loaded more meat onto it. "Beholden, mate. His Grace's fingers seem to be dipping everywhere these days, right up to his rings. He couldn't buy the Shadowshapers two years ago, he couldn't buy us last year, even with the offer of a theater built to our exact designs—"

"What?" Vered exclaimed.

"You didn't hear?" Rafe's smile was an intriguing combination of smugness and disgust. He told the tale briefly, finishing with, "So now he is, shall we say, not our most enthusiastic supporter, and anyone wishing his favor will be looking to interfere with us."

"A whole theater," Rauel murmured, a note of yearning in his voice.

"I shouldn't like that," said Sakary, quiet but adamant. "No, I shouldn't like that at all." When every man at the table stared at him, he went on, "It's the difference in halls that keeps us sharp. Playing the same place all the time, or nearly all . . ."

"Boring," Mieka interpreted. But he was wrong.

"Might get sloppy," Sakary said. "Complacent, like. Not pay enough attention."

"Not lose control, but forget to be as careful," Rafe agreed.

"Fettlers!" Mieka shared a grin with Cade. But in the next moment he remembered that Sakary was complacent enough about Chirene to make friends with Alaen and let him hang round the house. Admiration of a lovely wife was a fine and flattering thing, but if anyone took to visiting Hilldrop, he'd—

"Control is just the issue, though, innit?" Jeska asked. "The Archduke's control, I mean. Who will he try to buy next?"

Cade laughed quietly. "Isn't it obvious? Black Lightning, of course."

Sakary traded glances with Vered, then said, "That makes sense of today's announcement, then, doesn't it?"

They were told about another surprise, and not the good sort. Touchstone triumphant, Touchstone celebrated, Touchstone recognized wherever they showed their faces in Seekhaven—but the coveted invitation to perform on the last night of Trials before the lords and gentlemen of the Court had gone to Black Lightning.

Five

"READY? C'MON, MIEKA—mustn't keep the Princess waiting!"

Mieka growled wordlessly over his shoulder at Jeska. The masquer's reply was a laugh and an echo of footsteps down the hallway. Mieka went back to fumbling with his jacket buttons. They seemed to have multiplied since the last time he'd worn it—what had been one dozen now had become at least three—and his mother-in-law had been careless about the laundering as well, because the damnable thing had shrunk a bit. Not through the shoulders, which would have interfered with his glisking and annoyed the piss out of him, but around the ribs. Which was just as annoying in its own way. Giving up at last, he wrenched the thickly embroidered silk from his arms and grabbed a green brocade shortvest to wear over his white shirt. He wouldn't match the rest of Touchstone, and they wouldn't present the elegant picture Kearney Fairwalk intended when he ordered the clothes, but that was just too bloody bad.

Always refurbishing their stage clothes, was His Lordship. White, black, various shades of gray; one set of outfits that featured the same jacket in four different but harmonious jewel tones; shirts, trousers, longvests, tunics—but not, praise to all the Old Gods, any more of those silly neckbands with the pleats. There was a newer fashion now, featuring cascading lace at the throat and, for the truly stylish, at the wrists as well. The former itched, and the latter was impossible to work in. Every time Mieka considered complaining, however, he made himself recall last summer's little foray into a corseted blue gown and high-heeled shoes. Gods, what women had to put up with.

The green vest looked fine with the ruffledy shirt, he decided, although he had his doubts about keeping the lace cuffs out of the soup. He was trying to fold them up a little when a bellow of his name sent him running for the stairs.

His arrival was greeted variously. Jeska, who never cared what he wore because he always looked perfect, rolled his eyes. Cade, who fussed over his wardrobe in the belief that if people were looking at his clothes, they wouldn't notice his face, frowned. Rafe merely arched a brow. Mieka glared at them all, daring them to say anything.

But as the silence lengthened—and he knew how effective a silence could be in theater, making an audience more and more nervous until people were positively aching for more words—he finally burst out, "There was a smudge on me jacket, all right?"

"I thought your mother-in-law took care of your frustlings and fripperings these days," Rafe remarked.

"She does," he affirmed.

"Not very well, evidently."

"Not this time." The slander made him feel a bit guilty, so he added with a grin, "But she's a fantastic cook!"

Rafe's mouth twitched. "Obviously."

Stung, Mieka poked a finger into Rafe's stomach. "Hark who's talking!"

On the walk to the castle, Jeska shared the Court gossip one of his many lady friends spent her days collecting—for anonymous publication, and not in the *Court Circular*. Princess Miriuzca had recently been made a Duchess in her own right. "A title and the wherewithal to support it," Jeska explained, "to pass on to any daughters. Not at all like Princess Iamina, who has naught of her own."

Mieka laughed. "But she's rich! Like all the Royals!"

Cade regarded him with something that wasn't quite condescension. "The dowry all went to Lord Tawnymoor when she married him, didn't it? And if she divorces him, he keeps it all."

"So she's stuck with him," Jeska said. "And has to plead with her brother the King when she's out of money. He must be tired of it, so he settled a Duchy on the new Princess to prevent the same thing happening with her."

"That's a scandal," Mieka announced.

"In the impossible event that Blye and Jed divorced," Rafe challenged, "who d'you think would wind up with the glassworks?"

"Blye," Mieka said at once. "Because my brother knows I'd kill him."

"Tell that to the law courts."

"But it's not fair!"

"So now you see why King Meredan dredged up one of the old extinct titles and gave it to Miriuzca, with all its lands and—" He broke off as Jeska smirked. "No lands?"

"No lands," Jeska affirmed. "And there's the real scandal of it, according to Court thinking. Instead, he gave her full interest in ten ships."

"A Princess engaging in trade!" Waving a hand in front of his face like a lady fighting off a fainting fit,

Cade grinned. "Once my mother hears, she'll take to her bed for a fortnight with the shock!"

Another shock was waiting at the castle. Though Mieka saw it at once, none of his friends did. They were escorted to one of the small walled-in gardens that afforded what passed for privacy in regal life, made their bows, and accepted seats at a prettily decorated table under a chestnut tree. There were six of them at table, Touchstone and the Princess and Lady Dylas Clickpine, a dark, shy little girl of about eighteen who said exactly nothing the whole while. Such seclusion from prying eyes and eavesdropping courtiers was a signal honor for which Jeska expressed their gratitude with one of those just-shy-of-incandescent smiles he used on lovely ladies who belonged to other men. A casual lunching of sliced fruits, chopped vegetables, breads, cheeses, and the latest in savory jellies was placed before them—no soup, Mieka was grateful to note—and as the conversation progressed along entirely conventional lines, Mieka decided that if the Princess wasn't saying anything about it, then neither should he. But he knew now why she had a new title.

Only the thought of how excited his wife would be when he told her all about their lunching with the Princess kept Mieka from succumbing to boredom. He forced himself to pay attention to most of the talk, added a few stories of his own (those suitable for polite company), but was struggling against yawns by the time the sweet was served.

The servants withdrew to the doorways. So did Lady Dylas, at a signal from the Princess, with the only words she had spoken that afternoon: "Yes, Your Grace."

Rafe smiled at Miriuzca and said, "Begging your pardon, Your Highness, but how do you keep track?"

She widened limpid blue eyes. "Of what?"

"Of who you are. In the last hour I've heard people call you six different things. Your Royal Highness, Princess, my lady, Tregrefina, Duchess, Your Grace—does anybody ever call you by your name anymore?"

She looked surprised for an instant, then burst into a deep, throaty laugh completely at odds with her cream-and-sunshine beauty. A girl who looked the way she did ought to giggle. That laugh of hers belonged to a much older woman . . . and a much happier one, Mieka realized with sudden shock of insight. Then he reminded himself who she was married to—to whom she was married? Was that the right way to say it? Curse Cayden for making him worry about such silly things.

"One of these days," Mieka said, "my lady Duchess Highness Grace Tregrefina Princess and all the rest, you'll have yet another name." When they all looked at him, he smiled. "There'll be a little bit of a somebody racing about the Palace yelling 'Mum!' at the top of his voice!" He took it as a sign of how quickly and completely she'd learned to mask her true feelings that she didn't blush, only laughed again. But she couldn't quite conceal the sparkle in her eyes, and he took the wicked liberty of giving her a grin and a wink.

On the walk back to their lodgings, Rafe said, "All right, then, out with it. What was all that in aid of?"

"All what?" Mieka asked innocently.

Cade eyed him sidelong. "You know something."

"I know many, many things!" He danced lightly round a watering trough outside a riverside tavern, like a Piksey round a wishing well—until Rafe grabbed him by the scruff of the neck and threatened to dunk him.

"River or trough, your choice."

Mieka struggled, Rafe shook him, and finally he yelled, "All right, all right! I'll tell you when we get back to our place!"

"You'll tell us now!"

"Not in front of everybody in Seekhaven, I won't!"

Upstairs, in private, with the door shut, he gathered the three of them close with a crooked finger and whispered, "The Princess is in pig." When they all looked shocked, he made a face. "Thunderin' Hells, couldn't you see it?"

"Somehow," Rafe mused, "the words 'Princess' and 'in pig' don't exactly dance trippingly from the tongue."

"Call it what you like. She is. Takes an experienced father to see these things," he went on, and instantly regretted it when Rafe's blue- gray eyes went blank.

"So that shine in her eyes is her husband's doing," Cade murmured, "but nothing her husband's done—if you see what I mean."

Jeska was frowning. "Why haven't they announced it?"

"How should I know?" Mieka shrugged. "But she is, and it's a thing I'm thinking will make us a nice profit from a few discreet wagers."

"No!" Cade exclaimed, recoiling. "That's disgusting!"

"It's worth money," he replied flatly.

"It's also illegal," Rafe said.

"So?"

"Don't do it," Cade warned. "I'm serious, Mieka. There's no bookmaker in the Kingdom wouldn't report you for trying to place a bet like that." Pointing a long finger right at Mieka's nose, he went on sternly, "Bailing you out of quod isn't on my list of lovely ways to spend an evening. And lawyers come expensive."

Another shrug, and a regretful sigh; might have been nice to make a little extra cash on a sure thing. He bared his teeth and pretended to nip at Cade's finger. "Oh, all right. But here's another thought. Briuly's here, yeh? Let's have him come on right after us when we do the show at the Pavilion, and sing them all out with a lullaby. The Princess will appreciate that."

It was a feature of Trials that minstrels of all sorts roamed about, playing the taverns in hopes of attracting the notice of some lord who would offer employment. Most of the great landowners already had their own pet musicians, but there was always a chance of picking up some work. Briuly Blackpath was as little to be bought as Touchstone or the Shadowshapers, with whom he'd hitched a ride to Seekhaven this year, so despite his brilliance with the lute, he didn't have a noble employer. Like his cousin Alaen, he played when and as it suited him. Rich he was not, but he kept himself in strings and tavern patrons kept him in beer, and he was just as happy to have it so.

Briuly had an advantage possessed by no other musician: He was known personally to Princess Miriuzca, for last summer he had been one of the party sent to escort her to Albeyn. Word had got round that at this, the first Trials she would ever unofficially witness, she had asked for him to be present, just as she had asked for Touchstone to be the theater group sent to her homeland. It was Hadden Windthistle's opinion that Briuly was too unworldly to take advantage of this preference; Mieka understood this to mean that, like Cayden at times, Briuly was too full of himself and his notions of the Purity of Art to attend to the practical side of life.

When Touchstone reached the castle on the night they were engaged to play for the ladies, Briuly was already there, seated on the edge of the stage, spindly legs dangling as he played whatever pleased him at the moment and ignored the milling throng of Court ladies. Cade went over to him, bent to murmur something in his pointed Elfen ear, and Briuly nodded without breaking the complicated rhythm of his fingers on the lute strings.

Watching this, Mieka shook his head and sighed resignation as he mounted the side steps and approached the glass baskets full of withies. The Blackpath cousins were two of a kind, no matter how little they resembled each other physically. Both were deeply in love—Briuly with his lute, Alaen with Chirene—and neither of them had any time or thought for anyone or anything else. In fact, Alaen had stayed in Gallantrybanks during Trials, for Chirene was there and Sakary was here and the silly giddiot continually cherished hopes of seeing her alone.

The ladies began to settle into their seats at the Pavilion, eagerly anticipating the shock of what they were about to see. They all wore the usual masks and veils, pretending that nobody knew anybody else and none of them were really here. Princess Iamina was as always identifiable by the jewel of yellow diamonds and pearls that fixed a thin silk veil to her high-piled braids, but this year she had competition regarding rank. For the first time in Mieka's experience—admittedly not extensive—the Queen was present at a performance. He'd never heard of Roshien's attending one of these late-night pretend-secret shows. But that pudgy morsel of rose silk and wispy gray veils could only be the Queen, for everyone curtsied as they passed her, and again to the tall, masked girl in blue beside her. Mayhap Roshien was here because of the play's historical importance. Mayhap she had been persuaded by her new daughter-in-law. Mieka smiled to himself, wondering how much of the Court shared Miriuzca's secret.

Near Princess Iamina, and also providing competition, was the new Archduchess, flagrantly waving to someone. Had she wished to remain anonymous—and Mieka couldn't think of a single reason why she would—she would have done better than to wear her husband's colors. Included in this tribute of gray and orange was her wedding ring: a great lump of gray pearl surrounded by orange topazes. The thing reached almost to her fingernail and looked heavy enough to anchor a ship. Much had been made of this gift in the broadsheets, and it served to make her as recognizable as did Princess Iamina's gaudy yellow flower. Honestly, Mieka thought to himself as he mounted the steps to the stage, the things women did to outshine each other. Rather than turning at once for the glass baskets that had already been set up for him, he walked over to where Rafe stood at his lectern.

"I think the Archduchess needs a bit of excitement, don't you? For her dear husband's sake, if nothing else."

The fettler licked his lips and nodded slowly. "Iamina will be relieved not to be the focus tonight."

"Oh, you can spare a touch for her, too. But have a care with Miriuzca. And with the Queen. They're right next to each other, the ones in blue and pink."

"The Queen?" After a quick glance into the audience, Rafe smoothed his beard with one finger. "Hmm. So *that's* why the Stewards are here tonight."

"What? Where?"

"You really do have to start noticing things that aren't shoved directly under your nose. Four of 'em, tucked behind pillars. They'll be protecting the Queen, if necessary."

"But they never before—I mean, Iamina always comes to these things."

"Yeh, but who cares about her? Nobody that I've ever heard of. Roshien and Miriuzca, though, they're important. Even if they're not officially here."

"It's insulting," Mieka grumped.

"Yeh, it is. But the Stewards are here on somebody's order, so we'll just have to treat the ladies as delicately

as mistflowers." He chuckled. " 'Cept for the Archduchess, of course."

"Fine it down to a needle point and stick it to her,"
Mieka agreed.

He darted to the back of the stage, stretching his
shoulders loose as he went. Blye's beautiful glass baskets awaited him. The usual fond smile never reached
his lips, however. Laid across the black-rimmed basket
was a huge feather, all iridescent blues and greens and
touches of gold. A peacock feather.

He backed off, one hand groping towards Cayden.
Mastering himself at once, he snatched up the feather
and threw it to the far back of the stage. The others
mustn't see it, this traditional symbol of bad luck, this
worst thing that could ever be discovered in a theater.
He knew that the superstition was irrational, ground-
less, ridiculous, childish . . . and he felt a shiver down
his spine anyway as he took up position and flexed his
fingers. He would pay no attention to the peacock
feather. Touchstone would be as good as ever—*better*,
by all the Gods.

The play began with wind and rain, progressed through
the hiding of the Rights of the Fae beneath the tumbling
wall, the capture, and the scene inside the castle, with
everyone gasping in all the right places. But when the
cloak fell from the Fae's shoulders, instead of wings—
minutely described to him by Cayden from his observa-
tions of his ancestress—instead of delicate iridescence
Mieka created long, lush, gorgeous, many-eyed wings
made of peacock feathers. From the corner of his eye he
saw Cade's startled blink, and grinned to himself. Someone had thought to unnerve Touchstone with a single
peacock feather; Mieka created two dozen of the
damned things, just because he could.

The Fae's arrogance and contempt (and perhaps a bit

of Mieka's as well) spread through the audience, emotions that had put sneers onto other faces during other performances, though here, of course, expressions were invisible behind the veils. One of the tricks of the piece was the transition from the righteous defiance of the Fae to the righteous anger of his judges. However justified the Fae felt in hiding the Rights, what the Fae Folk had done in starting a war that killed thousands was an unforgivable crime. Lives broken and ruined, all for the sake of a few bits of gold and silver and glass, and the magic they represented. What merely mortal being—Human, Wizard, Elf, Fae, Piksey, Sprite, Goblin, Gnome, Troll, Giant—could justify destroying so many lives for his own ends? It was intolerable, and it was wrong. And Touchstone always made sure the audience knew it.

Mieka was gentler than usual with the transition to the grim finality of the condemnation, but added a droplet of fear just before the Fae was hanged, knowing Rafe would direct it at the Archduchess. Yet as Jeska spoke the last lines from the shadows, something odd happened. Mieka's tutor had once likened the art of glisking to a river, in which one must be careful not to drown an audience. One slid emotions, sounds, tastes, sensations into that river—Mieka always thought of them in terms of colors added to clear water, or pinches of different spices that subtly altered the taste of a sauce—and blended them together. But all at once it was as if the fear he had just conjured was a trickle of bitter blood seeping into a stream, and something—someone—beneath the surface was sucking it away with a ravening thirst. Sometimes a few people in an audience clutched at an emotion, so impatient to feel more or so empty of feeling themselves that instinct yearned beyond their controlling. Mostly they grasped at love, or happiness, or giddy laughter; at times there would be someone eager to experience the thrill of more brutal emotions, and this was why a fettler exerted such powerful control on the magic. But this was different. This seized on the fear and demanded more. He'd sensed something akin to it in only one place before: that weird old mansion outside New Halt. Twice now Touchstone had performed for an audience of a single mysterious person swathed in furs, but the feeling of being devoured was the same. Odd, though, that it was only fear that was so fiercely consumed.

He was too good at his work to allow this to distract him. As the piece ended, he paused to catch his breath. Then, as the applause swelled, he found the peacock feather and broke it off up near the eye, tucked it behind one ear, and leaped over the glisker's bench to join his partners.

Cade flinched back like a spooked colt. "What in all Hells—?"

"Later," he replied as they took their bows. He found the tall blue figure next to the short pink one, and chuckled; the Queen was applauding politely, but Princess Miriuzca was jumping up and down and clapping her hands like anything. It occurred to him that this was the very first time she'd ever watched a play from somewhere other than behind a screen or up in a minstrels gallery. He made sure their next group bow was directed right at her, and wished his ears were sensitive enough to hear that deep-throated laughter.

Briuly ended the evening with a lovely lullaby as the ladies left the Pavilion and Touchstone packed away their glass. Mieka had just finished nesting the second crate of baskets when he heard Cayden say, "Hope you enjoyed it, sir."

Mieka glanced up to find one of the Stewards nearby— not the white-bearded one whose wife had knitted him, though equally old to judge by the wrinkles all over his paper-fine skin. He was leaning on two intricately carved canes, and so bent in his spine that he had to twist his neck awkwardly to look up at Cayden.

"Always do, my boy," the man rumbled in a voice surprisingly powerful for one so frail. "Always do. Knew your grandsir, I did."

"Cadriel Silversun?"

"Well, him, too—I meant your lady mother's sire. Lord Isshak Highcollar." As Cade gave a little start of surprise, the old man went on, "Last of his line. Fine man."

Husband of Lady Kiritin Blackswan, she who had invented new and horrifying ways to use glass withies in war. She was the reason glasscrafting was forbidden to Wizards. Mieka gulped and bent over the crates, and tried to pretend he wasn't listening.

"Good man," the Steward was saying. "Got the children spared—though you'd know all about that."

"Yes. I know all about that," Cade said in the rigidly controlled tone that meant he wanted to smash his fists into something.

"Well, then." He cleared his throat. "Splendid to see the talent in you, boy. Excellent show tonight. Well-played. The ladies were impressed—or would have been if they were ever officially here, what?" He wheezed a conspiratorial laugh and limped away.

Mieka bit both lips together over the questions that stung his tongue. This was the Elsewhens all over again, he thought resentfully. Cade had secrets that it seemed everybody knew except Mieka. There were two methods of discovery, as far as Mieka was concerned: Wait for him to tell, or bully him into telling. Though patience was not one of his prevailing virtues, he always felt guilty whenever he worried at Cade like a dog with a sheep shank in its teeth.

He'd forgot that he had his own telling to do. They hadn't taken more than ten steps into the night-dark castle grounds before Jeska snatched the feather from behind Mieka's ear and ground it under his boot heel.

"I don't know where you got that from," he said, his voice low and shaking, "but I don't ever want to see one of those things near me again!"

"It's naught but silly superstition!" Mieka protested. "Did anything go wrong tonight? Did it? No! And anyways, what makes you think I had anything to do with it? Laid across the baskets, it was—d'you think I'd do such a horrid thing deliberately?"

"'Silly superstition'?" Cade quoted back at him.

"Yeh, well—it surprised me a bit," he admitted. "Still and all—"

"Who put it there?" Rafe growled. "Who'd like to throw us off our stride?"

Given a mystery to solve, Cayden forgot about the significance of the feather's meaning and occupied himself with sussing out the significance of the feather's presence. Mieka hid a smile and kept walking.

"Oy, Mieka!" a voice called from behind them. Turning, he peered at the three servant boys carrying the crated glass baskets—no, two boys and a young man of about his own age. A young man he knew: tall and thin, though not so tall as Cade, with badly kagged ears and a hint of Goblin about his uneven teeth.

"Dak?" Mieka was abruptly embarrassed that this person he'd once performed with was now fetching and carrying for him, the Master Glisker.

Dak revealed all his teeth. "What's been, mate?"

Cade said pleasantly, "Oh, we've been here and there. Introduce us, Mieka."

"Erm—Daksho Webholder. We—uh—"

"We were players together," Dak said, hefting the crate

casually higher in his arms, bouncing it a little. The crate
with the precious glass baskets Blye had made—

"And who are you with now?" Jeska asked, all politeness.

Dak ignored him, his brandy-brown eyes fixed on
Mieka. "Had a show, didn't we, one night in Gallybanks,
and there we all were, everything wonderful about us—
except for lack of a glisker."

"Rough luck," Rafe commented.

"Never told you, did he? Bloody little snarge!"

"Told us?" Jeska inquired, still cordial.

Mieka could stand it no longer. "The night in Gowerion! That very first night! I know it wasn't right of me,
Dak, but—"

Now the Goblin teeth were displayed in a sneer. "We
were gonna be famous! We—"

"No, you weren't." This from Cade, looking down
his considerable nose. "That was more than two years
ago. If you had the goods, you'd've found another glisker
by now and been invited to Trials."

Ruthless, pitiless fact. It was one of the things Mieka
most disliked about Cade, this cold and brutal instinct
for cutting to the bone with no concern for the blood
loss. He'd known the sharp side of Cayden's tongue
often enough himself; now, used against somebody
who didn't really deserve it—all Dak had ever wanted
was what Touchstone now had.

And then he remembered those boys on the Continent, the ones who'd stolen a withie. They'd thought
the glass twig would make them players. But it wasn't
in them—the ability, the magic—any more than it was
in Dak. Not really. Cade was right. As usual. And that
was probably the most annoying thing about him.

It was a confusing mixture of compassion and disdain Mieka felt as he said, "I'm sorry, Dak." Sorry, because it was more than the magic and the withies and even the skill and the talent and the ambition. "I really am sor—"

"Shut it, Mieka." Cade hefted the crate from Dak's startled grasp. "Perfectly lovely of you to stop by. We'll take it from here."

"Fuckin' Touchstone!" Dak shouted, and the two boys carrying the other crates and withies flinched. While Rafe and Jeska relieved them of their burdens, Dak went on, "Greatest in the Kingdom, swigging tea with the Princess! Oh, I was there, I saw you—I'm a *player,* but here I am toting trays from the castle kitchens! It shoulda been *me* there, it shoulda been *me*!"

"It would never have been you," Cade told him.

The cruelty of it didn't strike Mieka the way he thought it probably ought to have done. It was only the truth. Ruthless, pitiless fact. Cade's instinct. Part of what made him brilliant. Just as Mieka's instinct had compelled him to skive off the show in a tatty Gallantrybanks tavern and head for Gowerion, certain sure that he was good enough, that he was their missing piece. Ruthless. Pitiless. Monumentally arrogant.

At bottom, he and Cade were a lot alike.

He became aware that his partners had walked off, leaving him and Dak and the two frightened boys, all of them empty-handed. Mieka dug into his pockets and came up with a dozen or more coins, which he pressed into Dak's palm. A terrible struggle showed in the man's face: fling the money contemptuously onto the grass, or keep it because he needed it?

"Bastard," Dak said, and kept it.

"I really am sorry," Mieka mumbled, and made his escape.

They were waiting for him by the castle gate. Jeska gave him the velvet bag of spent withies and said, "Webholder. Not Spider Clan, I'm thinking."

Rafe snorted. "Think I'd be caught dead related to a third-rate fritlag like that?"

"Nothing to do with your clan," Cade soothed. "Webholder is one of those names like Jeska's. Foreign soldier, stayed here, took a name people could understand—"

"Like in that play, the one about the battle!" Jeska exclaimed. "The siege engine—there's them as loads it, and them as pulls back the netting that holds the rocks or fireballs—"

Rafe interrupted with a question directed at Mieka. "Was it him?" When Mieka stared at him stupidly, he said, "The peacock feather. He obviously has access to the Pavilion. Does he hate you enough?"

"I don't know."

At the same time Cade said, "Who gives a shit?"

"You know all the stories," said Jeska. "Peacock feathers are hideous bad luck in the theater. Everything from withies the tregetour forgot about priming to men in the audience run mad."

"None of that happened, though, did it?" Cade tightened his hold on his glass baskets. "Besides, it couldn't have been him behind it, even if he was the one who put it there. Where would he get a peacock feather? How could he afford one? Isn't it plain who's responsible?"

"Y'know," Rafe muttered, "I really consider hating you when you're smug."

"The Archduchess," Cade finished. "Not her husband's favorite play, not her husband's favorite players—how charming if there's a cock-up! And in front of the Queen, too!" He gave a harsh, haughty laugh. "A try at—what'd you call it, Mieka? Talking to the Archduke that time, you remember! Comparing various players' techniques to various methods of murder."

"How adorable of you," Rafe drawled. "What are we?"

"Slow poison," Mieka told him. "But him—a knife in the back."

Cade nudged Jeska with an elbow. "All she could manage was a peacock feather. Not so scary now, eh?"

Later, back in their room after a few celebratory drinks, Cade shut the bedchamber door, turned to Mieka, and said with absolute seriousness, "Don't ever apologize. Not ever, not to anyone, for going where your dreams take you."

"Wasn't nice, though, what I did to Dak and the rest." He stripped off his jacket and shirt, unwilling to look at Cade. When there was no reply for a time, only the sounds of water splashing in the basin, he finally had to turn. "And it's not like your Elsewhens, is it? You can't help having them. Me, I made a choice, to find you in Gowerion." Although it hadn't felt like a choice at the time. It had felt . . . inevitable.

Cade reappeared from behind a towel. "What I meant was that you shouldn't be sorry for something there's no fighting against. What we have, it's not kind to other people. It can't be, I think. Not if it's honest."

Ruthless. Pitiless. It took more than magic and talent, ambition and desire, or even instinct. It took the supreme arrogance of a belief so powerful that nothing and no one could shake it, not for an instant. Yes, he and Cade were a lot alike.

"And talking of honesty," Cade went on, "I'm sure you're just bursting to know about my grandfather." He picked up his nightshirt and began pleating the fine linen between his fingers. "Kiritin vanished towards the end of the war. Killed, probably. Maybe suicide. Nobody

knows. Her husband, Isshak Highcollar—he wasn't involved in the war at all, or so everybody in the family
says loud and clear if his name ever comes up, which it
doesn't, much. The King let him live, anyway."

"Wizard?"

"Mostly." He sat down, shoulders rounding. "He made
a bargain with the King to save himself and his daughters. They could live a nice, quiet life in the country—
part of the deal was he could keep one of the ancestral
estates, the worst of them, as it happens, awful old pile
on the side of a windy moor. But the price of survival
was their magic."

"Their magic?" Mieka echoed foolishly.

"There's stories about what spells were used and
who used them, but the fact of it was that he wore the
steel rings—you've heard of those?" When Mieka nodded, he went on, "His daughters had hinderings put on
them, and whatever magic they might've had . . ." He
finished with a shrug.

"What's a hindering?" Mieka shivered. It sounded
grisly.

"Imagine that you're outside a shop, looking in the
window. You can see everything—good food, warm clothing, shoes, a soft bed—but you can't go in. Ever." He
paused. "No, that's not right. You're not outside looking
in, you're *inside* a place with a big window, looking out
at life all around you—all the people and colors and
trees and wind and everything, just *everything*—but
you can never touch any of it. You can put your hand to
the glass but you'll never feel the warmth of the sunlight. You'll never hear people laughing, or taste the rain.
It's all there, you *know* it's all there, but you can never
get at it. That's a hindering."

"Gentle Gods," Mieka whispered. "And somebody
did this to your mother?" He began to understand why

Lady Jaspiela was the way she was. And had he really thought there would be no surprises at Trials this year?

"And her sisters. It happened with other families, too."

"But not the Archduke."

"Once he got to be a little older than Dery, they started testing every way they knew how. But he has nothing."

Mieka thought about all this for a few moments. "What was your grandfather's magic? The Steward made it sound something special."

"Not very, not in everyday life, unless you like to amuse yourself watching other people thrash about in bed."

"Quill, make sense."

"It was useful enough to the Archduke's father. If he tried hard enough, Isshak could see through stone walls."

"Oh, right," Mieka scoffed. When Cade was silent, he reconsidered. "He could? Really truly?"

"As I said—useful. The family all deny it, of course, but I've heard one or two things. You needn't bother putting spies in a castle when you've got somebody can look right into the courtyard and count the soldiers. Took a lot out of him to do it, though. Once he decided that Lady Kiritin had chosen the wrong side, it's said he started pretending that he'd worn himself out, so knackered that he couldn't hardly stay awake, much less do magic."

"He couldn't just lie about what he saw," Mieka reflected. "Easy enough to catch him at it. Compare notes after the battle was lost, and all that."

"He didn't exactly work towards the victory of the King's forces, but at least he stopped helping the Archduke. Which was taken into account when the war ended, and why he got to live, and his daughters with him." He snorted a laugh. "You think *you've* got interesting relations—my darling aunties are the original Gorgons."

"Still out on the mists of the moor?"

"One of them. The other married a local lordling and spends her time making life a foretaste of one of the nastier Hells for him, her four sons, the girls unlucky enough to be married to them, whatever children they spawned, and anybody else in a ten-mile reach."

There wasn't much to be said to that. They made ready for bed: shucking off clothes, having a quick wash in the basin, donning nightshirts, sliding between the sheets. A warm breeze through the half-open window brought the scents of flowers and the nearby river. Mieka knew by the sound of Cade's breathing that he wasn't anywhere near sleep. But he said nothing, because waiting for Cade to share what was on his mind had worked so far today. Patience was boring, but sometimes it was worth it.

Finally: "Don't you want to know if I've any more secrets stashed away?"

Mieka grinned to himself, but kept it from his voice as he said, "Did I ask, just then? No. I did not."

"But you wanted to."

"You always tell me things eventually, Quill. Because you know I always know when you're lying."

"Not being able to lie isn't the same as not telling the truth."

"Isn't it?" he asked innocently. "Sweet dreaming, Quill."

Six

DONE WITH TRIALS and onto the Royal Circuit. Done with performances for the judges and the ladies. Done with two appearances at High Chapel (which also counted as performances, in a way, at least for Mieka—keeping a pious and reverential face on wasn't easy, and Cade had absolutely forbidden him to play any of his tricks to get them out of it). Done with everything at Seekhaven except one last thing.

"C'mon, Quill. Don't you want to see what they've got?"

"No."

"You know you want to."

"Not interested." He turned a page in the book he'd picked up someplace or other in Seekhaven. A new book, *A Natural History of Dragons* or some suchlike. Mieka supposed he'd say it was for research and accuracy—as if Touchstone didn't already do the biggest, finest, scariest, most spectacular dragon ever seen onstage. Or offstage, for that matter. He reminded himself to borrow the book so his mother could read it to Tavier, his dragon-mad littlest brother.

Jeska came into their room, dressed to the tips of his kagged ears in a sky-blue silk tunic belted in purple leather. "Isn't he coming with?" he demanded, seeing Cade lounging in the window seat.

"He says not." Mieka gave a shrug. "You'd think," he went on, suddenly remembering what Yazz had advised on the drive here, "that he'd want to see them. Evaluate the competition, like."

Cade snorted and turned another page.

Their masquer bristled. "As if Black Lightning could compete with us on the best day they ever had while we were drunk to the eyeballs!"

"Well, of course, they're not *real* competition," Mieka soothed. "It's just that they *think* they are."

Rafe returned from the garderobe, straightening his belt. "Is he ready yet?"

"He says he's not going."

Rafe glared at Cade. "But don't you want to see what—"

Cade glared right back. "I do not give the tiniest pile of warm wyvern shit what they've got, or think they've got, or indeed have anything to do with them at all." And he made an ostentatious show of writing a few notes on the sheet of paper at his side.

"Hm." Rafe inspected his fingernails. "It innit so much that, is it, as what everybody *else* thinks they've got."

Cade put down his pen. "What d'you mean?" he demanded.

Seeing Jeska hide a smile, Mieka wondered what was going on. They'd both known Cade longer than he had, of course. Still, he couldn't quite see where this line of attack would get them.

"This is their first big show for the gentlemen of the Court, right? Grand expectations, and all that?" Rafe picked at a loose thread on one cuff. "Everybody's already seen their 'Dragon,' and they did all right with the Twelfth this year."

"At least it wasn't as awful as that 'open things and things will be open to you' drivel," Mieka remarked, trying to be helpful.

Rafe ignored him in favor of polishing the buttons of his jacket with a careful finger. "But everybody's seen all that. They have to do something new tonight, something original. Something to astonish every man in the audience—the way the Shadowshapers do."

"The way *we* do!" Mieka couldn't help but exclaim.

Once more Rafe ignored him. "People know what Black Lightning has done in the past—but now they're expecting something way beyond that. Something to set people chavishing all the way back to Gallybanks. Something to make Tobalt Fluter write a whole page about them in *The Nayword*."

Cade looked bored. "What would my presence at this show have to do with any of that?"

"We could laugh in all the wrong places," Mieka suggested, earning himself a stern frown from Jeska. Rafe, who seemed to have all this well in hand, went on ignoring him.

"If you're there to see it for yourself, you can have an opinion."

"Why should my opinion matter?"

"No idea, personally. But other people seem to think it does. Tobalt's rather substantial readership, for instance."

"And so?"

"So if you aren't there, you can't have an opinion. And people will want to know why. Lacking any other explanation, there's those as will be eager to speculate."

"About what?"

"About maybe you didn't attend the show because you're scared of them."

"Me?" Cade was on his feet, the book tumbling to the floor. "*Me*, afraid of *them*?"

And that, as the saying went, was that. Mieka grinned his congratulations at Rafe. Jeska was already out the door. Cade grabbed his jacket, hauled it on, and followed.

Halfway to the castle, Cade snarled at Rafe, "Don't think I don't know when I've been cozened."

"All I did was give you an excuse to do what you wanted to do anyway."

Mieka decided to be helpful again. "Just think how sweetly condescending you can be when Tobalt asks your views on their performance."

"Right!" Jeska smirked. "Printed up in *The Nayword* for everyone to read and ponder."

"Not ponder," Mieka scolded. "Marvel at. The whole world knows that Cade is a *thinker*."

Rafe nodded. "So long as he does it in words everybody else can understand, and leaves the dictionary of pompous vocabulary at home. We do want them to get the point, after all."

Last year, at the Shadowshapers' performance, they'd had personal invitations and prime seats. This year they were relegated to the back, and if the guards at the door hadn't recognized them, they probably wouldn't have got in at all. Scrunched together with minor functionaries and servants, Mieka wriggled his impatience and discomfort until Cade elbowed him a good one.

"Stop it! People know who we are!"

"Mayhap so," Rafe whispered, "but tonight nobody cares."

Mieka was not disposed to enjoy that notion. After nearly a fortnight of being recognized everywhere they

went in Seekhaven—he'd signed his name to more placards than he'd thought Kearney Fairwalk ordered printed
up—the only nods and smiles he'd seen directed at
Touchstone were the ones from the guards at the door.
He found he didn't much like being anonymous.

"It's said," a man in Prince Ashgar's livery whispered
excitedly to his companion, "that when the Lightning
strikes, no man is left unscathed!"

Jeska muttered, "Is that what they're putting on their
placards now? *The* Lightning?"

Another man was saying, "Saw them in Stiddolfe last
year, with my brother who's a gatekeeper at the University. And I'll tell you one thing for certes. Nobody who
sees them once can see them *only* once."

Cade murmured, "No, they just keep coming back to
haunt you—like a bad lamb stew."

"Your Majesty—Your Royal Highness—Your
Grace—my lords and gentlemen!" bawled the Master
of Revelries. "Black Lightning!" And as the curtains began to part, he scuttled off the stage as fast as he could.

Kaj Seamark, the thin and pallid masquer, had barely
taken up position when Mieka had to catch his breath,
staggered by the strength of the magic that suddenly
saturated Fliting Hall. It was impossible to tell right now
the nature of that strength. The fettler, Herris Crowkeeper,
could be keeping tight hold on exceptionally powerful
magic, or their glisker, Pirro Spangler, could be using
withies spelled with tremendous energy by tregetour
Thierin Knottinger, or a combination of these. Master
Glisker though he was, Mieka had trouble sorting it.

And he wanted very much to stay as detached from
the performance as Cayden always did, so that he *could*
sort it. In the presence of the Shadowshapers, he inevitably gave in to the skill of the players and went wherever
it pleased them to take him, as compliantly swayed as

any member of an audience totally ignorant of how it was all done. What they wanted him to feel, touch, smell, see, taste, and hear, these things he willingly gave himself to—because with the Shadowshapers, he knew he was safe. He'd worked with them once and knew how heedful they were of every fine distinction; he knew them personally and trusted their magic and their intentions. It should have been the same with Black Lightning, or at least regarding Pirro Spangler—he and Mieka had taken lessons from the same tutor, after all. But these first few instants, with the fierce glut of magic produced by Black Lightning—this felt dangerous.

"'The Lost Ones,'" proclaimed Knottinger, and Mieka was surprised yet again. Seldom performed these days, never a part of Touchstone's folio—he knew the story, and that was all. What Black Lightning would do with it, and how they hoped to impress the audience, was beyond his imagining.

The way the traditional tale went was that one day the chiefest of the Old Gods, tired of his daily duties and longing for some quiet family life, went to call upon his wife. She was busy bathing their children. She hadn't finished when he presented himself at her door, for she had so very many children, and so she brought into the room only those that were already clean. When her husband asked if she had no other offspring—for he seemed to recall a few more—she replied that she had none, for she was ashamed to show him all the little unwashed children and had hidden them away. But he heard them crying for their mother, and became angry, and said, "What woman hides from me, I will hide from men." His wife ran back into the kitchen, and discovered that all the little unwashed children had vanished to the hills and moors and woods and the lonely places, to live there apart from their brothers and sisters, invisible and abandoned. The sobbing mother bemoaned the loss of her children, while the wails of the forsaken ones echoed in the distance. The father, moved by their cries, regretful of his tantrum, vowed to help her find each and every one of their offspring, which he declared were as dear to him as all the rest.

It was a very old tale and a very old playlet, said to be written by a King who himself had the blood of Wizards and Gnomes, and was supposed to be a reprimand to parents who kagged an Elfen infant's pointed ears, or bleached a Goblin's red-mottled skin to purest white, or otherwise changed or disguised the physical signs of magical heritage.

Black Lightning made "The Lost Ones" into something very different.

In their version, it was not one of the Old Gods but the Lord himself who came to the Lady's residence and asked to see their offspring. Seamark was at first the Lady, robed and hooded in green, presiding over an unruly tribe of children: small flittering shapes easily seen to be Gnomes and Trolls, Pikseys and Sprites and Goblins, every magical race except Wizards and Elves. At the sound of the Lord's voice, she kicked aside the unwashed children and scolded them into silence as waves of annoyed disgust washed over the audience. Seamark made the change to the Lord, garbed in blue, thundering his rage at seeing all the dirty little children. And what happened once the Lord had banished them had the audience gasping. In a trice, he became once more the Lady, who neither wept nor pleaded. Instead, she nodded and bent her knees, praising the Lord's wisdom in rejecting the imperfect and the soiled.

All at once Seamark allowed the Lady's hood to fall back, revealing gracefully pointed ears. Knottinger suddenly stepped from behind his lectern, clothed in the

Lord's sky-blue robes, tall and Wizardly and holding out his hand to his Elfen wife. The whines and whimpers of the vanished children trickled away into silence. Then the Wizardly Lord said things that had never been part of the script before.

"And best riddance to them all—neither good enough for Heaven, nor bad enough for Hell. Mischievous Pikseys and troublesome Trolls and gross misshapen Goblins. Blood-soaked Redcaps, sullen Gnomes, and gobble-tongued Giants—all gone. So, too, the cunning Merfolk and hideous Harpies and especially the treacherous Fae—all invisible to the eyes of common man. But who was left? Which of the children did the Lord not curse?"

Onstage there appeared two swirls of white smoke. Lightning—jagged splinters of black, of course—stabbed first one column of smoke and then the other. The audience cried out as two figures appeared: an Elf and a Wizard.

"These, the favored children, the clean and virtuous children, the blithe and the wise! The children who alone resembled the Lord and Lady in looks and in merits! These, the only children seen by ordinary honest Human souls! Look upon these children who alone could be seen, who alone were washed by the Lady's own loving hands, cleansed of all taint! These, the givers of all music and poetry, art and crafting, knowledge, magic, and everything worth anything in life!"

Joy and gratitude, and awed delight—the tregetour had primed these into the withies, and the glisker conjured them, and the fettler let them rush across the audience in torrents. There was a taste of honeyed wine, a scent of rain-washed roses warming in the sun, and the figures of the Elf and the Wizard glowed as if the lightning lingered in their bodies. But when the tregetour finished his recitation, the emotions changed violently. Needle-prickles of panic and dread swept the hall. And to either side of the Elf and the Wizard other swirls of smoke appeared, black and brown and dirty, and the taste was of mold and the scent was all decay.

"But terrible things transpired," the tregetour breathed. "The Elf, the Wizard, they alone could look upon their lost brethren—the Troll and the Gnome, the Piksey and the Sprite, the Goblin and the Giant, and especially the Fae. And these jealous beings stole Elf and Wizard and even Human children away from here and there, taking them without warning into their invisible world to steal pieces of their clean-washed souls. From these they bred the halflings. And as years stretched to centuries, the descendants of the halflings lost their wings, their claws, their taste for blood and living flesh, and became almost . . . almost . . . *almost* Human."

Knottinger's voice softened so that all strained to hear him whisper those last two words: *almost Human*. The fear was raw, visceral, no subtlety about it. As powerful as Cade's own magic was, as intimately as Mieka knew the tricks players used to produce such effects, still he could not fight off this cold terror.

Fear of himself. Of what he was. Of those other races whose blood commingled in his body. Of Piksey and Sprite and Fae, the dirty unwashed banished children . . .

He sensed warmth next to him, and huddled closer to it—to Cade, who never allowed himself to succumb to anyone's magic, who always held himself apart and scarcely touched. He felt thin fingers lace with his own, and the terror began to drain away. Quill was here. He was safe.

The Lordly Wizard held aloft a glowing golden withie, and lightning once more flashed across the stage. He flung the shining glass twig towards the Elfen Lady in a graceful arc, and quick hands caught it, and black flame flared from the withie, annihilating the groupings of murky smoke all around. But then it did more: the fire reached far out into the audience, above their heads, banishing the fear, replacing it with pleasure, leaving behind a scent like new leaves and fresh bread, and the caress of soft summery rain, and the distant sweet sound of Minster chimes. The release was like surcease of pain, like warmth to shivering limbs. Mieka clung to Cade's hand and felt like weeping.

And then darkness, and silence. No one breathed. All at once a dozen strokes of black lightning split the air, and the tregetour and glisker, the masquer and fettler, all four were there onstage, clothed only as themselves in harsh black, shoulder to shoulder. Grinning.

Touchstone walked back to their lodgings in silence, applause that belonged to someone else still thundering in their ears. Their first round of ale was consumed without comment. At last, in the empty taproom, Cade stared into his empty glass and spoke. Cade the analytical; Cade the intellectual; Cade the one who never let himself feel the entirety of anyone's performance.

"I don't know how they did it, and I'm thinking I don't want to know. They targeted magic tonight, specific magic to specific bloodlines."

"I was ashamed of what I am," Mieka said. "Piksey, Sprite, Fae. The words were in my head like curses—like the way those people looked at me in that tavern last summer."

"I didn't hear myself being called any names, and I didn't feel anything except the washing water." Rafe downed the rest of his drink. "Wizard. That's all I am, besides Human."

"Nothing else at all?" Mieka clucked his tongue against his teeth. "Now I know why you're so boring."

Feeble joke, feeble smiles. But he had to admit he wasn't much in the mood for laughter, himself.

Cade turned his drink this way and that, staring at the patterns of color in the glass. "Any man in that audience who's got only Human or Wizard or Elfen blood—he felt the washing. He knows he's 'clean' according to this new version of things."

Jeska knocked back alcohol in a manner uncharacteristic of him. "I didn't feel any water."

"And thus you didn't feel 'clean.' The man beside me, the one who said about not being able to see Black Lightning only once, he felt it. He was smiling. Someone behind me and to the right, he was squirming. He's partly Gnome or Goblin or what-the-fuck-ever, and he felt dirty. Ashamed, like Mieka said."

"But how could they have specified the magic?" Rafe asked. "They can't possibly know any of those men. How could they target that way?"

Cade shook his head, still speaking to his drink. "It isn't a matter of having people at the doors making note of ears and teeth and skin and the way someone walks—that would be impossible. They'd have to identify everybody, and where exactly they're seated, and get the information to the group right before the show and that's just not possible."

Mieka was only on his second ale, but suddenly lost his taste for it. "They've got some sort of magic that tells them who's what without all that bother."

"Almost, but not quite right," Cade said. "The magic is specific and targeted, like Rafe says. But it—" Suddenly he raked both hands back through his hair. "It *seeks*. That's the only way I can describe it."

Rafe held up a palm as Mistress Luta approached with more ale. "Beholden, no," he told her. "Mayhap later." Then, to Cayden: "There's always been ways of sussing out who's what. Indicators of what kind of blood a person's got. Mieka's ears give him away, but even if they were round as any Human's, there's other things about him that scream *Elf*. And even if all those weren't present, you put him in total darkness long enough, and he'll conjure up a nice little golden light, sure as eggs is eggs."

"I'm not afeared of the dark," Mieka said curtly. "It's one Elfen thing I missed, praise all the Old Gods."

"Well, then, we'd just have to sit around and wait to see how slow your beard grows. Same for Jeska, that way. There's always something physical, isn't there? Those with Troll blood can train themselves to walk different, but when it comes to running, there's no concealing the way they move. What I'm saying is that however somebody tries to hide whatever shows up on the outside, there's ways of finding out what they really are."

"This is different." Cade took a swallow of ale, as if to get a foul taste from his tongue. "It's magic meant for particular kinds of people. If I'd got caught in it, I would've been thinking like you, only it would be Fae and Troll and so forth."

Jeska said slowly, "I've always known about the Elf—no other reason to kag my ears."

"Except mayhap Fae," Rafe reminded him.

"And yet you felt unclean." Cade looked over at him. "Goblin?"

Jeska nodded. "How did you know?"

"You come back from visiting your mother seaside, you're sun-browned. But you never stand too near a blazing fire, do you? Mottles your skin. Blye's the same way, if she stands too long too near her kiln. And the fair hair—there are a dozen Goblin lines that breed true for being blond as butter."

Mieka wanted to ask a sudden inappropriate question: How had all these races got mixed up together in the first place? But he knew Cade would only look down his long nose and say something like, *"Why, how very prurient of you, Master Windthistle!"* And Rafe would give a derisive snort, and Jeska would snigger and say, *"If you have to ask, it's a wonder you ever became a father!"* So he kept quiet. But he couldn't help wondering, all the same.

"How could this magic know what I am?" Jeska paused. "And why did *you* never say anything?"

"Because it doesn't matter." Cade stood, kicking back his chair. "It doesn't fucking *matter!*"

Mistress Luta glanced up from sorting herbs on a table, startled. Cade righted his chair and sat down again, managing a smile of apology in her direction.

"It doesn't matter," he repeated more quietly. "All the Wizardly Clans—Falcon and Spider and Elk and so forth, all the ways Elfenkind describe themselves with Water and Air and on, whether a Troll family comes from the mountains or the flatlands or has tended the same bridge for generations—none of it matters. It isn't a man's abilities that count. It's what he does with them, what he makes of himself and the world around him. It just doesn't *matter* what someone's born—but now I think it's going to. And I don't know why."

Mieka pushed his glass away, for probably the first time in his life. "Great-great-great-grandmother, the Clinquant House Horror, says there's sounds only purebred Elves can hear. She might be right. If she is, then that's like this, innit? Some things only Goblins can sense, or Gnomes, or Fae—only it's magic, not a sound or smell. Something that says to them, *This is what you are.* Does it talk back?"

"Magic heritage responding to the seeking magic? Interesting thought," Cade mused. "Why would they do such a thing, though? What's the point? It's magic I've never heard of before."

"Pity you're not in contact with your Sagemaster Emmot anymore to ask him," Rafe said. "According to you, he knew everything there was to know about magic."

"Liked to pretend he did." Cade shrugged. "I'll take a look in some books when we get home. But right now I have to decide what to say when Tobalt asks me for an interview. And he will, y'know. Rafe was right, earlier on."

"Well, you can't tell him this!" Mieka exclaimed.

"And I can't tell him what I really think, either." He traced the rim of his glass with one finger. "The Crystal Sparks turn the traditional inside out, but they don't make much that's original. They're for those who want to play at being rebels, for the unruly who don't really want to defy the world, just sneer at it. The Shadowshapers, they innovate. Style, substance, performance—they're artists who make the art understandable."

"But it's safe," Mieka blurted. "I don't mean the feelings, sometimes those aren't comfortable at all. But you always know they're in perfect control of what they do."

Cade nodded. "With Black Lightning, it's the chance that things *could* get out of control that brings people to see them. It's the danger. The feeling that you're on the edge. You heard what that man said—nobody goes to see them only once. You can go to them over and over again for that same thrill. Like dragon tears. They're a group for addicts."

"And us?" Jeska asked. "What about us?"

"We're as good with the conventional things as anyone. We don't do what the Sparks do, turning everything inside out. We come at the old plays from a different direction. New perspectives, so audiences see things a new way. As for the original plays—"

"You make them *want* to think, Quill," Mieka interrupted. "It's not just offering it up, like Vered does, throwing it out there for them to do as they like. He lets everybody know what *he* thinks, but he doesn't much care if they understand it. If they do, fine—doesn't matter to him one way or the other. But you—you're daring them to understand, to work it out for themselves."

Rafe said, "We showed them the whole story of 'Treasure,' but putting in the words that condemned the Archduke's father—that makes for a different sort of resonance. Both in emotions and in thoughts. It's there every time we perform it."

Cade gave a self-conscious little shrug. "It seemed right to do it that way."

"It was brilliant and you know it," Mieka told him.

"Whether it was or not, you're right that it *is* different from the way Vered works. I want them to understand. To think about what they've experienced."

"Changing the world?" Rafe asked softly.

"I was drunk when I said that. Tobalt never should've printed it."

Jeska glanced over to the door as it opened and let in a burst of vehement conversation. "Talking of whom—and I mean not just Tobalt but also the Shadowshapers and the Sparks—"

As the new arrivals piled into the taproom, calling for drinks and food, Cade looked almost panicky. Mieka patted his arm. "No worrying. I'll get Tobalt so drunk, he won't be able to hold a pen nor remember a single word you say."

Seven

ALTHOUGH TOBALT FLUTER hadn't even brought a pen that evening, and didn't get quite drunk enough to forget all he heard, whatever was said featured not at all in the long article he wrote for *The Nayword*. The pages (two and a half of them) of his report about Trials detailed each performance according to its eventual importance (the Shadowshapers, as First Flight on the Royal, got the most space, but Touchstone wasn't far behind). There was a stark description of Black Lightning's new piece, but no commentary. This didn't surprise Cayden. That last night in Seekhaven, Tobalt had said quite frankly that he didn't know what to make of the thing and would have to see it again before he could form an opinion. That this was a tacit invitation to make his own opinion known did not escape Cade, but all he did was smile and say he looked forward to reading the broadsheet once Tobalt had made up his mind and written a review of "The Lost Ones."

Cade had an opinion, of course. He didn't intend to share it with Tobalt. And though most of the talk that night was about Black Lightning, he didn't share his thoughts with anyone else, either. Just Touchstone; just the people he completely trusted. Looked at sidewise, that meant that he did trust Mieka with the truth of his thoughts, in spite of what the Elf revealed to his wife about the Elsewhens. Mieka hadn't meant to do that, and even if he had meant it, Cade would have forgiven him. Chances were that he'd forgive Mieka anything, and he considered himself mature enough at twenty-one to realize that this probably wasn't good for either of them.

Reconsidering the Elsewhen where the old woman snarled about how drunk and angry Mieka had been when he'd betrayed Cade's secret, Cade understood something else: that if Mieka felt himself to be included in Cade's confidence, there would be no more similar episodes. Treat him like a child, and he behaved like a child. Trust him, and he was trustworthy.

Or so Cayden had to believe.

If he accepted that Mieka was Mieka, and trying to change him was doomed to failure, then perhaps he'd never become angry enough to batter that beautiful Elfen face to a bloody ruin. The Archduke could believe about the Elsewhens or not; that didn't matter much to Cade. What did matter, what he feared, was the violence that could come of fury.

It wasn't the actual coming to blows that frightened him. He'd slugged enough other people in his life—and been clobbered in turn for it—that he knew whatever scrapes and bruises or even broken bones that ensued would heal, given time and a good physicker. (Or, he thought with a reminiscent smile, Mistress Mirdley, who had patched him up when one of the local boys needed lessoning about keeping his slurs about Goblins to himself. Not that Cade had done the teaching; it was Blye who'd got in a good swift kick where it mattered most after the boy had blacked Cade's eye. They'd been six years old.) No, it wasn't physical damage he feared. It was what losing control would mean inside, in his heart and in his mind. It would mean that he'd given up. And that, he would never do.

But Mieka wasn't his main worry on the drive back to Gallantrybanks. The subject occupying his mind was something he'd overheard in a Fliting Hall corridor just after their performance of "Treasure" at Trials. He was fully aware of the hypocrisy of keeping this to himself while deciding he ought to share everything with Mieka and Jeska and Rafe. Still, he wanted to think it through before he spoke—something he would never as long as he lived expect Mieka to do. But that was simply the way Mieka was.

What Cade overheard had startled him at the time. Later, once he had the chance to ponder a bit, it made him furious.

"Do you s'pose that's the true way of it?"

"Was that meant for a joke? How could he possibly know what really happened?"

"There was a lot of detail, and it felt true."

"They're players! It's meant to feel true! And Cayden Silversun, he's a writer, isn't he? Makes up stories all day and half the night. All of them do. It's what they're paid for."

"But—"

"But bollocks! It all came out of his head. He imagined the whole thing. It's no more real than the so-called Rights of the Fae. Dreamshine, that's all it is."

Once he'd thought about it, and got beyond anger, he realized something that he finally shared with his partners the morning after they left Seekhaven.

"Nobody really believes us, you know. About the Treasure."

Mieka and Rafe glanced up from their card game.

Jeska came out of a half-doze in his hammock, mumbling, "What? Are we there?"

"There's no proof," Cade went on. "They think it's naught but a story I made up." He set aside the book he'd been pretending to read. "We didn't identify the exact place with a name. We never called it Nackerty Close. We've never been there in person, so we couldn't show them anything they could recognize through visual clues. We didn't put in a damned thing that makes it believable, that convinces people that it's a real place and those were real events and that it all really happened the way we showed them it did."

Mieka was scowling. "Briuly and Alaen—"

"—can't be bothered," Rafe finished for him. "The one's too busy being an Artist, and the other's too busy being forlorn over Chirene."

"So let's go find it ourselves! That'd show everybody!"

Jeska said, "We've been through this before. It doesn't belong to us. We can't be the ones to find it."

Cade shocked them all by saying, "We may have to."

"Just to prove you're right?" Rafe slapped his cards onto the table and leaned back in the low, soft chair. "You'd diddle two friends and their families out of whatever the King would pay to have the Rights in his own hands, just to bloat your reputation?"

He felt his face burn crimson. "I didn't say we had to keep it."

"Why not?" Mieka demanded. "If we're the ones to find it, then why not?"

"Because it isn't ours," Jeska said again.

"Ooh, and isn't it just the most upright honorable little subject of His Majesty!" Mieka sneered. "We'll split your share, then, if you've such scruples!"

Cade ought to have known any attempt to talk about

this would degenerate into a verbal brawl. He sat there
listening to them squabble, looking only at Rafe, whose
disapproval stung.

Jeska and Mieka shut up only when Yazz roared
from the coachman's bench. "By Gods, have done!"

Mieka unhooked his hammock, fastened it into place,
and didn't bother with the mattress. "Wake me when
we're home," he growled, and turned his back on them.

Nothing was said for another hour or so, not until
Yazz stopped to give the horses a breather. Cade descended the wagon steps, stretched, and walked a few
paces down the road. Rafe was right behind him.

"So you want to show everybody, like Mieka said."

"I want them to know it's the truth."

"Why?"

"Because it is. Because the truth is important."

"You already gave the Archduke one in the eye, quoting those words at the end of the play. What is it you're
really after?"

"Just what I said. That everybody knows it's real."

"What does that get you, besides a swelled head?"

He turned to confront his old friend. "If the truth
doesn't matter to you, fine. I'm not made that way."

"Oh, and which part of you will you credit with this
devotion to what's real and true? Is it something in
your Elfenblood—which, thanks to Black fucking
Lightning, we all know now that I've none of? Or mayhap the Troll? The Fae? That must be it. Going to claim
the Rights for yourself, are you? By reason of exalted
heritage?"

"Damn it, Rafe, you know that's not it!"

"Then tell me what it is."

Jeska said behind them, "He wants everyone to know
he's right. It's that simple, Rafe. He wants to find the

carkenet and crown, with independent witnesses to confirm how and where he found them, and then he wants to hear it proclaimed the length and breadth of Albeyn that he was *right*."

"And what does that gain him? Not the money."

"No." Jeska kicked at a rock in the road. "I doubt he's thought it out this far, but what it really gains him is a thousand people at his door, wanting him to find a missing this or long-lost that. Another thousand who want to show him jewelry what's been in the family forever, with appropriate old stories, and have him say it's Fae-wrought. The Royal Librarian will want him to rake through every ancient text in the Archives, searching for clues to any other little dibs and daubs nobody's been able to figure out before. And then there'll be those who actually do some thinking about it." He gave Cayden an upslanting smile. "The ones who'll want to know how you knew, and won't take scholarship or research for an answer. And then you'll *really* be in the shit, won't you?"

No, he hadn't thought it out that far.

"Leave them lie, Cade," Rafe said. "If Alaen or Briuly want to play the bright lad and go looking, fine. Content yourself with good reviews, can't you?"

He usually had plenty to say about just about anything. He had no reply for this. They returned to the wagon and occupied themselves in individual pursuits—Jeska with totting up his own bank account, Rafe playing cards against himself, and Cade with a book he didn't read. Mieka was sleeping, or still in a snit pretending to be asleep. It didn't matter. They were only a few hours from home.

Yet *home* was not the refuge of solitude, high up in his fifth-floor room, that it had always been. They had exactly four days before they'd start out on the Royal Circuit, and in those four days, there were at least four hundred things to be done.

Packing. Making sure there were withies enough and to spare. Finalizing their portfolio. Playing a last show at the Keymarker before they left Gallantrybanks for the summer. And a long consultation with Lord Kearney Fairwalk in strictest privacy.

He had no intention of leaving before he'd arranged the transfer of his grandfather's legacy to a new account, nice and legal, with only two people having access to it. Kearney was all agog at his explanation of the bargain he'd made with his mother, but the look Cade gave him when he was about to ask why Lady Jaspiela's name would not also be on the account guaranteed that the question was not asked. They paid a visit to Kearney's lawyer, and then to the bank, and all was put in order. Bills for Derien's school and books and suchlike would be sent to Kearney's clerks, and anything questionable— payment demands from Lady Jaspiela's favorite dress- maker, for instance—would be forwarded to Cayden or His Lordship to be approved . . . or not. The final pa- pers were signed the day before the Royal Circuit started. And, as things had taken a bit longer than anticipated, Cade had Kearney drop him off directly at the Key- marker. He watched the carriage move cautiously down the narrow street, then remembered something and ran after it.

"Did you arrange for horses along the route?" The huge white animals belonging to the Shadowshapers would not be available to Touchstone, for of course the Shadowshapers would be using them all.

"Everything perfectly in order," His Lordship assured him, leaning out the window of his carriage. "Don't fret, Cayden, I know what I'm doing!"

"I know, I know—it's just—"

"You can't help yourself. You worry about your art, my dear boy, and let me take care of everything else. Hurry, now, or you'll be late for the performance!"

He wasn't late, but it was a near thing. Because of their early start on the morrow, the show tonight would be an early one. The placards announcing it read: THE DOORS OPEN AT SIX. THE TROUBLE STARTS AT SEVEN!

"New barmaid," Mieka commented as they took the stage. "Not their usual. Must be a cousin or something who needs the work."

Cade glanced over the settling crowd and picked out the new girl at once. The Keymarker had recently decided to specialize in leggy redheads. This girl wore the same black skirt, green blouse, and white apron as all the others, but she was a pocket-sized blond with a thick braid swinging down her back to her waist. As the barmaids finished delivering orders and gathered along the back wall to watch the performance, the new one looked ridiculous amidst all the tall, lissome young women with masses of red hair. Mieka must be right: cousin or niece or friend-of-a-friend needful of a job, or filling in tonight for one of the regular girls.

He did his usual survey of the audience as Rafe and Mieka set up the beginnings of the magic. Nobody here was particularly sensitive, so he relaxed. In spite of what Mistress Mirdley had said about various combinations of bloodlines producing unpredictabilities (such as Cade himself), he tended to agree with Sagemaster Emmot: Whatever magic each of the old races had, each generation saw it diluted just a little more. The play they were doing tonight was a perfect demonstration. "Dwarmy Day" involved a haughty Wizard who refused to pay the bridge passage fee to an understandably irate Troll. The spells they used could still be found in reference books, but nobody Cade had ever heard of could conjure them for real nowadays. Lack of skill, lack of education, or lack of sufficient specific magic?

Traditionally this was a "glisker's choice" sort of playlet. No group attempted it that did not trust absolutely in its masquer's ability to improvise. Accordingly, Cade had primed the withies with all sorts of things for Mieka to play with, and Jeska did his partners proud.

The first gambit was a cloud of grayish smoke called by the Troll so that the Wizard couldn't even see the bridge. Jeska made a great show of coughing and waving his arms about, then took in a huge breath and blew the cloud out over the audience, where it turned to sparkles like glass shards. Triumphant, he spit into his hand. A swirl of moisture rose from his palm and became a rain cloud. It hovered briefly over his head while he grinned—but before he could use it, the Troll's laughter (Rafe, over at his lectern) boomed through the theater as the cloud burst and the Wizard was drenched in his own spit. The audience chortled—Mieka had evidently decided to save the sensation of being soaked to the skin for the end. Sure enough, he could hear Mieka chuckling to himself as the infuriated Troll finally stomped out from his den beneath the bridge. When the Elf was feeling especially playful, he gave the audience not just the feeling of water but sopped undergarments as well when the Wizard hit the river. Tonight he had the audience squirming.

The play ended, a couple of withies were shattered in midair between Jeska and the glisker's bench, the applause began, and Cade was about to walk out from behind his lectern to join his partners in their bows when he sensed a snag in the magic. Frowning, he looked immediately to Mieka. If the Elf had been drinking too much again, or pricking some new kind of thorn—

But those changeable eyes were very nearly sober. Not Mieka, then. Cade glanced at Rafe and nearly tripped over his own feet. Calm, laconic Master Fettler Rafcadion Threadchaser was as close to sizzling furious as Cade had ever seen him.

They bowed, and again, but Rafe didn't stay for a third. He was down off the stage and striding to the back of the room, where the barmaids had dispersed to refill glasses.

"What's wrong with him?" Jeska asked.

Mieka raked sweat-damp hair off his face. "Thirsty, mayhap? I know I am!"

Cade's progress through the crowd was delayed by compliments and backslaps. When he finally found Rafe over near the side door, the fettler was pointing a long finger in the blond barmaid's face.

"—d'you think you were doing, girl? Do you have any idea how dangerous it is to twiddle about with magic? And don't tell me you didn't know what you were doing, neither!"

"I won't tell you that because it wouldn't be true," she replied coolly. "You know that as well as I do."

"Then what in the unholy fuck was all that?"

"There's a girl here tonight who's barely twelve. Right on the verge of her magic. So she's a little delicate."

"Girl? What girl?"

"Her older brother sneaks her in dressed as a boy. Not the first time, probably not the last. I've had words with him, but he's responsible for her—if you can call it that—while their parents are out at work until midnight. He's sixteen and perfectly besotted for theater, so whenever he can, he slinks into the Keymarker by working an hour or two carrying crates up from the cellar."

Cade nodded his understanding. "He brings his little sister along with him to sit in a corner out of the way, and when the place starts to fill up, everyone's too busy to keep an eye on either of them. So he sees a show for free—no, he actually gets paid, doesn't he, for the work done beforehand? Smart lad! And then he scarpers as quick as may be, to get home before his parents."

She gave him a glance from bottle-green eyes flecked with gold. "Not half stupid, are you?" Tossing the braid of dark-blond hair over her shoulder, she looked up at Rafe again. "Anyways, if I hadn't put up a bit of a guard between her and that mad little glisker of yours, and done it before your magic even began, what her screaming would've done to your concentration I don't like to think."

Amused, Cade watched Rafe's face as insult competed with outrage. Cade could guess what was running through his mind—Hells, it was clear enough in his face. Bad enough was the implication that a fettler of Rafe's talent and experience wouldn't sense a vulnerable child in the audience. Worse: that he in fact *hadn't* sensed it, because this girl had established a buffer before the first magic swept through the Keymarker—and he hadn't sensed that, either, until the very end. (Neither had Cayden, not until that little hitch.) Worse still was her insufferable cheek in thinking he not only wouldn't recognize frailty but couldn't adjust for it. But worst of all, she was a *girl*.

Rafe was drawing breath to express himself on any or all of these points when a barman yelled, "Megs!" and the girl flinched.

"Rafe," Cade said mildly, "we're keeping her from her work."

Finger in her face again, Rafe snapped, "Just don't you interfere in mine anymore, understand me?" He pivoted on one heel and made for the tiring room.

"Ale, please," Cade said swiftly, seeing she was about to escape. "Four, actually. Could you bring them backstage? Beholden." As he watched her go, he gave in to the smile that had been twitching his mouth. Though it was Mieka's opinion that there were seven sorts of female, Rafe recognized only two: Crisiant and everybody else. Each might have her individual place—mother, shopkeeper, glasscrafter, princess—but those places were to be kept to and no arguments about it. This barmaid who appeared to have the skills of a fettler . . . this wasn't something to which Rafe would raise an approving toast.

In the tiring room, Rafe had sprawled in a low chair as Mieka and Jeska finished packing up the glass baskets and spent withies. Cade saw the questions on the faces of his glisker and masquer, and wondered why neither had felt that little hiccup in the magic. He had no chance to say anything, because Megs was right behind him, expertly lofting a tray of four ales and a bowl of the Keymarker's special baked pompkin squash, a delicacy from the Islands provided at great trouble and expense, according to the owner, but in reality available at several dockside markets, according to Mistress Mirdley.

Rafe glared at the girl. Mieka looked more bewildered than ever. Jeska polished off his charm, as usual when around a girl whether she was pretty or not. Cade watched, fighting another smile, as he helped distribute the glasses and serve little plates of food.

"Beholden," she muttered.

"And what might your name be, darlin'?" Jeska asked.

She kept her gaze on the empty tray in her hands. "Megs."

"Megs what?"

With a long-suffering sigh: "Knolltender."

Jeska smiled. "And are you?"

She gave him a broad, toothy smile. "Congratulations! You're the five thousandth person who's tried to make that pun!"

"So what have I won?"

"A vocabulary lesson," Cade said. "It's tender as in 'minder,' not 'affectionate.'"

"I said he *tried*," Megs reminded him. "I didn't say he succeeded." Tucking the tray beneath her arm, she bobbed a mocking curtsy and strode out.

"Nice exit line," Jeska remarked.

Cade said, "Let's finish our drinks and get out of here. If I know you lot—and I know you very well indeed—you still have packing to do, and we leave tomorrow early."

"On the Royal Circuit," Mieka said with a contented sigh. "Y'know, I don't think I'll ever tire of saying that!"

* * *

IT OCCURRED TO Cayden on their fifth day out that he'd seen the Continent bedecked in summer, but not his own homeland. He'd never gone traveling like this before. That first Winterly, in the King's Coach, had been at times a sheer cold-clotted misery; the second, in the Shadowshapers' wagon, had been much more comfortable, but still . . . the *Winterly*. Landscape swathed in snow, roads knee-deep in mud, skies shrouded in dismal gray, and not much scenery even on the better days.

But Cade discovered, on Touchstone's first Royal Circuit, that his country was magnificently beautiful. He had seen only its autumnal gold and brown, its wintry gray and white. Sitting up on the coachman's bench with

Yazz, wind gusting through his hair, the boisterous drench of summer colors amazed him.

Green, for instance. It had only ever been a color of coolness to him before; he learned that it could be warm, drowsy, richly scented. Wheat rippling in endless fields; fruit trees bursting with pears and walnuts, apricots and almonds; dignified oaks quivering slightly with the chase and dance of foraging squirrels. *Green* was the tart juice of gooseberries picked sun-warm from stream-side bushes, and the moist tang of grass crushed under-foot. It was the emerald flash of dragonfly wings, the limp drapery of a woman's skirt rucked up into her belt as she worked, and waves of tangleskein moss clinging to river stones.

And there was noise, too, infinitely more noise than in winter. It was the animals, mainly. A Gallybanker, in the usual daily run of things, heard horses, dogs and cats, and the occasional caged songbird trilling in somebody's open window. Out here in the fields there were horses aplenty, of course, and dogs and cats, and a profusion of birds. But the lowing cattle, bleating sheep, grunting swine, and whatever sound goats made when provoked—for which Cade had no word, and this irked him—these things, although not precisely new to him, were in summer a raucous counterpoint to the flurrying wind and rushing streams.

There were people sounds, too: Workers calling to each other, laughing, singing. Steady hammering that meant a new house or barn, hacking axes that felled a tree, the clack of bricks being piled into small burnt- red mountains, the clanging of blacksmiths at the forge, the creak and groan of a grinding mill.

The stillness and silence of winter had its match, though, in the lazy quiet of a country road at late twilight.

All the workers were at their dinners; all the day's outdoor toil was done. Cade envied these people nothing about their lives except the scant hour of twilight hush, when all the world was drowsing.

Except for the insects. Hum, whine, buzz, click-snick, drone—in winter there were spiders and bedbugs, ground-bound and silent. In summer things flew all over the place, flies and bees and wasps and gnats and other things he didn't recognize but instinctively didn't like. Was it better, he wondered, to get bitten by something you never heard coming, or to have the warning of whirring wings so you could make a fool of yourself trying to slap away something you couldn't hardly see?

The Royal Circuit was different from the Winterly in other ways. Without snow and mud to slog through, travel time was cut by about a quarter. And because travel was easier for everyone, there were more shows at each venue. Farmers could bring their families into town for a little overnight holiday, leaving the crops to the hired hands, and the next day give their fieldmen a treat in town likewise. The Royal and Ducal Circuits were timed to coincide where possible with local fairs and festivals—from something as simple as a local lord's Namingday to the annual celebration at New Halt of the Miraculous Mending of the Sails by some Angel or other. (Nobody had ever made a play on the subject, which was odd, so Cade really didn't know much about it.) There were also more opportunities for private shows, because during the summer the nobility went on progress to their estates or traveled to visit friends and relations. This year, for example, Lord Coldkettle's nephew was being married; the Shadowshapers would perform on the first day of the festivities, Touchstone on the last.

There wasn't much overlap among the three groups on the Royal. A few times the Shadowshapers' wagon would be rolling out of an innyard just as Touchstone's wagon was rolling in. They crossed paths with the Crystal Sparks only once. Third Flight on each circuit went in the opposite direction from the first two, so rather than heading north on the route from Shollop to Dolven Wold to Sidlowe and so forth, the Crystal Sparks began in Stiddolfe and went to Frimham, Castle Biding, Lilyleaf, and north from there. Cade had to admire the logician who planned this out for all three Circuits. The whole of Albeyn loved a play, but there had to be enough time between performances to whet the appetite again.

Taken all in all, Cayden was highly satisfied with the Royal. Touchstone was a proficient, creative entity now; each man enjoyed his work more than ever; audiences were large and approving; the wagon was nigh on perfect; Cade had no complaints. There was even a set of Rules, framed and nailed to the inside of the wagon door.

Abstinence from liquor is discouraged.

No unsanctioned plays are permitted. This includes unfunny farces, mawkish melodramas, pointless poetry, and anything featuring the deflowering of a giggling moronic virgin.

At all stops, refrain from the use of rough fingernails in the presence of ladies and children.

Hammocks are provided for your comfort. Do not abuse the privilege by hogging all the pillows. The offender will be tied up inside his hammock for the duration of the journey.

Do not snore *at all*. Do not accuse your Master Glisker of snoring. He never snores. *Never*.

In the event of runaway horses, remain calm. Leaping from the wagon in panic will result in being laughed at by your fellow passengers.

Should the driver (who is taller than you by half a mile and outweighs you by half a ton) judge a passenger guilty of any of the following offenses, that person shall receive chastisement as the driver determines.

1. Foul farting
2. Sobriety
3. Good manners
4. Inaccuracy in aiming at the pisspot
5. Unwarranted celibacy
6. Endangering the sanity of fellow passengers

The Rules are brought to you by Mieka Windthistle. Obey them or suffer.

"Suffer what?" Rafe wanted to know when first he read through them.

"Dire things," Mieka promised.

"Such as?"

"Dire, dreadful things."

"I'm waiting."

"Dire, dreadful, disgusting, damaging—"

"Good Gods!" Cade exclaimed. "He swallowed a dictionary!"

"—distasteful, deplorable, despicable—"

"And is yarking it up out of order," Cade went on.

"—damnable, despoiling—"

"Enough!" Rafe begged.

Mieka cocked an eyebrow at him. "Am I to understand that the Rules will be obeyed?"

Rafe drew himself to his full six feet two inches and stared down at the Elf. "Or what?"

"Hideous, horrible—"

"All right, all right!"

"Especially the part about snoring."

Eight

LOOKING BACK, CADE found it extraordinary that no one had asked Mieka how he would amuse himself now that he'd rewritten all the Rules for his own convenience.

They really ought to have known.

He behaved himself, more or less, from Shollop all the way to Scatterseed. But on the road up the Pennynines, either boredom or the unwonted burden of being good became too much for him.

They really truly ought to have known.

The first thing he did was to complain that everyone was getting a bit whiff, so he suggested they take advantage of the brook running alongside the road. The water was chilly, but the sun was out and the air was warm, and he further suggested that it might be a good idea to rinse out some of their clothes. He even darted back to the wagon—twice—to gather armfuls of laundry. Yazz was enlisted to rig up drying lines inside the wagon. Negotiating the flapping criss-cross of shirts and underthings was a bit tricky for the rest of the day, but Mieka solved that problem by hanging all their damp underclothes out the windows. Though daytime in the mountains was pleasantly warm, nights could grow very cold indeed until high summer, and by morning they had the choice of wearing what they'd been wearing for three days or waiting for their linen to unfreeze.

Taken to task for this, Mieka seized a blanket and went to sit up on the coachman's bench with Yazz. After a few desultory games of cards, Cade, Jeska, and Rafe climbed back into their hammocks for a nap, listening as the Giant and the Elf sang a series of intricate roundelays. The sound of Yazz's deep, gravelly voice paired with Mieka's light and surprisingly sweet singing was no stranger than the friendship between them, and Cade smiled.

And then the firepocket began to smoke.

Putridly.

Windows were opened. Fragrant candles were lighted. It was discovered that just beneath the steel bracings of the firepocket, where it could be heated to a nice smoky glow, was a lump of pasture coal—otherwise known as cow shit.

Even when the smoke had cleared, the interior of the wagon stank. With the windows open to the breezes in hopes of airing the place out, the three of them huddled in their hammocks, wrapped in blankets. Cade buried his nose in a sachet of herbs Mistress Mirdley had packed in with his clothes, and cursed the mad little Elf for a full hour.

The following afternoon they happened upon a long, narrow lake tucked prettily into a fold of the mountains. The Master of the King's Roads and Byways had been inspired by the scenery to build a little projecting platform halfway across the bridge so travelers could pause to admire the view. At Cade's request, Yazz halted the wagon at this convenient balcony. They used it to introduce Mieka to the lake, kicking and yelling and fully clothed. While he spluttered and shivered and flailed back to shore, they debated whether or not to leave him there.

"Dunno," Rafe mused. "Gliskers might be pretty thin on the ground at New Halt."

"Cade can do the work until we send to one of the Gallybanks agencies for somebody else," Jeska pointed out.

Rafe was looking over the bridge's low parapet at the infuriated Elf. "Not much of a swimmer, is he?"

"Puppy-paddler," was Jeska's scorning verdict. "Not much use, taken all in all. Can't swim, can't ride, can't drive a carriage—"

Mieka had reached shallow water and was slogging through reeds and muck, cussing the whole while.

"Now we know why he changed the Rules," Rafe remarked. "That one about foul language—fluent little bugger."

"Done yet?" Yazz rumbled from his bench.

"Almost," Cade called back. "I don't think we can sack him, Jeska. What would we tell his mother?"

"All she'd say is that it's a wonder we didn't do it sooner."

"I—hate—you—*all*!" Mieka bellowed. *"Forever!"*

Every so often on the rest of the drive to New Halt he rather ostentatiously unfurled a white silk pocket square, with which he gently and tenderly dried his ears.

The weird old place outside New Halt was a different experience than it had been on the Winterly. Reassuring, to have their own safe and snug wagon waiting for them in the courtyard rather than someone else's carriage; bizarre, to find it was just as cold in the cellar as it had been in winter; startling, to see that there was a second member of the audience this time, also wrapped head to boots in furs and woolen blankets. Seated side by side in cushiony chairs placed in the exact center of the vaulted undercroft, they said nothing and reacted not at all as Touchstone set up glass baskets and lecterns. They didn't even move. It was like playing to corpses. Cade had raised the subject of this yearly engagement with Vered at Trials and found out that the Shadow-shapers dreaded it just as much as Touchstone was learning to. It paid magnificently, but to Vered's mind it wasn't worth it—and he was just as glad that he and Rauel and Chat and Sakary could charge enough for their other private shows that they'd be returning a po-lite regret to this year's invitation.

It was with real perplexity that Cade had found out in a gloating letter from Kearney Fairwalk that the Shad-owshapers had not received an invitation this year at all. Crystal Sparks, Black Lightning, and Touchstone would be playing here, but not the best group in the Kingdom. Most curious, and completely unexplained.

As they set up, Cade wished that Touchstone could afford to turn down this performance and say they were busy—polishing their withies, trimming their toenails, anything to avoid this. The chill, damp cellar with its gloomy stone vaulting was eerie enough, especially af-ter driving through a bright summer afternoon, but their audience of two, shrouded and muffled and absolutely silent, was downright unsettling when one was accus-tomed to playing to hundreds. Still, the money was nec-essary, and it would come to them personally in little bags full of coin, rather than being deposited in their bank accounts. So here they were.

"Treasure" had been requested, and thus "Treasure" they would perform, but scaled back and toned down. For one thing, they were coming off five exhausting shows in New Halt. Two of those audiences had been com-posed of sailors off fortyered ships, rowdy and drunk

and contentious. Tomorrow night they would appear
before at least four hundred men from ships belonging
to the new Duchess of Downymede—Princess Miriuzca—
who had specially arranged this treat for her sailors. A
kindness, Rafe observed when Kearney sent them notice
of the engagement, and a very smart move on her part;
perhaps, he suggested, she wasn't so ingenuous as she
seemed. Mieka had given a snort and replied, "Marriage
to Prince Ashgar would make for rather a swift grow-
ing-up, don't you think?"

On this night, which should have been their time off
to rest and relax, they were instead playing yet another
show. The magic would be narrowly focused, and not so
powerful as needed for a large audience. Jeska wouldn't
have to work his voice so hard. Rafe wouldn't have to
monitor the distribution of magic through a vast hall.
Cade had primed the withies with just enough and no
more. Mieka had to produce only minimal effects. Still,
when the Elf offered bluethorn all round, they took him
up on it.

In the play, the cloaked and hooded Fae had scarcely
reached the wall, intent on hiding the Rights, when
with senses heightened by thorn, Cade felt it begin: a
twitching, a quivering, not of weariness in Mieka or
Rafe or Jeska, but of eagerness. It wasn't of his making;
he had put nothing of that into the withies. Fear and
defiance, rage and resolve—these things, yes, as the Fae
heard the crashing hoofbeats and the resonant belling
hounds of his pursuers, and toppled the stones onto
the bright gleaming carkenet and crown. But Cade had
not primed the magic to produce this fervent expectancy, this *hunger*. Tending to the general surrounds as
he always did, as any good tregetour must do, he was
aware of ripples in the ancient stone cellar, things that

had nothing to do with what was happening in the play. Eager anticipation became growing need, and then blatant demand.

As quickly and deftly as magic flowed through the cellar, it was absorbed. Soaked up. Devoured. The painstaking structure of the play held, all the sensation and emotion Cade had put into the withies and Mieka released and Rafe modulated and Jeska used, but the demand for more and yet more increased by the minute. Mieka had abandoned his usual light, limber dance and was grabbing each successive glass twig with grim resolve. Rafe had to struggle to adjust the magic, not through any fault of Mieka's but because the insistent hunger grew and grew. Jeska skipped lines here and there, which confused and then alarmed Cade until he realized that the masquer was editing as he went, dumping anything that wasn't absolutely necessary to the piece, hurrying ahead to the verbal cues that would prompt the change of scene to the trial and hanging. Mieka responded to those signals: bluethorn kept him alert; consummate professionalism kept him in control. Yet as Cade watched his glisker at work, he saw the strained jut of his jaw, the frown knitting his thick black brows.

〔**Cade gripped the tregetour's lectern in both hands, watching in horror as Mieka's dance became a lurching, flailing stagger. Drunk on whiskey or thornlost, or both, he missed his grab for a withie and as the magic surged and faltered, endangering three people onstage and three hundred people beyond it, Cade lunged for the glisker's bench and—**〕

No! he told himself desperately. *No! Not now!*

The Elsewhen faded before it had truly begun.

He had no time to believe or not believe what had just happened to him. Mieka was gritting his way through the forming of the castle walls and the shadows that implied the condemning judges, but he was soaked in sweat and there was something wild and despairing in his face that made Cade's decision for him. Striding over to the glisker's bench, behind the illusory wall where the captive Fae stood, Cade took the withies right out of Mieka's hands and shoved the Elf to one side. Mieka stumbled, then fell to his knees, gasping for breath, those eyes blank and staring. He wasn't drunk; the bluethorn had worn off; he was simply and utterly exhausted.

The magic was faltering. Though it was Cade's own magic inside these glass twigs, Mieka's passion and skill were needed to transform it into sound and sensation, experience and emotion. Cade could do a glisker's work. He'd done it before. But he wasn't Mieka.

The least of his problems right now was the performance itself. He didn't care if there was a juddering in the scenery, if the sensations wavered and weakened. He pulled back on the emotions and concentrated on hanging the Fae while Jeska, coping as always, jumped to the final speech. Cade couldn't just tear the magic back from the grasping need; to do so would risk not just their audience—about whom he gave not the slightest damn—but Jeska and Rafe as well. It was for them, and for Mieka slumped nearly senseless on the floor beside him, that he worked. He wrestled with that ravening hunger, and each time he drew back, it lunged forward, wanting, needing, demanding, draining. And angry, so angry at being denied a feed.

He untangled Jeska from the magic, and then Rafe, sensing their shock and their gratitude. And as Jeska gasped out the final words of the play, Cade simply and brutally ended it. The cellar was emptied of all magic. It was like being pulled by someone's hands, someone who suddenly let go, so that balance was lost and it was all Cade could do not to stagger back and fall.

Mieka, still huddled at Cade's feet, whimpered softly. Jeska, over by Cade's abandoned lectern, grabbed at it for support before straightening his spine. Rafe's head was bowed, his chest heaving, as if he had battled a dragon.

Neither of the two fur-swathed occupants of those chairs moved.

Cade would never know how they got their glass baskets packed up. He was numb, emotionally hollow. He was aware, sporadically, of Mieka swaying upright beside him, of Mieka and Rafe stacking glass baskets inside their crates, of Jeska wedging a shoulder under Cade's arm and gripping Mieka around the waist to guide them both towards the stairs. All he could really sense was the presence of those two silent, motionless watchers, who had somehow fed off the magic. They were still hungry. He heard, as if from a vast distance, the jangling of spent withies in the velvet drawstring bag Mieka clutched to his chest, trembling.

The chill of the cellar was no less than the chill in the huge hall where, as twice before, a laden table awaited. Food on golden platters, wine in silver cups, candles in crystal branches, and places laid for four. The sight of it sent a spasm of nausea through Cade's stomach. Rafe, arms full of crated baskets, walked right past it out the door. Jeska took the withies from Mieka and followed Rafe without a pause.

Mieka wobbled a bit, then made it over to the table, where he seized all four purses. "We bleedin' well *earned* these!"

That he didn't seize a bottle or two of wine as well was testament to his fatigue. He nearly fell on the way to the door. Cade, none too steady himself, met him half-way and wrapped an arm around Mieka's shoulders.

"I'm sorry, Quill," came the dismal whisper.

"Not your fault, Elfling."

With a flash of his usual spirit, he asked, "You *admit* to that?"

Cade hugged him tighter. "Not your fault this time, anyways."

After a few more steps, Mieka said softly, "You did good."

"I pay attention to you, y'know. Every show. But nobody's as good as you."

"Not thinkin' of sacking me, then?"

"My glisker you are, and my glisker you stay—no matter how often I want to strangle you."

Content, Mieka rubbed his cheek to Cade's shoulder and was asleep on his feet before they were out the front door. Yazz was suddenly there, lifting Mieka, carrying him to the wagon. Cade found a convenient pillar and leaned against it, closing his eyes, wondering if there was enough bluethorn in the world to perk him up for tomorrow night's show. Worry about that some other time, he told himself, when he could knit two thoughts together without unraveling half his brain with the effort.

Hugely muscular arms surrounded him, picked him up. He was too light-headed to protest. Time slithered around him so that the next thing he knew he was tucked in his hammock hearing the slam of the back door. A few moments later there was the soft trilling sound Yazz made to alert the horses, and the wagon began to move. But Cade didn't feel that. The delayed Elsewhen had claimed him.

[Cade gripped the tregetour's lectern in both hands, watching in horror as Mieka's dance became a lurching, flailing stagger. Drunk or thornlost, or both, he missed his grab for a withie and as the magic surged and faltered, endangering three people onstage and three hundred people beyond it, Cade lunged for the glisker's bench and shoved Mieka out of the way. The Elf didn't even protest as Cade grabbed up first one withie and then another, so completely lost that all he did was sit on the floor and start counting his fingers like a toddling child.

It was a long-familiar play, "The Dragon," and Cade knew what he was doing at the glisker's bench—he'd done it before, even though he wasn't the artist wielding the withies that Mieka was. If there were snags in the magic, it could be attributed to the unfamiliarity of the new Downstreet Theater, although the very thought of Touchstone's being considered so unprofessional that they made such amateurish mistakes clawed at Cade's pride.

They finished the performance. The Prince spoke his final, weary words as the Dragon lay dead at his feet. Cayden left the wrap-up of the magic to Rafe, knowing he could count on his fettler the way he would never again count on his glisker. He ought to join Rafe and Jeska to take their bows, but the only thing he could think of was beating the living shit out of Mieka Windthistle.

He turned, fists clenched. Those eyes were looking up at him, big and bewildered, like the eyes of a hurt child. But something caught at Cade's gaze in the off-stage shadows, and he glanced round. There stood Thierin Knottinger of Black Lightning. From the tregetour's wrist dangled a little gold velvet pouch. He waved it gently to and fro, a gleeful taunting grin on his face. In his other hand was a glinting glass thorn. Holding it between thumb and forefinger, he lifted it slowly, making sure Cade was watching, and placed it against his own neck, not quite touching the skin. And then he began to laugh.

Cade knelt beside Mieka.

"Quill? What's—I don't—Quill, what happened?"

"Shush." Taking Mieka by the jaw, he turned his head to the left, then the right, and saw it: a tiny puncture mark above his collar, a delicate drop of blood. *Lord and Lady and all the Old Gods and Angels damn them, damn them to each successive Hell for all eternity—*

"I'm sorry, I'm so sorry—"

Smoothing the sweat-limp hair from Mieka's face, he shook his head. "No, Elfling, it's all right. Let's get you someplace quiet, shall we?"

"But I don't understand—I couldn't—"

"I'll explain it later. Come on." He got Mieka upright, nearly losing his grip as the Elf shivered. "Easy now, easy—"

"Quill, I'm sorry!"

"I know. It wasn't your fault."

* * *

"THEY'LL BE REBUILDING the Downstreet."

Morning, and breakfast, after a night's crushing sleep. Cade was still sodden with weariness. There were many long hours before their show tonight, and he intended to spend more than a few of them curled in his hammock. But he had to talk about this.

"Mmph?" Mieka swallowed a mouthful of bread and cheese. "Rebuild it?"

"As a real theater. There'll be some sort of big opening performance, with us and Black Lightning and I'm not sure who else, but—"

"And you know this because why?" Jeska answered his own question. "Saw it, did you? Were we any good?"

"We would've been, if Thierin Knottinger hadn't stung Mieka with some seriously nasty thorn." Cade swirled tea in a lovely blue glass cup, part of the set made by Blye. She'd also given them two of the silver serving bowls that were part of the collection of ancient family plate that had been a wedding present from Kearney Fairwalk. There were eight bowls, she'd told Cade, and it wasn't as if they got used more than twice a year, so Touchstone might as well have the benefit of them. At the moment one of the bowls held porridge. Personally, Cade couldn't face it, and made do with bread and tea. "Crumpled up like a snarl of knitting yarn onto the floor, our glisker did, leaving all the magic to swirl about every whatever whichway. Not a pretty thing to see, even if it hasn't happened yet."

Rafe sat back at the table as if recoiling from the words, and bumped his head against a shelf. All these weeks in the wagon, and he still hadn't quite got used to it. He rubbed the back of his head and with an attempt at his usual composure said, "And it won't happen, by Gods. Good of you to warn us. Something of a departure for you, isn't it?"

"Thierin is a bloody bastard," Mieka growled. "I'll break every withie he owns."

Cade went on, "I don't know when the new Downstreet will be built, but when it does, none of us gets anywhere near Black Lightning, right? We'll bring Yazz to the theater as protection if we have to, or arrive half a minute before we go on, or—or *anything*, just so we don't get in arm's reach of any of them."

"What exactly went on?" Rafe asked.

"Mieka lost control of the magic. I had to take over."

"Like last night." Mieka winced and took a sip of hot cinnamon tea. "I'm sorry for that—"

"I keep telling you, it wasn't your fault," said Cade. "We all felt it."

"I should've been able to—"

"With those two leeches sucking us dry?" Rafe poured out more tea. "It felt like my bones were bleeding."

"All the same—" But Mieka didn't finish the thought.

Instead, he demanded, "Why would Black Lightning want to do such a thing to me? Everybody knows we're streets better than them, even on the worst night we ever had."

"If we'd really lost the magic," Cade began, "if it had gone wild on us—"

"At an important show like that," Jeska interrupted, "it could ruin us."

"There was a group, years ago," Rafe said slowly. "Before your grandfather's time, Cade. Nobody ever knew what really happened, whether the tregetour had primed the withies wrong or the glisker made a mistake, or maybe the fettler couldn't keep a good enough hold on the magic. But a dozen men in the audience that night went mad, and dozens more didn't speak for a fortnight. Nobody actually died, though it was probably a near thing."

"The Gallymarchers," Jeska said.

Cade nodded. One reason there were Stewards at Trials was to ensure that groups who would be playing to larger audiences actually knew what they were doing. A tavern with a few score patrons was one thing; a venue holding three hundred or more was quite another. The magic had to be stronger, and therefore under stricter control by the fettler.

"So what has to change?" Mieka asked. "We'll have to play the show, that's not in question. We made our start at the Downstreet."

"And the owner's wife likes you." Cade smiled. "No, I wasn't thinking of not performing. But the piece we did was 'Dragon,' so maybe if we do something else, that will be enough."

"I don't agree," Rafe said. "What we do or don't do onstage doesn't affect what happens before we're onstage."

"Ha! I know!" Mieka exclaimed. "Let's get Auntie Brishen to cook up something really vile, and give a little thornprick to Thierin instead!"

"As wild as they already are, do you think anybody in the audience could survive them losing control of the magic?"

"Enough sleepy-stuff, and he'd never even take the stage."

Jeska shook his golden head. "And what's the first rule of all theater folk?" He lifted a hand as if swearing an oath and declaimed, "'If you're drunk to the eyes or bone-weary/ If your folio's lost, stolen, or strayed/ If your withies are scarred/ Or your memory's marred—/ The play must always be played.' Black Lightning would still perform, and we'd all end up gibbering."

"Rafe has the right of it," Cade said reluctantly. "It's not onstage that matters, it's what happens before."

"Where did he get me that I didn't feel it?" Mieka wanted to know.

"In the neck. But if you're planning on a collar that reaches to the tips of your ears, I remind you that there's lots of other bits of exposed skin—"

"I could wear a full suit of armor. Just until we got onstage." He slid out of his chair and struck a pose in the middle of the wagon. "Always fancied meself with a sword and shield, clanking about like a walking steelworks!"

They'd manage to think of something, Cade knew—preferably something that didn't involve a hundred pounds of plate armor. But something else had occurred to him. He had actually refused to see an Elsewhen.

Sagemaster Emmot had told him—and how long ago it seemed—that the foreseeings might change as he got older. That he might even be able to control them. That they might increase or decrease in frequency, that the content might be more detailed or less—all of which only meant that Emmot had as little idea about what exactly this "gift" of his would do as Cade himself did.

But this Elsewhen he had refused to see. Refused to give in. Refused, because his presence in the *now* was vital.

When it came back, as insistent as that hunger last night in the cellar, he'd learned something about a possible future. The blood chilled in his veins when he thought of what might have happened in that future if he'd resisted again.

What if he'd refused to watch, that second time, and they'd gone to the opening of the Downstreet Theater ignorant of Thierin Knottinger's intent? Professional disaster, emotional danger—

If Knottinger would dare some kind of disruption, and stand there bragging about it with his little green bag and his glass thorn, then what else might he try?

Why not just kill Mieka? So simple, so final. No more Touchstone at all, not without Mieka.

"When Touchstone lost their Elf, they lost their soul."

Think it through, he ordered himself. If he was right about Black Lightning, then the Archduke was even now courting them to become his own pet theater group. They'd agree; of course they would. A theater built to their specifications—but what would the Archduke receive in return? Chat had told Mieka about great lords and princes on the Continent who owned performers for the reputation it gave them. The Archduke was known to be theater-mad, but—what else would he gain?

No way of knowing.

Very well, then, what else about Black Lightning? The odd and eerie trick of identifying each man's bloodlines—how did that work? How had they targeted specific magic to specific races? Mieka had sensed everything else he was besides Elfen; Rafe had sensed nothing at all, being nothing other than Human and Wizard. And that made sense, didn't it—the subject of the play itself was how all the various races had come to be, a twisting of the old story, making Elf and Wizard the only clean blood, the only pure children of the Lord and Lady—

The answer was there someplace; he knew it was. But he was just too tired. Abandoning his breakfast and his puzzlings, he crawled back into his hammock and slept.

Nine

TOUCHSTONE'S PERFORMANCE BEFORE the Princess's sailors in New Halt went very well, even considering a lingering collective exhaustion. Bluethorn all round, enhanced by the cheers of an enthusiastic, roisterous crowd—they were so pleased with themselves that after "Dragon" they decided to give the men a rousing version of "Sailor's Sweetheart." Even better, after the show, an official wearing Princess Miriuzca's new badge (a blue forget-me-never on a silver ground, with a three-pronged coronet above) appeared and handed Cayden a little purse of gold coins.

"Lovely!" Mieka exclaimed when handed his split. "Something to spend at the Castle Biding Fair!"

"Are you sure you'll be able to hang on to it that long?"

"Well . . . you're right. You'd best keep it for me, Quill. And my mother's letter as well—she sent a list, and I know I'll mislay it and buy all the wrong colors and such."

Cade wanted to say, *Why not keep your mother's letter with your wife's?* But he didn't. Mieka had a small wallet of iris-blue leather in which he carefully folded his wife's few letters. It never left his pocket except when he was onstage.

Neither did Mieka wear anything she'd sewn for him while he was working. Bearing in mind what Mistress Mirdley had told him about Caitiff spellcastings, Cade wondered whether this was why Mieka could so unthinkingly bed whichever girl took his fancy after a show. Hadn't there been something, though, about such spells lasting only a month? Thinking back, he recalled that Mieka had taken to coming in well after midnight only after the first few weeks on the road. If there had indeed been magic, it had worn off by now, and young Mistress Windthistle must be anguishing herself something to behold. She must know at this point that Mieka had no more been born to be faithful to one woman than to become Royal Librarian. It simply wasn't in his nature—and if she was trying to change him, as in the smaller matter of correcting his speech, she was destined to fail. Evidently *knowing* wasn't the same thing as *understanding*. Mayhap Blye had been right about what constituted a happy marriage.

He thought about the marriages he had observed at close view. Rafe and Crisiant; Hadden and Mishia; Jed and Blye. Yes, there was both knowing and understanding between the partners in each, and acceptance of dreams and desires, and all of them were happy unions. Then there were his own parents. Lady Jaspiela knew and understood very well what her husband did at Court. As far as Cade had ever been able to tell, she was neither happy nor unhappy about it; she simply ignored it. Was that *acceptance*? Presumably Zekien Silversun was contented in his life as Prince Ashgar's First Gentleman of the Bedchamber—although Cade supposed he was more circumspect now that the Prince was a married man. Still, the Palace was a big place, and aristocratic couples always had separate bedchambers. Now that Miriuzca was pregnant, Ashgar could use this as an ex-

cuse to absent himself from her bed and return to his
bachelor habits. Which meant that Zekien would be consulting with the Finchery and suchlike places to supply
the Prince's bedwarmers.

Cade hoped that Miriuzca didn't know. If she knew,
would she understand? And even if she could understand
it, would she accept it? Perhaps she was the kind of
woman who found her happiness in her children. And
possibly her friends, he thought, remembering Lady
Vrennerie, now married to Lord Eastkeeping. Perhaps
they were happy. He hoped so. He hoped so very much.

Well, none of it was his problem, nor was it likely to
be. Who would ever marry him? Gone on the Circuit for
months at a time, constantly performing while in Gallantrybanks, vanishing to a rehearsal or the Archives or
his own library the rest of the time . . . it would take a
rare woman indeed to tolerate that sort of marriage,
much less find happiness in it. Chat's wife, Deshenanda,
seemed content with her home and children; the Gods
alone knew what Sakary's wife, Chirene, thought; Cade
had never met Vered's wife, or Rauel's, but apparently
they had worked out their own manner of dealing with
their husbands' long absences. Crisiant, he understood
more and more, was a woman in a million and Rafe was
a fortunate man. Cade always had in his mind that
Elsewhen, about the woman who lived with him and
had borne his children and didn't want to be bothered
with anything to do with how he made the money that
supported the family. It was warning enough, wasn't it?
Taken together with Blye's merciless words about his
never being able to live an ordinary kind of life, it was
certainly warning enough.

Besides, he thought wryly as the wagon rolled towards
Castle Eyot and a five-day holiday from the Royal Circuit, he spent more time with these three quats than

most wedded couples spent together. Was Touchstone a happy marriage? Onstage, absolutely. They knew and understood each other perfectly. Offstage . . . they bickered and sniped, took care of head colds and hangovers, yelled at each other for being late or being sulky or just being themselves, discussed and listened and commiserated and accepted (however grudgingly) each other's foibles. And created. And protected each other.

No, it wouldn't be his problem, marriage to a woman. This marriage that was Touchstone was trouble enough.

Well, as long as there were pretty girls around to serve drinks and his other needs, of course. Cade enjoyed that aspect of being a famous player very much, and almost every night.

Castle Eyot was even more beautiful in summer than in winter. Blooded horses frolicked in green velvet pastures, the orchards were heavy with ripening fruit, and on the island mid-river, the castle glistened white as a wolf's tooth. Their stay overlapped that of the Shadowshapers by a day, and all eight players took full advantage of Lord Rolon Piercehand's hospitality and especially his wine cellar. The last night of the Shadowshapers' holiday, they all went up to the top of the tallest castle tower with a dozen bottles of the finest Frannitch brandy, which rendered Cade drunk enough to broach the subject of the mansion outside New Halt.

"Creepiest shows we ever played," Vered said with a shudder. "Heaps of money for it, of course—"

"And every penny earned twice over," Mieka put in. "Mayhap thrice."

"Can't say as I won't miss the coin," mused Rauel. "But we decided after last year that we'd never do it again. It was a relief not to be invited."

"Good eats," Sakary offered. "But not worth it."

The tower room was a hideaway that had nothing in

common with Mieka's little aerie at Wistly Hall. For one thing, it was securely attached to the rest of the building. For another, it was sumptuously furnished with deep couches, velvet pillows, patterned carpets strewn one overlapping another, delicate little tables, and gigantic hanging lanterns lavish with faceted crystal drops the size of a fist. Cade made mental note of these, thinking that perhaps Blye might enjoy making them. They weren't hollow, so they would be perfectly legal.

"Who really got fed?" Rafe wanted to know. "Thrice now I've felt as if the marrow was being sucked out of my bones."

"Yeh," Mieka said, "but it's what all audiences do, though, innit? Not like *that*, I mean, but—" He stopped, frustrated, and appealed to Cade with a glance.

"In a way, you're right," Cade allowed. "The difference is that they take what we give, and there's none of that demand to be fed—"

"But there is, y'know," Vered interrupted. "More and more and more, and the groups that don't or can't provide aren't booked much, are they?"

"Not everybody's like that," Jeska protested. "Not everybody is there just for—for—"

When he seemed unable to find a word, Cade finished for him, "For an hour's swilling at the trough? I agree."

"More 'communal experience,' is it?" Vered teased, rolling his eyes. "Shared occasions creating a bond, and all that?"

"Have done," Sakary said with a rare grin, "or I'll tell 'em all the truth about you."

"You wouldn't!"

"Wouldn't I, though?"

Vered made a hideous face at him, then laughed. "He's got nothing on me—been threatening that for years, just to see if I'll go all cowardly craven. But that's what some people in the audiences are, aren't they? Too spineless to feel things in their real lives, and our job is to do their feeling for them."

Cade frowned at this characterization, but not because he entirely disagreed with it, not if he was being honest. He simply preferred what Mieka had said to him years ago—that players did the audience's *dreaming* for them.

"In that cellar," Rauel said, "that man, whoever he is, wants more and yet more—and knows how to get it. And *that's* the difference."

Vered nodded agreement with his partner. "And now you say there were two of them?" he asked Cade.

"Like Vampires, only it's not blood they're after."

"Funny you should mention Vampires," said Chat, staring into his drink. "Where I come from, there are stories—"

"Quick!" Mieka cried. "Get the garlic!"

"Like I said—*funny,*" Chat growled, blue eyes dancing. But only for a moment, and his face was solemn again as he went on, "There came an invading army from the East—likely you people here never even heard about it, it being that long ago and naught to do with your tidy little Kingdom anyways. It was back when magical folk still lived in the open, and did their work whatever it might be, and nobody thought much of it. Oh, they kept themselves mostly to themselves, but things went along just fine until these *balaurin* swept in with their war chariots and monster-sized horses to pull them. Ancestors of Rommy's breed, y'know, but with the demons bred out of them by now."

"Demons?" Jeska asked, startled.

Vered rolled his eyes. "Now you've done it. He's

about to tell you all about all those filthy Eastern knights and their filthy Eastern ways."

"Been nagging at us for years, he has," Rauel confided, "to write it all up as a play."

"Why don't you?" Rafe asked. "Even the tiny piece you've let him tell sounds a good story."

"And I'd tell the rest of it," Chat said pointedly, "if this lot would shut up."

"Something to moisten your throat, then," Mieka said, passing over a bottle.

When Chat—and everyone else—was sufficiently lubricated, he went on, "The *balaurin* invaded, and the Humans were losing, and even alliances with Wizards and Gnomes and Goblins and Elves and all other magical folk couldn't help. There were great battles and small skirmishes, and every day the *balaurin* killed more people and took more land. So the wisest elders of all the races had a lengthy and worried talking, and it was decided that a special order of knights should be created, and bestowed with powers given by each of the magical races according to their ability."

"Like 'The Pikseys and the Sunrise Child'!" Mieka exclaimed. "You know, the one nobody does anymore, about the baby and the gifts the Pikseys gave her, and the Fae weren't invited to the Namingday and got all huffy and then—"

"Tripe," Vered sniffed.

"Twaddle," Rafe agreed.

"Twee," was Sakary's verdict.

Mieka sulked. "I *like* that story."

"Let him get on with this one," Cade said. He rested his head against the piled pillows of his chosen couch, watching the lantern crystals spin rainbows over the ceiling as a breeze drifted through open windows. His imagination supplied what Chat's narrative talents did not, and he began to see what a true storyteller might do with it.

"Where was I? Ah. It's not known exactly what skills and powers were given these knights, or who gave what, or how it was done. There was a mighty battle, and once the dust blew clear, the *balaurin* were all dead, except for a few that were sent back to their Eastern homeland in silver chains." He glanced at Mieka and added, "And draped in necklaces of garlic, because, it was said, that was the only plant with a scent strong enough to counter the stench of demons."

"So how did garlic get linked to warding off Vampires?"

Chat gave a shrug. "Hells if I know. Anyways, once the *balaurin* were defeated, the knights were so exhausted that none of them lived much longer. All of them died within weeks of each other. They were buried in a single huge tomb with a stone monument above it, and a shrine that got added to as the years went by. The shrine's a ruin now, of course, after all these centuries. But spellcastings were put onto the tomb and the stones have never so much as quivered in an earthquake— and that part of the Continent gets earthquakes every few score years or so. They say the locals talk of a curse being put on it by the few *balaurin* who survived, and they won't go near the place."

"And from that," Vered said, "he wants us to write a play."

"It could be done," Cade mused. "Pick one of the knights to be the hero, do the scene with the giving of powers—"

Sakary gave a soft, heartfelt groan. "You're about to suggest the big battle, aren't you?"

Rafe nodded in sympathy. "Dust, blood, wounds, terror, clashing swords and screaming horses, shouted orders, thirst, confusion, spellcastings—and that's just for starters. It'd be a horror for a glisker, even worse for a fettler."

"One of the stories," Chat said stubbornly, "says that some of the new-made knights were given silver arrows. Some others were given wooden lances. And one of them, who'd had his hand lopped off in an earlier battle, he got a replacement hand made of wood that worked as well as his real one."

"Not with the girls, I'll bet," Mieka said.

Jeska was unamused and saucer-eyed. "But—garlic and silver, and a wooden spike—those are all to do with Vampires!"

"Exactly." Chat drained his drink and wrapped his arms around a huge crimson pillow. "Which is why it's so odd that tales about Vampires linger on the Continent, and even crossed the Flood to Albeyn. If the *balaurin* were all killed, except those few who were sent back, and there were never any more of them seen again, why do we know about garlic and silver and wood?"

"We like nightmares," Cade mused. "The more scared we are, the better it is to go home to our nice warm safe beds."

"The way I hear it," Rauel said with a sly grin, "no bed is safe from Mieka Windthistle. There's a girl in Sidlowe—"

"Which one?" Mieka asked innocently.

Rafe drained his drink and pushed himself upright amidst his nest of pillows. "By your kind leave, gentlemen, I've heard enough stories for one night. I make my living by them, 'tis true, but there's naught in my contract says I have to listen to *him* any more than absolutely necessary. I give you good evening," he finished, and fell over onto the carpet.

Yazz was summoned to carry him off to his chamber. The Shadowshapers' driver, Rist—also part Giant— came to help, but Sakary, Rauel, Chat, and Jeska departed under their own power. Mieka lingered a while, finishing off a bottle, then made his slow, lurching ramble to the stairs.

Vered waited for him to go, then turned to Cade. "Learned me lesson, finally, about drink," he confided wryly. "One glass of wine with dinner, one glass of brandy after, and I'm done."

Cade grinned. "Keep it quiet, though, or you'll ruin all our reputations." So saying, he upended the last of a bottle down his throat.

"Can you keep it quiet that I've been working on the very tale Chat told us tonight?"

"Have you, now?"

"I know a good story when I hear one—even if it's been mangled in the meantime. Like your 'Treasure' piece. That's what gave me the encouragement." He hesitated. "Mieka says you have a lot of old books."

"Ah." Now Cade understood. "Anytime. For an appropriate fee, of course!"

Vered threw a pillow at him. "You'll be in luck if I don't hold them to ransom, once I've got me hands on 'em! Where'd they all come from, anyways?"

"They belonged to my grandsir, who was a fettler."

"Not a Vampire tregetour, like you and me and Rauel?"

Cade spluttered with laughter. "Where'd that notion come from?"

"Think on it, son. When we prime the withies, is it just our own experiences we use? No. It's observing other people. Taking note of how they react. Gathering up bits and pieces from all over the place to put into the plays. We take, whether people want to give or not—and if they don't want to be giving of it, we know how to be taking of what we need anyways."

Cade had never thought of it like that before, and said so.

"Like the knights in the story," Vered went on, speaking to the starlight outside the windows. "They were given powers and spells, I reckon, just like us. They used them, just like us—"

"And knackered themselves unto death! Not one of my ambitions!"

"Yeh, but—I've a thought that perhaps they took, too, mayhap what they weren't supposed to, and there's more to their dying after the final battle than Chat ever heard the telling of. So I'd like a look into your books, if I may. Something's there in that tale that niggles at me brain."

Cade tried to weave his own brain around it, and for a moment thought he knew where Vered was going. Then the last swallows of brandy hit him, and he lost the threads.

{"—writing about the Knights of the Balaur Tsepesh, Your Grace. At least, that's what I gather from what my daughter's husband has said."

It was a dim little room, scarcely more than a cubbyhole, with no windows and no furnishings. But although it was very cold, she wore only a thin cloak. She stood with hands folded and head raised high, an interesting combination of servility and arrogance. The disparity of emotions on the man's face was more complex: impatience, a contrived boredom, alert interest, and annoyance at his dependence on this person he despised and needed.

"Tell me precisely, woman."

"Yes, Your Grace. Vered Goldbraider has borrowed

books from Cayden Silversun. One afternoon Gold-braider arrived at Wistly Hall, where Touchstone had gathered for rehearsal, to return several of these books and request several more. His words were these: 'Anything to do with the Knights of the Balaur Tsepesh, the ones with a red dragon as their symbol.' My daughter's nephew-by-marriage is a child fascinated by dragons, so she looked into one or two of the books, thinking most kindly to find a story to tell him—"

"I care nothing for tales told to children at bedtime," the Archduke snapped. "What else did Goldbraider say?"

"He asked if Silversun has any books dealing with your part of the world, Your Grace. He meant, of course, the lands your ancestor came from. Silversun replied that he might have better luck at the Royal Archives. It was mention of Your Grace's name that alerted my daughter, you see, and she paid attention, but nothing else of interest was said."

"I have told you before, *everything* Silversun says and does is of interest to me."

"And I have reported what I have been able to discover, Your Grace—"

"All of it?"

"All of it, Your Grace."

"Goldbraider," he murmured then. "Pity he's so stubborn. So volatile. He would have been useful."

"But the Shadowshapers refused Your Grace's offer—"

"How did you hear of that?" he demanded sharply.

"The Elf."

"Of course. The Elf. Always the Elf." He pulled from his coat pocket a folded piece of parchment, extending it to her as a wary kennel-master extends food to a bitch known to bite.}

"Cade? I asked what you think, and you haven't said a word."

He looked over at Vered: the white-blond hair, the dark skin, the combination of Elf and Wizard and Goblin and who knew what all else—except that Black Lightning with their magic could have touched whatever was in him and he would feel it, sense it, know what exactly he was, just as Cayden had felt and sensed and known the Fae and Troll and Goblin blood in himself—

"Sorry," he managed. "Just thinking it over."

—the *dirty* blood, just as Piksey and Sprite and Gnome were *dirty*, children of the Lord and Lady yet banished as unworthy in Black Lightning's version of the story—

"Sounds interesting," he said at random.

—Black Lightning, who either had been or soon would be approached by the Archduke, Cade felt certain, even though he'd never seen it in an Elsewhen—the Archduke who wanted to know everything Cade said and did, and had Mistress Caitiffer in her hooded cloak of thin black velvet that kept out the cold with warming spells to spy on him through her daughter, the way her daughter had told of Mieka's drunken rant that revealed Cade's foreseeing—

"Of course. The Elf. Always the Elf."

"How—how would you go about it?" he asked, abjectly grateful that the question seemed to have some meaning for Vered, who started talking again. Not that Cade really heard him.

—and did this all mean that the Archduke actually believed? Cade had reassured himself for months now that the notion was too outrageous to evoke aught but laughter. But what if the Archduke *did* believe?

With an effort he collected his scattered thoughts and concentrated on what Vered was saying. The night breeze had freshened, tinkling the crystal drops with a noise that hurt his ears.

"—mainly through the eyes of the Wizard who gives one of the knights a silver hand."

"I thought it was made of wood."

"Rotten stage effect. Can't think yet what a silver hand might do, but it's a much better visual than wood. And the knight—"

"The Knights of Balaur Tsepesh," Cade heard himself say.

"Of what?"

"I–I heard it someplace. Vered, I'm sorry, but I'm too paved right now to remember. I need some sleep."

Eyeing him, Vered nodded agreement. "Might be an idea to follow my example, y'know, about the drinking," he suggested. "You're not so luffed that you'll forget about the books?"

Cade shook his head and pushed himself to his feet. "I'll remember. Come see me at Redpebble when we're back in Gallybanks. And lend us a shoulder, eh? There's too many stairs between me and my bed."

* * *

HAD THIS BEEN the Winterly, Mieka would most likely have been in the throes of his annual head cold and spent their time off recovering. This year—healthy and ready to have some fun—he was relentless. Rising at noon, he ran through the gardens, the castle, the nearby village, and the serving girls until well after midnight, and he did this for five solid days.

Jeska occupied himself most days with riding, professing himself sick to the eyeballs of any company but his own—but of course he found congenial female company by night. Jeska, Cade was convinced, could find congenial female company in the middle of a desert. Rafe

explored the castle between penning a long letter to Crisiant, appearing each evening at dinner to detail newly
discovered amazements. Lord Rolon Piercehand's ships
traveled all over the world, and constantly brought
back the latest in beauties and oddities to amuse him
and his guests. Rafe (and Mieka) devoutly avoided the
room with all the stuffed animal heads; these had a tendency to roar. In his meanderings he found an upstairs
chamber full of glass cases containing lidded baskets of
all sizes made of all sorts of things: reeds, rope, beads,
bones, spun silver, and something he swore looked like
hair. Another room was devoted to rock specimens,
some of them as large as a horse trough. There was a
collection of weird white marble figures, all of them
with folded arms and blank faces, in the same chamber
as about a hundred little black metal figurines with elon-
gated spidery limbs. A smallish chamber contained an
assortment of human skulls, some of them painted or
decorated with beads. The display of clocks had been
added to, as had the roomful of musical instruments.

"And somebody's bespelled it," Rafe concluded, "so
that when the door opens, everything there plays the
same note. As for the room with the skulls—"

Mieka shuddered. "They open their jaws and yell.
Been there. Not going anyplace near it again!"

Most interesting to Cayden was the library, which
somehow he had missed entirely on his previous two
visits. The reason for this turned out to be simple: Lord
Piercehand had only this spring ordered the transfer of
all the books from his Gallantrybanks residence here to
Castle Eyot.

"Quite a lot of work for you, I'd imagine," Cade remarked to the servant who was cleaning the windows.

"We're used to it, Your Honor. Every time His Lordship's fleet sails in from the Lord and Lady alone know

where, crates and crates and more crates arrive once the fortyer is over, and places to be found for it all. This chamber, for an example to Your Honor, used to hold His Lordship's array of bowls. Clay, glass, silver, gold, and I've no notion what all else. So the shelves were already here."

Looking around at the thousands of volumes now on those shelves, Cade said, "That's a lot of bowls."

"There's a lot of practically everything here at Castle Eyot, Your Honor. And it's been a puzzle to us, finding a new place for them all. But as it's books that's fancied, let me fetch my son. He had the arranging of them. Managed it in a fortnight, he did," he finished proudly.

And managed it very badly, Cade didn't say. It appeared that "arranging" meant putting all books with similarly colored bindings together regardless of subject or language. It would take a real librarian to sort all this out.

Aware that the lack of organization made it futile, still he spent three afternoons searching for any reference to the Knights of Balaur Tsepesh. He found nothing, of course. Several volumes about Vampires, all written in the last fifty or so years, including a book of stories that quite obviously built on what little was demonstrably true. He found these surpassingly silly, not vivid enough to give him even the smallest of nightmares, but he read them to make sure there mightn't be something useful tucked away. There wasn't.

There were hundreds of books in languages he didn't know, and while trying to convince himself that some of the titles stamped in gold or silver on the spines looked familiar from the months on the Continent last year, he suddenly thought of Drevan Wordturner, the librarian who wanted to be a cavalryman. Drevan had made a prize fool of himself at the marriage-by-proxy ceremonies, and not even Kearney Fairwalk's interest in him had saved him from banishment to the Archduke's remotest estate, presumably to continue studies he hated in books only his family could now read. Perhaps he might be appealed to for information about the Knights.

The instant this absurdity occurred to Cade, he laughed aloud. But the more he considered it, the better the idea seemed. Who would ever think that anyone could be stupid enough to ask the Archduke's own librarian for information the Archduke did not want known?

Cade was sure that whoever and whatever the Knights had been, they meant something to the Archduke. He had been—would be—rattled good and proper when told that Vered Goldbraider was researching them. Perhaps Cade could drop a casual word to Kearney, who would most likely be thrilled at the chance of seeing Drevan Wordturner again. It probably should have disgusted Cade that he was about to use Kearney Fairwalk's bedroom preferences to his own purposes. It put him on a level with the Archduke—who, if Mieka was right, had brought Drevan Wordturner along because he looked enough like Cade so Kearney could do some pretending when the lights were low. The Archduke had tried to use Drevan to get to Kearney to get to Touchstone; Cade planned to use Kearney to get to Drevan to get to the Archduke, or at least get to some information the Archduke wanted kept secret. There was an agreeable symmetry about it that pleased Cade, and far from being ashamed of himself, the scheme amused him.

The Royal Circuit continued with shows in Bexmarket and a long, tiring drive to Clackerly Minster through ripening fields under a sultry sky constantly threatening rain. A large parcel was waiting for them at their inn just outside Clackerly Minster. In addition to the usual family letters, there were gifts for all four of them as well. Mieka, recognizing his wife's handwriting on the individual packages, tossed them in each recipient's general direction before ripping the muslin wrapping off his own. With a glad cry, he flourished a new shirt made of forest-green silk, with laces up the front of thin golden braid.

"Ah, me darlin' girl's been missing me!" he crowed. "Where's her letter?" After a rapid perusal, he said, "For the wedding performance at Coldkettle. What's she sent you lot, then?"

The gifts were shortvests of the same material for Cade and Rafe, an embroidered neck cloth for Jeska, all with gold embroidery. Jeska was already swirling the silk around his neck, stroking the lush folds.

"That's very thoughtful of her," Rafe said, fingering the subtle embroidery on the vest. "Beholden to your lady, Mieka."

"Yes, much beholden," Cade said. He wrapped the muslin carefully around the garment—which he had not actually touched—and retied the string. And all the while he was thinking that it really was a beautiful vest, and it was going to be a real shame to shove it down the garderobe and pretend he'd lost it.

Ten

RAFE WAS SERIOUSLY peeved, and Cayden didn't know why. It wasn't as if Touchstone hadn't been welcomed with flattering attention, and by Lord Coldkettle himself. The stage had been specially built for the wedding festivities, out in the main courtyard with a whole castle wall as a backdrop—and wasn't Rafe always delighted when they had an outdoor venue, with no stray support beams or odd walls to deal with, and a freedom that let him and Mieka stretch their strength? Jeska was the one who always worried that his voice and gestures might not project well enough to the back rows. They had one performance on the last night of the celebrations, and one the night after, and would be spectacularly well paid. Cade simply didn't understand what Rafe's problem might be, and a few hours before their show he finally confronted his fettler.

"Didn't see her, did you?" Rafe growled.

"See whom?"

"The little blond who thinks she's a fettler."

"She's here? Whatever for?"

"One can only speculate," he snapped, and refused to say anything more.

Not being entirely stupid, Cayden could guess. The

girl—what was her name? Tegs? Kegs?—was likely here
to provide protection for guests who might be too sensitive to magic. Who had hired her? Lord Coldkettle
himself? One of his friends? A guest? Keymarker barmaids didn't invite themselves to noble weddings.

This would be the first time Touchstone would perform outdoors at Coldkettle, and mayhap someone was
nervous about whether or not they were up to the challenge. The Stewards took such things into consideration
when awarding points that would put a group on the
Ducal or Royal—all the Winterly shows were performed
indoors—but until a group proved itself, there must be
doubt. Touchstone had already played several outdoor
shows on the Royal with no problems whatever. Whoever had hired this girl, the implication was enough to
exasperate Rafe, and Cade couldn't blame him.

Touchstone would perform to a crowd consisting of
the nobility and Coldkettle's general population from
miles around. Special arrangements had been made for
women to watch. Viewing stands holding a few dozen
seats each had been constructed here and there, fitted
with thin gauzy curtains that fooled nobody. As Cade
stood with his partners offstage, waiting for the huge
assembly to quiet down, he bit back renewed impatience with this silliness about not allowing women to
witness theater performances. Surely by now, after all
these years, someone ought to have acknowledged that
theater didn't shatter their poor fragile little minds. Barmaids had been witnessing performances for years.
Mayhap they were considered to possess a lower-class
gristle that rendered them insensitive. Ridiculous notion, but who knew what the Stewards were thinking?
Somebody ought to have made the official decision
that permitted women to attend openly, rather than

sneak behind veils or dress up as boys or huddle behind curtaining wisps of material. Perhaps it was more fun for them, the way the ladies of the Court enjoyed the pretense regarding performances at the Pavilion, but it annoyed Cade.

Picking out by sight one small girl with dark-blond hair, possibly disguised in boy's clothing and wearing a cap of some kind, was hopeless. Using magic, however, would be easier; he had only to supervise Mieka's and Rafe's efforts a little more closely than usual, and find out where the resistance or protection was. If any.

There was none. "Dragon"—truly dazzling when performed outdoors under the stars—was a smashing success. "Hidden Cottage" had been specially requested (the funny version, complete with near-sighted lordling and squealing pig), and had the audience in whoops of laughter. But no sooner had the glittering motes of Mieka's high-flung shattered withie drifted to the stage than the glisker leaped over the glass baskets and grabbed Cade's arm as they took their bows.

Smiling all over his face for the cheering crowd, Mieka demanded, "What in unholy Hells was *that*?"

"What was what?" Cade parried, trying not to wince at the grip on his arm. The slight little Elf was stronger than he looked.

"Is it me you don't trust, or Rafe?" Mieka smiled and waved, and kept hold of Cade as they left the stage. "Keeping watch over everything like that, putting yourself betwixt the magic and the audience more than you've ever done since that very first night in Gowerion—"

"Mieka—"

"It can't be Rafe you were worried on, so it has to be me." They had reached the guards' room built into the walls that had been set aside for their private comfort before and after the show. Mieka dropped the smiling mask and confronted Cade furiously. "After all this time, you don't—"

"It wasn't either of you, I swear. And let me go, damn it!" He wrenched his arm free. "You remember that girl at the Keymarker?"

Rafe handed each of them a cup of ale. "I appreciate your caution, but it wasn't necessary. She didn't do anything."

"I know."

"What the fuck are you talking about?" Mieka demanded.

Rafe explained; Mieka became mollified.

"Are you absolutely sure you saw her?" Jeska asked.

"Down in the village yestere'en, wearing go-to-Chapel best, trying to look as if she can afford to do more than gape at the goods in the windows."

"I keep wondering who hired her," Cade mused. "I mean, it's not as if a Keymarker barmaid gets invited to—but, come to that," he interrupted himself, "how could anybody know she has the skills and could be hired at all?"

No longer interested now that his pride had been soothed, Mieka said, "You puzzle it out as you like. I'm for the party. Good drinking, this," he finished, and emptied his glass, and went in search of another.

It might have been the new green silk shirt, and it might have been the ale, but Mieka was in his own bed that night on the opposite side of the chamber from Cade's.

The disappearance of the shortvest stitched for him had provoked jeers about how he couldn't be trusted to remember to pack anything but the glass baskets and withies. Jeska fretted a bit about visual harmony gone all to Hells because of Cade's carelessness, but then recalled that he had a velvet scarf almost the same shade of green—it was indeed his color—and lent it for the show. Cade promised to look for similar silk at the Castle Biding Fair, but told Mieka he'd have somebody else do the sewing. Mistress Windthistle couldn't be expected to do all that work again just because Cade was too much the dizzard to treat the garment with the respect it deserved. He was very careful to say all this while pretending to search through his things one more time, not looking at Mieka; he wasn't exactly lying, but the Elf could always tell if what he said wasn't exactly the truth.

The next morning the happy couple—Cade hoped they'd be happy, at any rate—departed on their wedding trip. Touchstone would play one more show, inside the castle this time, for Lord Coldkettle's lingering guests, then leave the next day, bound for Lilyleaf, Castle Biding, Frimham, Stiddolfe, and home. Cade was helping Rafe pace out the dimensions of the vast entry hall, calculating the height of the ceiling and the distance from the makeshift stage to the grand staircase and balcony where the guests would sit, when a familiar voice spoke his name just behind him.

"I hope I'm still allowed to call you Cayden," she went on. "Or it is Master Tregetour Silversun to everybody now?"

He turned, genuinely glad, and said, "Only to people I don't like. How are you, Vrennerie?"

"Very well, much beholden to you." Her smile was as delightful as ever, and the look in her eyes as she glanced at the tall, smartly dressed man beside her indicated that here was most definitely a happy marriage. "Have you met my husband? Kelinn Eastkeeping, this is my friend, Cayden Silversun."

They bowed, and smiled, and Cade was favorably

impressed not just by Lord Eastkeeping's gracious, open manner but also by his own ease in meeting the man who husbanded a woman he had almost been in love with. No envy here, no heartbreak—which meant his heart couldn't have been so very much involved.

"I would have come to greet you before," Vrennerie was saying, "but in this crush there'd be no chance to be talking."

And that put an end to whatever suspicion might be in his mind that she subscribed to his mother's notions of propriety, and believed that titled ladies did not seek out the hired entertainers for conversation. The thought, however fleeting, was unworthy, and he covered the rush of shame with a smile. "We've been busy working."

"Fascinating work, too," Eastkeeping said. "We're so remote at our holding that, if you can believe it, I didn't see a play until I was twenty years old!"

"Shocking," Vrennerie said. "Or would be, if the same wasn't true of me." Sweetly and demurely lying through her teeth, she added, "Or would be, if ever I'd actually seen a play."

"Which she never, ever has done," said His Lordship. "Of course."

"Of course," Cade echoed, repressing a grin. "I think—" But Rafe called impatiently from the bottom of the stairs, interrupting him.

"Ah, but we're intruding on your work," said His Lordship. Turning to Vrennerie, he said, "Weren't you going to ask about travel plans?"

"We leave tomorrow's dawning for home, Cayden, and our way is taking us on the road to Lilyleaf. Would Touchstone care to ride with us for a day?"

"Cade!" yelled Rafe.

"Keep your hair on!" Cade yelled back. To Vrennerie, he said, "Tomorrow at dawn—only be sure not to listen for the first hour or so, while Mieka lets everyone know his opinion of rising before noon."

"Oh, I'm knowing all those words now," she laughed.

"She made me teach her," groaned Eastkeeping. "She heard most of them on board ship, then at the Keeps before the wedding, and then at the Palace. She threatened to use them in polite conversation if I didn't give her definitions *and* rules for usage." He shook his dark head, and to Cayden's surprise, the shifting of thick curls revealed the tips of pointed ears. Elfen, probably—or, considering the location of his holdings, Piksey. "These modern young women—scandalous, simply scandalous."

"I completely agree with Your Lordship. At a guess, she then gave instructions to the Princess?"

"*Cade!*"

"The name's Kelinn, and quite frankly I've never gathered up courage enough to ask. Until tomorrow morning, then? I'm looking forward to the show tonight." With an innocent smile and dancing dark eyes, he added virtuously, "And I'm sure Vren would, too, if she could."

Cade nearly choked on a snort of laughter, and decided he liked Kelinn Eastkeeping. Then again, he couldn't imagine Vrennerie marrying anyone who lacked a sense of humor.

As usual, Mieka's protests ("Gods-damned fucking asscrack of *dawn* you wake me up?") lasted only as long as it took him to crawl into his hammock and go back to sleep. Cade and Jeska took advantage of Lord Eastkeeping's offer of horses to ride, and a cheerful little procession left Coldkettle just after dawn. Shortly before noon, one of the outriders reported a fine stag not two miles off, and a brief debate was held over whose lands these were and whether a hunt would be legal. Vrennerie used the map on the side of Touchstone's wagon to calculate where they might be, deciding that they were likely still within Lord Coldkettle's domain.

"He won't begrudge you some sport, I'm thinking," she told her husband.

"Care to ride with us, Cayden? Jeska?"

Obedient to a sidelong look from Vrennerie, Cade said, "Beholden, but no. I'm not that good a rider."

"And I've never been on a hunt," said Jeska, but he looked tempted.

"Then you must join us! Weren't you just telling me that every experience adds to your skills onstage? Coming, Vren?"

"Not this time. Have fun, dearling." She watched them gallop off into the forest with a few men-at-arms, her smile indulgent. "It doesn't matter whose land it is. He never kills anything," she confided, smoothing the material of her dark red linen skirt, split so she could comfortably ride astride. "It's the chase he enjoys, and the wildness of the riding. And then, if they do corner the animal, he just sits there to be admiring of it."

"I like your Lord Eastkeeping," Cade said impulsively, and she laughed.

"So do I! Come, let's ride on. They'll find us later." After a slight pause, she said, "My lady enjoyed the lunching at Seekhaven. She wrote to tell me so."

"It was very kind of her to invite us." He paused, adjusting the reins in his hand. His mount was a good, steady, serviceable brown mare, easy to ride and with no nonsense about her. The chase, he surmised, would not appeal to her any more than it did to him. "She seemed very happy. I assume there's an announcement will be made soon."

"How did you—?" She caught herself, then shook her head, the white ribbons of her plaited straw hat dancing around her cheeks. "No, don't tell me. Yes, the proclaiming will be made within a fortnight. She wanted to make sure, and to send a letter to her father first."

"Mieka was sure the instant he saw her."

"Then he must not have a look at me," she told him shyly. "If Kelinn knew, I'd not be riding in the fresh air but suffocating in one of the wagons on piles of pillows."

"But that's wonderful! Not the pillows or the suffocating, I mean, but—"

"Shush!" She grinned over at him. "It was my secret, and now it's yours—and I know you are a man to hold secrets close. Now, tell me how your Royal Circuit has been treating you."

"Very well indeed." As he ran through their itinerary, it occurred to him that there were tales Vrennerie had heard in her country that might enlighten him. At which point he wondered if he was curious for Vered's sake or for his own.

At noon they stopped to rest and water the horses, and to wait for the hunting party to return. Yazz put sprags around each wheel to keep the wagon from rolling, then set up their camp table while Rafe brought out chairs.

"Still snoring," he told Cade when asked about Mieka. "We'll give him an afternoon nosebag. May I offer you a glass of wine, my lady?"

"Beholden, and please call me Vrennerie. How do you sleep, though, with the bumping of the wagon wheels?"

"The Elf is useful for a few things—not many." Rafe grimaced. "Good as the springs are on the wagon, we bounced about quite a bit to and from Trials. But his mother has a cushioning spell, and whereas she did the main working of it, she taught it to him and he renews it now and then. So now we float along serene as a barge on a canal."

Cade watched the effect of this information about magic, so casually shared. Then he reminded himself she'd married a man with ears seen only on a Piksey or an Elf. Or a Fae.

Vrennerie squinted at the wagon wheels, as if the spell might be visible, then nodded. "My husband's gifts are of a growing sort. Our land at Eastkeeping is rocky and the soil is poor, but somehow he can encourage the wheat to grow and ripen. I believe," she said in a conspiratorial whisper, her brown eyes laughing, "that he sings to it!"

"Mieka has a sister who's rather agricultural," Cade said, tearing off a hunk of bread to dip in a sauce thick with chopped vegetables. "I'm told it's the Greenseed line of Elfen blood."

"Kelinn's grandmother—or was it great-grandmother?—was a Grassdew. Odd about names, isn't it?" she went on, cutting into the round of cheese to serve all three of them. "The Human ones are all places, like Eastkeeping or Tawnymoor, or my lady's new title of Downymede."

"That's only the nobility," Cade said. "Mostly the Human lines are crafter names, like Goldbraider or Bowbender."

"Then it's the Wizard names that have hints of their Clans in them?"

"Sometimes. Rafe's a Threadchaser, Spider Clan. Me, I'm Falcon, though how Silversun came out of it I've no idea. And one of my lines is Watersmith, which could almost be a Human crafter name. But actually it's Elfen."

"*Their* names," Rafe said, "connect to the Elements. Earth, Water, Fire, Air. Windthistle is obvious, of course, and Greenseed. But one of our best friends is a Cindercliff, which is a place name—only she's mostly Goblin with a few streaks of Wizard in her and a bit of Piksey and even some Elf." He shrugged and smiled. "So names don't mean much, taking all into account."

"You are all so casual about everything," Vrennerie said. "Different peoples and such. It's such a nice change from where I was born."

"Has it taken you long to get used to it?" Cade asked.

"Not so long as it might, if I hadn't fallen in love with a certain set of ears!"

If Mieka had been with them, he would have smirked and said something about the multitudinous irresistible qualities of Elves, beginning with but by no means limited to the elegancy of their ears. Cade was just as glad Mieka was still asleep.

After the simple meal, Rafe went for a walk. Vrennerie wondered if it might be possible for her to look inside the wagon.

"I can give you a tour, if you like," Cade said, swinging the door open for her. "Don't worry, we won't wake the Elf. When he sleeps, he *sleeps*."

Still, she kept her voice low as she commented on the tidy arrangements, the charming conveniences. Mieka was curled in his hammock, oblivious. Cade invited Vrennerie to sit down, and poured more wine. With all the windows and the back door open, there was breeze enough through the wagon to stay cool—and to provide ample evidence to anyone outside who cared to look in that Lady Eastkeeping and Master Silversun were doing nothing but sharing a glass of wine in the company of a snoring Elf.

"I've been wanting to ask you," Cade began, "about something I heard a friend talk about. Have you ever heard of the Knights of the Balaur Tsepesh?"

She widened her eyes. "Good Lord and Lady, where did you ever hear of such awfulness?"

"The invasion from the East, you mean?"

"That, yes, of course. But what the Knights did to gain themselves power to defeat them—" She set her wineglass on a shelf and folded her hands in her lap. "What was your friend saying?"

"That Wizards and other magical folk gave the Knights spells and suchlike for the battle." Although it seemed odd to him, suddenly, that if people with magic had been so essential in defeating the invaders, why had they been persecuted and expelled in later years?

"No, no, that wasn't it at all! It wasn't the people with magic who were giving them their powers. They bargained with demons, the very ones who came with the invaders."

This was a new angle. "These demons thought to turn them to their side?"

"No one knows. It could have been the *balaurin* thought they might switch sides themselves. But the Knights took such power as was being offered, and even though their aims were noble, to drive out the invading evil, their souls were forever forfeit."

"Times were desperate, though," he suggested.

"Very much. The only strength that could defeat the *balaurin* was strength like their own. And when the Knights had this strength—"

"I was told that all of them died soon after the final battle."

"Not all of them," she said grimly. "Some lived on, despised and feared."

Ah! So that was the reason for banishing the magical folk, who had given spells and such to the Knights. He did believe Chat's version and he believed Vrennerie's as well, easily seeing how it could work into the tale. The Knights becoming greedy for more power, making a bargain with the demons . . .

"So nobody ever goes to their tomb and shrine?" Cade swirled wine in his glass. "Shrine to what? A God? The Lord and Lady?"

"To the victory they won. To themselves, I suppose. There were offers—offerings? Yes—I have learned much but sometimes I get confused. I still don't quite think in Albeyni!"

He didn't take her up on the change of subject. "What sort of offerings?" Thinking of the flowers that were a standard gift at roadside shrines.

"Dead animals." She shivered in the afternoon warmth. "Just barely dead, and the blood still warm and flowing."

Oh, what Vered would make of *that* onstage.

Vrennerie wore a worried frown. "Why are you wanting to know about this? Surely you won't make theater about it!"

"No, of course I won't," he said honestly. "It was just such a strange tale, and one I'd never heard before. Since it comes from nearer your part of the world than mine—"

"This country, Albeyn—this is my part of the world now."

He accepted the rebuke with a small bow of apology. "Forgive me. My curiosity leads me a lot of places, and sometimes into rudeness."

"You would not be who and what you are if you were not filled with questions about everything. So to answer—yes, offerings of fresh blood were made, and some say it was to satisfy the doomed souls of the Knights so that they would not leave their tombs and—"

Outside the open windows shouts were heard, and galloping hooves. Mieka suddenly jerked upright in his hammock, flailing in alarm, and somehow managed to twist himself around into a cocoon. "What?" he exclaimed, struggling to get free. "What's all the racket?"

"Just His Lordship returning from the hunt," Cade said, for the shouts were of greeting and there was no urgency to the hoofbeats.

"Whose Lordship?"

"Lady Vrennerie's."

"Vrennerie?" Mieka asked, peering through the mesh. "She's—what are you doing here—damn it!" He had rolled himself over, hammock and all, so that he was staring at the floor. "Get me out of this!"

"No, leave him be," Cade told Vrennerie. "It's a good place for him."

"Cayden!" he wailed.

Laughing, they managed to extricate him. Cade was grateful for Mishia Windthistle's strictures on sleeping in nightshirts; otherwise, Vrennerie's modesty might have been affronted. Mieka, of course, had none to affront. He made it to his feet, gathered the knee-length garment and his dignity about him and bowed to Vrennerie.

"Gladdest greetings, my lady. I am beholden to you for your help." Glaring at Cade: "You, I'll deal with later."

Lord Eastkeeping was calling for his wife. Mieka handed her gallantly to the door. She paused to whisper something to him that Cade didn't catch. Mieka looked startled, then guilty, then began to laugh. So did she. Before Cade's curiosity could trounce his manners again with a demand to know what had been said, she had descended the steps and was striding to meet her husband.

Mieka was rummaging in piles of discarded clothing. "Where's me trousers, eh? Oh, here—no, those are Rafe's—"

"What did she say?"

Yanking his own pants free, he smirked. "I'm not telling."

"Come on, Mieka!"

"No." He tried stuffing all those folds of bleached linen into the waistband, then cursed and hauled the thing off, looking around for a shirt. When he found one, he shouldered into it. "But one thing I'll say, Cayden Silversun, and it's that those stories you two were talking about, they crept into my dreams and it's a marvel and a wonder I didn't wake up shrieking!" He bounded down the steps, begging for something to drink.

The hunting party returned, as Vrennerie had predicted, without the stag. Jeska returned with a torn shirt and scratches all over his face and arms and a vow, once he was in the wagon applying salve to his cuts, never to participate in such folly ever again.

"All this anguishing yourself," Cade scoffed, "over a few scrapes?"

"It's not just that," he replied, and gingerly rubbed his backside. "I'll be sore for a week!"

"You can visit the baths in Lilyleaf," Mieka suggested. "That ought to help." When Jeska continued to grumble, he went on, "Only think on it—all that lovely hot water, all those lovely bath girls to rub your back—"

"It's not me back that hurts!" But the masquer began to look interested.

"I'm sure they'll rub whatever needs rubbing," Mieka soothed. "And very capably, too." He stretched and scrubbed his fingers through his hair, saying, "I'm for a ride up top with Yazz. And I really ought to meet Lord Eastkeeping afore their road splits off from ours."

The introductions were performed just as everyone was mounting up to continue the journey. Mieka was all charm and smiles, but as Cade watched the usual process, he discerned a subtle shift in the Elf's demeanor from *This is someone who must be won over* to *This man is someone I like;* from master manipulator to real person.

Cade walked with him over to the wagon, intending to give him a leg up to the coachman's bench. Mieka hesitated, gave Cade an oblique glance, and said softly, "He seems nice."

"Yes."

"She looks happy."

"Yes. Are there any other trite social niceties you'd like to trot out for inspection?"

"I just meant—" He gripped the handhold on the side of the wagon. "You're not bothered. Them, I mean. It doesn't bother you."

"Not at all."

"Well . . . good, then." Without another word, and without looking directly at Cade, he climbed up to sit beside Yazz.

With a wry smile and a shake of his head, Cade went to check his horse's girth. For all that Mieka's antics could render him speechless with fury at times, there was yet a kindness about him, a gentleness unexpected in one so madly brash. But Cade still wanted to know what Vrennerie had told him. Not that he'd ever find out, of course.

They parted from Lord Eastkeeping's party at dusk. Camp was set up and dinner was set to cook, but Touchstone's wagon rolled on to the night. Farewells were warm and promises were made to meet again in Gallantrybanks this winter. Cade got back into the wagon and found a glass of ale already poured for him, and Rafe frowning across it.

"What's all this about that story Chat told us? Mieka says you asked Vrennerie all about it. You're not thinking of making us do a full-stage battle and all that goes with it, are you?"

"No." He watched an apple orchard go by outside the window, heard the sounds of Lord Eastkeeping's camp fade into the distance.

Mieka slouched in the opposite chair and poured more ale. "We should've stayed for dinner."

"Lilyleaf tomorrow," Cade reminded him. "Mistress Ringdove will have fresh trout in lemon sauce and those mocah candies you like."

"Stop tormenting me!" Mieka scowled at the left-overs of bread, cheese, and vegetables that would be their evening meal. "Croodle's cooking—the very mention of it in the same breath as such chankings as this just isn't decent—"

All at once Jeska began burbling where he lay in his hammock, swinging gently back and forth. "*Croo*dle, *Croo*dle," he sang, a sweetly silly grin on his face. "Croo-dle cooking cooing cuckoos—"

Cade stared. "What's wrong with him? Swallow the same dictionary Mieka did?"

Rafe said, "A little something of Auntie Brishen's finest in his ale. So he'd stop carrying on about his sore bum."

"Don't worry," Mieka assured them as Jeska went on crooning. "It'll really hit him in a few minutes and then he'll shut up. Thorn's different when you drink it—not like sliding down a hill, more like falling off a cliff."

"Croodley, crudely, rudely, lewdly, cutely, toodley-dum-de-doodley—"

"Oh Gods," Cade moaned. "How many minutes is a *few* minutes?"

"—lumpety-thump, clumpety-rump, teedley-wheedley-boo!"

Cade pointed a finger at Mieka. "Make it stop. Now."

"Dumpety-crumpush, Duchess on crutches, luscious, mush . . . m-m-m-mushes . . ."

Silence.

Cade peered at his slumbering masquer. "Will he be all right in the morning?"

"No reason why not." Mieka plunged his fork into a hunk of cheese and regarded it resentfully. "We'll throw him into the baths, shall we, first thing after lunching?"

Eleven

EARLY TO RISE, *early to bed* only made a man bored out of his head, as far as Mieka was concerned. Whilst he'd still lived at Wistly Hall, his bedchamber had been far enough away from everyone else's in the vast barracks of a place that he wasn't bothered by other people rising at repulsive hours of the morning. In his new home, his wife had thoughtfully arranged the baby's cradle in her mother's room at the opposite corner of the house from their bedchamber. When his daughter squalled for her morning feed, Mieka heard her, but only at a distance.

His partners in Touchstone weren't so obliging regarding his comfort. Rafe, the baker's son, still woke early, noisily, and inconsiderately: banging about the wagon, opening or closing windows, muttering to himself, searching with an unjustified amount of racket for this or that or something to eat. Cade, bless him, usually sprawled silently in his hammock, thinking Great Thoughts or reading, for an hour or so after waking. Sometimes, though, he was as rude as Rafe, especially when he couldn't find the book he'd been reading the night before. Jeska would slide quietly enough from his bed, but the splashing of his morning wash, the cursing that always came with negotiating the cleft in his chin on a shaving day, and the debating he did with himself about which of his score of equally gorgeous outfits he would wear that day invariably interrupted Mieka's sleep. A discreet application of redthorn at night didn't last until dawn.

So Mieka never minded that much when Yazz got them to their next stop while they were all still abed. He could wake up enough to climb stairs to their allotted rooms, or elect to stay in the wagon while the others went into the inn, and then cuddle back to sleep with little or no memory of ever having woken up at all.

Yet when the wagon pulled into Mistress Ringdove's establishment in Lilyleaf at dawn, Mieka was wide awake and had been for quite some time. This annoyed him. If he didn't get some decent sleep, he'd be nigh on useless at their first show tonight—or would be, without some of Auntie Brishen's bluethorn. The reasons why the night had been fitful and fretful were only partially clear to him, but he was sure all of them were Cayden's fault. The man's habit of thinking too much was, unfortunately, contagious.

Mieka wasn't quite sure how they'd come to be traveling with Lady Vrennerie and her husband—he hadn't even known she was at Coldkettle for the wedding—so her presence in the wagon yesterday had been a shock. Not the shock that had twisted him up in his hammock; that maneuver had been deliberate, an example of the *clever and mad* Blye had recommended years ago. He'd actually been awake for some time, listening to the conversation. And grisly talk it had been, too. He'd decided when they got to the dead animals part that it was time to put a stop to it before he lost his appetite.

There had been a second shock when he was handing her down the steps. *"Just to be letting you know,"* she'd whispered, *"that green shirt from last night suits you much better than all that velvet last summer—such a difficult shade of blue, don't you agree?"* He'd nearly collapsed with the knowing that she had recognized him last summer behind the blue gown and heavy veil. How had she managed it? He hadn't a clue. But if he ever did such a thing again, he'd make sure to keep a withie up his sleeve and use the magic inside to create an appearance for himself that would keep him mysterious. And all at once he resolved that he would indeed do such a thing again, just to see if he could.

Thus decided, he'd settled himself for sleep. But his brain was too engaged in poking around various other things, all of them to do with Cade and Vrennerie.

He still didn't understand why Quill hadn't pursued the girl. She was attractive and he'd been attracted. She laughed in all the right places, they were compatible— what was Cade's problem? Mieka had thought, for a time, that Vrennerie would become a presence in Cade's life, and therefore in his own. But it seemed she was naught but a passing digression.

Had this been a play, he thought suddenly, one thing would follow another in nice, logical, and even predictable order, all of it leading to culmination and resolution. Happily ever after wasn't a strict requirement, but nothing in the script would have anything to do with aught other than the stated plot.

But this wasn't a play. Life was messy, illogical, unpredictable, and things and people happened that had nothing to do with each other, leave alone the basic plot. How did you apply a *plot* to life? You couldn't, not without warping things out of their proper proportions. Events that ought to be significant turned out to be trifles; people one met seemingly at random turned out to be central to one's life. People came and went, things that had once been vitally important became trivial, what you thought would come of something—or someone—never happened the way you thought it might. Mayhap by the end of one's years, one could look back and make sense of everything. But not necessarily—and certainly not while it was all happening. There was no predictable plot to the events of a life.

Lady Vrennerie, for instance. Had this been a play, Cade would be sighing right now at losing her to Lord Eastkeeping, who would of course have been infinitely less agreeable and perhaps even sinister, as befitted the standard story of a hero's heartbreak (casting Cade as the Hero, naturally).

In a romance, something would happen to His Lordship to make Vrennerie available again, and she would come running to Cade for a scene of tearful, joyful reunion. Applause, take the proper number of bows, curtain down. In a tragedy, Vrennerie would be very unhappily wedded and stay that way, and Cade would keep sighing for the rest of his life—but *nobly* sighing, for as the Hero, he must do the honorable thing and not tempt her away from her marriage vows.

Cade evidently did not feel inclined to sigh. Why should he? Vrennerie was clearly happy in her marriage and he was clearly happy for her—which automatically disqualified him from the role of Hero, because even the noblest of that breed must needs sigh. Lord Singleheart, for instance; in a rather stupid little playlet, upon realizing the superior suitability of his lady's husband, he became so depressed that he rode off to fight wyverns and, needless to say, managed to get himself killed.

Nowhere in any play or poem or tale Mieka had ever heard of—and in his profession, he'd encountered most of them—not in romance or tragedy or anything in between, did the Hero stay friends with the lady who married another man. This was *life,* not a play, and Mieka concluded that it was much better that Cade was happy for Vrennerie and remained her friend rather than sighing (nobly) or riding off to get himself killed.

Not that Quill would ever do anything that idiotic, or that vulgar. Mieka could see Alaen doing it, though—a much deeper streak of the romantic than Cade had Alaen Blackpath, pining after Chirene. His wife had mentioned in her latest letter that the poor fool had shown up again at the house. Thorned, of course. Her mother had had the fright of her life when she came upon him, sleeping curled up like a child with tears still on his face, in a corner of the bedchamber Chirene occupied whilst she and Sakary had rented the place. When he woke, humbly apologetic and meek as a lamb, they bundled him into a hire-hack back to Gallantrybanks, but in Mieka's opinion the man really ought to pull himself back into one piece.

He simply couldn't imagine Cayden doing something that silly. He had better taste.

Still . . . was there no feeling that the man would surrender to? Not love, obviously. Nor rage, neither. Mieka couldn't have counted the times he'd seen fury flare in those gray eyes, only to be doused almost immediately. Sometimes he deliberately provoked that anger, just to see if Cade would succumb. He never did.

It wasn't that Cade was heartless. His love for his little brother, for Mistress Mirdley, for Blye—he *could* feel. He wouldn't be capable of priming a withie if he couldn't feel. Mieka's job was to take those feelings and use his own to build on them, focus them, accentuate them, use them to beguile their audiences. But with Cade there was always the caution, always the control. Not even Black Lightning's disgusting play had shaken him, though it had shaken everyone else who'd seen it. But not Cayden, not he.

Well, Mieka told himself as he trudged up Croodle's back stairs and fell onto a bed, at least Cade had learned how to laugh. On first meeting him, Mieka hadn't been entirely sure Cade knew what laughter was, leave alone how to do it. *Took me awhile, though,* he mused. *Clever and mad . . . that's the ticket.* And on this thought he finally drifted off to sleep.

Late that afternoon, Cade, Rafe, and Jeska yielded to Mieka's persuasions and accompanied him to the nearest baths. There were a dozen or so of these scattered throughout the city. Some were just ranks of wooden tubs, but some boasted marble pools and three different temperatures of water. One could loll in water cloudy with minerals, herbs, or, in the really expensive places, milk. In some places the rubdown girls were for hire; in others, they provided a massage but nothing else—though Mieka had found on previous visits that a bit of cajoling usually overcame their professional scruples. Not that he'd ever had to pay for that sort of thing ever in his life, of course, or ever would.

It was a glorious summer day as they walked the two blocks to the baths. Neither the most exclusive nor the least, decorated with a few fallen columns nicked from elsewhere to give it an impression of age and dignity, there were two mineral pools for bathing (one cool and one hot) and rooms with individual tubs where a patron could select the type and temperature of the water. On Croodle's advice, Mieka had chosen the hour when most of the bath attendants took their break, before everything was cleaned up following the men's afternoon hours and just before the time allotted to women. Whether it was Touchstone's name or Croodle's that got them special treatment—or the simple fact that the girl on duty was young and responded with giggles to mild flirtation—they were escorted at once into the changing room. Rafe chose a private bath; Mieka, Cade, and Jeska plunged into the hot pool. The masquer immediately began swimming lazy laps.

"Nice," Mieka remarked as he floated on his back within easy reach of the side railings; he could swim, but not very well. His voice echoed up to the arched ceiling, painted deep blue with silver and golden stars. "All to ourselves! Makes me feel a right prince, it does, with half the world to command."

"I'll take the other half," said Cade, who sat on a step, waist-deep in hot water. He waved a languid hand. "And an age of marvels shall ensue!"

"Free whiskey," Mieka said at once, "and a real theater in every town!"

"At reasonable prices. Women will be allowed to craft whatever they like, as professionals *with* a hallmark."

"*And* attend the theater openly." He gave the matter due consideration, then added, "No more anguishing over having to do any of The Thirteen at Trials."

"Vered's got you thinking about that, has he?" Cade grinned. "What grand ideas you and he have got! I'd settle for hot cinnamon mocah every morning for everyone as wants it—"

"And whatever the Archduke wants, by law he'll never have it!"

"Talking of law," Jeska said, "while you're sorting out the world to suit yourselves, do me a favor and put an end to all writ-rats."

Cade frowned. "Trouble with Airilie's mother?"

It took Mieka a moment to remember that Jeska, too, was the father of a little girl. Mieka had seen her a few times, but never met the mother, to whom Jeska had not been married.

"I've gone through her accounts and my accounts,

and they don't add up straight. She says she's not received even half what she's owed. Kearney's clerk says she must be mistook. But she has lawyers now, y'see."

"I'd been wondering," said Cade, "about all those letters you keep getting. The ones with the seals and ribbons."

Mieka growled low in his throat. "D'you want me to send Jed and Jez to loom over them until they give in?"

Jeska swam towards them, muscular arms taking long, slow strokes. "Beholden, and it's a lovely image to hold in my head, but no. I won't have it said that I've shorted my daughter of her rights." He stopped near them and submerged, then surfaced with his hair slicked back from his face. It immediately began to spring up in curls again. "Can't believe how big Airilie's getting," he said wistfully. "And but for a few days every few months, I've missed all of it."

"They grow," Mieka said. "No stopping it, whether you're there to watch or not." He hesitated, because his next question was highly personal and Jeska had never been all that forthcoming about his private life. "Not to be nosy, but—why don't you and your mother have the raising of the girl? I mean, the law being what it is, with fathers having all the rights to the children and such—"

"That's only if the parents are wed and then divorced," Cade told him. "He's on the document as legal father, and Airilie has his name."

"Mum saw to that," Jeska said. "One of her cleaning clients was a justiciar, and she got his advice. Wanted us both to have the right to see her only grandchild."

Mieka sighed. "But now it's come back to bite you in the bum. Not that you wouldn't have supported them anyways, of course," he added hastily. "And talking of your bum, are you feeling better?"

"You promised *girls*," Jeska grumbled, sparkling

blue eyes giving the lie to his tone. "Girls with lovely soft hands, rubbing whatever I want them to rub. Where are the girls?"

The girls—well, one girl, petulant at being interrupted during her dinner break until she saw her client—duly produced, Jeska vanished into one of the private rooms. Mieka and Cade lingered for a while in the water, then braced themselves for the required plunge into the cold pool. Emerging with shivering swiftness, they wrapped themselves in towels and went in search of their clothes.

The wood-paneled changing room was empty. Every shelf, every hook, every bench.

No shirts, no trousers, no stockings, no boots, no nothing.

They had just turned to face each other when Jeska wandered in, went to the shelf where he'd left his clothing, and stood there for a moment staring at it.

"Not him," Mieka concluded. "Rafe."

"Rafe," Cade echoed in a tone that promised grim vengeance.

Not if Mieka found him first. Hitching the towel tighter round his waist, he strolled out to the reception area, smiled sweetly at the blushing giggler, and said, "Whatever the man with the beard paid you, I'll double it."

"Nobody p-paid me, Y'r Honor," she stammered. "I'd be losin' me place, I would, to take extra from a customer!"

Cade called from the inner doorway, "But you *did* see a bearded man walk out of here with more clothes than he came in with? Carrying them, I mean?"

She nodded. "I didn't think much on it."

If she'd bothered to think at all, Mieka told himself; she didn't look the sort to have the wherewithal for much thinking.

She cast an anxious glance at the wall clock and said, "Beggin' Y'r Honor's pardon, but it's nigh on time for the ladies—"

Right on cue, the front door opened and a brace of respectable middle-aged women in large, fussily feathered summer hats entered. With another of his most adorable smiles, Mieka dropped his towel.

"Gracious!" one of the women cried, unabashedly looking him down and up and then about halfway down again.

The other didn't bother with the down-and-up part. "Hired a new bath boy, have you? I quite approve."

Not much in this naughty world could bring a blush to Mieka Windthistle's cheek, but these brazen ladies had managed it. He scooped up his towel and fled for the changing room. Cade followed, looking torn between laughing at Mieka and setting plots to kill Rafe. Jeska merely looked bleakly determined.

"There'll be nothing to wear, count on it," he said. "Nothing of our own and nothing to borrow. But it's only two blocks to Croodle's."

"You're joking!" Cade exclaimed.

"No. I'm not." Taking a deep breath, he secured his towel as best he could and marched into the hall and out the front door.

Resigned, Mieka and Cade followed him.

Two blocks of whistles, laughter, shocked faces, cheers, and lascivious propositions later, they were scrambling up Croodle's back stairs. Halfway up, they bumped into Jeska, who didn't seem able to move.

One glance up at the landing told Mieka why. The second-most-beautiful girl he'd ever seen stood there, delicate black brows slightly arched above eyes as big and brown as a doe's. She was tall and slender, with a heart-shaped face, full lips, high cheekbones, a broad nose with thin, flaring nostrils, and skin the color of a cup of hot mocah mixed with a dollop of milk.

"Your pardon, I'm sure," Mieka said to the girl, pushing past the unmoving masquer. A quick glance at Jeska's face showed a man so utterly gobsmacked that he didn't even remember how to breathe. "Slight problem with our clothing—won't take up a moment of your time—"

Cade followed, and when they both stood on the landing near the girl, they looked down at Jeska. His towel was securely in place, but there was a bump in front. Mieka clapped a hand over his mouth to stifle a giggle. Cade snarled Jeska's name, and when there was no response, he jumped down the few steps and hauled him up by the arm, stumbling and slack-jawed.

"Sorry," Cade mumbled as they passed the girl, who was biting her lips together, dark eyes twinkling. They were in their room with the door almost shut before she began to laugh.

Mieka would have joined in, but was distracted by the sight of Rafe lounging in a chair by the window, at his knee a little table bearing a tray with four pints of ale. He waved graciously, like King Meredan acknowledging a crowd of cheering subjects.

"Make no mistake," Cade intoned. "You *will* die for this."

"You can't kill me tonight, we've a show in four hours. Have a drink, whyn't you? And I'll tell you who I saw on my walk back from the baths."

Mieka grabbed up two glasses and shoved one at Jeska. "Here. Down this, and then go do something about downing *that*." He nodded to the now very obvious result of staring at the girl.

Rafe had noticed. It was difficult not to notice. He smiled sweetly and observed, "I see you've met Kazie.

She's only just arrived this past spring from the Islands, and she's Croodle's cousin, so hands to yourself, Bowbender—and, like Mieka, I do mean that literally."

Having emerged from his daze, Jeska glared at them all, took a few swallows of ale, and snatched his clothing from a chair. "To Hells with you, then," he said, and betook himself off to the garderobe down the hall.

"Who'd you see?" Mieka asked, discarding his towel and stretching out naked on his bed.

"The little blond. The one from the Keymarker. Again. She saw me, as well, and hurried the opposite direction."

"Delusional," Mieka said sadly. "How *will* we break it to Crisiant and his mother?"

"I saw her," Rafe insisted.

"Of course you did," Cade agreed. "And when you find her again, you can hire her to protect *you*."

*   *   *

SOMETHING WAS WRONG with this audience. Mieka suspected it almost from the start of "Hidden Cottage," but he knew it for certain sure when nobody laughed at the pig.

He'd been casting worried glances at Rafe since the evil sisters spirited away the beautiful bride. By the time the young lordling went in search of her, Mieka was watching Cayden as well. Nothing was different from how they usually played the piece. Jeska was spot on with his lines and gestures. Mieka created and Rafe managed the magic with all their customary skills. But Jeska was having to work hard at winning the audience—something he *never* had to do. Rafe was having to struggle with the flow of magic—and not because it was irregular or Mieka was bungling it. Cade was knot-browed, hands gripping his lectern as his gaze swept the audience again and again, searching for Mieka knew not what.

People simply weren't responding. Moreover, they knew they ought to be responding, and were becoming restless.

Mieka didn't have the skill to probe the audience the way Rafe and Cade were doing. All he could do was his work, although the temptation to ratchet up the intensity of the magic was nigh on irresistible. The bluethorn meant he could do it if he chose. He held off, sweating and baffled, until all at once there was a roar of laughter and everything was suddenly, simply, completely fine.

They got through to the end of the playlet and the applause was, as he'd come to expect, deafening. If the audience didn't note the grimness of the smiles as Touchstone took their bows, mayhap it was because Rafe had left lingering laughter in the hall.

There was no laughter on their walk back to Croodle's.

"That performance," Jeska said wearily, "was *not* fun."

"That performance," Cade announced, "was interfered with, and by somebody with only half an idea what he was doing."

"It wasn't a 'he'!" Rafe snapped. "I *told* you I'd seen her—and now look what she did to us tonight!"

"Erm . . ." Mieka plucked at Cade's sleeve. "What exactly happened? I mean, I felt it, but I'm not sure what was going on."

"Nothing like what she did at the Keymarker. This was—it was like a wall between us and the audience. Nothing was getting through. Oh, bits and pieces here and there, but—no, it wasn't a wall, like," Cade said, searching as always for the right words. "More of a—"

"Like somebody'd wrapped the audience in wool,"

growled Rafe. "Things were getting through, but no-wheres near the way they ought."

"I couldn't get them to laugh," Jeska muttered. "Not like they usually do."

"Not your fault, mate," Mieka reassured him.

"It wasn't the visuals or the sounds or anything that got muffled," Rafe said. "It was the feelings. It must be the same as seeing a play on the Continent, one without any magic at all."

They walked on in silence for a while. Then Mieka said, "The one Vered and Rauel did that time—in the first part, eating breakfast and whatnot, there wasn't any emotion. That made people restless, too."

"That was on purpose. Designed so." Cade shook his head. "And whether they were aware of it or not, the audience knew there'd be a—a balance. Culmination. They trust the Shadowshapers."

"Was this done to make people not trust us?"

"When I catch up with that girl—"

"So *now* you believe me," Rafe grumbled.

"Is she following us around?" Jeska asked. "Has she been trailing us all through the Royal?"

"How could a barmaid afford all that travel?" Rafe countered.

Mieka gave a shrug. "How could she afford to be at Coldkettle, and now in Lilyleaf? Somebody's paying her."

"And when I find her," Cade finished ominously, "I'll find out who."

They were nearly at Croodle's place. Mieka eyed Jeska sidelong and said, "Gods, what a look on you! Put on your pretty-face, old son, or Mistress Kazie won't recognize you."

Even in the uncertain lamplight on the street, he could see the masquer's blush. Schemes flittered through his head, but he rejected them firmly. Rafe was his target for the next little while; Jeska could woo the luscious Kazie in peace.

Three days later, the masquer still hadn't managed it. This was unprecedented. The lady seemed equally smitten—when she thought nobody was looking at her, of course. Curiously enough, none of them ragged on Jeska about it. They all knew *serious* when they saw it. More to the point, perhaps, they all knew what Croodle would do to them if her cousin or her favorite player were mocked in any way for their feelings. And feelings there definitely were; proof enough was that neither could talk much around the other.

Mieka found this amusing. All those words Jeska had memorized over the years, and he couldn't think of anything to say? He was discussing this with Cayden one afternoon over a pint out back—Croodle had added a brick courtyard with tables and chairs, with big earthenware pots of flowering plants—when Rafe strode out from the taproom with the girl in tow.

"Tell them what you told me!" he commanded as he hauled her down the steps.

"Leave me be and I might consider it!" About halfway to their table, she managed to reclaim her wrist.

Mieka leaped up, got another chair, and flung Rafe a chiding glare as he settled the girl into it. "Go get her a glass of wine," he directed, "and go find your manners while you're about it!"

"Pegs, isn't it?" Cade said.

"Megs," she corrected. "Beholden, Master Windthistle, but I'd rather have a pint." She pushed up the sleeves of her blouse—a fine, thin white linen, almost a man's shirt, lacking decoration or embroidery—and tucked stray strands of dark-blond hair behind her ears. Human ears, Mieka noted, and in all other respects a wholly Human girl. Except for that fettling ability, of course, and a certain lightness to her bones that hinted at Piksey or maybe even Sprite. But where the Wizard in her might show, he'd no notion. And partly Wizard she had to be, to have the fettling talent.

Cade hadn't stood to greet her, nor even shifted from his lounging pose, long legs extended and crossed at the ankles. He sipped his ale and looked for all the world as if a friend had just dropped by for an afternoon visit. "Lovely day, isn't it?" he observed.

Megs didn't bother to reply to this inanity. She glanced over at Mieka. Her eyes were the deep clear green of a glass bottle with that sparkly white wine in it. A glint of gold here and there, shadowed by thick dark eyelashes. She wasn't terribly pretty, not by Mieka's standards, but there was something interesting in her face. Again he thought Piksey, perhaps, or Sprite.

Black Lightning could have found out in an instant. There was a thought hiding behind that, but he had no time to coax it out.

"Beholden for quieting Threadchaser," she said to Mieka. "He yelled at me for five blocks."

"Why's that?" Cade asked in that perfectly amiable tone that always meant trouble.

Mieka was interested to see that the geniality didn't fool Megs one bit. Shrugging, she said, "Because he thinks I was at Coldkettle—"

"Weren't you?"

With another glance at Mieka: "Can't you shut him up, too?"

It pained him to admit it. "Short of stuffing a gag down his throat . . . no."

"Shame, that." She looked over her shoulder to the back door.

"You were at our show a few nights ago," Cade said. "Why?"

"I wasn't anywhere near your show. How could I be? I'm a girl."

"Girls have been known to dress as boys to get into the theater."

"Not this girl. I was at the White Columns, and I can prove it."

Cade hooted with laughter at this reference to Lilyleaf's most exclusive and expensive inn. "Swanning about the best chambers, no doubt, with two maidservants to wait on you hand and foot!"

"I didn't say I was *stopping* there. I said I *was* there. For a tregetour, you're not very precise about words, are you?"

Mieka waited for the explosion, which to his mind was as inevitable as if Cade were a pile of black powder and she'd just scraped a flint-rasp in his general direction. Rafe came up then and deposited a pint glass on the table. He sat down, folded his arms, and glared at her.

She took a pull at the drink. With venomous sweetness she said, "Beholden, kind sir. Dragging a girl through the streets is thirsty work—won't you get something for yourself?"

He went on glaring. "Talk."

"I was about to. I don't know what happened at your show, but I gather that it had something to do with interfering in your performance." She paused for another swallow. "All I can tell you is, it wasn't me."

"Don't you mean 'it was not I'?" Cade asked, all treacle pudding with candied raisins drizzling honey. It made Mieka's teeth hurt just to hear him.

"What are you doing here, then?" Rafe demanded. "If it's not to mess about with our magic—and for that matter, why were you at Coldkettle?"

"For the wedding, of course."

"Invitation personally signed by His Lordship, I take it?"

"His steward hired more servants for the banqueting. Notice any of the Keymarker's tall redheads?"

"Certainly not!" Mieka said. "He's a happily married man." This dim attempt at humor earned him a kick under the table from Cade.

Rafe was saying smoothly, "None of the Keymarker's tall redheads ever mucked about with a performance."

"I already told you why I did what I did!"

"Oh," Cade said, "and your fragile little friend just happens to be in Lilyleaf taking the waters, so you thought you'd come along and see her safe?"

"I had enough money after Coldkettle for a little holiday. You ought to've been lawyers, the both of you!"

Mieka reflected that observing this conversation was a bit like watching a three-sided game of battledore. And it was giving him a headache. So he said, "May I ask something?" He kept his voice gentle and polite, winning another grateful glance for his manners—which concept would have had his mother fainting with shock. "I gather Rafe described what happened the other night. What do you think it might be about?"

"It's something only a fettler could manage, if I understand correctly?"

Rafe nodded. "Not a very good one, but—"

"But good enough to give you some trouble?" A tiny smirk twisted her lips. "Not for very long, I'm sure. You're *Touchstone*, after all. I'd look for someone who wishes you ill, first off."

"Funnily enough," Cade drawled, "we managed to suss out that bit."

"And then find out if they've any unemployed fettler friends willing to come make some mischief."

Black fucking Lightning, Mieka thought instantly.

He knew Cade and Rafe were thinking it, too. Aside from personal experience and mutual loathing, there'd been that Elsewhen of Cade's, about Thierin Knottinger giving Mieka some vile sort of thorn that toppled him in the middle of a show.

Megs had finished most of her ale. "May I go now?"

"With Rafe's apologies," Mieka prompted.

"I can talk for myself," the fettler reminded him. "And I am sorry. But you have to admit that after what happened at the Keymarker, and then again the other night . . ."

She stood, shook out her skirts, tried again to tuck her hair tidy, and said to Mieka, who had risen to his feet, "Beholden, Master Windthistle, for your kindness and the ale. No, I can manage quite well without an escort. I give you gentlemen good afternoon."

She crossed paths with Croodle, who was coming out with fresh pints. They exchanged a few words Mieka didn't hear; Croodle laughed and nodded.

"Spicy little piece," Rafe observed as Mistress Ringdove set their drinks before them.

"That she is." Croodle nodded and sighed. "If I had her working here, I'd not be having to rise up my voice half so often. She's the sort keeps 'em sorted."

"You could probably hire her away from the Keymarker," Cade said. "She doesn't much fit in with their usual barmaids."

For some reason this struck Croodle as hilariously funny, and she walked back to her kitchen door still laughing.

Twelve

"YOU HAVE TO hear this," Rafe said, waving a broadsheet as he entered Croodle's taproom.

Cade looked up from the letter he was writing to Derien. The boy was fretful about starting at King's College next month and was positive of three things: The sons of the nobility would despise him, he didn't know half of what he ought to know, and he'd be absolutely miserable from the instant he set foot outside Redpebble Square each morning until he returned home each night. *And besides all that,* Dery had written, *some of them will have magic and use it on me and nobody even knows if I even have any magic or not and even if I do it won't happen for years yet!*

Cade couldn't play the hypocrite by reassuring Dery that highborn ancestors didn't matter; in such a setting, blood counted. Neither could he tell the child that all he need do was study as hard as he could and he'd be fine; considering his own rather sketchy academic career, he'd look a right fool harping on the virtues and rewards of dedicated scholarship. As for the magic— the least said about that sort of thing, the better. Not that he had any doubts that his little brother would turn up with something interesting and useful and perhaps even powerful. With their background of talents on both sides of the family, it would be extraordinary if magic had passed Derien by. But whereas Cade might easily mention their grandfather the fettler and all the other Wizard and Elf and so on blood in their veins, he reasoned it would be for the best not to bring up their mad uncle Dennet, or their even madder great-grandmother Raziel Watersmith, and especially not their mother's mother, Lady Kiritin.

What he'd decided to write about instead was how this was Dery's first step to independence, and how much Cade envied him setting out so young because he'd been almost thirteen before he'd gone to Sagemaster Emmot's Academy, and surely there'd be at least one boy willing to make friends. The words were coming slow and thin and unconvincing, and thus it was with relief that he set the letter aside and turned to Rafe.

Lilyleaves was the isn't-it-just-*too*-cute name of the local broadsheet, which during the summer catered to out-of-town visitors. Interspersed with adverts for various baths and inns and shops were articles sketching week-old news from Gallantrybanks, cullings from the *Court Circular,* advice columns on healthful habits and the latest fashions, and reviews of local taverns, musical performances, fortnightly public balls, and theater.

"They didn't write about that first show, I hope." It still troubled him, that muffling of their magic. They were no closer to learning who had done it or exactly why. At least it had not happened again. They were scheduled for one more performance in Lilyleaf, and then tomorrow would be off to the Castle Biding Summer Fair, then the seaside town of Frimham, and finally the University at Stiddolfe, and home.

"No, last night's." Rafe sat with him at a corner table and beckoned Mieka to join them. There was a gleeful glint in the fettler's blue-gray eyes that alerted Cade at once. But he held his tongue, because the sparkle wasn't directed at him.

Mieka slid into a chair and distributed cold beers. "Say on, old son," he invited with a smile.

Gleeful became positively evil. "'Yestere'en at the Baths, the gentlemen of Lilyleaf were treated to a fine performance by Touchstone,'" he read aloud. "Let's see—we were superb, blither blither, we were brilliant, more blither, we put a stimulating new twist on—ah, here it is." He folded the broadsheet, cleared his throat impressively, and read, "'As regards the glisker, Mieka Windthistle—'"

"They got your name right, anyhow," Cade observed.

Mieka scowled at him. "Shut it! I want to hear what it says!"

"'As regards the glisker, Mieka Windthistle, the superiority of the work must be experienced personally, for she handles the withies with such delicacy and assurance—'"

"*She?*"

Rafe nodded, a little smile twitching his lips beneath his beard. "I'm sure they don't really think you're a girl. But there it is for all the Kingdom to read."

Mieka snatched the page from Rafe's hand. "*She?*"

〔Mieka stormed into the dim wood-walled offices of the *Lilyleaves* and bellowed for the broadsheet's editor. "Get him! I don't care if he's making love to his wife or his sister-in-law or his favorite whore or all three at once! I want to see that miscreated crambazzle and I want to see him *now*!"

Within moments a crowd had piled up in the reception room. A balding, middle-aged man pushed through and demanded, "What's all this, then? I'm the editor. Who're you?"

"Mieka Windthistle!" He tore off his shirt, buttons pinging off desks, chairs, windows, and the eyeglasses of one startled scrivener. "Master Glisker for Touchstone!" He started in on his trousers, yelling all the while. "And your stupid rag of wastepaper not fit for wrapping rotted fish called me a *girl*!" Shirt discarded, trousers tangled at his ankles, horrified workers shrieking all round him, he yanked down his underdrawers and roared, "Does *this* look like something that belongs on a *girl*?"}

Cade was laughing as the Elsewhen faded, and Mieka turned on him in a fury. "What's so bleedin' funny?"

"You!"

"And what if it'd been *you* they called a girl?"

"It was just a printing error, Mieka, don't be so touchy!"

"Two printing errors," Rafe pointed out helpfully.

"What?" He scanned the rest of the article. "'In a style not often seen, Windthistle practically dances her way through—' *Her!* Gods' bollocks!"

"I dunno," Rafe mused. "You might look right fetching in a skirt and one of those frilly blouses."

Cade pretended to consider. "You may be right about that. Something in pink, p'rhaps."

{Mieka swanned into the broadsheet's offices, flicking a lace fan here and there by way of greeting. And it *was* Mieka. Despite the full purple skirt, matching tight-laced bodice, and ruffled pink blouse; despite the padding that filled out that blouse; and even despite the long black curls cascading down his back and the globs of makeup on his face, it was indeed Mieka. Those eyes were unmistakable. He trilled a request to be directed to the editor. Some hapless functionary in a brown jacket led him to the far corner of the building. A door was opened, the functionary made a jerky little half bow, and a balding, middle-aged man rose from behind the desk.

"Who's this, then?" he demanded after gaping at this apparition in pink and purple.

"So tremendously delighted to meet you!" Mieka sang out. "Frightfully grateful, don't you see—not until your article about Touchstone's performance last night was I entirely sure. But now you've unconfused me—eternally beholden to you!"

"Sure? Of what?"

All smiles, Mieka flung his arms wide, endangering a shelf and two stacks of books with his fan, and twirled round on his toes. "My friends say it was only a printing error, but it happened twice, so I knew there must be something in it. Fingers of the Gods pointing the way, don't you see!"

"No, I don't see!"

"Isn't it obvious? You called me 'she,' and everything finally became clear! I really do believe I'll just *adore* being a girl!"}

This time Cade had to brace himself against the table, he was laughing so hard. "Oh Gods—Mieka, I'm sorry—it's just—"

"What did you see?"

Cade shook his head and tried to catch his breath. "Nothing awful. But you don't have to give them such a shock, you know. A polite reminder would suffice."

"What in all Hells are you talking about?" Then he crumpled the page in his hands. "Never mind. I don't care. Where do I find these—"

"—miscreated crambazzles?" Cade asked, unable to resist. Should he let Mieka go now, and outrage the hired help by stripping off? Or should Cade try to calm him down and wait for Rafe's teasing to suggest the notion of dressing up as a woman?

{It was a bizarre little group strolling towards the theater: three boys who didn't move like boys at all, and one gaudily clad woman who didn't move anything like a woman. She didn't sound like one either as she—he—chivvied the trio through the crowd and past two constables more concerned with the free show they would soon see than with keeping the uninvited back from the queue. The "boys" slipped past on a signal from the theater's chucker-out, who was grinning. The "woman" was about to join them when one of the constables finally paid attention.

"Here, now, Mistress!" he bawled, reaching out to grab at a sleeve. "What're you thinkin' of doin'?"

"You'd best leave your hands off, my good man, or you'll be answering to someone more important than you ever dreamed you'd meet in your whole miserable life!"}

Mieka was still ranting about the printer's error, but at a lower volume. *Mieka.* Of course it had been Mieka in that Elsewhen of more than two years ago—how could he not have realized it? As for the three "boys"—Blye, Jinsie, and—Megs—

Megs?

Cade reached reflexively for his ale and took a big swallow.

There were differences between that Elsewhen and this. He brought out the earlier one to examine it, and found that not only didn't he know who the third girl was in the other one, but Mieka's outfit had changed from bright green with beet-red lace to turquoise with pink ruffles and so many gold chains that he clinked when he walked. And the three girls (*Megs?* his astonished brain kept nattering) actually made it into the theater before just one constable, not both, accosted Mieka.

Yet how any of it could have changed because of something Cade himself had done or not done was a complete mystery. For that matter, how he might influence Mieka in this ridiculous affair of the mistaken pronouns was likewise baffling.

He really ought to be used to this by now.

"Cade?" Rafe rapped his knuckles on the table.

"What is it, Quill? You saw something more, didn't you?"

They were looking at him, knowing that another Elsewhen had just surprised him. For once, none of what he'd seen was horrible or threatening—unless one counted the possibility of Mieka's spending a night or two in quod for attempting to get into a theater dressed as a woman—

—but he *wasn't* a woman, and therefore what he wore had nothing to do with whether or not he was allowed inside a theater.

Cade began to laugh again. He could see it now, or at least as much as would get Blye, Jinsie, and Megs (*Megs?*) into a performance, and Mieka as well in all his flashy finery. What would happen next, he didn't yet know. But oh, it would be a grand and glorious lark finding out.

* * *

CADE HAD BEEN working on a new play. Well, he was always working on a new play—he couldn't seem to help himself—but he did want to have something definite to show Kearney Fairwalk when His Lordship met them in Frimham. But dedication to the work couldn't compete with the prospect of watching Mieka descend on the offices of the *Lilyleaves*.

The Elf had abandoned his grumbles and withdrawn to Croodle's chambers upstairs. Between the two of them, possibly with help from Kazie, they'd decked him out very prettily in a butter-yellow skirt and a rose-pink blouse. This intrigued Cade; in the Elsewhen, Mieka had been in purple. Something had changed, something Cade had said or done had altered the future. He was at a loss to think what it might be, but fascinated to see how it would all turn out. He'd had no subsequent Elsewhen to let him know, which must mean that whatever happened from now on was Mieka's choice.

When Mieka came downstairs, festively clothed, with Croodle and Kazie laughing behind him, Cade bowed and offered escort. It occurred to him as they walked towards the *Lilyleaves* offices that it was a good thing the old rule about improper attire no longer applied. A few days ago, it had been towels. Today, mercifully, he himself was fully dressed in trousers, shirt, and jacket. As for Mieka—it wasn't just the skirt and frilly blouse and feathery fan and huge straw hat decorated with a trailing green silk scarf. There was a glisten of magic in the air that grew stronger as they approached the address gleaned from the broadsheet. Cade recognized it as Mieka's own magic.

As long black curls began to appear below the hat and the blouse filled out in front, Cade asked, "All right, where is it?"

"Where's what?"

"The withie."

"Pocket." He patted his thigh. "Something left over from 'Sweetheart' last night." Spinning round on his toes, he demanded, "Well? What d'you think?"

"Lip rouge. And not so much with the eyelashes."

"I didn't do anything to me eyelashes." The smiling mouth turned bright pink. "Darker? To match the blouse?"

Cade sighed. "You are entirely, thoroughly, completely, utterly, absolutely, appallingly mad, you know."

"Ah, but fiendishly clever with it!" A laugh, and a few more steps, and: "We're here. I'll do the talking. You just stand there and look worried, eh?"

"I'll do my best."

Mieka swanned into the office as in the Elsewhen, deploying the fan in a flutter of white feathers, bestowing his sweetest smile all round. There was just enough magic altering his appearance to make the impersonation almost credible. Cade saw confusion, suspicion, apprehension, distaste, and even a bit of alarm in the faces of those who gathered in the reception area. None of them knew quite what to make of this apparition—or even what this apparition might be.

"I give you glad greetings, all and each and every one!" Mieka trilled—a line stolen from one of the Mother Loosebuckle farces. "Such a lovely day outside, such lovely people inside! It would be the pinnacle of my existence to have a long talk with each and every one of you, but I simply must see your editor, the darling man! Where may I find him?" When a jumpy little personage in a brown jacket glanced involuntarily to the left, Mieka beamed at him. "So very good of you! Infinitely beholden!" With a playful flourish of feathers, he sailed unescorted in the indicated direction, skirts swishing, the fan held aloft like a triumphal banner. Cade followed, and observed that the fan seemed to be molting.

In the back corner—where Cade could have told him to go, if he'd had a mind to it—a door opened and the expected middle-aged, balding man stepped out. "What's all this, then?" he shouted. "Get back to work, all of you!"

"The *editor*!" Mieka cried, clasping both hands together in raptures. "How exciting!"

"Who in all Hells are you?"

"That's *exactly* what I wanted to speak with you about."

Cade had thought there were two different directions this could go: Mieka stripping and demanding to know if the revealed equipment belonged on a girl, or Mieka pretending to be thrilled that his personal confusion had been cleared up at last. He really ought to stop underestimating Mieka.

The Elf pranced uninvited into the office, then whirled round and gestured expectantly at Cade. When all Cade did was stand there, befuddled, he snapped in his own voice, "Oy! Chair!"

Cade pulled a wobbly wooden chair from a corner and handed him into it. The fan lost a few more tuftings that drifted to the floor.

"Beholden," Mieka said sweetly, and then graciously invited the editor to be seated in his own office. Arranging his skirts, he folded the feather fan and leaned anxiously towards the desk. "Now. Shall we be direct and forthright? I always feel that's for the best when dealing with the press. Whilst I do realize that I'm quite enchantingly favored in form and feature, even for an Elf—"

"What?" the man asked, sinking into the chair behind his desk.

"He's pretty," Cade translated.

"Very," Mieka agreed. "But whereas I'm sure you didn't *really* mean to make out that I'm a girl—"

"A printer's error, I told him," Cade put in.

"Yes, yes, we've been through all that. The fact remains, however, that there are those who will suspect that Touchstone is—that I—that we—oh, how shall I put it?"

"That there really is a female onstage," said Cade. He began to see where Mieka might be taking this, and set himself to aid and abet.

"Exactly!" Mieka leaned even closer to the desk, and in a confiding tone said, "I've found that having a Master Tregetour at one's beck and call is the most useful thing imaginable when one is attempting to explain oneself. Always looking for the right word, that's my Quill!" He rapped Cade on the arm with his fan, fondly, leaving behind a few flecks of feather. Then, sitting back again, he frowned his distress. "I can't disguise that I'm rather worried. The notion that Touchstone has been gulling the whole Kingdom all this time by putting a *girl* onto the stage when such things are just so entirely, thoroughly, completely, totally, and—what was the rest of it, Cayden?"

"Utterly and absolutely," Cade supplied.

"Utterly and absolutely and *appallingly* forbidden, don't you see—well, that could get us into some real trouble. What I mean to say is, will they think I'm really my third cousin once removed, whose name is Miekella?" Looking up at Cade: "Stunning girl, by the bye—looks just like me, only even prettier. I must introduce you soon."

Cade solemnly bowed his gratitude.

"As I was saying—will people think that I've been onstage this whole time really as a girl and—what's worse—traveling about with three young men—three rather attractive young men, I might add, all the ladies say so—staying at inns, all night, in upstairs rooms— well, I'm sure you understand the potential scandal of it," he concluded.

The editor's jaw by this time was slightly open. His fingers scrabbled feebly at some papers on his desk.

"In any case," Mieka went on, rising to his feet with one hand in the pocket of the skirt where Cade knew the withie had to be, "I'm here to demonstrate as convincingly as I can the truth of the matter." With an endearing smile, he spread his arms wide and announced, "*This* is how Miekella Windthistle would look."

Then he let the magic fade.

Gone were the extravagant curls, the pink lips, the full bosom. Gone as well, Cade saw with a shock, were the clothes. Skirt, blouse, hat, scarf—he stood there stark naked with the feather fan gripped in his fist. The fan lost its garnishings and became a slender glass withie.

Mieka's smile became truly Angelic. "*I*," he announced, "am Mieka Windthistle."

"Oh dear Gods," Cade breathed. The mad little Elf really had come out onto the street dressed in nothing but magic and a pair of knitted blue silk socks. Cade had known from that very first night in Gowerion that Mieka was good, but he'd never imagined he was *this* good.

Or this crazy.

"Any questions?" Mieka prompted. "Doubts?" No response from behind the desk. "Mayhap an admiring adjective here and there? No? Well, much beholden to you for your time and understanding. We'll leave you to your work. Cayden, old dear, shall we?"

"Get some clothes on!" he hissed.

Mieka glanced down as if only now realizing he wasn't wearing anything at all. He examined the withie, shook it once or twice, held it to one ear to listen to it. "Oh, my. I seem to have run out of magic." Turning back to the editor, he asked, "You wouldn't happen to have a spare pair of trousers hanging about, would you?"

Cade snatched the withie from his hand. It was hard to concentrate enough to prime it, for the editor had recovered his powers of speech.

"Get out of here!" He pushed himself up from his desk, leaning heavily on it, and roared, "This instant, d'you hear me? Right now!"

"Love to," Mieka told him. "Slight problem."

"Out! *Out!*"

Mieka shrugged. "If you insist."

Cade grabbed his arm before he could stroll through the doorway. "Here—use this—there's not much, but you can wear my jacket—"

Taking the withie, Mieka favored him with a radiant smile and fluttering eyelashes. "Oh, Quill! You're so good to me!"

Within moments Cade was following him back through the *Lilyleaves* main room. If anyone was startled to see that the young woman who had entered wearing a yellow skirt and pink blouse and carrying a hugely feathered fan was now a young man, barefoot, wearing gray trousers and a blue jacket much too long for him, it didn't make the next day's edition.

*   *   *

"DAMN IT TO all Hells!" Mieka whined on their walk back. "The paving's hot enough to burn holes in me feet!"

"Should've thought of that, shouldn't you?" Cade asked with no sympathy whatsoever. The sunshine was in full spate by now; they'd stuck to the shady sides of the streets on the walk here, but now there were no shady sides. He just hoped the magic lasted long enough to get Mieka upstairs at Croodle's. "You lied."

"I'm known to do that, on occasion."

"About the withie."

"Among other things."

"Cousin Miekanna?" Cade asked pointedly.

"Miekella," he corrected. "I only lied that she looks like me. I'm *much* prettier."

He kept his gaze on the paving stones directly in front of him, as if he might be able to judge which would be cooler than the rest. The absurdity of his little jumps from one to another was getting him stared at by passersby. Cade told himself he ought to be grateful they weren't staring at him for other reasons.

"And you don't want to meet her, believe me," Mieka went on. "Dreadful creature. She lives at the Clink now, with Granny Tightfist and Uncle Breedbate." All at once he gave an exclamation of delight and jumped into the gutter, feet splashing. "Ooh, that's much better!"

Cade glanced up ahead of them and finally broke down laughing. Mieka looked up and wailed aloud. The small gutter river was the accomplishment of a fat gray horse who, by the looks of the production, hadn't taken a piss in at least three days.

Thirteen

JUST THIS ONE last show in Lilyleaf, Cade told himself, just another few hours to get through, and he could laugh himself silly all the way to Castle Biding. He had not the slightest confidence, however, that he or Jeska or Rafe would be able to get through tonight without collapsing every time they even glanced at Mieka. Throughout the afternoon somebody broke into sniggers every few minutes, and on the walk over to the Baths for the performance, Mieka made them laugh apurpose when he slunk along the sides of the buildings as far away from the gutters as possible.

They were still grinning when they took the stage.

All humor was gone by the end of the first two minutes of "Dragon."

Someone was mucking up their magic again. Cade sensed it, knew Rafe and Mieka and Jeska did, too, and fought it to the final lines.

A few nights ago, the muting of the magic had been general, spreading over the whole audience. That time at the Keymarker, when Megs had been protecting the young girl (or so she'd said), the obstruction had been specifically localized. This leaped all over the theater, from group to group with no anticipating where it would be next. The audience saw the Dragon spread its great wings, smelled its fetid breath; heard the rasp of the Prince's labored breathing, tasted the copper of blood and fear on his tongue, felt the heft of the sword in his hand—all these things were as usual. But the effects were deadened by that leaping, infuriating barrier.

Cade called up everything his grandfather had ever told him about fettling, everything he'd observed Rafe do over the years, everything he'd ever read about technique. He kept seeking the source of the obstruction, trying to track it back from the area it affected to its origin, and could not. What he found he *could* do, after a while, was to scare it off, pitting his own magic against it, projecting strength and a lethal threat. It would falter, then vanish, only to rise in another part of the theater. Cade began to be distracted by fear that Rafe and Mieka, frustrated and angered, might pour more emotion into the piece and concentrate it more keenly to get past that infuriatingly skipping barrier, and overwhelm the audience to its peril and their own exhaustion. Still, as furious as both of them were, they were professionals. They had to get through the play, and somehow they did.

And although they were wrung out by the futile effort to find and negate the muffling magic, they agreed backstage amongst themselves that they owed the audience one more playlet. Nobody would be expecting it, so there was a good chance that whoever had set up the strange, frustrating barrier had left the theater. So had a goodly number of other patrons. A little over half of them lingered, complaining about Touchstone's undeserved reputation or arguing that they'd been superb the other night and this was just a fluke, everyone had off days.

When the manager stepped onstage to announce a

second play, there was applause, of course. The theater
had been packed to bursting, patrons doubtless drawn
by the glowing review in that morning's *Lilyleaves*.
Those who had stayed were getting twice the value for
their money—although many of them would have said
they'd not yet got much for their money at all. So there
was also jeering, and Cade flinched when he heard it.

"We'll have to give them 'Doorways,'" he said. He
expected groans of dismay; what he got were curt nods.
"And if any of you sense anything, anything at all, we
stop right in the middle of whatever it is and—"

"—and demand to know who's trying to fuck with
us?" Rafe shook his head. "No weakness, Cade. We do
it. Whatever happens."

At the glisker's bench, Mieka had selected the withies
for him. "I need whatever you can give me," he said
quietly, those eyes narrowed and furious and grimly determined. "We can sleep it off all the way to Castle Biding if needs must. But it has to be a spectacle, with all the
flash we've got, and powerful enough to overwhelm the
bastard if he's still out there."

"Do it fast," Jeska put in nervously. "He might've gone,
then heard we're doing another play, and be coming
back."

So Cade primed the withies as quickly as he could, and
with more than he'd thought he had in him. He'd never
been so tired in his life as he was when he trudged back
to his lectern. If Mieka had brought his thorn-roll to
the theater, they could have pricked some bluethorn and
got through this. Where Rafe and Mieka and Jeska
would dredge up the energy for this without thorn, he'd
no idea. He only knew—they all knew—that it had to
be done.

The Sleeper began to dream. The doors lay before him.
He opened some, backed away from others. Scenes of

home, family, richly ripe fields; despair, degradation; idleness and apathy; accomplishment and wealth and fame. All the effects were there. The tastes and scents of fresh bread and butter, of sour wine, of flowers and rotting fruit and spring air. The feel of rough sacking, smooth silk; the sounds of lutes and Minster bells and maddened dogs and happy laughter and terrified screams. And the emotions: smug satisfaction, colossal boredom, elated triumph, drunken befuddlement, quiet pleasure—with an undercurrent of dissatisfaction beneath it all, until the last door opened and Jeska spoke the final line, and vanished into *This life, and none other*.

The audience got what they came for. The volume of the applause was all out of proportion to the number of people still in the theater. No one had attempted to dampen down the magic. The intensity of what Cade had put into the withies, and that Mieka had extracted to make the scenes within the open doors, Rafe had tempered and adjusted to spread evenly throughout the hall without hindrance. There'd been more anger than usual in the mix, and mayhap the images had not been so precisely detailed, but there'd been no snags. They were *Touchstone,* and by the time they walked offstage, every man in the place knew it.

Jeska took care of them on the way back to Croodle's. He steadied them when their steps faltered, hired a couple of lads to carry the glass baskets and withies, demanded a pair of hire-hacks to convey them all, yelled for Croodle and Kazie to help them upstairs.

"What about you, then?" Cade heard Kazie ask worriedly.

"I'm fine. Not much for me to do in 'Doorways' except remember the lines. They did all the work."

That wasn't strictly true. Tonight Jeska had added what Elfen magic he possessed, and edited the play as it had progressed to shorten it as much as he could without damage. He'd run the show tonight, with Mieka and Rafe taking their cues from him rather than the other way round, as was usual with "Doorways." Cade kept putting one foot in front of the other up the stairs, one arm around Mieka's ribs and the other draped across Croodle's strong shoulders, mindlessly grateful for a masquer who was a true artist and an even truer friend.

He fell across his bed and felt somebody haul off his boots. Croodle said something about food. The mere mention of eating made his stomach heave.

He must have groaned, or maybe whimpered, for Jeska said hastily, "Not just now. In the morning, maybe."

"You have a good long lie-in," Kazie advised. "We'll keep the place closed until noon."

"But—"

Croodle interrupted him. "You boys will be needing the quiet more than I'll be needing the morning drunks."

Cade tried to rouse himself enough to express his appreciation for this generosity. All he managed to do was get his eyes open. Standing there, arm in arm, were Jeska and Kazie. They made a striking couple, his limpid-eyed golden good looks the perfect contrast and complement to her darkly exotic beauty. There was a steadiness about them, somehow, a feeling of stable ground underfoot. He'd never seen this expression on Jeska's face before, and all at once he envied it ferociously.

Stability? In the life of a traveling player? Gods and Angels, he must be getting old.

As his eyelids slid shut and he plummeted into sleep, he tried to understand how a day that had been so much fun at noon could become such a nightmare by midnight. *This life, and none other* . . . He grimaced, thinking what a Hell this life could sometimes be.

* * *

CADE WENT TO sleep exhausted and woke up angry. So did his partners. It wasn't quite noon when they met downstairs for something to eat before piling into the wagon for the journey to Castle Biding. Cade forced himself to make the usual polite farewells, to which Croodle merely arched a brow before giving him a hug that nearly snapped his backbone.

"You stay safe," she whispered in his ear. "I'll get word to you if anyone else has to go through what you boys did."

It was the first time it had occurred to him that whoever this was, he might have other quarry in mind besides Touchstone. Mulling this over took him out into the courtyard and into the wagon. He glanced out one of the windows in time to see Jeska kiss Kazie in full view of anyone who cared to watch. She was wearing the green scarf he'd lent Cade at Coldkettle.

"Serious, then," Rafe murmured beside him.

"Looks to be."

"We've a spare chamber over the bakery," he said enigmatically. "Or there's always room somewhere at Wistly."

Cade frowned at him. "Jeska has his own place now, so she can—oh," he finished lamely, as it finally struck him that this was not one of the masquer's many dalliances. If Kazie came to visit in Gallantrybanks this winter, it would all be proper and respectable. Because it *was* serious. Memory of how Jeska had looked last night confirmed it.

Mieka climbed up the wagon steps, moving as if he were older than his great-great-grandmother. Hefting a huge basket into a corner, he said, "Lunching," hooked up his hammock, crawled into it, and curled up to sleep.

As urgently as Cayden wanted to discuss what had happened, he didn't begrudge Mieka the rest. Yazz had scarcely got the wagon moving when Jeska and then Rafe follow the Elf's example. Cade made himself comfortable in one of the cushioned chairs, but did not sleep. Because of their late start today, they'd have to travel relentlessly in order to reach Castle Biding in time for the Summer Fair. The horses were fresh, but Yazz would never overstrain them; they'd arrive at Castle Biding when they arrived at Castle Biding, and there was an end to it. For himself, Cade was still so weary and empty that he didn't much care if he ever stood on a stage again, though he knew that this feeling would pass. What would not go away was the need to figure out who was doing this to them, and why.

It was midafternoon when Mieka rolled over in his hammock, squinted at Cade, and said, "Stop all that bloody *thinking* and get some sleep."

"I can't help it."

"I know. Try anyways."

He smiled, and shrugged, and said, "Maybe in a while."

With a grunt of disgust, Mieka extricated himself from the hammock and went to the washstand to pour out some fresh water into the glass bowl and splash his face. "It's too hot in here. Let's walk for a bit."

The wagon wasn't moving quickly enough to make it difficult to jump down from the back door. Cade jogged forward to alert Yazz that they'd be on foot for a while so he could keep on giving the horses a breather; the Giant nodded acknowledgment and returned his attention to driving.

"Somebody's out to get us," Mieka said without preamble.

"Mayhap not just us." Cade told him what Croodle had said, and added, "But when you put it alongside the peacock feather, I tend to doubt it's anybody but us they're after."

"Still think it traces back to the Archduke?"

"He doesn't much like us, for several reasons. We turned him down about the theater, we used words in 'Treasure' that were the same as condemned his father—"

"We spoiled his plan to take Blye's glassworks," Mieka reminded him.

"I'd almost forgotten about that."

"Jed wrote," he said, scuffing dust up from the road with the toe of one boot. "The Glasscrafters Guild came round again, checking the stock to be sure Blye's not making anything hollow. 'Twas a bit of a rush-about, hiding the withies and such—did you hear she's making them for Hawk's Claw now, too? I don't know any of them much, but Chat vouches for their glisker."

"Good enough for Blye, good enough for me," Cade said, reminding himself to learn as much as he could about Hawk's Claw anyway. Just in case.

"The Guild didn't find anything. Problem is, come Wintering tax time, she'll have to explain how she makes the money she makes without making things she's not s'posed to be making."

Cade nodded slowly. That first Wintering after her father's death, Touchstone had been Blye's partner in the glassworks and shared payment of the taxes. Their wedding present to her and Jedris had been the majority of their shares in the business. Kearney Fairwalk's clerks had managed to trick up the books, first to hide that Touchstone took its share of profits in illegally made withies, and then regarding the transfer of ownership and the value of the business.

"We still have an interest in the glassworks, all of

us," he mused. "Kearney's people can play around with the numbers, like they've been doing."

"If the Archduke is behind it," Mieka warned, "then backspanging the accounts, no matter how clever they do it, won't put them off. And Chat mentioned that there's been a bit of talk about where they're getting their withies, now that they don't use Master Splithook anymore."

"Well, as long as nobody finds out she makes them—"

"You're not listening. Jed's pretty well certain they'll demand a look at her books. At the very least, there'd be a fine."

"We'll pay it."

"At the very worst, she could lose the place."

They walked for a time in silence. Then Cade asked, "Why are you telling me this now? How long have you known?"

"Forgot to read the letter," Mieka admitted. "I only remembered it when I was looking for clean stockings yesterday." There was a brief reminiscent flash of a smile.

Cade snorted a laugh. "They'll never be the same."

"Chucked 'em, in fact. Total loss. But that's when I found Jed's letter." He sprang ahead a few steps, turning to walk backwards as he talked, but the usual energy was missing. "It'd been such a *good* day, all in all, y'see. Everybody laughing . . ." He sighed. "I didn't want to spoil it."

"No, other people are perfectly capable of doing that. But why mention the letter now?"

"Because we can't do sweet fuck-all about whoever's trying to ruin us. Blye's problem is something we can solve. And not just for this year, but all the years to follow."

"I'm not understanding you," Cade complained. "What

could we possibly—besides Kearney's clerks, I mean, there's nothing—"

Mieka had tilted his head to one side, a little grin playing about his lips. Those eyes were suddenly dancing with mischief.

"What?" Cade demanded.

"The Princess is having a baby."

"And?"

"The baby needs a present."

*   *   *

MIEKA SPENT THE whole evening composing a letter to his brother by lamplight in the wagon, pausing to think every so often while chewing on the end of Cade's pen. Cade didn't admonish him. If what he was scheming up helped Blye, he could chew the pen to splinters for all Cade cared. Besides, it was only something his parents had given him, and easily replaced.

Meantime, Rafe and Jeska discussed with Cade what they had done last night and how they could do it better if it ever happened again, which none of them doubted it would do. When Mieka finally finished his letter and joined in, he had a further suggestion.

"This winter, on the nights we're not playing, I'll make the rounds of the taverns."

"How is this different from your usual nights off?" Rafe asked.

"Snarge! I was thinking that after the amateurs finish, I can buy them a drink, like, and move the talk round to fettlers needing work."

"Ah," Cade said. "So you were listening to what Tegs said."

"Megs," Rafe corrected. "And how are they to know that Touchstone isn't looking for a new fettler?"

"Hmm." Mieka considered. "Hadn't thought about

that. But you'll admit that once word goes round regarding what's been happening, they'll all be thinking that a new fettler isn't such a bad idea—" He cringed back, laughing, as Rafe lifted a threatening fist. "Joking! Joking! You can come along with, and make sure nobody thinks any such thing!"

Rafe made a face at him. "Actually, it might be a good idea to hint that you *are* looking for a new fettler. If the purpose behind this is to put us all wrong-footed, then a rumor here and there would get back to—"

"The Archduke," Cade said.

"We don't know that for sure. But whoever it is would be pleased to think it's all working." He paused for a sip of his drink. "What about that lad with the peacock feather at Seekhaven?"

Mieka shook his head. "Masquer. And before you ask, the fettler went back to his ancestral pigsty north of Scatterseed a year or so ago when his father died."

"Ask around anyway," Cade said. He swirled liquor in his glass, staring at the last swallow and wishing there were enough left in the decanter to pour another. It had become their custom to save Auntie Brishen's whiskey for late evening before they went to bed, and Yazz carefully siphoned out sufficient for two glasses each so the barrel would last. "Why does the Archduke want us ruined?" he asked suddenly. "Spite?"

"He wanted to own our glasscrafter," Rafe mused, "and then he wanted to own *us*. I know what Chat says about great lords on the Continent buying their own pet players—"

"If you can call them players," Jeska scoffed, "with no magic to their work."

"—but there's plenty of others to choose from. And it seems a thin reason, doesn't it? Hacked off just because he can't get the group he wants?"

"The Shadowshapers turned him down as well," Cade said. "But I'll take oath on it, Black Lightning will have accepted."

"So why haven't there been any rumors about the Shadowshapers? I can answer it," Rafe went on. "They're the best in the Kingdom—yeh, Mieka, even better than us, and everybody knows it. If they suddenly started snagging up their magic, nobody'd believe it. Nobody'd *dare* mess with them."

"Then it comes back to *Why us?*" Cade said. But he knew. He knew.

"We could always ask him," Rafe drawled.

"You do that, old son," Cade told him. "You spend the next few nights working out just how to gain admittance to the hallowed Halls of Threne. It's off the road to Stiddolfe, I'm sure we can make time for it, and he's probably at home enjoying the glories of summer and his new wife. You can also decide how you'll be persuading your way past the guards to the presence of Himself. And then when you settle on just what words to use, you can figure out how you plan to escape with a whole skin." He tossed back the remains of his drink and stood, swaying slightly with the movement of the wagon. "And after you've made up your mind about all of *that*, you can tell us what we're to say to your lady wife when we bring you home in more pieces than are generally recommended for survival. Yeh, you enjoy yourself working all that out. Me, I'm for some sleep."

He had hooked up his hammock and was arranging the thin mattress atop it before Mieka broke the silence. "Eloquent, that's our Quill. Sweet dreamings, all—though I dare you, after that little recital."

"What're *you* snarking about?" Rafe muttered. "*I'm* the one he just dismembered into component parts."

* * *

THE PERFORMANCES AT the Castle Biding Summer Fair were maddening. Not that anyone interfered, not once during the five shows. It was the grinding dread of interference that sharpened their tempers and wore them out. Cade had learned on Touchstone's two Winterly Circuits that towards the end, a kind of undercurrent of exhaustion dragged at them constantly, but surely he was much too young at twenty-one to feel this bloody tired all the time.

Bluethorn, as ever, helped.

Once again their schedule overlapped that of the Shadowshapers by a day, and Cade made no excuses for dragging Vered off for a private talk once the Shadowshapers' performance had, as always, been applauded to the open skies. As at Coldkettle, the venue was outdoors. The stage had been set up in a corner of the fair's sprawl. Ordinarily Cade would have looked forward to the opportunity to expand beyond the confines of a theater or guild hall. All he could manage was an inner wince for how weary he would be after priming the withies with magic enough for the extravagances the audiences would expect. "Dragon" would do very well here.

"What's been, Cade?" Vered asked pleasantly enough as he was pulled along a torchlit path through booths shut up for the night. "Where are we off to? Have you discovered where they're keeping the naked dancing girls this year?"

That such entertainment existed at all, outside some exceedingly rough taverns and a few exclusive gentlemen's clubs in Gallantrybanks, was a surprise to him. But then, he'd only ever been at Castle Biding during the winter, when it was a bit chilly for that sort of thing. "If that's what you're after, talk to Mieka. He's got an instinct for finding the prettiest girls within ten miles."

"I thought that was Jeska."

"The girls find *him*. No, I want to talk of the Knights you want to write about."

He told it succinctly, not mentioning his source. Or, rather, his sources, plural; no need to let Vered in on the secret of his Elsewhens. When he'd finished, Vered sighed gustily.

"So the Knights were real, and it happened." His long white-blond hair was almost luminous in the darkness. "Beholden, Cade. You've given me a lot to work from."

"You have to keep it close," Cade warned. "I'll lend you all the books you like, but don't go near the Archives. And especially don't ask to search the library at the Halls of Threne or the Archduke's city residence. He can't know what you're up to until you present it onstage."

"Like you with 'The Treasure,' eh?" Vered chuckled. "But if I'm to compete with such distinguished historical precision—" He broke off when Cade didn't laugh. "You're serious."

"Dead serious. And don't ever come to any of our rehearsals. All my books are at Redpebble Square, you can get them and return them from there—I know, I know!" he cried, frustrated. "It sounds completely mad. But it's just as mad that somebody's been messing us up while we're onstage—"

"Messing you up? How?"

Cade explained that, too, and why he suspected that the Archduke was behind it—well, *some* of why he suspected it, anyway.

Vered said nothing for a time. They had walked deep into the deserted fair, where torches were few and far between. Up ahead, Cade could just make out placards nailed to a booth: Touchstone, half-covering the

Shadowshapers, with a wedge of the Crystal Sparks peeking out beneath.

"When I was starting out," Vered said at last, "before Chat came along, even before I met Rauel and Sakary, we were playing one night in a village outside Clackerly, a tavern I wouldn't send my precious old father to have a pint in—and he's the one what stranded Mum without a clipped copper pennypiece before I was even born, so you can guess just how precious I hold him. I was doubling up, tregetour and masquer, just like now, only it was because our masquer had got himself into a right brawl and while his bones were mending . . . well, it was me priming the withies *and* acting the plays for a fortnight. So at first I thought I was just awearied. But what I'd put into the withies—costume and scene and such—I could feel it wasn't coming out quite rightly. Some rude old so-called comedy, it was, and me capering about stage front, speaking lines to the audience while things went on behind me. They laughed, to be sure, but as I say, it didn't feel right. I turned for a look—and instead of the pretty girl in a blue silk gown s'posed to be preening behind me, there was this horrible drazel-woman with a face on her that'd terrify small children and large dogs, and a green velvet hat sprouting three tattered feathers that the swan who'd grown them would be ashamed to admit. The fettler lost his hold on the magic, the glisker simply gave up, and everything just sputtered to a stop while I stood there all flummoxed. Then this farmer-type gets up from his chair, right at the front, and bows, slaps down his tankard, and betakes himself off out the door with everybody cheering. The innkeeper told me later that the fetching little charmer conjured up onstage was the image of the man's wife, who'd died the week before, communally reviled, and this was his manner of bidding final farewell."

Cade had run out of patience about halfway through this story, but was hiding it as best he could. This was Vered Goldbraider of the Shadowshapers; one didn't interrupt Vered Goldbraider in the middle of a story, no matter how little that story had to do with anything relevant to the topic at hand.

But even in the dark and off a stage, Vered could sense the mood of his audience. "Now, you're asking yourself, 'Why the fuck is he telling me this boring old fable?' The point, mate, is that there are people out there who can mess with your magic whether you will or no. Most of 'em refrain. They're not professionals, and they know it, and when they come to a tavern or theater, they've come for the show just like anybody else. This particular yobbo, he did it apurpose. Who knows where he got the magic from, or what he did with it— probably nothing, not in everyday life, though in his younger day he might've been an amateur player of some sort. There's hundreds like him. But it's like when you sing along under your breath whilst a minstrel's playing—there's people as don't realize they're doing it until somebody gives 'em an elbow and says 'Shut it!' So it's possible that somebody in your audience was like that, using fettling magic without the full knowing of it."

"No," Cade said firmly. "This was too definite. Too deliberate."

"All right, then. That's why I told that story. Clear in your own mind now, yeh? There's more to the tale, though. Whilst I was staring like a fool, I got a taste of the magic he was using. Bitter, it was, and sharp like an unripe plum."

"Magic has a taste to you?" Cade asked, bemused. He'd recognized Mieka's magic on their little foray to the *Lilyleaves* offices, but he'd thought it was because he was so used to working with the Elf.

"Sakary will tell you that we couldn't work that well with Mieka because nobody can control him—nobody except Rafe, evidently. But you ask a little deeper, and he'll admit that the taste of it wasn't right for us. Rauel, he describes it in sounds, how things are in tune or not in tune. Can't understand that, meself, because I'm like Sakary that way, I s'pose. I *taste* other people's magic."

All Cade could say was, "How?"

"What got taught in this swagger-and-strut Academy of yours, eh?" He nudged Cade with a shoulder. "How you do it—you just *know*. It might be that we all perceive it different, but the fact of it is that with some practice, you can identify the person using the magic." He paused, taking Cade by the arm and turning him so he could peer into his face. "You didn't know? Nobody ever told you this?"

Cade shook his head. Then, in a rush: "That first night Mieka played with us—Rafe said that he just *fit*."

"Maybe he understands it in shapes. There's them as knows it by the feel—rough, smooth, silk, wool carpet—and I know a girl who describes it as temperatures. She and me, we do conjure up some heat," he added with a self-satisfied sigh.

Uninterested in tales of conquest, Cade said, "What's mine like?"

"Not a clue."

"But you've been to our shows!"

"Have I? Hmm. Don't really recall."

Outrage competed with sudden panic. The Shadowshapers had never seen Touchstone onstage? It was a warning about the abrasion of his nerves that it took him a moment to hear the wicked grin in the man's voice. And, too, the stupidity of thinking that the Shadow-shapers hadn't seen them perform many, many times: Touchstone was, after all, the Shadowshapers' only real rival, and the Shadowshapers knew it. Grateful for the darkness that he fervently hoped had hidden his reaction, Cade managed a casual, "Well, then, you must stay another day and watch us tomorrow. I'm sure you'll learn something."

"Winding you up is a lot of fun—no wonder Mieka enjoys it so much!" Then his voice changed, and he said seriously, "Understand, Cade, it's your magic inside with-ies used by Mieka and adjusted by Rafe. I don't know the taste of your magic, because it's never just your magic, if you follow. I'd recognize Mieka's. I worked with him once. See?"

"Yeh. Were you at Black Lightning's Seekhaven show? Did you sense what they were doing?"

"No, and no. Heard about the play, but—"

"They've got some way to direct specific magic at people. Whether you're a Wizard or Elf or Goblin or whatever—" He explained how, at the climax of the piece, everyone in the audience who had a glimmer-ing of anything but Wizard or Elf had felt dirty and ashamed.

"Gods damn," Vered breathed when he'd finished. Then, seeming to shake himself, he continued briskly, "You know what comes next, don't you?"

"Next?" Cade felt stupid. Vered was one of the few people who could do that to him. Their minds worked differently, even though they were both tregetours; Cade often had the sensation that Vered was at least one step ahead of him, sometimes half a dozen. He'd never liked it much.

"Pinpointing what someone is, through magic—next

comes magic directed right at those aspects of each man."

Belatedly, Cade caught him up. "If somebody's part Goblin, magic specific to Goblins can—do what?"

"Whatever. Give him a thirst for more beer, drive him gibbering into the night, make him piss himself in public. And it would be *only* those with a particular sort of background, y'see. Magic directed at specific—"

Cade interrupted. "Can you tell *what* someone is by the taste of their magic?"

"Not generally. Sometimes."

"Teach me how."

Vered laughed, startlingly loud in the darkness. "Are you always this gracious? D'you show your partners this level of refined manners? And you a sprig of the nobility!"

"Please," he added, face burning with mortification.

"Teach you how to do it, add something new to your stash of tricks and skills—and you our biggest rival." He snorted.

Cade ought to have preened himself over this open admission. He couldn't be bothered right now. "I have to know. I have to find out who's doing this to us." Calming himself, he glanced sidelong at the white-headed shadow that was Vered. "Teach me how, or no books."

"You already agreed—"

"And you said you'd owe me. Well, this is how you pay me back."

"What'll you do if you find the cullion and put a name to him?"

"Ask who he's working for."

"And then beat the shit out of him. All right, when we're back in Gallybanks, I'll have a go at showing you how to identify somebody else's magic. But you may sense it different-wise than me, y'know."

"Doesn't matter. I just need to know how to do it."

"Some people can't. Chat, f'r instance. You might not be able to, either."

"If not me, then Rafe or Jeska or Mieka." But he was sure he could do it. He'd learned how to do so much—and abruptly he wondered why Sagemaster Emmot had never taught him how to do this. How to recognize an individual by his magic.

And then he wondered what else Emmot had never taught him.

He'd learned so much at the Sagemaster's Academy. How to work spells appropriate to his gifts as Wizard and Elf. How to survive and organize the Elsewhens. How to structure a play, words and magic both, even going so far as to hire a retired tregetour for a few months to teach him the formalities and the techniques. How to ride a horse and flourish a cloak and prime a withie and the basics of glisking and which fork to use with the fish. But not this.

"I'll learn," he said. "I *will* learn."

Fourteen

ONLY HE *DIDN'T* learn.

To him, a specific individual's magic had no distinguishing taste, color, shape, smell, temperature, texture, noise, or other characteristic of any kind. It simply *was*. He knew Mieka's magic, and Rafe's, and probably Jeska's (though he'd never actually thought about it and Jeska didn't use his own magic all that often). After an aggravating morning in his company, he knew Vered Goldbraider's. But he couldn't have said exactly how he knew, except for the fact that he did know. This was an offense to a mind that had been taught to analyze and categorize.

Mieka had said during the first week or so of their acquaintance that he and Cade saw magic in the same colors, and that would make organizing the withies easy. Evidently, Cade told himself in frustration, he saw magic itself in colors but couldn't apply the theory to an individual's magic.

"Instinct, mate," was Vered's conclusion. "Beholden for the books."

Would he recognize the source of the hindering magic if it happened again? He had no means of knowing.

The muffling barrier had not made an appearance since Lilyleaf. Which was just as well, because the rest of the Royal Circuit had been a soggy, rain-soaked wretchedness, except for the second night at the University in Stiddolfe when a cluster of admiring students took him out for a drink following the show. After the first few beers, it seemed that he had expounded on a variety of topics in a manner suited to a hundred-year-old retired tregetour lecturing aspiring stagecrafters and playwrights. The resulting article in the next day's University broadsheet ran to four solid pages, and had Mieka in whoops of laughter.

Cade admitted, privately and ruefully, that it was good to have something to laugh about again, even if it was himself for being pompous. After Lilyleaf, and the subsequent tensions of every performance for the rest of the circuit, grins were few and far between.

For one thing, it rained. Nothing torrential, just slow, steady, monotonous, incessant rain that revealed the wagon roof to be not quite watertight. The *drip-drip-drop-oh-Gods-damn-it!* was maddening. Every so often Yazz rerigged some sort of covering that kept out most of the water, wrapped himself in a hooded cloak that could have served as a mainsail on the average cargo ship, hunkered down, and drove.

For another thing, Mieka became nauseatingly sentimental when they got to Frimham. If he had roamed the byways of the Castle Biding Summer Fair to revisit the exact spot where he first clapped eyes on his wife, Cade knew nothing of it. But in this town of his courtship, he was forever wandering off to some spot that held special memories, returning just in time for their shows with a sighing slump of an attitude that really was most annoying. Rafe finally snarled at him about it. Mieka's reply was another sigh, and then a momentary kindling of those eyes as he replied, "You just wait. We still owe you about the towels."

But nobody had the heart or the energy to do anything about that. Cade agreed, their fettler was definitely due a little something in retaliation for the bathhouse stunt. He had relied on Mieka to dream up a scathingly brilliant revenge, but Mieka's dreams were concentrated on past delights and future pleasures, and he couldn't wait to get back to Hilldrop Crescent—where, Cade was certain, he would exile his mother-in-law and the baby to Wistly for a week while he renewed intimate acquaintance with his wife.

Cade proved to be correct, except in judging the time span. After the Royal finally came to an end, it was almost a fortnight before Mieka showed up again in Gallantrybanks, sleek and complacent. He returned only because Touchstone was booked at the Keymarker for five nights, and his brothers Jed and Jez had gone out to Hilldrop to remind him of this and drag him back by the ears if necessary.

As usual after a circuit, Cade slept for a few days, couldn't find anything to do with himself for a few more, and finally got back into his city routine of writing. He knew he ought to be out during the day, trying to find a new place to live, but he just couldn't. Derien, who had started at his grand new school, needed him too much.

Things weren't as bad at the King's College as the boy had feared. He had even made some tentative friends. Two of these turned out to be infinitely more interested in Derien's brother, the famous Master Tregetour, than in Derien. It was their misfortune to show up at Redpebble Square on one of Cade's go-away-and-leave-me-the-fuck-alone days. Dery and Mistress Mirdley were at the glassworks and Lady Jaspiela was paying afternoon calls, so the footman climbed upstairs to ask Cade what he was to do with Their Young Lordships. Cade clattered down the wrought-iron stairs from the fifth floor, curious in spite of his foul mood about what sort of friends his brother was making. He summed up the pair instantly as being just old enough—about fourteen—to get into a theater. A tavern, no. (He conveniently forgot his own forays into both sorts of establishment at that age.) Derien was the most wonderful nine-year-old in the world, but he *was* only nine years old. Boys of fourteen didn't cultivate friendships with nine-year-olds.

Giving them a toothy smile that hid his anger, he told them to stand very, very still. They did so, awestruck at being in his actual presence. After a very long minute, he expressed his gratitude for their cooperation in providing him with the perfect portraits of arrogant little quats deeply infatuated with their own struggles to rise above abject privilege. He'd be using them as characters in his next play.

"And by the bye," he finished as he showed them to the door, "I have, as the ancient Wizardly saying goes, 'the knowing of you' now." He gave them another smile: fewer teeth, more menace. "So it might be that you'll want to behave yourselves. I trust you understand. Good afternoon."

A bluff, of course, but they couldn't know that. All he was interested in was keeping them from sucking up to Derien.

He had underestimated his brother's shrewdness. When he mentioned at tea that a couple of the boys from school had shown up a bit earlier, Dery's face screwed up into a comical grimace.

"I know *exactly* which ones. Crackbough and Hammerfall. Hinting for an invitation to tea, right?" Then

he grinned. "Or didn't you let them get that far? Or—
wait, I know! They were so overcome to be in the presence of the great Master Tregetour that they couldn't
even talk!"

Cade laughed for what felt like the first time in weeks.
Blye, who had joined them for tea by the kitchen fire,
immediately slipped from her stool into a curtsy,
hands clasped before her, silver-blond head bowed in
reverence.

"Forgive me, O Exalted One, for not properly expressing my own wonderment at being allowed to breathe
the same air as Your Brilliantness!"

"Oh, leave off," Cade told her. "The curtsy's all right,
but the trousers and boots spoil the effect."

"Jed's been making me practice," she said, resuming
her seat and deliberately sprawling her legs. "Mysterious allusions to a special event, and all that." Eyes suddenly
narrowing, she looked at Cade and then at Derien.
"You know something, don't you? Where is he taking
me that I need something so useless as a curtsy?"

"We know nothing," Cade proclaimed.

"And if we did, we wouldn't admit it," Dery added.

Blye growled.

Mistress Mirdley, ever unruffled, applied the teapot
all round. "Have you decided yet what you'll make for
that commission?"

With an arch smile for Cade and Dery, Blye answered,
"If I had, I wouldn't admit it."

"Come on," Cade coaxed. "I know Mieka wrote to
you about it—surely he had a suggestion."

"Did he? You know, I just can't remember."

There followed enough pleading from Derien to
make her relent. Eventually. From her pocket she pulled a
folded sheet of paper. On it was a drawing.

"A pottinger? Of glass?" Cade stared. A practical and traditional gift for a baby's Namingday, along with a matching spoon, pottingers were made of anything from tin to pewter to solid silver or gold. Historically, and in the cases of the poor, they were carved from wood. But *practical* and *traditional* were not words one associated with Mieka Windthistle.

"And why not a pottinger?" Blye demanded. Then, more thoughtfully, she said, "I thought you'd exclaim over its being hollow."

"The man who buys your withies?" Mistress Mirdley snorted. "A fool and a dimwit he may be, but not yet a hypocrite." She paused, eyeing Cade. "Not *yet*," she repeated.

"I'm young," Cade observed dryly. "Give me a little more time."

Blye went on, "Mieka's had an idea for the spoon—curve the handle round and back so the child can get a good grip, rather than having it slide out of his poor little fingers all the time. I'll etch the Princess's forget-me-never on the bowl of the spoon, and another at the bottom of the pottinger—Mieka says it'll be encouragement for licking the spoon clean and finishing the soup!"

Jindra must be a picky eater, Cade thought vaguely. Was she old enough yet to use a spoon? He knew so very little about babies. Happily, he wouldn't have to worry much about this one until she was older. But how old would she be before her parents began shouting and then screaming and then hitting each other and—no, he'd definitely worry about that some other time. Schooling his mind to the subject at hand, he said, "I have a suggestion. Have Jed make a second pottinger—out of wood. The glass one can nest inside it."

Blye and Dery looked confused. Mistress Mirdley looked her congratulations and said, "A connection with the common folk."

What he didn't mention was that once the gift was given—and he'd make certain it was given personally, not lumped in with the thousands of presents the good people of Albeyn sent when an heir to the throne was in the offing—and the Princess learned that the glasscrafter who had made the little magical box had also made the pottinger-and-spoon set—but did she yet know enough to know that women glasscrafters could not possess a hallmark, and without a hallmark, making hollow things was forbidden? He realized Mieka was gambling (and the odds were long, but when had that ever stopped Mieka?) that she *didn't* know, and would be so delighted with the gift that she would accept it, and once she had accepted it and thus implicitly given her approval, Blye would be safe. With Royal patronage, even of a casual kind, Blye would be safe.

He could imagine the scene: Blye and Jed and the Princess and himself and Mieka—Blye would have good use for that curtsy she'd been practicing, appearing before Royalty—

And then he wondered if Mistress Caitiffer and young Mistress Windthistle would also be making something to give the Princess's baby.

They wouldn't dare.

They dared with me.

According to Mistress Mirdley.

Whom I've known all my life and who's taken care of me and protected me and raised me and Derien when our parents couldn't be bothered and wants only the best for me and—and—why am I constantly trying to defend that girl?

Because Mieka loved her. He had chosen her and

married her and she was the mother of Jindra. And they were all stuck with her ... for a while, anyway. Cade realized, quite coldly, that he could afford to be patient. One of these days, one way or another, young Mistress Windthistle would be out of their lives forever. And the laws were such that she wouldn't be taking Jindra with her.

For the present, though, there she was at Hilldrop Crescent, with her mother and her baby and Mieka's mindless devotion, which was unabated and even enhanced, to judge by the look of dreamy pleasure on his face when he sauntered into rehearsal that next afternoon at the Keymarker.

Cade had anticipated the absentminded languor. They had five shows in seven nights ahead of them and no room for further self-indulgence. So he and Rafe and Jeska had arranged a little something to wake their glisker up. Remind him why he'd been born, so to speak, before his daydreaming made them angry enough to make sure he wished he were dead.

"I've had an idea," Rafe began when they were all supplied with beers. They were seated on uncomfortable chairs onstage, ignored for the most part by the barmaids and stock boys who were readying the place for the night's trade. "Something out of the usual, but it might work."

"Pray silence for Master Threadchaser," Cade intoned.

"It's a play for children," Rafe explained. He was trying for his customary casualness and achieving only diffidence. "That window at High Chapel in Seekhaven, the one with all the Clan emblems—Elk and Salmon and so forth—I was thinking we might do up a little rhyme for each, use the window as a backdrop, make it sort of a teaching play, if you see what I mean."

"But children aren't allowed in theaters," Jeska said.

Rafe shrugged. "What does anybody perform that children would want to see? But if we do this, and it gets known that an afternoon performance, say, would be a nice thing for the little ones—"

"Pull them in early," Cade interpreted, "so that when they get older, they're already of a mind to attend as many plays as they can."

The fettler looked annoyed. "I thought that with your grandfather's inheritance in your pocket now, you'd stop thinking about everything in terms of money. What I'm thinking is that it would be something fathers and sons could do together."

Mieka looked up from his beer, frowning. Then, wrapped in smiles, he cried, "Crisiant's pregnant!"

"How do you *do* that?" Cade blurted. For the sudden blush on Rafe's cheeks told him Mieka was right.

"Wasn't me!" The Elf chortled. "I didn't go anywhere near the girl!"

"Oh, funny," Rafe remarked. "Just side-splitting."

"Excellent work, mate! *Oy!*" Mieka bellowed in the direction of the bar. "Another round, darlin'!"

"And *fast* work," Jeska said, clapping Rafe on the shoulder. "We've only been home a fortnight."

"I'm efficient," he replied calmly. "Yesterday when I woke up, there she was hunched over a basin, poor sweetheart." A little smile flashed in his beard. "I said there must've been something off in the fish we had the night before, but she said that by now she ought to know the difference. She's consulting with her mother and my mother today. So we'll wait and see."

"Congratulations. I'm sure it'll all go well this time." Cade distributed fresh beer all round and raised the toast.

"Beholden, beholden," Rafe said. "But as for the play—it won't be anything scary, just the images, the sounds and things. A tickly spider in their hands, the feel of a swan's feathers, whinnying horses, mostly visuals with gentle effects."

"Can I do a lion?" Mieka asked. "I'd love to do a lion."

"One of the best plays I ever saw," Cade mused, "was 'Shamblesong'—the Mazetown Players—Gods, that was years ago now! It was for children and exactly the wrong sort of thing to do in a tavern, but I loved it."

"And a woodpecker!" Mieka chortled, and tapped a withie on the arm of his chair.

"Mazetown Players? You couldn't have been much more than a child yourself," Jeska said. "They were lost at sea ages ago."

Mieka was still beating out an irregular rhythm with the withie. "Bit of a poser, though, doing things like butterflies and fish. I mean, what sort of noise does a fish make? What would we do for a fish?"

"Even if we can't put children in the audience right away," Rafe went on, "we can do it as a play for adults, and once they talk about it enough—"

"Print the rhymes!" Jeska exclaimed. "That's how to do it—print it up as a book of rhymes that they can take home with them and show the little ones!"

"With pictures," Rafe agreed, looking startled that somebody else had guessed where he was going with this. "I've done a few sketches, talked with some art students while we were in Shollop and Stiddolfe—"

"You've been working on this quite a while, haven't you?" Cade asked, amused and impressed.

"Well, Crisiant was expecting before we left."

He hadn't said a thing: not before they left on the Royal, not when the letter had surely come to tell him their dreams were again disappointed. Twice now that he hadn't been with her when she lost a baby.

"We'll be home all winter this year," Cade said impulsively. "This time everything will be fine."

"Bees would be fun, too," Mieka was saying. "Lots of lovely noise. And peacocks. Let's do a whole flock of—"

"No!" Jeska snapped. "Absolutely no peacocks."

"Actually," Cade said quickly, interrupting whatever protest Mieka might have made, "ever since that show in Lilyleaf, I've been thinking about doing a play where we take out one or another of the elements. Get rid of all the emotions, for instance, like you suggest with this play, Rafe—not the way the Shadowshapers do it with 'Life in a Day,' with the payoff at the end, but *nothing* during the whole piece. It would make more work for Jeska, of course—"

"I did just fine that time," their masquer stated. "I can work with anything you care to give me—and even when I can't get at it to work with."

"I know," Cade soothed, "and that's what got me to thinking about this. What if we snipped out all the visuals? Have it be sounds, smells, tastes, emotions—"

"And words, of course," Mieka reminded him. "Can't have a play without words."

"Can't we?" He smiled. "It would make my life a lot easier!"

Rafe sat up a little straighter and opened his folio across his knees. "Interesting stuff to think on, but don't we have some work to do?"

"That we do, lads, that we do." Resisting a glance towards the bar, Cade, too, opened his folio.

This was Jeska's signal. "What's *she* doing here?"

Cade pretended to notice Megs, as if Rafe hadn't just indicated she had arrived. "She works here," he replied mildly.

Rafe growled. "Not when *we're* working here, she doesn't!"

"Oh, untwist it, would you?" Mieka rose and beckoned the girl over. He pulled up a chair and handed her into it, chattering all the while. "Nice to see you again! Did you have a good time in Lilyleaf? Back here to earn enough for another holiday, eh? Never mind them, you sit right here and watch and listen all you like."

Thus far, Mieka was reacting precisely as hoped. Their rudeness had produced an instantaneous urge to contradict them, and he was always polite to girls. Things might get dodgy with the next bit, though Cade and Rafe and Jeska had enough experience of the Elf by now to guess pretty accurately what he would do. A request made through the Keymarker's owner had been several days waiting for the girl's reply, but it seemed Megs had been unable to resist coming early to watch their little rehearsal.

With a rustle of wrinkled linen skirts, Megs sat down. She had tied up all her hair to keep it from getting dusty as she worked, and the head scarf, patterned in turquoise and yellow, did nothing for her green eyes or her pallid complexion. In point of fact, she looked rather like a sack of laundry cinched with a blue leather belt. Without expressing her gratitude for the chance to observe Touchstone at work or even for the chair Mieka had pulled over for her, she said, "Did you ever suss out who was mucking up your magic?"

"Let's not discuss unpleasant things," Mieka admonished with a comical grimace. "What d'you say, mates— shall we do a quick run-through of 'Treasure'?"

"'Silver Mine,'" Cade told him. "Somebody asked for it special tonight. Why don't you sit over near Rafe, Megs? That way, you can observe what he's doing a little more closely."

Rot, of course; she'd be able to sense his work even on the other side of the room. But it was all part of the plot.

Mieka once again played the gentleman and moved the chair for her. She eyed Cade with suspicion, then shrugged. Not much to say for herself today; good.

Cayden talked it through as Jeska murmured the lines and Mieka provided a few shards of magic, just enough to suggest the cold, damp darkness of the mine, the despair of the trapped and doomed miners.

"You see how he adds impressions," Cade said softly, "one at a time, making sure each is distinct while blending into the others. I haven't fully primed these withies yet, so there isn't much power in the workings. Still, it's giving you the idea, yeh? You can feel what Rafe is doing as well, making sure everything stays smooth and even, that the back of the room receives the same flow as the front and the middle. He knows what Mieka will do next, and he's ready for it—but a really great fettler is always ready for anything."

There was that in her eyes that invited him to shut up so she could concentrate better and understand without his having to tell her. Cade smiled, leaned forward, elbows on his knees, and kept talking.

"When the switch is made from the trapped miners to their sons waiting up on the hill, that's when the work gets tricky for an inexperienced fettler. There's a different essence to the anguish, and the transition has to be subtle. And of course there's the change in backdrop—a touch of a breeze, the taste and smell of the air, mayhap some lights in the village far down below. Their legs are tired from climbing so quickly up the hill, and there's another difference from the men inside the mine, whose arms and backs are aching with trying to shift the rock. You can hear that Jeska has made the voice younger. What happens in a real performance is a shift in costumes and faces as well." He paused, glancing over at Mieka. "Show her a bit more, why don't you? Just a touch. If you think she can handle it, I mean."

Megs ground her teeth and glared. Mieka sniggered, plucking another withie from the glass basket at his feet. Rafe sat back slightly, as if withdrawing physically as well as magically, while Jeska, nearing the end of the first son's speech, sat up a little straighter, alert to what was about to happen.

The idea had been to fool Mieka into thinking that Megs was doing it all: that Rafe had ceded control of the magic, which admittedly was a stingy shadow of what would be used in a real show. Then they would tease Mieka that although the *Lilyleaves* had dubbed him the first "girl" in theater, now he had some competition.

That had been the plan.

They'd neglected to include Megs in their calculations.

Well, how were they to know she really *was* good enough to take control of the magic for real?

And it wasn't as if Rafe were giving her anything. She simply took over. Jeska made the switch back to the collapsed cavern with barely a flicker of reaction—ah, the agile and accomplished Jeska, forever prepared to turn on a pennypiece. Rafe's big hands clenched and he looked for a moment as if he'd wrest control back from Megs, physically if necessary. Cade shook his head slightly; too risky, to fight over the magic with someone so blazing-eyed determined to hold on to it, even if she was only an amateur. There wasn't all that much to battle over, still just traces and tinges, nothing of the all-out intensity that marked a real Touchstone performance. Yet Megs was doing most of what Rafe usually did, and doing it rather well.

No changes of costume or feature, not in rehearsal, but a full range of other effects. The taste of stale, dwindling air; the ache of exhausted muscles and the deeper ache of grief; shards of panic, quickly repressed; the gradual flickering-out of the lamp, leaving only the sheen of stacked piles of glinting silver ore (inaccurate, but everybody understood it to be symbolism: the price of the miners' lives—it really was a rather subversive playlet); the increasing cold; the hitch of each breath in the throat; the soft, ominous clatter of stones presaging the mine's final collapse.

Megs handled it all. The barmaids and stock boys who had strayed closer to the stage now stood transfixed, caught, watching mere shadows, feeling only trifles, affected all the same.

Mieka hadn't noticed a thing. Lost in his own delight at creating—for this was naught but a rehearsal, after all, so he needn't be as vigilant as onstage—he rocked lightly in his chair and smiled happily and enjoyed himself.

What was bound to happen did happen: Megs began to lose her nerve, compensated, *over*compensated, drew back, adjusted, regrouped, tried for a stranglehold. Rafe, as alert and adaptable as Jeska, was ready. He gathered up the magic and at the same time did to her something of what she'd done to him all those months ago: set up a protective barrier. As the piece drew to a close and Jeska whispered the last lines, Megs stared at Rafe, anger and betrayal snapping in her eyes. All the magic drained away. Cade hauled in a deep breath, ready to say he knew not what, when she sprang to her feet shaking with rage.

"I had it!" she shouted at Rafe. "I *had* it, and you took it away!"

"Had what?" Mieka asked.

Rafe leaned back in his chair. "Not bad. Not bad at all, for a first real effort."

"Real—?" Mieka looked from him to Cade to Jeska and then back at Cade again. "What the fuck—?"

Jeska clucked his tongue against his teeth. "Mieka! Language!"

Cade addressed Megs, who was still furious. "You really shouldn't have done that, y'know. I realize it must have been a dreadful temptation, but—"

"I was doing it! It was *mine*!"

"For a little while," Rafe said. "And don't ever take it again without permission. That's the sort of silly trick can get you tossed out of class forever."

Mieka stuck his fingers into his mouth and gave a piercing whistle. When he had their attention, he asked, "It was *her*?"

"Of course it was me!" she snarled, and paced to the edge of the stage, arms folded around herself as if hugging the lost magic tight.

"*You!*" For a breath and a half Mieka looked as if he wanted to punch everybody in the room, including Megs. Then he collapsed into laughter. "That's me made a fool, right enough! I should've known! Cade's determined to get girls onstage as well as into the audiences—I should've *known*!"

Rafe arched a brow at Cade, who resisted the impulse to squirm in his chair. This hadn't been their plan at all. It was supposed to have been Mieka fooled into thinking Megs had done the fettling. None of them had thought that a girl could actually do it. Megs had. And if girls could do that, they could do all the rest of it—with proper training, of course. The prospects were . . . unnerving. For all that he was the ready champion of a girl who had proved herself an expert glasscrafter, this was different. This was *his* profession. *His* art.

"Girls onstage as players," Rafe was saying softly. "Cayden Silversun, what will you think of next?"

Megs swung round. "I don't want to be a *player*! Gods and Angels, what a horrid life you people lead! I want to be a *Steward*." Then, with a mocking smile for their gasps of disbelief, she said, "Much beholden for the lesson, gentlemen. Drinks after the show tonight are on me."

Fifteen

HANGOVERS WERE, PRAISE be to Auntie Brishen Staindrop, largely a thing of the past for Cade. Granted, the thorn she had only this spring concocted, and that Mieka highly recommended for the purpose, didn't work on Cade the way she thought it would, but that was usual for him. His strange brew of bloodlines still baffled her, and in her last letter accompanying a month's supply of the necessities—blockweed for dreamless sleep, bluethorn for working a performance even though he was exhausted, a few other mixtures that he enjoyed when he had the time and the inclination—she mentioned she was blending up something that he might find interesting. When he remembered to, he kept track of his reactions and occasionally wrote them all up so she'd have an idea of what to try next. Still, he continued to be a puzzle, and thorn that was supposed to alleviate if not actually cure a hangover instead gave him hives. (He discovered this on the Royal Circuit the morning after Mieka's Namingday. Mieka had turned twenty; Cade had turned bright red and bumpy.) What did work, and what he asked for a goodly supply of, was a combination that Mieka used for something else entirely. He never would say just what.

Megs stood them to as many drinks as they could swallow, and the four of them had to be poured into hire-hacks without much idea of their ultimate destinations (other than Mieka's one-word command, "Home!"). They were in luck, for the owner of the Keymarker knew their addresses and they all made it into their own beds before dawn. Cade retained just enough functioning brains to remember to prick the hangover thorn before diving onto his bed for a few hours of oblivion.

The next morning he was fine. The vaguest of head-aches was eased with several cups of strong, hot tea. Then he climbed back up to his room for a quick wash and a long debate with himself over which jacket he ought to wear, for this afternoon he would be making An Appearance.

Cade and Derien knew very well why Jed had urged Blye to learn a proper curtsy. Each year, after the hottest part of the summer was over, a week or so of gorgeous weather always preceded the arrival of serious rain across the Flood. During this interval a two-day racing meet was held on the grounds of the Palace. It was dis-tinct from the fair and horse market that took up ten days and twenty acres in spring, and to which Cayden had often escorted his mother and brother. This year, because he wasn't readying for the Winterly Circuit, he would be taking Derien and Lady Jaspiela to the late-summer races. Jed and Blye would be joining them.

Blye had figured it out that morning, when at break-fast her husband presented her with a hat. Not just any hat; a *hat*. All the ladies, from Royalty to merchants' wives to daughters of the horses' trainers, would be wear-ing white dresses, the better to appreciate their hats. Blye marched through the back door of Redpebble Square, through the kitchen and hall, and into the vestibule wear-ing a new white skirt and blouse with a thin purple ribbon around her waist, and an expression that dared anyone to comment on what was on her head.

It was deserving of comment. Jed had good taste, Cade decided, and told him so as he followed, grinningly pleased with himself, behind his wife. He'd had the sense to recognize that a woman as little as Blye couldn't possibly wear one of those extravagances of silk flowers and frills that Cade had seen before at the races. (Most other women shouldn't wear them, either, but that was just Cade's opinion.) Neither was Blye the sort for fussy lace or soaring feathers, broad brims or cascades of beaded fringe. Jed had gifted her with a close-fitting cap of dark purple velvet, decorated on one side with an embroidered thistle in the same purple picked out in tiny black glass beads. The rich color made her pale skin and silver-blond hair glow, and even allowing for the uneasy look in her big brown eyes, she looked genuinely pretty.

Cade knew better than to tell her that. She'd find it out anyway, when admiring glances were directed her way at the races. Neither did Derien make any remarks, but his elegant bow—with wrist flourishes worthy of Mieka at his grandiose best—was eloquent enough. When he straightened up, Blye suddenly laughed and swept him a curtsy, good humor restored.

Lady Jaspiela's white gown was lace-over-silk, buttoned to the throat and almost to her fingertips against any encroachment by ill-mannered sunshine. Her wide-brimmed green hat formed the basis for a display of silk clover dotted with white flowers, rather like an itinerant lawn. Dery wore his favorite blue velvet peaked-and-billed cap, ornamented today with a silver falcon pin to match the one he'd given Cade a couple of years ago; it had been Cade's Namingday gift to him this year and he was tremendously proud of it. Cade showed up downstairs wearing his pin in his jacket lapel. But as for a hat—

"Absolutely not. No. I refuse. Jed's not wearing one and neither am I. We're both tall enough without putting an upended vase on our heads!"

Jedris was just as adamant. "I don't care if they're made out of straw or covered in silk or rabbit fur—they look like exactly what Cade said. Vases turned upside down, with our faces growing out of the bottom."

"Like flowers," Blye cooed, patting his cheek as they went through the front door of Number Eight, Red-pebble Square.

"Nothing to worry about," Dery observed. "Mieka will make up for it."

"Mieka's joining us?" Lady Jaspiela so far forgot herself as to sound almost eager. She had greeted the appearance of Blye and Jed in her parlor with a scant nod, then ignored them in favor of adjusting her gloves. But the prospect of an afternoon in the Elf's company nearly made her smile.

"And his wife," Jedris said. "They were supposed to be here by noon—and there's the Minster chime, and here they are!"

"Mieka?" Cade opened his eyes as wide as they would get. "On time?"

"I heard that!"

The Elf leaped from Kearney Fairwalk's second-best carriage, lent to them for the occasion. Kearney was at Fairwalk Manor for a month or so, doubtless something to do with the harvest or the hunt or whatever it was noblemen did on their estates at this time of year. He had evidently taken his regular coachman with him, for the youth handling the reins was dressed in a groom's deep blue coat that lacked the oak-leaf buttons and pin of senior Fairwalk servants.

"Greetings, all!" Mieka caroled, sweeping them all a bow. "Your Ladyship, you're looking a right portrait, you are. Jed, unhand that girl—oh, wait, never mind, she's your wife! Make yourself useful, Cayden, and climb up top with the driver—there's not room enough for us all and your legs are too long. Unless you'd prefer to be stuffed into the boot?"

Cade approached in genuine awe. "What in the name of everything holy is that thing on your head?"

Mieka grinned. Tilted at a rakish angle was a cap rather like Derien's in design, but on an ostentatious scale. Well, this was Mieka. The peak was at least a foot tall, the bill looked as if half a dinner plate had been glued on, and the whole had been executed in cloth of gold, with a purple feather sweeping from one side to the other.

"I didn't make it," his wife called anxiously from inside the carriage. "I had nothing to do with it!"

"No one would ever think that you did," Jed assured her. "You have taste. That thing—it's—"

"Words fail you?" Cade squinted and held a hand up to shade his eyes. The thing really was blinding in the sunlight. "Me, too."

"Envy," Mieka said with airy unconcern. "Sheer envy." He turned to Lady Jaspiela. "Don't you think so, Your Ladyship?"

She considered. "I think," she said at last, "that it will be much remarked upon." And she was inside the carriage before Cade could decide whether or not she had just made a joke.

No. Impossible. His mother had no sense of humor.

Neither did most of the people attending the races that afternoon, not if their hats were anything to judge by. They all seemed sincerely pleased to be wearing gardens of flowers, orchards of fruit, feathers enough to stuff a thousand mattresses, jewels (both real and fake) accented by lace veils and silk ribbons and beads in all the colors of the rainbow. Several of these concoctions, on women and on men, sported what looked at first to be small animals clinging precariously to their skulls. Flattened circles of straw or silk seemed popular, though to Cade they all looked like decorated pancakes. From the brim of one gentleman's yellow silk hat, strongly reminiscent of an overturned pisspot, dangled talons that might once have belonged to a very large hawk or a very small wyvern. And one lady had braided her pale brown hair into a nest that formed a cozy perch for two improbably colored birds, fully feathered.

Mieka, who had never been to the races before, pouted a bit when he saw how many people, male and female, had outdone him. None of them, however, wore anything as glaringly bright as his golden cap.

"I made a perfectly fine hat for him," his wife fretted to Cade after he'd paid their entry fees and they were strolling the lawn towards the stands. "He wouldn't even consider wearing it."

"That doesn't surprise me at all. Please don't worry about it," he added as she looked so downcast that even he was moved. "We can pretend he's a country cousin in the city for the first time, and more than a little touched in the head!" When he saw that this did nothing to lighten her mood—evidently she had little to no sense of humor, either—he went on, "And anyway, nobody, man or woman, will be looking at him once they see you."

He'd meant it for a compliment—that the women would all be envious and the men would all be covetous. She truly was the most beautiful girl he'd ever seen. But she met his gaze with renewed anxiety in her iris-blue eyes.

"Is there something wrong with my gown? Or my hair? Is my hat not right?"

"No, no," he soothed, "your gown is lovely, and your hair, and that red silk hat is perfection. There's not a woman here who won't be wishing she'd worn something else, and not a man who won't be wishing he'd come here with you."

"Do you really think so?" she whispered.

"Yes," he said, quite honestly. Everyone would be talking about her—and it would be churlish of him to believe that this was her principal ambition. Still, this was precisely the place for the socially striving to see and be seen.

The Palace in Gallantrybanks had been added to at various times through the centuries, mainly by kings who wished to impress the populace (and provide productive employment) or queens who had tired of their old apartments and wanted to start fresh and fashionable. Thus the building was really a series of buildings, some connecting and others not, with so many ginnels and breezeways and staircases and tunnels that even the Royal cats and dogs were said to lose themselves in the maze. This was true only of the part that most people didn't see, for King Cobin had begun, and his son King Meredan had finished, a frontage that actually made logical sense. Visitors entered through huge wrought-iron gates in the shape of dragon wings into a vast courtyard giving a view of the river. The new three-story frontage had been tacked on to the old confusion of stones and styles, presenting an orderly row of white columns holding up a roof of rich cinnamon-brown tiles. Every so often a broad grand staircase led up to doors and windows, all topped with pointed arches. Today these stairs formed the basis of the stands (with barricades behind to prevent people from wandering into the Palace itself, of course). And the cobbled courtyard, a good quarter of a mile long, had been fitted out with a fenced-in oval racecourse. A few inches of sawdust cushioning several more inches of packed dirt made up the track. In two days' time, everything would be shoveled back into carts and taken back to the Palace gardens. Nobody envied the workers this toil, which had to be finished before the rains blew in or the whole courtyard would become a sea of mud.

Today the weather was very fine, with only a few unenthusiastic clouds drifting past: no threat to the track. Or to the hats. This was a real shame, Cade thought as he shepherded his mother and brother and friends through the crowd towards the stands. Most of these hats deserved nothing so much as a drenching that would obliterate all traces of their existence.

All at once his attention was caught by the ugliest headgear he'd yet seen this afternoon. Hugely brimmed, made of straw, it looked like roof thatching dotted with turquoise flowers. Turquoise ribbons looped in ever-lengthening tiers down the lady's back, enough ribbons to wrap up the Palace like a Namingday present. Her white dress was no better, with flounces from knees to hem that made her seem even shorter than she was; as she walked past, the ruffles puffed out with each step like the froth at the base of a waterfall. The thick hair done in a single plait over her shoulder very much wanted to be blond but couldn't quite manage it. Suddenly he realized that he knew that braid, and the face beneath the hideous hat. Turquoise, he mused, definitely was not her color; hats of any kind were not her style. Green eyes flashed recognition for an instant before she looked right through him and continued on her way.

"Cade? Cayden!"

He remembered his manners and made his apologies to his mother. "I'm sorry—I thought I saw somebody I know. What were you saying?"

Not that he cared. He was too busy wondering what Megs was doing at the races. Granted, anyone with money to buy a ticket could get into the general stands, and a barmaid with fettling skills (who wanted to be a Steward!) had just as much right to enjoy the races as anybody else. But somehow this sort of gathering didn't seem to be her style, either. Just exactly what her style might be, he had no idea, but what he'd seen thus far wasn't particularly promising.

Jed spied a section of seats that might suit them. Cade was just about to agree when portions of the crowd shouted and surged towards the track as ten horses thundered past. Somebody bumped into him, which made him lose his balance, which sent him a stumbling step towards Mieka's wife. She was so small and dainty that any attempt to brace himself on her shoulder would not only be terrible manners but likely send them both tumbling to the ground. He tried to get both feet under him and succeeded only in tangling his legs like a newborn colt. And here he'd thought adolescent awkwardness safely relegated to the past along with hangovers.

"Cayden!" She put a steadying hand on his chest—and her other hand, delicate and determined, closed around his crotch.

"Steady on, Quill," Mieka said from behind him. As Cade flinched, he felt the Elf's hands at his back to prop him up. "Frightful crush here, eh? Let's find someplace where we won't be trampled at every other step."

Cade stood there, stunned silent but blessedly secure on his feet again, and watched the girl smile at Mieka. So lovely, so innocent, so adoring, so adorable. He felt like throwing up.

He had no time to indulge. A young man wearing the Princess's blue-and-brown livery and forget-me-never badge shoved a path to Cade's side and, just as a roar sounded the end of the race, tried to bellow something in Cade's ear.

Cade thought it unseemly to shout. He waited for the noise to subside. "Could you repeat that?"

"Master Silversun?" When Cade nodded, the young man looked pleased with himself. "Thought I recognized you. Saw Touchstone at the wedding celebrations last spring. Brilliant show." Then, remembering his errand, he said, "Her Royal Highness would like a word, if that's agreeable."

And thus Cayden and his entire party were escorted towards the Royal Ring, where it would soon be in his power to introduce his mother to Princess Miriuzca, future Queen of Albeyn.

It would be an acute pleasure to include Derien, Blye, Jed, and Mieka and his wife, mainly because their inclusion would cause Lady Jaspiela acute mortification. Of course, she was thrilled to her gloved fingertips by the invitation, but too haughty to show emotion except for a slight flush on her cheeks. As they were walking, she began to speak in a low and rapid voice for Cade's hearing alone.

"Is it finally obvious to you that you could have a position in her household at the flick of a finger? With your father attending on the Prince and you placed with the Princess, our family would stand to influence the entire Court—especially once they inherit."

Mieka, on her other side, listened with his sensitive Elfen ears and made rude faces at Cade behind her back.

"I don't know why you don't take advantage of the favor she's showing you. It would be the easiest thing in the world—"

"And what would you have me do for her, Mother?" Cade asked sweetly. "For I can tell you with absolute certainty that she doesn't require anyone to do for her what your husband does for the Prince."

Her color deepened a trifle. Mieka grinned from ear to pointed ear.

A little while later they were being admitted through a short white wooden gate and climbing a dozen or so steps. On the way up, they passed a gentleman on the way down, who arched his eyebrows at them.

"Amazin'," he drawled from beneath a towering hat that closely resembled a thick orange spike flattened on top by a clumsily wielded hammer. "The sort they allow into the Royal Ring these days!"

Mieka's wife whimpered softly with nerves. That, at least, was honest, Cade noted as he glanced at her for the first time since she'd groped him. She was ice-white and saucer-eyed, and clinging to Mieka's arm with both tremulous hands. Even the bronze-gold curls beneath her red silk hat were quivering. Cade took a quick look over his shoulder at Blye and Jed. She was in a state of shock and trying not to show it; he was trying to be not quite so tall. Derien alone was undaunted, and Cade spared a moment of admiration for the serene self-confidence of the very young.

The Royal Ring was a large platform constructed in a half circle out from a floor-to-ceiling window of the Palace, right on the finish line. That little white gate and the awning above it set it apart. Princess Miriuzca, visibly pregnant, was seated in one of a pair of almost-throne chairs, dressed in white with a wide-brimmed blue hat trailing sea green silk veils. The empty chair was of course for her husband.

The Princess smiled as Cade and his little group approached, and held out a welcoming hand. He took her fingertips and bent over her wrist, as a cultured gentleman ought. He performed introductions, starting with his mother. Then Derien, whose bow was a great deal more accomplished than it used to be before the King's College had got hold of him.

Amused, Cayden let his sense of humor a little off its lead. "And now that you've met the Silversuns, it's time for all the Windthistles. This one"— he pointed at Mieka, who doffed his preposterous cap —"is my glisker, as you may remember. That one is Master Jedris Windthistle, who is in business with his twin brother, who's just as tall and redheaded. In fact, all the Windthistles are twins but for the newest one, and *this* charming lady is the Windthistle who is her mother."

The girl sank into a flawless curtsy, blushing as the Princess smiled and said, "All best wishes, Mistress. I'm sure your little girl is a joy to your heart." Looking up at Cade, she asked, "How many Windthistle twins are there?"

"Four sets. Alarming, isn't it, to think there's a second one of him?" He grinned at Mieka. "But the Lord and Lady were good to us all, and his twin is a sister named Jinsie, and much the nicer of the set."

"Better-looking, too," Derien piped up.

Cade concluded, "And *this* Windthistle is Jedris's wife, my old friend Blye, whose work Your Highness saw last summer."

After a momentary puzzlement, she laughed in delight. "The glasscrafter? Oh, but I have been hearing of you from *my* old friend, Lady Eastkeeping! Are you not usually wearing trousers?"

Lady Jaspiela went from mortified to horrified.

Most unexpectedly, Mieka's wife saved the situation with, "And very lucky that she does, Your Royal Highness. Why, it would be as if my husband tried to do *his* work on the stage in a corset and silk gown!"

"With lace to his fingertips!" Miriuzca giggled. Then, her mouth tucked into a sly little smile, she said, "But of course, we only speculate. We ladies have never seen players on a stage."

Mieka's wife looked torn between terror of her own boldness in addressing Royalty uninvited, uncertainty about whether or not she was supposed to laugh, and an agony of bliss that a Princess had called her a *lady*.

Miriuzca then turned her attention to Lady Jaspiela, as was proper, and complimented her on her two fine sons, her distinguished husband, her lovely gown, and her beautiful hat. Blye began to breathe again. Jed looked as if the effort not to laugh would soon give him an attack of some kind. Mieka, curiously enough, was still looking stunned that his quiet, modest, shy little wife had dared to open her mouth. Cade decided it was a good look on him. Anything that kept him silent was a good thing.

Velvet-cushioned stools were arranged at the Princess's gesture. Cool drinks were handed round. Blye found herself seated at Miriuzca's knee, telling her—haltingly at first, then with bright fluency—all about glasscrafting. Cade stood slightly apart, surveying the little scene with satisfaction. The pottinger wouldn't be necessary, though it would certainly be given at the appropriate time. With the Princess's personal esteem between her and the tax collectors, Blye would be safe.

While everyone was waiting for the fourth race—bemoaning their losses on the third and hastening to place bets—the clouds that had been milling about in the distance began to blow closer. A brass gong sounded to call the weathering witches to push them away. Everyone in Gallantrybanks was more or less familiar with this, but, judging by the startled widening of her eyes, Cade was certain that Miriuzca had never seen it before.

She might have heard about it, but hearing and seeing were two different things. He had been amusing her with tales of the Royal Circuit when the gong rang out, and as the weathering witches swarmed to the center of the track to work their magic, he saw her begin to tremble.

Very quietly, he said, "It will take them a few minutes to finish their work. They use their personal affinity to water and air—they're mostly of Elven blood—to coax clouds away. When they get rid of snow, it's the weathering witches with an understanding of fire who melt snowbanks so the water runs down the drains."

She nodded, a stiff and unconvincing smile on her face.

Derien returned from fetching more fruit juice, and overheard the last bit. A swift glance at the Princess told him what must be wrong, and he proved himself a promising candidate for a diplomatic career by leaning comfortably against Cade's shoulder and taking her hand to comfort her. "There's nothing spectacular about it, you know. Nothing like what my brother can do onstage!"

With visible effort she asked in a whisper, "Can every magical person do this kind of thing?"

Cade shook his head. "No, not everyone. All the gifts and specialties are different amongst the magical races, and for each individual. There's never much telling what will show up. With this one, for instance—" He rumpled Derien's hair. "We live in deepest dread of what mischief he might be able to do with his magic, once he comes into it in a few years." Dery made a face at him, and the Princess began to relax. Cade continued, "I know the concept behind what the weathering witches do, and I can melt a bit of snow from the front walk at home, but I can't do what they're doing with those clouds, for instance."

She looked in the direction he pointed, and caught her breath as the clouds slowly backed away. All at once she chuckled that deep, throaty chuckle of hers. "Weathering witches must be coveted guests at outdoor parties!"

Though he joined in her laughter, he was writhing inside, too embarrassed to tell her that weathering witchery was very low on the ladder of magical accomplishments.

"But I have been rude," Princess Miriuzca said, "taking up all your time like this. I'm sure there are other friends you wish to be talking to." It was polite dismissal, and Cade knew it—had been expecting it, in fact, for the last half hour. What he didn't expect was her murmur of, "And I see my husband about to arrive with far too many people, who are believing that their titles give the right to bad manners and claiming all the chairs and footstools for themselves."

"I know the type," he assured her. "You have my sympathies!"

She gave a guilty little giggle, then composed her features to regal calm. She was very good at it by now, he noted with a pang of regret.

Gratitude was expressed and leave was taken, and they were almost out of the Royal Ring before Prince Ashgar and his retinue arrived. Trailing behind was the Archduke. As they passed him, he gave Cayden a genial nod, but his words were for Mieka's wife.

"Your mother's artistry is sorely missed by the Archduchess these days. May I attribute the beauty of these ladies' gowns to her skills?"

Cade had less reason than ever to come to the girl's defense, but everything about Cyed Henick annoyed him. And it would be a heart of solid rock that could remain unmoved by her sudden cringe as snideness couched in compliments put her and everyone with her in their proper places: very near the ladder's bottom, a rung or two above peasants, charwomen, and the men who drove the dung carts.

Before Cade could speak, Lady Jaspiela favored the Archduke with her notice and said, "Pray give my greetings to Her Grace. I so enjoyed our talk at the milliner's last week, where we were both choosing hats. I had hoped to see her here today. I have the card of my own dressmaker to give her, as she requested."

Cade had the sense not to gape. The Archduke had the sense to say only, "Regrettably, Her Grace is indisposed. I shall convey your good wishes." With a nod, he rejoined the Prince.

"Insufferable man," mused Lady Jaspiela. "Derien, please find me someplace shady to sit down."

"Your Grace, the child is born."

The Archduke looked up from his desk, brows arched in a silent question.

The servant—the chamberlain, to judge by his fine silk shirt and silver chain of office—cleared his throat, then admitted, "A girl, Your Grace. Her Grace is well, and sends her apologies."

"Ah well—a son next time, I'm sure. Be so good as to open as many bottles as you like downstairs and toast my daughter."

"Your Grace is all kindness. Congratulations, Your Grace. I give Your Grace good night."

When the man had departed, His Grace took up pen and paper. After scrawling the date at the top, he began immediately, with no salutation:

Just after midnight last night my daughter was born. My wife has apologized. She has not the wit to understand that a girl can tidy things up genealogically.

Let us hope she turns out pretty enough to interest
Prince Roshlin when they grow up—though ultimately
that has nothing to do with the matter. They will do
as they are told. As for the events at the Downstreet,
I think you will agree that Silversun's cleverness in
outwitting the constables a few weeks ago went
a long way towards preventing an actual riot. I
believe—}

But whatever the Archduke believed was not visible
to Cayden as the Elsewhen faded out.

"Cade?"

He glanced down at Blye's worried dark eyes. Of the
two others present who would recognize an Elsewhen,
Derien was chattering to Jed, and Mieka was whispering soothing words to his wife. "Never mind," Cade
murmured. "As Mother says—insufferable man. Let's
find somewhere to sit down."

During the time it took to accomplish this, his mind
worked feverishly at trying to comprehend what he'd
seen and why. First, whether she was aware of it yet or
not, Archduchess Panshilara was pregnant, not indisposed. The date on the Archduke's letter was three weeks
shy of nine months from today—the day after Cade's
own Namingday, in fact. Second, she would have a girl—
which would make things "tidy." The Princess's child
would be a son—Prince Roshlin, who could be married
to the Archduke's daughter. The man's schemes certainly
were far-reaching, Cade thought sourly. What influence
he himself might have on that midnight scene completely escaped him. How could what he did or didn't
do possibly affect when the Archduchess delivered her
child?

But as Jed and Mieka hauled him off to place bets on
the next race, he suddenly realized how he could turn
this knowledge to his financial advantage. And Mieka's,

because the girl really was owed some sort of compensation for the humiliation she'd suffered.

He had never done such a thing before in his life. He had never used his foreknowledge to make money. To get himself out of unwanted personal futures—such as servitude to Master Honeycoil—yes, he'd done that often enough. Still . . . how many times had he experienced an Elsewhen that offered this sort of opportunity?

And on that thought another Elsewhen flitted across his mind. Just a glimpse, just a swift impression of himself and Mieka in the drab little office that belonged to Slips Clinkscales, the odds-man who lived at the bottom of Criddow Close.

During the rest of the afternoon, Jed broke even, Cade lost a bit, and Mieka came out ahead by a tidy little sum that, uncharacteristically, did not put him in a cheery mood. Cade didn't understand this until they were leaving. It was quite simple, really: The sidelong glances and frankly admiring stares directed at his wife annoyed him. He held her by the waist, close to his side, and glared at any man who looked more than a second or two. Cade shrugged it off, thinking that if a man didn't want other men to look at his wife, he ought to keep her immured at home or marry somebody plain.

Everyone was tired by the end of the day. Having had experience of the impossible traffic around the Palace gates, Cade had arranged with Kearney's coachman to bring the carriage round to the Hestings, a few blocks away. Lady Jaspiela and Derien lagged behind a bit, and Jed and Blye outpaced them some, so Cade, a step or two behind Mieka and his wife, was the only one who overheard what she said to him.

"I don't understand why the Princess talked so much to Blye and not me. She's not nobility or anything. We're both crafters and married women—and *her* craft-

ing isn't even done by women. And I've had a baby and
the Princess is about to have one and it isn't as if Blye is
ever going to, poor thing, so what could they find to
discuss? And besides," she finished artlessly, "I'm much
prettier."

Mieka laughed briefly, and Cade swore it wasn't just
imagination that lent the note of disapproval to his voice.
"Oh, *much*. Did you think that might be the reason?
The Princess is a lovely girl, no doubt of it—but you're
something the Gods made personally and with infinite
care to every perfect detail, and mayhap the Princess
didn't like being outshone."

There was more on this theme, but Cade stopped listening. A minute or so later, Jed waved from a corner
and soon they were all piling into the carriage. Cade
elected to ride up top with the coachman to give the
others more room, and stared at the passing streets of
Gallantrybanks unseeing, occupied with some very unpleasant thoughts.

"... it isn't as if Blye is ever going to, poor thing." He
would have to ask Jed if presents came regularly from
Mieka's wife—a pillow slip, a scarf, a blouse, sheets.
After realizing that the arrival of the green shirt had
curtailed Mieka's nocturnal entertainments for about
a month, Cade wasn't disposed to doubt Mistress Mirdley any longer. And with the thought of the Trollwife,
he felt the tension seep from his shoulders a bit. She
loved Blye; she would be on the lookout for any "gifts"
from Mistress Windthistle—the gorgeous little bitch. He
found all at once that despite feeling outraged on her
behalf at the Archduke's rudeness, her snobbish envy of
Blye settled the matter for him for good. It was a relief
finally to give in to his dislike.

Not that she'd ever attempted to win him over.
He counted for nothing as far as she was concerned; a

temporary distraction in her husband's life, an annoyance but nothing more serious. He remembered the look on her face in the back alley of the Keymarker, when he pretended he'd not seen Mieka kissing her. He saw again, as if in an Elsewhen, her smug certainty that she was winning and that eventually she'd win. But it hadn't been an Elsewhen. It had been real. And there was very little he could do to thwart that anticipated victory.

She thought it would be a victory. He knew otherwise. There'd been that other Elsewhen, the one where Mieka had come home drunk, thorned, belligerent, and the pages of Touchstone's folio had been burned in the fire by his pregnant wife, and they'd battled each other bloody—

Only that had been in the other house, the one Mieka hadn't bought. It hadn't been Hilldrop Crescent.

Hilldrop Crescent, he had blown up with black powder and with Cade's help.

Of all the Elsewhens he'd ever had about the girl, a few were comprehensible in light of subsequent events. Her sewing, for instance—and he reminded himself once more to ask about anything sent to Blye. But there was one that he hadn't thought of as being about her at all, just a fleeting flash on the way back from Seekhaven after their very first Trials.

It had been night, and he'd been seated on a bench very like this one, having taken over the driving from Kearney's coachman. Mieka was beside him, and they were talking, and all at once the carriage lamps had illuminated the startled shape of a fox in the middle of the road.

{A flicker of white at the tip of a fox's tail, and screams rippling through an immense room crowded with revelers and ablaze with candlelight. A girl with gold-and-bronze hair sobbing into Mieka's shoulder.}

Cade had lost his grip on the reins. The Elf had grabbed them, slowed and finally halted the horses, lied fluently to the coachman, and said nothing about the weirdness of it all as Cade rummaged through his satchel for Mistress Mirdley's little kit of necessaries for a soothing salve. Cade could still see Mieka's hands as he smoothed the ointment onto his palms, the red welts left by the leather reins, the single blood blister. Mieka had never said a word about any of it, and Cade had never told him about that Elsewhen. It had happened before Mieka knew about Cade's foreseeings. It had happened even before Mieka met the girl at the Castle Biding Fair. And it mystified Cade still, the fox and the ballroom and the girl weeping against Mieka's shoulder. He'd never seen its like since, which he knew from experience meant nothing. It might happen; it might not. Some decision of his had made it possible, and it might come true.

Sixteen

NOTHING IN THE past three days had gone right for Mieka.

Well, one or two things had been tolerable, but that wasn't the point.

First, those hulking great bullies, his big brothers, had shown up at Hilldrop Crescent at some vulgar hour of the morning to drag him back to Gallantrybanks. Neither Jedris nor Jezael had shown any sympathy when he yelled out the window at them for interrupting the sleep he needed if he was to perform well at that night's show. They stood in the courtyard and yelled back that the show wasn't until the *next* night, and in view of his inability to figure out the days of the week, it was lucky he had big brothers to remember for him. Mieka yelled back, rather incoherently. This woke the baby, who started to cry, which got everybody out of bed.

Then Jed mentioned that he was taking Blye to the races, and that set off wheedling and then tearful appeal from his wife to join the outing. The frantic packing that went on after this didn't bear thinking about.

Neither did the journey to town, with three of them plus the baby crammed into a hire-hack (Jez rode up top with the driver, and how Mieka envied him). The only good thing had been leaving his mother-in-law behind, waving to them from the gate. Jindra had been lulled to peaceful sleep by the vehicle's motion, so that was a good thing, too. But there'd been a bottleneck on the road into Gallantrybanks, caused by dozens of other carriages and carts heading into town, adding at least three hours to the journey. The street traffic had been horrendous. By the time they reached Wistly Hall, they owed the hack driver a small fortune and their dinner was cold.

Mieka sought relief and a better mood in a discreet thornful while his wife began hasty construction of a hat—of all the idiotic things to occupy herself with—and his mother and sisters cooed over the baby. His father was closeted in his workshop, polishing wood and plunking strings. On the main stairway, Mieka saw several people, presumably relations, he didn't recognize and who didn't recognize him as the famous son of the house. He felt like a stranger in the home he'd grown up in.

The next day he rose early—for him—and escaped to the shops, where life improved with the discovery of the cloth-of-gold cap. Then he betook himself off to the Keymarker and what he anticipated would be a quick rehearsal before drinks, dinner, more drinks, and yet another brilliant Touchstone performance. Only that would-be fettler girl had shown up, and he'd been made a fool of. They all had, truth be told, but Mieka felt it more than the others. He was angry with himself for not realizing what Megs was doing, and angrier still for being angry with her, and angriest of all at how forced the laughter had felt when he finally managed to laugh. Jokes weren't supposed to be *on* him; they were supposed to be *by* him.

His wife had been vexed when he wouldn't wear the hat she'd made for him—an unadventurous reworking of one of his father's old caps with a fresh ribbon-band and some feathers. And then, despite Lady Jaspiela's assurances, his own golden cap hadn't been much remarked on at all. As for the things that *did* catch people's attention—he wouldn't have worn any of those hats at moonless midnight into an unlighted coal mine, but that wasn't the issue. And *then* his mother had caught him pouring a whiskey to get him through the first part of the day, and snatched it away from him with a stern warning to be on his best behavior—and no thorn, either, Mieka Windthistle, are you understanding me?

Not that anybody paid much heed to him at all, not even Cade—who prevented him from having any real fun with dire looks from those gray falcon eyes of his. And talking of eyes, every man who passed by stared at his wife, which was gratifying for about ten minutes and then became an irritation, then an exasperation, and finally a genuine infuriation. They had no right to look at her like that, no matter how beautiful she was, not with undisguised lust in their eyes and practically licking their lips. When she gathered up the pluck to speak to the Princess without having first been spoken to, he was stunned; his shy, gentle little darling! And in defense of Blye, too, which ought to be his and Cade's and especially Jed's job.

His temper had nearly exploded at the Archduke's malicious little gibe. That Lady Jaspiela had got her retort in first—even before Cade—was startlement enough. That she had come to her own defense and nobody else's with that claim about having met the Archduchess shouldn't have wounded him, but it had; he thought she liked him.

Winning a nice sum at the races had improved his outlook. But on the walk to Lord Fairwalk's carriage, his wife had gone on complaining that the Princess had paid more attention to Blye than to her. He had soothed and complimented and wished he were on the Keymarker's stage, where he could forget everything except the joy of doing the work he'd been born to do. Then he remembered that their next show was tomorrow night, and even then there'd be Megs the Fettling Barmaid to worry about, and whether she would play her tricks on him again.

Not an enjoyable three days.

At Wistly Hall he made straight for a liquor bottle before giving in to the urgings of his parents and siblings to be told all about the races. His wife told them breathlessly about the Princess. Neither of them mentioned the Archduke. After a time, his mother suggested that they both must be tired, and ought to have their supper on a tray upstairs. Mieka was grateful for the escape. In his old bedchamber, redecorated with new curtains and counterpane that his wife and her mother had made, he sought refuge in his thorn-roll.

She came in a little while later with a dinner tray. The whiskey bottle was half-empty and he wasn't much interested in food by then. Besides, a fortnight at Hilldrop had made his clothes too snug again. He'd felt a bit sluggish last night in performance. It wouldn't hurt to skip a meal or three. He watched through slitted, drowsy eyes as she fed Jindra, put her into the cradle that had snuggled three generations of Windthistles—and that was quite a lot of Windthistles—and sat down to have her own dinner.

"Good time today?" he heard himself ask.

"Lovely! Meeting the Princess—" She put down her fork and gave him such a look of loving delight that all his moodiness vanished. "Oh, Mieka, it was wonderful! And everyone was so kind—well, almost everyone— and so many people nodded and smiled—"

Especially, he thought with a cynicism he knew was borrowed from Cayden, after they'd been seen in the Royal Ring. "Glad you had fun."

He sprawled on the bed, a pillow behind his neck, taking an idle swallow of whiskey now and then as he watched her undress and put away her things. She moved so gracefully, so delicately. He knew it must be an effect of the thorn, but it seemed to him quite natural that soft swirls of white, like smoke, like feathers, like fog, trailed behind her every gesture. It would be nice to be wrapped up in that pale iridescence, like being inside a pearl. She sat beside him and upended her reticule onto the bed, sorting through coins and little pots and vials of makeup and scent, a handkerchief, a flat green wallet of sewing things, the ticket for the races to be kept as a remembrance, a folded business card, a few wrapped sweets. He was about to ask how women could cram so much into such tiny bags when his eye lit on the business card and he reached out for it and opened it and read through bleary eyes *The Finchery*.

"Wh—what's this, then?"

"That? Oh, just something some man gave me today at the races. I took it just to be rid of him. Lady Jaspiela was talking, and me and Blye—I mean, Blye and I—that sounds so silly, doesn't it? We were trying to listen to her but a man came up to where we were sitting and he was bothering me, he kept trying to give me his card. So I took it and he finally went away. Why? Who was he? Do you know him?"

He could always tell when Cade was lying. Something about the eyes. He wasn't sure what. But he always knew. He knew now. Nothing to do with her eyes; she wasn't looking at him. With her, it was her voice. The light quick eager rush of words. Too many words.

Whatever she was telling him, it was a lie.

He would never be certain of exactly what happened then. The next thing he knew for sure was that he was shouting and his wife was weeping and the baby was screaming and he was standing in the middle of the room, accusing her of being a whore or wanting to become one.

"Mieka! Stop it!"

He'd heard his father raise his voice mayhap four times in his life. Hadden Windthistle was bellowing now. He turned to the doorway, where his father stood, and realized there was a glass in his hand and he was about to throw it, just as it seemed he'd thrown plates and teacups and a half-empty bottle of wine.

"*Mieka!*"

It wasn't that he had any memory of throwing these things. It was that there were smears of food on his fingers, and broken crockery on the floor, and a dark stain of wine on the blue silk counterpane where she huddled and wept.

Someone in skirts pushed by him and picked up the baby. Jinsie, long pale hair streaming down her back and tangling in the baby's waving fists. "There, lovey, it's all right now, I promise it's all right—"

"No!" his wife sobbed. "Give me my baby! Give her to me!"

"Not just now, my dear," Hadden said softly, gently. "You're too upset. And you're bleeding."

It was true. There was a smudge of blood at her mouth.

He had done that. He had slapped her. He could feel the sting of it now on his fingers and palm. And he had said things—horrible things.

But—*The Finchery*—

Almost like one of Cade's Elsewhens, or what he imagined an Elsewhen might be, he could see the two of them standing in the night-dark street outside the Kiral Kellari, and the gray coat Cade's father had given him, and the card inside a pocket that Cade had thrown to the street, and reading the card with the girls' names on the back and little stars drawn beside the names. And Cade saying viciously, *"You can compare notes on what makes a 'refined' fuck."* The Finchery was a whore-house, frequented by Prince Ashgar himself.

He heard the muted patter of glass onto the carpet and half an instant later felt his hand sting anew. Not with the bloodied punctures and gashes of having broken it in his fist; no, this was a burning that left no blood and no visible wound, for he had done to the wineglass what he did almost every night to a withie. He had shattered it with magic.

Jinsie hurried from the room, carrying her wailing namesake, and cursed him as she went past. Hadden clenched his fingers around Mieka's shoulder.

"Mieka. Come with me."

He stared at his father, befuddled, thorn and liquor roiling in his brain, and remembered suddenly a time long ago when he'd been fighting with Jinsie—children, they'd been, ten or twelve years old—and his father had told him that any man who hits a woman was no man at all.

"Y–you don't understand," he mumbled. "The card. She—" Fury welled up in him again, a flood tide of it, acid burning his blood. "She took the card! She *took* it!" And he wrenched away from his father and towards the bed, where his wife screamed and flinched. "Bitch! Whore! You took that card!"

"That's enough, little brother," said a new voice behind him—Jezael, wrapping both arms around Mieka as he'd done to tease him all their lives. Mieka struggled, kicking and shouting, as Jez simply picked him up with his arms pinned to his sides and carried him out of the room. All at once he couldn't breathe. Gasping, light-headed, vision darkening around the edges, he tried to keep fighting but felt his limbs lose their strength.

He woke on a hallway floor.

"No, don't try to sit up just yet," said his father. "Drink this."

Anticipating alcohol, he swigged water and choked. He glared up at his father, feeling betrayed. He was helped into a chair. Jez had vanished, and so had Jinsie with the baby, but Mieka heard his mother's murmuring, soothing voice down the hall. Everything being taken care of, just like always; everything would be all right.

Not by bloody half, it wouldn't.

"You said something about a card."

His father always could read him like the headline of a broadsheet.

"Is this what you meant?"

"The Finchery," he blurted. "It was—"

No, it wasn't.

FINICKING
Elegant Apparel for Ladies of Style
657 Kirtlers Lane

"I'll admit," his father said quietly, crouching beside the chair, "it does look rather like 'Finchery' if one takes but a passing glance."

He held the card, examined it. Smooth and white, printed in deep blue ink. *Finicking.*

"From what she tells your mother, a man admired her gown and was hoping she would visit his shop. She took the card just to—"

"—to be rid of him," Mieka whispered. "She told me. I didn't listen." He frowned at his father. "But—it *looks* like 'Finchery,' don't it? And everybody knows what that place is."

"Do you think that justifies what just happened?"

"I'm sorry! But I saw the card and I just—I couldn't—I was so *angry*—" He gulped. "Fa, I'm sorry."

"Mieka. I'm not the one who needs an apology."

"I can't go back in there—I can't face her—"

"You can, and you will. Right now."

"Fa," he moaned, "I'll say I'm sorry, I really will—I just can't do it now, I'll do it tomorrow—"

"No. Tonight." Hadden stood. "No son of mine will do what you did and not make amends as soon as may be. I won't have it."

Mieka nodded, and pushed himself out of the chair. No charming himself out of this one. No laughter, no jokes, no taking his usual role of family clown.

But she'd been lying to him; he'd heard it in her voice. She'd lied about how she got the card.

The card that said *Finicking,* not *Finchery.*

He didn't know which part of it she'd lied about. He couldn't ask. He didn't want to know.

His mother had left the bedchamber. His father paid him the undeserved compliment of not waiting to make sure he apologized. Mieka heard the door close with a little creak of ancient hinges and dragged his gaze up from the floor. She curled on the bed, her beautiful eyes bloodshot and drowning, the left corner of her mouth swollen. One slender bare foot and ankle peeked out from beneath her hem. So fine and fragile, so exquisite, so thoroughly his—but she had lied to him. He no longer knew whether he'd slapped her because of the card or because of the lie.

"I'm—I'm so sorry," he whispered. "Please—forgive me, I'll never do it again, I swear—"

She flinched at the sound of his voice. He had sense enough not to approach her, even though he was sure that if only he could hold her and kiss her and make love to her, everything would be all right again.

"I swear," he repeated. "By all the Old Gods, I swear I'll never—"

"You hit me," she breathed.

"I know, I know, I'm sorry—I love you so much—it will never happen again, I promise—I'll do anything, *anything,* if only you forgive me—"

Her soft lips trembled, and after a long hesitation she nodded. And began to cry again, very quietly.

He couldn't stand it. He took a few steps towards her, intending to comfort and promise—and she cowered back. He couldn't stand that, either. He turned and fled the room, slamming the door behind him, and didn't stop until he was in his tower lair.

Hunched in a corner amidst threadbare old carpets and pillows leaking feathers, he remembered that the thorn-roll in his bedchamber wasn't his only supply. He supposed it was awkward, preparing the mixture with spit instead of water, and having no brandy or whiskey to cleanse the glass thorn before or afterwards. He didn't much care about any of that. All he really wanted was to sleep, and dream pretty dreams, and have his hand stop hurting, and forget this awful night had ever happened.

* * *

TWO OF HIS wishes were not granted. He slept, but didn't dream, and when he woke midmorning his hand no longer hurt from too-close proximity to his own magic, but he still remembered everything.

By now he was hungry. He couldn't go downstairs; he couldn't face his wife or his parents or his brothers and sisters or anybody. He just couldn't. He wanted to stay right here where nobody could find him and confront him with eyes that were angry or disappointed or hurt or frightened. So he fixed up another thorn and curled into a corner and slept again.

This time he did dream, and it was both comforting and terrible. He dreamed that Cade had found him—Cade, who alone knew about this aerie because he was the only one Mieka had ever shown it to—and was seated beside him with long legs folded, waiting for him to wake up. He was so glad Quill was here. His presence meant that Mieka was safe from everything and everyone. It had always been like that with them: Mieka never felt scared and Cade never had bad dreams. But the last person in the world he wanted to see was Cade Silversun, because he knew he would have to admit to what he'd done, and that would be worse than the look in his father's eyes last night, worse even than seeing her cringe away from him.

But maybe he didn't have to tell. Maybe he could keep it secret.

No. Not from Cade.

And Cade had seen much worse things about Mieka in the Elsewhens, hadn't he?

"I know you're awake."

No dream at all, of course.

"I can hear you thinking up excuses."

Oh dear Gods—did Cade already know?

"You missed rehearsal. Nobody here knows where you went—they all think you crept out of the house sometime early this morning. They thought you were with us. Your father is confused, your mother is worried, and your wife took the baby and went back to Hilldrop at noon." Cade stretched out his legs and sighed. "Nobody, not even Jinsie, will tell me what happened."

Famished—it had been a whole day since he'd had anything to eat—he sat up and wasn't at all surprised when his brain spun round a few times inside his skull.

"But I suppose it can wait until you're fed and watered. No beer," he warned. "Not on an empty stomach. We've a show tonight."

He scrubbed his fingers back through his hair and groaned.

Cade wore a tiny smile. "You *are* Mieka Windthistle, right? It's just that I've never heard you go so long without saying anything unless you're sleeping or passed out."

"Fuck off."

"That's more like it. Come on. Food and a wash, and a hire-hack to the Keymarker, and no bluethorn so don't even think about it."

Somehow Cade managed it so that he didn't have to see anybody. The climb out of his little tower lair; the walk to his bedchamber where all the evidence had been tidied up as if nothing had ever happened, though the blue counterpane was missing; a quick soap-and-rinse in the garderobe down the hall while Cade went for something to eat—within the hour he was clean, fed, and clothed, and all without having seen a single person except Cade. Incredible, in crowded Wistly Hall. As he crunched into an apple on their way downstairs, Mieka reflected that it would be a nice life, this. With the addition of liquor, it would be just about perfect. Food and drink, peace and quiet, Cade to talk with, nobody to perform for except their audiences. Well, except to be clever and mad every so often, for Cade's sake.

That night at the Keymarker wasn't their best show, but it wasn't their worst, either. Megs was not present. They did "Dragon" and "Dwarmy Day" and stayed for just one drink before Cade hauled him into a hire-hack.

"Redpebble Square," Cade told the driver. Then, to Mieka: "You're staying at my house tonight. I told your mother before we left."

He discovered in himself a sharp loathing for Cayden when he was being helpful and understanding. He didn't want to be helped or understood. He wanted a good bottle of whiskey and another night alone in his aerie with his thorn-roll. Performing onstage hadn't done for him what it usually did. There was little of the release, the relief of emotions spent, the fulfillment of knowing they'd done well.

"Had a fight, did you?"

Mieka turned his face to the window and said nothing.

"The Prince was angrier, and the Dragon was horrider," Cade went on. "So *you* must be feeling angry and horrid, and put that together with her going back to Hilldrop and you hiding in your tower all day—"

"We had a fight," he conceded.

The horse clopped on.

In a completely different voice, Cade asked, "You hit her, didn't you?"

Mieka's head turned so quickly that he was certain sure he heard his neck bones crack. But it was dark in the hack, and he couldn't see Cade's face.

"More than once?"

"No."

"Did she hit back?"

"No. But I think she wanted to."

"I don't blame her."

After another half mile or so, he heard himself whisper, "I slapped her—just the once, I swear—and I threw things and—and I broke a glass. With magic. I had it in my hand and I broke it."

"I wondered why you were a little wary tonight,

reaching for the withies. Actually, I'm surprised you still have the hand."

"Quill—I don't know what scared me worst. And that makes me a complete shit, doesn't it?"

"Yeh. It does."

Mieka sagged back into the worn leather seat. "Can we go right up to your room? Please? I don't think I can face Mistress Mirdley."

"She doesn't know. Nobody knows."

"She'll know there's something to be known, and I couldn't stand that."

The hack rolled to a stop. Cade got out, paid the driver, and preceded Mieka through the front door. The tall, narrow house was silent, all the way to the fifth floor. No sounds from the kitchen; none from Lady Jaspiela's chamber, nor Dery's. Just their footsteps on the wrought-iron stairs, just the hush of their breathing.

Cade lit a candle and closed his bedchamber door. He pointed Mieka to the overstuffed chair in the corner: a new acquisition, covered in nubby black wool, big enough to curl up in comfortably without cramping Cade's long limbs. Mieka hoped that Bompstable didn't sneak up here often for a nap; that white fur would be impossible to clean off the black upholstery. It must have been awful getting the thing upstairs, though possibly Cade had found somebody with a Hoisting spell to help. (Mieka supposedly knew one, but he'd never been much good at it—witness the Wintering Night when he'd tried to relocate just the blankets but instead moved the whole mattress.) Cade must be starting to gather things for the move to his own flat. Mieka had heard nothing about where.

"Sit down and start talking."

"I need a drink."

"Probably so. But not right now."

Mieka felt small and insignificant in the big chair. He folded his legs to one side and leaned on the padded arm and stared at his hands. "I found a card that I thought was from the Finchery, and I started yelling and throwing things. Fa came in, and Jez, and Jinsie took care of the baby. After I settled down, I told her I was sorry. I went to the tower and that's where you found me." He looked up, knowing better than to use The Eyes but needing to know if Cade was as disgusted as he feared. "Can I have a drink now?"

"No. You left out the part where you shattered the glass with magic."

"I shattered a glass with magic," he echoed dutifully.

"And the part where you hit her."

"I hit her."

Cade sat on the bed and propped his elbows on his knees.

After a long silence, Mieka burst out, "Why aren't you shouting at me? I'd be shouting at me right now."

A wry smile twisted his lips. "You've been shouting at yourself all day. And especially during the show tonight."

"I've been trying not to hear," he admitted. "But I don't understand why you're not—I mean, what I did, it was horrible—"

"Yeh, it was."

And then he knew he'd been right. "But you've seen me do worse. In an Elsewhen."

Cade nodded slowly. "Much worse."

"Why didn't you ever tell me?" he cried.

"Would you have believed me?"

Mieka wanted to fling back a *Yes!* He knew it would be a lie. He would not have believed Cade. He would have said that he did, just to shut Cade up. But he would not have believed.

It wasn't in Mieka's power to shock Cade with what he'd done. He'd seen Mieka do much worse. Cade was sickened and disappointed, but he'd been waiting for something like this. Mayhap he'd been waiting for years.

"And you *expect* the worst of me, don't you?" he challenged, sudden anger clenching his fists. "Whatever you saw—no warning, not a fucking word! You could change it—isn't that how it works? You only see things you have the power to change—"

Temper flared black in Cade's eyes. "What do *my* choices have to do with *your* marriage? If you can figure that out, you're a whole lot smarter than I am—and we both know you're not!"

"You're going to let it happen—you *want* it to happen because you hate what I have with her, you're envious, you can't stand it that we're happy!"

Cade met his gaze steadily, coldly. "Are you?"

Mieka pushed himself out of the chair. Before he could take more than two steps across the room, Cade added, "Planning on hitting *me*, now?"

He wanted nothing more in the world. Instead, he swung round and slammed the door behind him and ran down to the kitchen, where he knew he'd find the next morning's breakfast ale in a jug on a shelf.

He couldn't drink it. He couldn't even pick it up.

There was money in his pockets, his winnings from the races. He could find a hire-hack and go—where? Not to Wistly. He didn't want to see any of his family. Not Hilldrop Crescent. Gods, no. The Threadchaser bakery? Rafe would carve him into very small pieces with a very dull knife if he upset Crisiant by showing up at this hour.

Jeska was undoubtedly entertaining a lady friend—or, considering the effect Kazie had had on him, lying alone in his bed moping.

An inn where they didn't know him, where he could sit in the taproom half the night and drink himself forgetful and then somebody would haul him up to bed—if they didn't simply rob him of what was in his pockets as he slumped-inert over a table and then chuck him onto the street with the rest of the rubbish.

He sat beside the banked fire, listening as the mantel clock chimed one, and then two. At last he stumbled to his feet and climbed back up the stairs. Cade was in bed, asleep or pretending to be. Mieka was too tired to be more than remotely angry to find that a blanket had been spread on the shabby old couch. Cade had expected him to return. He knew as well as Mieka did that Mieka had nowhere else to go.

Seventeen

EARLY-RISING TREGETOURS were an abomination. Cade Silversun in a *Let's get going!* mood was an offense against nature, common decency, and especially his long-suffering glisker. It didn't happen often, this revoltingly cheery morning frame of mind, which was probably why he was still amongst the living. Cade with a purposeful glint in his gray eyes meant places to go or people to see, sometimes both, and Mieka knew the look well enough to know he had no chance of rolling over and going back to sleep. His last desperate gambit on such occasions was to suggest that Cade was looking a bit grubby and needed a shave. That usually got him at least another half hour or so while the water was heated and the straight razor stropped, lather was applied and whiskers were scraped off.

But today Cade only shook his head. "Nobody will mind, where we're going." He smiled slightly, adding, "And besides, you know it never matters what I look like, when I'm going someplace with you. Nobody ever even notices I'm there."

Mieka had always thought this attitude was just plain silly. During the last year or so, Cade had started to grow into his face. He would never be conventionally handsome, and there was that nose to consider, but he seemed to think he was the ugliest thing ever birthed with the possible exception of the average new-hatched wyvern. And he truly had no idea how beautiful his eyes were. It was rather akin to the way he didn't realize how brilliant he was. Sometimes Mieka was amused, and sometimes frustrated, by Cade's ongoing bewilderment at being in possession of a really remarkable brain. At his age, one would think he'd have got used to it by now, or at least accepted that it did in fact exist and it was indeed his.

All that aside, Mieka was grateful that Cade was speaking to him. They'd said some rotten things to each other last night and he knew they'd been on the verge of the unforgivable. Yet here Cade was, sunny and teasing. It was almost enough for Mieka to absolve him of getting up so bloody early in the morning.

"So where *are* we going?" Mieka asked.

The only answer was a shrug. Mieka was handed clothes and a towel, and told to hurry up because the kettle was already on the boil downstairs in the kitchen. After a quick wash—no shave, because although his beard was very thick for an Elf, it grew very slowly—he trudged downstairs to find that a gulped cup of tea was all he would get for breakfast, for the hire-hack had arrived.

"Where are we going?" he demanded again as Cade waved farewell to Mistress Mirdley and hustled Mieka out the front door.

"Someplace you've never even heard of. But we'll make a stop along the way."

"Food?" Mieka asked hopefully.

Cade chuckled. "Food."

But not for Mieka.

Long ago there'd been only one huge market in Gallantrybanks, but as the city grew, people began to complain about having to slog across town and back just for a few days' provisions. The problems of housewives and servants made no impression, of course, on anyone with the influence or the money to change this state of things. One evening, however, a middle-aged lord was presented with a dinner that consisted of nothing that had not been salted, potted, pickled, dried, or otherwise preserved, because by the time his cook and her kitchen maid had fought through the ever-increasing traffic to the market, everything fresh had already been sold. That this outrage occurred in late summer, when everything from lamb to lettuce ought to have appeared nightly on his table, offended His Lordship. What absolutely infuriated him was that he was not dining alone, and whereas housewives and other people's servants mattered to him not at all, to offer such a meal to his friends was insupportable. When told the nature of the difficulty, he ruminated for a few days, and then bought and razed an entire block of Gallantrybanks within easy walking distance of his mansion and set up an indoor market. His Lordship was in most other respects something of a moron, but he did know good food, and its lack on his table motivated him to exert himself for the first and only time in his life. He made a fortune and was never heard from again. His grandson, however, built a second, third, and fourth establishment, his great-grandsons a fifth and sixth and seventh, and every spring for the last 143 years, the old man's Namingday was celebrated with a minor parade through the stalls and free ale at lunching.

Mieka knew all this because of the annual excursion (*not* on the free-ale days) offered by the littleschool near Wistly that he and all his siblings attended. The children toured the stalls, were told where various fruits and vegetables and meats came from, and given free samples, and whereas Mieka had found all this most enjoyable at the age of seven, the next year he had matured enough to look on the outing as a lovely opportunity for some truly creative mischief. That year, Jez had been chosen to give the speech to the market guildmaster who always welcomed the children, and Mieka had been forced to listen to his brother practice it about a half million times. (Jez didn't mention it in his speech, but that the cook had deliberately chosen to serve no fresh foods on a night when guests were present was something Mieka took for granted; no fool, she. It was also his opinion that His Lordship had been mostly a moron, along with everyone else in the olden days, for it had taken them such a very long time to come up with the idea of multiple markets.) Mieka's antics on the day of his brother's speech had been comparatively tame compared to what he got up to in subsequent years. He always behaved himself perfectly at school during the week prior to the outing. He always spent the following week in disgrace and confined to his room at home, but this was a small price to pay.

When one of these markets turned out to be the stop Cade had mentioned, Mieka was delighted. But if he had thought they would be selecting their breakfast fresh off the carts, he was mistaken. Cade took him right past vendors of teas and mocahs, fruit pastries and buttered muffins, while Mieka entertained him with the tale of what he'd done on the school visit when he was ten.

"—great huge sacks of dried peas, like hailstones— Cade, don't those muffins look wonderful? Couldn't we—?"

"Maybe later. Come on."

"But I'm hungry!"

"What did you do with the peas after you stole them?"

"How did you know?" He grinned. "It was only a couple handfuls—handsful?"

"Handfuls."

"Oh. Anyways, there was a teacher everybody hated—a real snarge. Every day at *exactly* four he left his assistant in charge and went downstairs before everybody else to be first in line for the best cakes at teachers' tea."

Cade sidestepped a harried-looking matron with a huge shopping basket in one arm and a screaming infant in the other. "How far did he fall?"

"Only half a flight, bouncing on his great big bum. Not much of an audience for it, either. Just me, behind a pillar. But we were free of him for a whole fortnight!"

"Aggravating little smatchet, weren't you? I take it you didn't get caught."

Mieka laughed for what felt like the first time in weeks. "Me? Never!"

Cade murmured, "But then you grew up." He swerved towards a booth piled with sacks of flour. "Find us a handcart, there's a good lad. Good morrow to you, Mistress Tola!" he greeted the Trollwife behind the counter. "I'll be needing twenty pounds of your best."

"Quite a while since last I saw you, Cayden. Out gallivanting, I wager." She dusted down her apron and clasped one of his hands in both of hers. "How's Mirdley doing these days?"

"As charming and winsome as ever, beholden to you."

She snorted. "That's not saying much. Fifty pounds, you said?"

"Thirty."

"Oh, I thought I heard you say sixty."

"No, forty ought to do very nicely."

"We'll make it fifty, then, shall we?"

"I think that's fair." They clasped hands on it and Cade turned to Mieka. "Weren't you looking for a handcart?"

Mieka had never heard an odder haggle, but it seemed this was an old joke with them. Mistress Tola was eyeing him sidelong as she effortlessly hoisted ten-pound sacks of flour onto the counter.

"So that's your Elf?"

"That's him."

Mieka waited to be introduced.

"Mieka, go find a handcart."

He went to find a handcart.

When he returned, lighter by a couple of pence to hire it for an hour, he helped with the loading. Somehow in the interim, fifty pounds had become one hundred. He counted, then again: ten ten-pound sacks. But neither Cade nor Mistress Tola said anything about it, so neither did Mieka.

It took a little less than an hour for Cade to finish his shopping. In addition to the flour, other staples joined the haul: salt, porridge oats, loaves of sugar from the Islands. There were spices, too, and huge bags of tea, and boxes of sweets. At last Mieka helped roll the handcart back outside to the street, where Cade waved down another hire-hack and everything was loaded into it.

"*Now* do I get some breakfast?" Mieka asked.

"Worked for it, I s'pose. Here." He delved into a pocket for two slightly crushed muffins. Another pocket yielded a bottle of apple cider—the uninteresting kind, Mieka was unhappy to note when he pulled the stopper and took a swig. "All for you, glunsh," he mocked gently.

Mieka was too busy devouring the muffins to hear the address Cade gave the driver. A few minutes later he was feeling quite his old self and thinking that mayhap he wasn't such a horrible person after all. He'd seen Cade cut people dead with a single glance. But Cade was still speaking to him, even teasing him and including him on whatever mysterious errand this was. So he couldn't be so terribly awful, could he? Not if Cade was still his friend.

Anyways, plenty of men disciplined their wives—and their children, he reminded himself with a reminiscent wince for the swats on his bum he had to admit he'd earned. It wasn't as if he beat his wife on a nightly basis. He'd never hit her before, and never would again. He'd promised.

And it wasn't as if he didn't give her everything she could possibly want. A lovely house, a child, blue tassels for the curtains, even her mother living with them. She had money and a home and beautiful clothes and now she was even acquainted with Royalty. So he'd given her a slap—what of it? He'd been provoked. He'd been drunk. He'd made a mistake about the card but not about the way she was lying to him.

Gods, what a tangle.

He was about to say as much to Cade when the hirehack came to a stop. Eating and thinking had taken more time than he thought it had. When they emerged into a sluggish drizzling rain, Mieka saw with astonishment that this was the worst section of Gallantrybanks: clamorous manufactories and tenement blocks for the men who worked in them, men who used to be their audiences in the seedy taverns they used to play. Touchstone had got too grand and important and posh and expensive for these men nowadays. Somehow, this realization made Mieka feel a whole new sort of guilty.

Cade told him to stay with the hack. He went to knock on a wooden door that needed fresh paint set into a two-story brick building that needed fresh mortar and seemed to have been constructed entirely of clinkers fired in a kiln too long. Rain glistened on the blackened bits, shiny as glass. To either side were derelict manufactories, the signs on them so old that the words could no longer be read.

Within a few minutes a youngish man came out with a wheelbarrow, his powerful muscles and rolling gait proclaiming a goodly mix of Troll in his background. The transfer of goods began. It took four trips to get everything inside and stacked in a tiny vestibule. Mieka shook the rain from his hair and looked around the dim interior. A desk bare of everything but a pitcher and four wooden cups; two closed doors to the left; a short, narrow hall leading to a locked and bolted door; and a small, badly painted sign on the brick wall between two unlit lamps. GINNEL HOUSE.

He looked to Cade for an explanation. A ginnel was a passage between buildings, and Gallantrybanks was riddled with them. But how could a ginnel be *inside* a building? The implication was—what? He didn't have the sort of mind Cade did, able to play about with words and make peculiar connections.

The locked door opened from the inside, and a small, dainty woman came out, seemingly in danger of being bowled over on a wave of children's noises behind her: giggling, crying, yelling, singing. She shut the door behind her and touched her palm to a brick in the wall beside it, and suddenly Mieka knew that the steel lock was just for show. Whatever was behind that door was protected by magic.

"Master Silversun!" the woman exclaimed, holding out both hands. "You're welcome for just yourself, but look what you've brought with you!"

"Trying to make up for being gone all these months," Cade said, bending gallantly over her wrists. Each was circled by a thin, beautifully worked silver filigree bracelet; she was married, and to a man with taste,

Mieka decided. She could have been any age from thirty to fifty, her dark face unlined but for a few strokes at the corners of her deep brown eyes. "This is my friend, Mieka Windthistle."

"Ah, the glisker!"

Mieka received both hands as well, and noticed as he bowed over them that although her fingernails were scrupulously clean, they were cracked and ragged with hard work. "Delighted," he told her, stepping back.

"And puzzled, yes?" She smiled. Turning to Cade, she went on, "The tour, but it must be quick. There's a wagon due in about an hour."

"Of course. We don't want to trouble you."

She opened the magical lock, and the noise washed over them as they went through into a passage lighted by lamps at regular intervals. There were a dozen or so doors down its length—rather like Cade's "Doorways" play. But unlike onstage, where the doors opened onto various scenes, here the the scenes were painted on the walls between doors. Green hillsides with cows and sheep, houses with bursting rosebushes, fanciful trees bearing fruit in all the colors of the rainbow, a farm with goats and dogs and cats and a dragon, white-sailed ships on a brilliant blue ocean with a mountainous island in the distance. They weren't professional paintings, and none of them were magical—no movement, no changing colors—in fact, Mieka realized, they looked as if painted by children. Several of the doors stood partly open, and in each there were cots and a chair, a few toys, small stacks of neatly folded clothing. The brick walls within had been painted soft green or pale yellow, with counterpanes that sometimes matched.

The last door on the left opened into a playroom, whence the noise. Dolls and balls and a small menagerie of stuffed animals, tables and chairs, and children ranging in age from toddlers to ten-year-olds causing all sorts of happy racket. There were three middle-aged women in the room, but nobody would have said they were in charge; instead, they seemed to be guardians of chaos, not calm, and perfectly happy to have it so.

The door on the right led into a refectory. There was a mural all along one wall, of animals both real and imaginary. At the back was a wide window into the kitchen. Three of the seven circular tables crammed into the space were occupied. Mieka was trying to figure out how to ask Cade exactly what this place was and why they were here when he realized that not only were all the other people in the room women and children, but at the sight of him and Cade, all of them froze silent and stared.

He was used to being looked at. But not like this. Not with hunted eyes in faces bearing new bruises and old scars. Not by women—and some of the children— who had bandages on their jaws or their arms in slings or who limped as they rose from their chairs and backed slowly up against a wall. Staring at him.

"They're having a bite to eat before the wagon arrives," said their guide. "It's a long ride, where they're going. The others are back in their rooms, the ones who still need a few more days to heal before they go to their families or friends, or sometimes—like today—far from Gallantrybanks."

"With different names," Cade murmured.

"Oh, yes. It makes things impossible for them and their children legally, but their decision—and I agree with them—is that although they're not free to marry again, not under their own names, at least they're safe." She tucked a wayward strand of dark curling hair behind her ear. "We'll let them finish, shall we?" she asked softly, and they left the room. Out in the hall, as they walked she went on, "If you'll excuse me now, there are still some arrangements to make. They don't have much to pack, of course, but we did get two lovely big barrels of clothes last week from a friend." Her smile was a marvel as she looked up at Cade. "Someone you recommended, and much beholden to you for it, Master Silversun."

"A word here, a word there." Cade shrugged. "I wish I could do more without compromising your precautions."

"We have good friends, and they have friends who have other friends, and on the whole we do very well. A pleasure to meet you, Master Windthistle." With another smile, she opened the main door for them.

Mieka dug into his pockets. He still had his winnings from the races. All of it went into her hands. Then he undid his golden topaz earring and gave her that, too. As he gave it to her, he saw the glint of the silver bracelet on his own wrist, and his fingers twitched towards its clasp. But it wasn't just jewelry, it was his wedding jewelry, sealed with magic. All at once he knew that whenever he looked at it from now on, he'd be reminded of this place, and what he'd done.

The money and the earring went into the woman's skirt pockets, and she touched his arm gently, and then Cade was guiding him through the door.

It was raining harder now. He turned his face up to the sky and tried to remember other times when it had felt so clean to do this. Cade would scorn the image as trite, he knew. But while he was neither as smart nor as creative as Cade, he had brains enough to know why he had been brought here. He got into the hire-hack and hoped the rain would excuse the moisture on his face.

Cade told the driver, "Just take us anywhere, it doesn't matter. I'll tell you when to stop." He got in and gave

Mieka a handkerchief and sat silently in his corner of the hack.

Mieka struggled for a few moments, then curled up and hid his face and wept.

After a long while Cade spoke again. "The man who helped us unload the provisions, he's some sort of distant relation of Mistress Mirdley's. So is Mistress Tola—the lady who sold us the flour at half price. I don't know the name of the woman who runs Ginnel House. They tend towards privacy, as you can imagine."

Mieka had recovered himself by now. But he still couldn't look at Cade.

"Mistress Mirdley started helping them when they set the place up, about three or four years ago. I didn't even know about it until this year, when she asked me to take some money by on my way to the Kiral Kellari one night. And I didn't really know what Ginnel House was until a bit before we played at the wedding celebrations last spring. I've never asked how many women and children they help. From what we saw today, I'd guess it's a lot. More than anybody wants to admit. There are probably other places like it, safe places, in Gallantrybanks, but I don't know anything about those, either. It's not necessary for me to know. That's what Mistress Mirdley told me, and she's right. The only people who really truly *need* to know about it are the women who haven't anywhere else to go."

"You've been waiting for this, haven't you? Ready for it. Elsewhen."

"Yes. When I found out what the place was, I knew I'd be taking you there sooner or later."

He repeated his question of last night. "Why didn't you ever say anything? Why didn't you warn me?"

"Because even if you believed me, it's something you had to learn for yourself." Leaning forward, he opened the little grilled hatch beneath the driver's bench and called through it, "Number Eight, Redpebble Square, please." He sat back again, and they were both silent for a long time.

Then Cade said, "The other evening, back home after the races, Dery's legs were hurting. He's growing so fast." He paused for a fond smile. "I remember being that age, and my leg bones outgrowing the muscles and tendons. It hurt like twelve kinds of Hell. Mistress Mirdley and I rubbed liniment into his legs, poor little bantling, and she gave him something for the pain. We kept watch until he fell asleep, and then she said, 'That's the way of it with everything in life. When it hurts, you know you're growing.'"

Mieka scrunched farther into his corner. "I notice she did give him something for the pain."

Cade shrugged. "That's the kindly thing to do."

He knew where Cade was headed with this. He resented it. "I'll take the thorn over the hurting, beholden all the same."

"Most people would."

"Not you," Mieka accused. "The sort of anguishing you do over every damned little thing—it's not normal."

"*I'm* not normal—hadn't you figured that out by now?"

He heard the bitterness and, Gods help him, relished it.

"We learn only from the mistakes we make and the pain we endure," Cade said quietly.

Mieka said nothing. What he was thinking was, *So nobody ever learns anything from being happy? You're wrong, Cade. Gods, you are so wrong! And one of these days I'll prove it to you.*

The hack drew to a stop at Redpebble Square and they got out. Cade went into the kitchen for something to eat; Mieka went upstairs to sleep. He hadn't got much last night—this morning, really—and he suspected that anything he ate would come right back up again.

But of course he couldn't sleep. He kept seeing those women staring at him. He kept seeing her eyes with that look in them. He supposed all this meant he was growing, because—Gods, how it hurt.

At three by the Minster bells, Cayden appeared upstairs with a lavish tea: three sorts of muffins, baked eggs in little pastry shells with bits of ham and cheese, fried flatbread dripping in butter and jam, a bowl heaped with berries dusted with sugar, and a plate of sliced pears. Mieka discovered that he was ravenous and the instant Cade set the tray on his desk, he leaped on the food.

"Mistress Mirdley says not to be impressed," Cade told him. "This is what she made for our breakfast, if only we'd had the decency and manners to come downstairs early enough to eat without rushing off, so it's all reheated and stale and if it tastes awful, it's our own silly fault."

It was all delicious. A little while later, replete and sipping his fourth cup of tea, he nestled into Cade's new chair and sighed. All he lacked was a nice glass of whiskey, and he'd be perfectly happy.

Not that he deserved to be.

Cade had been alert to the change in his mood. "So can we really talk about it now?"

"Want to hear every sordid detail, do you? Or—wait, I know. After what you made me look at this morning, you want me to relive all of it and make all the right connections so it *hurts* again and the lesson sinks in." He met those gray eyes with a parody of a smile stretching his lips. "Fuck you."

"You said there was a card."

Relentless. Wasn't that what he'd thought once—more than once—about Cade? Ruthless and relentless and inexorable when it came to the truth. Of course Cade wanted all the details; that was how his mind worked. Pull apart each tiny little piece of whatever it was, even if it was Cade's own soul, for examination and interpretation, and only then could it all be put back together and understood. This was probably what made him a great writer. It was certainly what made him an annoyance.

"From the Finchery," Mieka heard himself say, giving in with poor grace to the inevitable.

"Tell me about it."

"What's there to tell? It was a business card."

Cade sighed. "What kind of paper? Typeface? Color of ink?"

"Just the usual paper—stiff but not rigid. Blue ink. I don't know anything about typefaces."

"Was it like the one I found in my father's old coat that time?"

"Yeh, of course."

"Are you sure?"

Mieka's patience, never very extensive, ran out. "It was a card, all right? I saw it on the bed and picked it up and unfolded it and I thought it said 'Finchery' but it really said 'Finicking' and who the fuck cares what kind of card it was?"

"You say it was folded? Was it a recent fold? Had it frayed? What about the edges? Were they sharp or dog-eared?"

"I don't remember."

Cade gave him a look that said, *Of course you do, you twit!* But what he said next was, "What did it smell like?"

"Smell? How should I know? Am I a hound on the hunting field, belling when I pick up the scent? I didn't go to your posh Academy and learn how to remember every stupid little—"

"Just close those incredibly unobservant eyes of yours and think about the card. You unfold it, you read it. What does it smell like?"

He did as told, shifting uncomfortably in the chair. "Her perfume. It smelled like her perfume."

"Violets or roses?" When Mieka opened his eyes and gaped at him, Cade gave an irritable shrug. "Like you said—I'm trained to remember things. She uses two different kinds of perfume. Which one was it?"

"Roses." He paused again. "I think. It's hard to tell. She was sitting near me on the bed and she—she—" *She was lying to me. I know she was lying to me—but about what?*

Into the sudden silence Cade said, "She was wearing the violets perfume that day. I remember it. She had a little vial of it in her purse and she took it out to daub some on her wrists. The Princess said how pretty it smelled. And it was in one of Blye's glass vials, so they talked a bit about that, too."

"So?"

"So it was violets that day," Cade said stubbornly. "But the card smelled of roses—"

"But how does that *mean* anything?" he exclaimed. "Violets or roses or cow shit, what does it matter? I saw the card and I thought it said 'Finchery' but it didn't, when Fa showed it to me it said 'Finicking' and what does it matter?"

With infuriating patience, Cade explained, "If she'd had the card longer than just that day, and kept it in another bag, then it would pick up the scent—Mieka? What is it?"

"You're on the wrong page with this," he said dully. "It's the card, yeh, but nothin' to do with the smell."

"How do you mean?" Wary, astonished and trying not to show it—it wasn't often he had the pleasure of outthinking Cade Silversun. It was no pleasure now.

"It wasn't folded. The card Fa gave me. It said 'Finicking' but it wasn't folded. The other one, the first one . . ." Mieka set his teacup carefully on the floor, knowing he was in danger of dropping it. "Quill, that first one really *was* a card from the Finchery."

A long, slow exhale. "I swear there wasn't an Elsewhen about this, Mieka. I just—I had a feeling—something not quite right—"

"She had a card from the Finchery. Why would she have it?"

"You can't seriously believe she'd—Mieka, it's a *whorehouse*."

"Why would she do such a thing? Why did she lie to me? I heard it in her voice, when she was saying about the card—and then it was a different card Fa showed me—why would she want to trick me like that?"

Slowly, reluctantly: "You're not exactly shy around girls when we're on the Circuit."

What a tactful way of putting it.

"This might be her method of showing you how it feels."

How a card from a whorehouse compared with a casual dalliance far away from her did not make sense to him.

"And . . . and you did slap her, Mieka. It doesn't matter that you were thorned-up. You hit her."

I was thorned-up, and drunk, and provoked, and—and—oh Gods, I hit her.

"Never again," he vowed. "No matter what she does or—or—" He stopped. "Is *that* what she wants? To hold this over me forever? Put a hand to her cheek and that'll remind me, and—"

"How should I know? She and her mother worked like all Hells to get you—" He broke off abruptly, as if fearing he might say too much.

Mieka surged out of the chair, furious. "Did you see that, too? And never told me? Gods fucking damn you, Cayden!"

"And again we get back to the real question," Cade snarled. "Would you have believed me? Given the choice between having her and what I might've told you, which one of us would you have believed?"

And that, Mieka suddenly understood, was why Cade hated her.

He didn't look round as he went to the door. "We've a show tonight," he said coldly. "I'll see you there, at the Keymarker—but don't expect me to talk to you. And don't you fucking dare talk to me."

The door didn't slam as loudly as he would have liked, but it would do.

Eighteen

No winter of Mieka's life had ever seemed to last as long as this one. There was work enough to keep him busy, shows at the Keymarker and the Kiral Kellari and Gallantrybanks' few small theaters and many private mansions; when he wasn't working, he was either at Wistly Hall with his family or at Hilldrop Crescent with his wife and daughter and mother-in-law, though these were more like visits than being in residence. More often than not, Touchstone had a week of performances in a row and it was impossible to go back to Hilldrop every night. So he stayed at Wistly, and life was just as it had always been before his marriage. But life at Hilldrop was just as it had always been, too.

There, he was husband and father and son-in-law, but only for a few days at a time. It took at least half a day to return to the rhythms of life in that house, and on the nights before he returned to Gallantrybanks, part of him had already left. He spent a lot of time with Yazz and Robel in their huge warm loft in the barn that combined bedchamber and sitting room and kitchen and, by spring of next year, a little sectioned-off space for their expected child. Sometimes, feeling nostalgic—which was ridiculous at the ripe old age of twenty—he even slept in Touchstone's wagon, with a bottle of Auntie Brishen's finest and a thorn-roll at his side.

At Wistly, he was son and brother and designated jester. In addition to his parents and siblings there were cousins, aunts, uncles, and complete strangers milling about the place, and no one ever knew who was going to show up or move out on any given day. His mother ran the house as best she could manage, while his father made lutes. The real changes were in his brothers and sisters. Jez had a new girlfriend (and seemed serious about her). Jinsie had become their mother's chief deputy around the house and was seeing five different young men (and professed to be bored with them all). Cilka was experimenting with encouraging small shrubs to grow into shapes Petrinka designed (both had been intrigued by Mieka's descriptions of what he'd seen on the Continent, and Grandsir Staindrop envisioned new and profitable ventures for his gardening enterprise; it wasn't just Derien Silversun who'd latched on to a possible career as a result of that trip). Nearly five years old now, Tavier and Jorie were attending the local little-school and bringing home friends who added to Wistly's anarchy. He didn't want to *be* a dragon anymore, just keep a few as pets, and she ignored everyone in favor of books, now that she had learned to read.

It seemed to Mieka sometimes that he had two distinct lives—three, if he counted the time rehearsing and on-stage with Touchstone. Occasionally these lives intersected. His mother and Jinsie would come to stay at Hilldrop, or he would bring his wife and the baby for a week at Wistly, and once in a while various Silversuns and Threadchasers and Jeska would come by for dinner. It was confusing at times, when he bothered to think about it. Mostly he lived as he had always done: moment to moment, on his instincts.

What made the winter so long was that there was no renewal of friendly relations with Cayden. The *don't talk to me* interlude lasted only a few days. Well, it would've been impossible to maintain it much longer. They worked together, after all. And it was easier to start speaking to each other again than to explain to Rafe and Jeska why they had stopped.

But the quiet talks, the late evening drinking, the sharing of interesting thorn, the laughter—Gods, how he missed laughing with Quill.

There was laughter enough in other places, but it wasn't the same. It was Mieka's nature to create merry mayhem wherever he went. He wondered sometimes if his restraint from even the mildest mischief at the races that day hadn't been his own sort of Elsewhen, a foreshadowing of misery-soon-to-come. He seemed to be lacking in ideas these days. That, too, was an odd reflection of Cade, who was having trouble with his latest creation. For all the busyness of that winter, things felt suspended, frozen in time, like they were all posing for an imaging that took forever to be finished.

Tavier and Jorie's Namingday provided a nice distraction—but only for one day. Mieka gave his littlest sister a pretty new dress that his wife had sewn. For Tavier there was a pair of silk-and-wire wings (their mother moaned softly at the sight until Mieka made Tavier promise on his hope of ever seeing a real dragon that he would never, ever, *ever* try to use them to fly). The boy seemed to get taller by the day, and once or twice suffered the same sort of pains Cade had described. Mieka rubbed liniment into his legs and assured him that the aches meant he would be as tall as Jed and Jez, not a runt like Mieka himself. But as he soothed his brother, he wondered how the pain of losing Quill's confidence and friendship could translate into growth.

There were means of easing that pain, of course, and Mieka availed himself liberally of them all. Thorn and liquor, and pretty girls after the shows, and going out with Rafe to various taverns, supposedly to have a look at new players but really to ask about unemployed fettlers. That last was a cover for their shared need to get drunk, for Crisiant had again miscarried. Mieka would have bet his own magic that Rafe would find no growth in that kind of pain.

Some of the groups weren't bad. Some were plain awful. They never did run across anybody who knew of a roving fettler. Mieka loved the attention and the flattery when he and Rafe were recognized. Kearney Fairwalk's placards served them well, for they were invariably greeted by name within minutes of walking in the door. They'd have a few drinks, watch the show, and afterwards invite the group to join them for a few more drinks. He loved, too, the respect verging on worship offered Touchstone. And when one or another of the lads made a joke about whether they were looking for a new fettler to replace Rafe, Mieka laughed uproariously and said yeh, but not like you're thinking, because me 'n' Rafe, we're lookin' to go out on our own with another masquer and tregetour but we're not likin' to leave Cade and Jeska stranded, right?

But they never did hear of a roving fettler, so Megs must have been wrong after all.

Cade got to hear about the imaginary breakup. One afternoon at the Kiral Kellari for rehearsal, he presented Rafe with a list of tregetours and masquers, saying that he and Mieka might find somebody to suit them better from amongst those names. Rafe glanced down the list, then handed it to Mieka and said, "All these men are dead."

Cade nodded amiably. "So they are."

The implication being that so would Rafe and Mieka be if they kept on telling that particular story.

It was necessary to rehearse at the Kiral Kellari, even though they knew the place very well, because the owner was in the process of turning it into a real theater and the alterations perforce altered the way magic here had to be done. Besides the structural differences, the huge painting on the side wall had changed. More to the point, its magic had changed. The old mural of the Mer King (who closely resembled Prince Ashgar) and the ladies of his court (who closely resembled some of his many mistresses) had been taken down. It was considered disrespectful, now that Prince Ashgar was married and everyone adored his Princess. But it had taken time to organize a new mural, for the proprietor of the Kiral Kellari had had some trouble finding commercial sponsors. Master Honeycoil the wine merchant, Franion's Finest Bottled Ale, and Bellchime Keggery had all been perfectly happy with the old one, saw no reason to finance anything different. It was Master Honeycoil's opinion that giving the Mer King more hair and a different chin would solve any problems of delicacy. The owner of the Kiral Kellari disagreed, and he was tired of the old mural anyhow. So he commissioned a new one.

Yet it kept undergoing alterations. He couldn't decide which court he wished to see. The basic theme of a royal wine cellar must be retained, for that was what *kiral kellari* meant, although in what language Mieka never did find out. The naked breasts had to stay—this establishment's customers were men, and men enjoyed looking at naked breasts—but nobody wanted to look at, for instance, half-naked Trolls except other Trolls. For himself, Mieka didn't much care what was decided on, as long as nothing about the cellar looked anything like that cellar they'd played three times at that mansion outside New Halt. He hadn't yet discussed it with Cade and Rafe and Jeska, but he was determined never to set foot in that building again, no matter how much money was offered.

Touchstone finished setting up—glass baskets, withies, lecterns—then took a look at the newest additions to the mural. For the last month or two a great burlap curtain was drawn across it after opening time; magic would have done as good a job at concealment, but that much magic would have interfered with performances. Nobody was working on the thing this afternoon, and Mieka could sense only a few new spells applied since their last engagement here. It was more Rafe's responsibility than his, anyway, figuring out how Touchstone's magic might bounce or slide.

The main mural was still of a cellar, but arched windows framed other scenes supposedly taking place outside. Lacking firm direction about what kind of court to show, the painter had concentrated on these images first.

Standing close enough to see but far enough away for some perspective, Mieka squinted at one of the window views. A road meandered between green fields under a cloudless sky. But in this placid rustic scene an emaciated little man in a bright red hat stood braced by the side of the road, carrying a sharp wooden scythe and looking furiously ready to use it. Confronting him was a Good Brother in traditional robes, hands folded piously, his very Human face pale but determined as his lips moved on the same words over and over again. The magic didn't include the sound of his voice, but Mieka could guess what was being said. Some quote from *The Consecrations*—for the little man was a Redcap, and the only method of thwarting a Redcap and escaping his sweeping scythe was to recite holy words. If a Redcap caught you without sacred texts to recite from memory, you were dead, for the red of his cap was dyed with blood. If it dried, he would die.

"Forever hunting fresh blood," Cade murmured at his side. "Charming, isn't it? Come look at this one over here."

Uncomplicated, this one. A Human girl slept beneath an apple tree in what ought to have been another pleasing little rural scene. But the fruit was falling from the branches as a hideous little creature in dark clothes and a tall hat laughed and spun something white and cobwebby in thick fingers, and let the resulting threads trickle down into the sleeping girl's ear. The magic hadn't yet been fully refined, so the fruit jerked about in all directions and the gossamer kept unraveling.

Mieka frowned. "What's that s'posed to be?"

"A Goblin."

"What?" No Goblin or part Goblin he'd ever encountered was as hideous as this creature. True, the teeth were yellow and crooked (easily remedied by a chirurgeon), and the single eyebrow across the forehead was a Goblin trait (even more easily remedied by a pair of tweezers). But there was a menace and a malice to the ugly face that made him want to draw back and shiver. "No," he protested. "Can't be."

"It's a Goblin." Cade pointed. "See how his laughter is making the fruit fall from the tree? And that little handweaving he's doing—those are nightmares he's sending into the girl's mind as she sleeps."

"But Goblins can't do that!"

"Legends say they can. Look over here."

A Piksey sat on a giant toadstool, hands wrapped round his knees. Dressed all in green, with an impudent pointed hat, he grinned a grin that crinkled the corners of his upslanting eyes as he watched a bewildered farmer try to coax a horse to the plow. The poor animal's head hung and his sides heaved and every line of him proclaimed total exhaustion—for of course the Piksey had been racing the horse across the fields all night long.

"But that's just stories," Mieka protested. "Makes a good playlet, and funny enough in the right hands"—he was thinking of one performed by the Shadowshapers, and another more traditional piece done by the Crystal Sparks—"but nobody actually believes that kind of thing. It's just silly. And those footprints leading to the toadstool, all gold and silver Piksey dust? That's naught but tales as well."

Making a show of looking at Mieka's feet, Cade said, "Are you sure? The boots hide it, I s'pose, but there've been times I could swear—"

"If you ever saw anything like that, you were pricking too much thorn. And I've enough Piksey in me to know!" He returned to the Goblin, shaking his head. "That's just—"

"Disgusting," Rafe said behind them. "There's a Harpy over in the other corner, playing cards with a Gorgon. Back turned, of course, but still—"

Mieka felt his hands clench into fists. "Can you imagine what this will be like when it's finished, and all the magic is working?"

"Finished is one thing this will never be," declared the establishment's owner, Master Warringheath. "An offense and a scandal, this is. I won't have it between my walls. I've sacked the painter and all his assistants."

Rafe clapped him on a shoulder. "Good man. I shouldn't care to do my drinking with a Gorgon nearby, even if her face is turned away."

He nodded emphatically. "Goblin nightmares, and fruit dropping from trees," he muttered. "My son's wife is a bit Goblin, and a sweeter, kinder, prettier girl never lived. Rafcadion, my friend, could you do something about the magic that's already been applied? Kill it off somehow?"

Rafe shook his head regretfully. "Not my specialty. Cade or Mieka could put something in its place, but why waste good magic on bad pictures?"

"I'm thinking you've the right of it there. Ah, well, the new painter comes tomorrow, and he can get rid of that muck."

It was at this same rehearsal that Cade began to hint at his most recent project. Not going well, was this new play, not at all, but he stuck at it and had a question for Mieka.

"Can you do thirsty?"

Mieka glanced up from the glass baskets, holding aloft his glass of beer. "Since I was fourteen, mate."

Cade pulled an annoyed grimace. "No, I meant can you make the *audience* thirsty?"

He felt like throwing the glass, but it would be a waste of good beer—and look what happened the last time he threw things. He flung words instead. "You think I'm some sort of backspanger hired by the management to waft a bit of dry-mouth round the tavern?"

Cade stared at him. "What are you talking about?"

Jeska enlightened him. "Never heard of that? Those of us Elves as has a bit of glisker magic, but too young or not good enough, tavern owners hire them—but not too often, mind, or it'd give the game away. Easier if you're kagged, of course," he mused. "Thuswise, nobody suspects *Elf* when all of a sudden they're perishin' for another drink." He shrugged. "Share of the takings for you, lad, back next week sometime for another go—and could you nudge them in the direction of the costlier ales?"

Mieka was wide-eyed. "You *never*—!"

"No, not me. Cousin on Mum's side. He wanted me to join him."

"But you didn't."

"I've better things to do with what little magic I've got."

Mieka ruminated on this for a time. "You've more than you know."

"Mayhap." A sunshine smile, not of the sort he used onstage but a real one. "I prefer having you lot doing most of the heavy lifting. Leaves me energy for more rewarding pursuits."

"And have you heard from the delectable Kazie this week?"

Jeska's smile widened. "She'll be here for Wintering."

"Excellent! Mum's putting together a party—you're all invited, Dery and Mistress Mirdley, too, if they've a mind to it," Mieka said in Cade's general direction, but didn't look at him. He did a lot of that these days; both of them did, this not looking at each other. Well, at least they were speaking.

"First Wintering in two years we'll spend at home," Rafe mused. "We ought to send something to our hosts at Cloffin Crossriver. Just to let them know we miss them."

"Already done," Jeska reported. "Hawk's Claw will be at Crossriver for Wintering, and their tregetour is by way of becoming a friend of mine."

"The Longbranch boy?" Cade asked.

"Trenal Longbranch," Jeska affirmed. "I sent some Frannitch wine and a pair of Blye's finest glasses with him. Not that she actually made them, of course," he finished with a wink.

"Are Cilka and Petrinka busy growing hothouse flowers?" Cade asked Mieka.

"Roses and hundred-petal daisies," he confirmed, surprised that Cade remembered that Elfen tradition from their midnight conversation. It seemed so long ago, that night spent lying in the darkness, talking, hearing the Minster bells. And that reminded him. "Jez is seeing a girl whose father's a bellwright. Not the great big ones, just handbells. Should make lots of lovely noise at midnight!"

"Talking of noise," Cade asked innocently, "will you be blowing anything up?"

"Oh, Gods," Jeska moaned. "Don't give him ideas!"

It was so good to be laughing again. But it didn't happen often enough, that winter.

At least he wasn't bored. Or plagued with his annual head cold, which was unusual enough that his mother decided he'd outgrown them, like losing baby teeth. And he wasn't poor, either. Kearney Fairwalk had been busy while Touchstone was off on the Royal Circuit, and during this, the first winter of their rank as Second Flight on that circuit, they were in constant demand. Whenever Mieka found himself almost dreading yet another show at yet another private party, he did two things: remind himself how much money was piling up in his bank account, and prick a nice armful of bluethorn to get him through the performance. Though every now and then he had to choose a vein on an ankle, because sometimes the skin of his arms was too reddened and raw to support another puncture.

Quite a few bookings took them out of Gallantry-banks for a night or three, so Yazz and the wagon were kept busy as well. Sometimes Robel came along to keep her husband company, but more often she stayed at Hill-drop getting ready for their coming child. When word had got round the village last spring that a Giant (or mostly) and his wife were living at the Windthistle place, once the alarmed whispers gave way to curiosity and then to familiarity, the neighbors decided it was a convenience, having someone like Yazz in residence. Not only could he be counted on for favors involving the moving of weighty objects, but he was also, to put it mildly, a deterrent to anyone who thought it might be amusing to cause trouble of any kind. Theft and commotion were rare occurrences in Hilldrop these days.

So everybody was gainfully employed and making money and happy as hogs in slop, and Mieka ought to have been well pleased.

At least he wasn't bored. Or not very often, anyways.

Some nights, when he was curled in his solitary bed at Wistly or staring at the ceiling of the wagon as they rolled home from a country mansion, he told himself he really ought to talk things over with his wife. He ought to ask her—calmly, gently, without threats or anger, just as a matter of information—why she had done what she'd done with those cards. Why she had lied to him.

He kept telling himself this, and that the next time he was at Hilldrop he'd make time to do it, and couldn't even fool himself. Every time he considered a conversation of the sort, he got queasy. Besides, she seemed perfectly willing to forget the whole thing. He had peace in his household when he was there, and even if it made him edgy sometimes to be in her presence, he just couldn't face talking it out with her. She would cry, he knew she would, and put a hand to her cheek, and once more he'd feel like a complete shit, and nothing would be resolved anyway, so why put himself through all that?

In his more cynical, Cade-influenced moments, he knew that if she discovered that he knew when she was lying to him, he would never be able to trust her again. If she knew, she'd be wary and guarded around him. This way, unaware that he could tell, she was still the guileless girl he'd married. She would never test the limits of his perceptions by lying just to see how much she could get away with.

It was the precise opposite of how he felt with Cade, who knew very well that Mieka always knew when he was lying and no longer bothered to try. Mieka remembered that first Winterly, when Cade had kept secret even the fact that he *had* Elsewhens, and how Mieka had waited with uncharacteristic patience for Cade to admit the truth. He couldn't stand a return to that. He needed to know that Cade would never even try to lie to him again.

Touchstone didn't spend all of Wintering at Wistly Hall. The early part of the evening was taken up with a performance at Kearney Fairwalk's town house. A select company of gentlemen had been invited, a tent had been erected in the back garden, firepockets kept everybody warm, fine foods and finer liquors were served, and Mieka saw Fairwalk thornlost for the very first time.

He wondered if Fairwalk, so obviously of Gnomish blood, knew all the strictures regarding various lineages— blockweed was a very bad idea for Pikseys; Goblins and bluethorn were a disastrous mix—but decided there must be enough Human in him to allow for just about anything. It happened that way for some people, the way it did for Mieka: he could indulge in pretty much what he pleased, for he was so many different races mixed together that any nasty effects on, say, Sprite were canceled out by his Elfen blood. Or so Auntie Brishen said, and he had no reason to doubt her. On this thought, he began to wonder who was providing Fairwalk's thorn. Master Bellgloss, perhaps, with whom the Shadowshapers and Crystal Sparks did business. Whoever had done the concocting, Fairwalk was well and truly thorned: pinpoint pupils, flushed cheeks, laughter rising to wild giggles, and a tendency to talk loudly and rapidly without making an uncomfortable amount of sense. Even his hair, usually limp and weary, seemed energetic.

They did a rather lengthy version of "Doorways" at Fairwalk's request. Cade had written some new lines for Jeska and given Mieka more than enough in the withies to indulge himself with: ten doorways, rather than the usual five or six, and more time spent with each. By the time *"This life, and none other"* was spoken, despite the bluethorn Mieka was exhausted.

Fairwalk had insisted on paying them for this performance, even though their audience of rich merchants and nobles were there not just for the party but with an eye to showcasing Touchstone in hopes of securing future bookings at private gatherings. Mieka was directed to be on his best behavior, and he submitted without too much protest—for his wife would be at the Wintering celebrations at Wistly, which was also the first anniversary of Jindra's birth, and he had no intention of letting a drunken tongue say words that wouldn't help anybody, least of all himself. The counterbalance for bluethorn was alcohol, but he'd used up everything the thorn could provide him, so he merely shook his head and smiled when one of the servants offered him a whiskey. He saw Cade's brows arch—for surely this was a first in Mieka's life, turning down good liquor—and didn't much feel like explaining himself.

If anybody suspected that there was a reason why there were no women present—not even serving girls—at Fairwalk's party other than the men-only conventions of theater, nobody mentioned it. Still, Mieka was interested to see the Archduke's librarian, Drevan Wordturner, in the crowd, though he was less pleased when Cade sought him out for a few minutes' conversation after the show.

"What'd you talk to him for?" Mieka asked in the carriage back to Wistly Hall.

"Just exchanging greetings."

It was dark, so Mieka couldn't see his eyes. Yet he knew Cade wasn't telling the whole truth. "It's about books, isn't it?"

"Imagine that!" Jeska said brightly. "Talking with a librarian about books!"

"Shut it," Mieka growled. Jeska had been deplorably chipper these last few days. Kazie was in town, staying with Croodle's friends down below the Plume. She would be at Wistly tonight for Wintering. An announcement was shortly expected, and then all of Touchstone would be married except for Cade. "I meant those books Vered wants, about the whatsis Knights."

"How do you know about that?" Cade demanded.

"Chat told me he's been impossible since we all got home from the Royal. They've turned down a dozen or more bookings, even a real money-spinner tonight at Piercehand's, just so Vered can hide himself away and think great thoughts."

"Let's go by his place next week," Cade suggested. "Take him out for a drink. His wife and the boys are probably sick of him by now—" He broke off as Mieka shook his head. "You don't want to take him out for a drink?"

"Love to. But part of the reason he's playing Hovelden the Hermit is that his wife took the boys off to her mother for the winter and maybe forever—some awful place that he was born in and couldn't wait to get out of. She hates Gallybanks, y'see, exactly as much as he loves it."

"Oh, dear," Cade sighed. "Well, then, he must *really* need a drink."

"You'll have to get past the new lady friend first."

The gray eyes opened wide. "Is there anything by way of gossip that you don't know?"

Mieka grinned. "I only know because they had a fight, and the dinnerware is not, shall we say, what it used to be. He came round to commission a service for twelve from Blye. Jed told me all about it. The new girl's a bit . . . umm . . . unpredictable."

"So he's all alone—with the new friend—at home on Wintering," Jeska said, "without his family. That's a sad thing. We ought to bring him to Wistly. And the new lady friend, too," he added generously.

But Mieka shook his head. "I already invited him—and her—and Mum's upset that he turned us down."

"Your mother," Cade remarked, "is an extraordinary woman. Eight children of her own, not to speak of all those people wandering about Wistly Hall, and still she takes in strays."

"If it's a peaceful and orderly home life Mum was looking for, she oughtn't to've married Fa. Besides, once you're dealing with fifty or sixty in the house, another dozen makes no nevermind."

But it was an odd thing, descending from Fairwalk's carriage in Waterknot Circle, to feel like a stray himself. A guest. The way he'd felt all winter. And that was foolishness, because he'd grown up here and this was his home. Moreover, he had another home that was all his. Most of the time he felt like a guest there, too. There was only one place where he felt he truly belonged: onstage with his partners. *"This life, and none other"* was a confusing concept when one had three lives at once and only one of them felt like home.

Nineteen

TOBALT FLUTER HAD made his name at roughly the same time the Shadowshapers and Touchstone were making theirs. It was a mutually beneficial relationship: he was a writer, and they gave him something to write about.

Tobalt Fluter wanted more.

"It's something you said, Cade," he confessed one afternoon at Redpebble Square. Weary of wrestling with a play that simply wouldn't come right, Cade welcomed Tobalt with gratitude for the distraction. Mistress Mirdley gave them tea in the kitchen and withdrew to her stillroom. Derien was due back from school any moment. Considering the rate at which Tobalt was going through muffins and pastries, the boy would be left with nothing but buttered bread to eat.

"Something I said?" Cade passed the seedy cakes.

"About theater and changing the world. I want to know what all of you think. I want to do an issue of *The Nayword* that's nothing but theater, nothing but tregetours. I'm giving a little dinner next week and I'd like you to be there. You and Vered Goldbraider and Rauel Kevelock, of course, Mirko Challender from the Sparks, and the tregetour from Hawk's Claw, Trenal Longbranch, he's got some interesting ideas—"

"I agree. I've talked with him a few times."

Tobalt beamed at him. "So you'll be there!"

"I didn't say—"

"They're letting us have the stage at the new Downstreet," Tobalt went on, and gulped the rest of his tea, and got to his feet. "Hoping you'll be so impressed that you'll agree to play at the grand reopening, of course."

"Tobalt—"

"It's to be a real theater now, and an inventive design it is, too." He pulled on his coat. "There's an outer hall with a bar at either end, and instead of one layer of seats"—a painfully colorful woolen scarf was knotted around his throat—"there's a sort of wide balcony with yet more seats, so they didn't lose anything by putting in the hall out front."

"Have I said yet that I'll be—"

"They're saying that capacity will be six hundred! Of course, the wife had to change the room she used to keep her little shrine in—"

"It was destroyed in the fire that burned the place down."

"Ah, but she's had another one made for the upstairs. She says none of her boys would know what to do with themselves if there wasn't that bit of stone and fire and water to allow for upstairs. 'Her boys' of course being you players, because she has only the two daughters of her own—"

"Tobalt!"

"—and the elder girl's had to postpone marriage because of the fire and lack of money, so her mother's more than eager for everybody's success at the new Downstreet. Anyways, we'll be dining onstage." He dug into his pocket for gloves and pulled them on. "You'll have the chance to get a feel for the place. Perfectly splendid that you'll be there, Cade! Can't wait! Beholden to your Mistress Mirdley for the tea!"

"By the Lord and Lady, you talk more and faster than Mieka! I don't think I'll be—"

But as Derien came in the back door, Tobalt took the opportunity to go out. Cade was left sitting there with teacup in hand as Tobalt called over his shoulder, "I'll send round with the day and time!"

"Day and time for what?" Dery wanted to know.

"It seems I'm invited to dinner."

The boy pounced on the scanty remains of tea and through a mouthful of apricot muffin mumbled something about Jinsie.

"What about her? Swallow first, smatchet."

He paused long enough to say "Glassworks," before attacking the tea tray again, with a piteous cry to Mistress Mirdley for more seedy cakes.

Cade entered the shop to find Jinsie gossiping with Jed and Blye, and marveled again that Mishia and Hadden Windthistle had produced four such totally different sets of twin offspring. Jed and Jez were tall, redheaded, entirely Human to look at. Mieka and Jinsie were all Elf, and reverse images of each other: he was black-haired and white-skinned, she had pale golden hair and a dark complexion and blue eyes. Cilka and Petrinka were Piksey-sized and Piksey-dainty; Tavier and Jorie were more Elfen in feature but growing so fast that it would likely be only a couple of years before they were looking Cilka and Petrinka in the eye, and Cade suspected that they would both turn out more Wizard than Elf. The vagaries of heredity, he mused, and smiled a greeting as Jinsie finally noticed him.

"Oh good, you're here," she began briskly. "Mieka says you've some notion about taking elements out of a performance—getting rid of the emotion, or doing a play without any words at all. I want to talk to you about that."

"You don't approve?"

Evidently he hadn't quite kept all the sarcasm out of his voice, for she made a disgusted face and replied, "Nobody has the right to an opinion but you tregetours, is that it? Well, it so happens I *do* approve. Only what I want you to do is craft a performance for people who are deaf. If you're going to do it anyway, why not do it so it's actually some use? I have a friend whose sister is losing her hearing and nobody can figure out why. All the physickers just shrug and say, 'Something in the blood,' meaning of course that they've no idea and want to blame her ancestry. Who knows but what they're right—but the point is that she wants to go to a play. She reads all Tobalt's articles about Touchstone and has copies of all your placards. So we'll come as boys to a show sometime this spring, I'm not sure when, but why can't the deaf go to theater performances meant just for them?"

The magic that produced visuals and sounds was on a different order from the magic that seeped into people's senses to provide taste and touch and smell and emotion. None of it was real, but making pictures and noise was distinct from techniques used to touch the other senses and evoke feelings. It was where *glisk* had originated, in fact. Plenty of magical folk could conjure up visual and auditory images. It took real skill and subtlety and training to be a glisker.

"But would it be possible?" he asked aloud. "To put the sounds directly into someone's head—I mean, it might be a similar process to how we do taste and scent and all that, but—I don't think I'd know where to begin."

Blye was shaking her head. "Not cause someone deaf

to actually hear, but leave sounds out altogether. Base the experiencing of the play on everything *except* sound."

"But what about the words?"

"Ah, now you've pierced him right where he lives!" Blye laughed.

"It could work for the blind, too," Jed offered. "No images at all."

"Mieka won't like that," Cade mused.

"Consider what it would be like," Jed went on, "being blind from birth and never having seen *anything*. And then all at once there are all these shapes and colors and things confusing your head—you wouldn't know what to do with it, would you?"

"It would be terrifying," Blye said. "Like when Bompstable was a kitten, and he'd never heard thunder."

Jed nodded. "He didn't come out from under the bed until the next day, poor little thing."

His sister suddenly grinned. "And how do *you* know he was under the bed all night? By the time you were married, he was a grown-up cat!"

With all the absolute—and absolutely spurious—innocence of their brother, Jedris said, "She told me, of course."

Cade shared an eye-roll with Jinsie, then said, "At Master Emmot's Academy we had to learn how to organize things inside our brains. That's what we do with sight and sound when we're infants, I suppose—learn to recognize patterns and such. It's the same with music, or learning to read. Finding out what the letters mean, and how they go together to make words, and—"

Jinsie interrupted. "I'd love to hear your theories of learning—some other time. Will you at least think about it? When Mieka said you were mulling over doing a play that leaves out one of the usual aspects—" She shrugged delicate shoulders. "I've been writing to some scholars at Shollop about it, who've been investigating causes of deafness. Leaving aside cases of accident, of course—something to do with the structure of the ear, tiny bones that grow together or something. It's all too complicated for me. When you're at Shollop next summer on the Royal, why don't you look them up?"

"I think I'd like that. Beholden, Jinsie."

"Now you're here, Cade," said Jedris, "would you have a look at my plans for the frames for your glass baskets?"

Mieka had been complaining recently that because all glisker's benches were different, setting the baskets atop them constituted a clear and avoidable danger. So Jedris had proposed a set of wooden supports. Cade spent a fascinating hour discussing the designs, suggesting changes, and deciding that combining wood and nails into a useful object was rather like combining a story and words and magic to produce a play. Everyone had his own tools. Tomorrow, he vowed, he'd polish up his particular set and get to work with renewed determination.

When he got back home, a letter was waiting for him. "Tobalt doesn't fribble away any time," he remarked, and explained Tobalt's proposal to Derien and Mistress Mirdley.

"Will you go?" Derien asked. "Who'll be there?"

"I won't be within five miles of the place if he invites Thierin Knottinger."

"All the more reason to be there," Dery urged. "Betwixt you and Vered and Rauel, he'll be demolished. There may be some bloodstains left on the brand-new stage, but demolished all the same."

"They can have a fine time doing it without me." He made as if to toss the invitation in the kitchen fire.

Dery reached out a hand to stop him. "You have to

be there, Cade. It's good advertising. And nobody will read the article if you're not in it."

He laughed and ruffled his brother's hair. "What makes you think I'll get a word in sidewise? Vered and Rauel will both be there, competing for attention!"

"And column inches," Mistress Mirdley observed.

In the event, Knottinger didn't show up. Many apologies, many regrets, many excuses—Tobalt read the note aloud, said, "Oh, that's too bad," and everyone promptly forgot all about Black Lightning.

The new Downstreet was indeed a marvel. Cade thought briefly about the Archduke's proposed theater, and decided he could do much worse than this. Mieka Windthistle, in fact, might have been the advisor regarding the bars at either side of the wide lobby, sparkling with mirrors (Blye's work) and expensive glassware (not Blye's work)—expensive because Touchstone wouldn't be shattering it. Reflected in the mirrors were dozens of square, squat, colorful bottles of brandies, dozens more tall green bottles of wine, and half-barrels of various beers and ales. As for the theater itself, there were two levels of seating and the stage was huge. Hanging from support beams were three large branch-lights like upside-down trees, brass polished to gleaming gold—nothing for Touchstone to shatter there, either. The beams were painted black in contrast to the eggshell color of the ceiling, which angled upwards to allow for the upper rows of seats. The swagged stage curtains were off-white velvet, as was the covering of the glisker's bench. A table set with silver plates and fine crystal looked terribly lonely in the middle of all that polished oak planking between the curtains.

"Welcome all!" Tobalt sang out from the front of the stage. "Come in, step up, sit down!"

When Cade arrived, Vered and Rauel were already

present, strolling down the middle aisle to the stage steps. Trenal Longbranch was—most professionally and quite unnecessarily, for he'd have the chance well before Hawk's Claw played the Downstreet—pacing off the distance between the back doors and the front rows. Mirko Challender of the Crystal Sparks slouched in a few minutes after Cade, looking elegantly bored.

When they were all seated, dinner was served by a pair of teenaged boys whose hands gradually stopped shaking with the excitement of being in the presence of so many celebrated players. The food was excellent, the sweets especially good: lemon custard flavored with clove, and elderflowers simmered in honey and poured over bread pudding studded with berries.

Like Vered, Cade drank very little—not because, like Vered, he was especially susceptible to liquor, but because Tobalt was making note of every word said. He remembered only too well other times he'd been drunk and Tobalt had had pen and paper to hand. And tonight there was no Mieka here to distract everyone with his clowning.

Mieka would have been welcome, Cade mused. Everyone seemed rather edgy. Each man present was aware of the others as competing playwrights, and even more aware that they were expected to say fascinating, startling things, unsure if they were to be baited like bears in a pit or encouraged to dance like lapdogs in ruffled collars. So all through the meal nobody said much of anything except for polite conversation about wives and offspring and the latest in fashionable boots and shirts. Several toasts were raised to the new little Prince, born a few days ago, named Roshlin for his grandmother Queen Roshien.

Tobalt started them off, once the dishes had been

cleared and they were left with bottles of brandy. "I hear from my sources," he said with an arch smile at Vered, "that your new play is so long that it'll take up a whole evening. Not even a break in the middle for a drink?"

Vered wore a *Wouldn't you like to know?* expression. "I never listen to rumors."

Rauel wore his most charming, wide-eyed smile. "Changing theater is what we do, isn't it? The Shadowshapers, I mean—though I'm sure all the rest of you are talented innovators as well."

Cade had known both of them long enough to know they were each in a mischievous mood. He settled back in his chair, sipped brandy, and prepared to enjoy the show.

Trenal Longbranch, a good-looking youth with the shoulders of a dockworker—or mayhap a Troll—and just a bit too much chin, was taking everything much too seriously, including his drinking. He filled his glass yet again and said, "It takes the Shadowshapers to get away with it. Any of us others, we change so much as a line in one of the Thirteen and we're booted off the stage. Except for Touchstone, of course," he added hastily, with a glance at Cade, who acknowledged him with a gracious nod. "It's the Stewards and the nobility who want everything just as it's always been. You take something new to anyplace outside Gallybanks, and they eat it up with a spoon."

"While the nobility sneers," said Mirko, "and compliments itself on its superior taste. The Sparks, we never introduce anything new at Trials. We wait until we're out on the Circuit, and by the time word gets back here about how good it is, the highborns have been outwitted."

"You're assuming they have wits to be outed of," said Cayden. "My mother's one of them, I ought to know."

"So's my cousin," Longbranch admitted. "A right pain in the netherparts, is His Lordship. Keeps reminding me who paid for my first withies."

"No objections to your profession, then?" Rauel asked, fully aware of Lady Jaspiela's attitude. Cade had whined to him often enough about it in the old days.

"As long as it keeps me away from his daughter," Longbranch said with a cross between a grin and a grimace, "he's thrilled."

"Ah!" sighed Mirko. "The lovely Lady Lellia Longbranch!"

Trenal responded with a laugh—a trifle forced, in Cade's opinion—and a warning finger like a threatening arrow. "You stay clear of her, too!"

Tobalt was uninterested in gossip. "Why is it that some people are so opposed to any alteration in how things have always been done?"

"We all resist change," Cade heard himself say. "One way or another, most of us want things to stay as they are. Familiar. Comforting."

"Society intends us to resist it." Vered ran a finger round the rim of his glass. "Wouldn't do to have everybody questioning why they have to do what's always been done, would it?"

"But in theater," Tobalt said rather desperately, "your introduction of two masquers at the same time, in 'Life in a Day'—"

"That wasn't innovation," Vered told him with a shrug. "Plays started out with one actor, changing characters with actual masks. Color was used as a prompt, as well— physickers always wear green, f'r instance, and Mother Loosebuckle's always in a red skirt. Then they added another actor, and then another—until some brainy little git thought of putting magic into it, so we only *need* one person onstage."

"After that, all the old plays—the really old ones—were probably rewritten back to their original forms," contributed Rauel. "Undoing the changes—"

"Bloody Hells!" exclaimed Mirko. "You mean we're not just doing *old* stuff, we're doing the oldest *versions* of the old stuff?"

"Yeh—gruesome, ain't it?" Vered grinned. "So what we did, putting a second masquer onstage—nothing radical about it, not at all."

"And yet," said Longbranch, "it's truer to your vision, and moves theater in a different direction. Cayden's right, we cling to what we're leaving behind, and making the changes is often painful—"

"But sometimes it's the necessary choice," Cade murmured.

"To turn back," he went on eagerly, "to forsake change—that's a betrayal of what we know we need to become."

"But why must it be painful?" Rauel asked, his big soft eyes honestly forlorn.

"You only know you're growing when it hurts," Cade told him, hearing Mistress Mirdley's voice in his head, and his own voice telling Mieka the same thing. And in Rauel's next words he heard echoes of what he knew Mieka would reply.

"But what about being happy? Doesn't that have anything to teach us? Can't we learn from contentment, from laughter?"

Vered shrugged. "If you have to ask yourself whether you're happy, most likely you're not."

"Gods!" cried Mirko. "You two would depress the Angels!"

"Talking of Gods—and the Lord and Lady and so

on," Vered went on wickedly, "let's do discuss how theater is the communal experience that Chapel is *supposed* to be."

Cade laughed and shook his head. "I've stumbled down that road before, my friend."

"And now," Rauel announced, "he'll draw the difference between the emotions and the intellect, and how rational belief is superior to instinct, and—"

Vered interrupted him. "It's no good kindling emotions just to see the pretty flames. That's religion at its worst. Using imagination in the theater to stir up the fire—that's just encouraging illusions." He smiled again, and in him Cade could suddenly see not Wizard or traces of Elf or Goblin but deliberate malicious Fae, intent with not-quite-innocent glee on making as much trouble as possible. "Of course, the first plays were based on tales from *The Consecrations*, so maybe it's all one and the same: imagination, illusion, religion, theater—"

Tobalt gulped audibly. This portion of Vered's remarks would not make it into any articles. Dancing close to blasphemy, he was. "But the emotion created by the imagination, by a tregetour and glisker in a play, is just as real as any other."

"Which wouldn't be so bad," Vered went on, "except that most people are scared half to death of their own imaginations—*and* their own emotions. So they feed off ours!" He toasted Cade with his brandy glass. "And we've had this talk, too, you and me. Bleedin' Vampires, players and audiences alike!"

He felt it then, an Elsewhen hovering closer, closer, and resisted it. There was no danger to giving in, not when he was safely seated amongst friends, but he had no intention of arousing their curiosity or their alarm by turning all blank-eyed and distracted, and then having to explain himself somehow. Besides, if what

he saw and heard was even half so horrific as some of
the other Elsewhens had been . . . he was no masquer,
to contrive a convincing face and manner on the turn of
one word in a play.

Vered was still talking. "I read somewhere that
there's actually something immoral about imagining
yourself into different times and places—"

"That musty old book of Chat's?" Rauel asked. "From
someplace on the Continent," he explained to the others. "The point of it was something like, 'You are who
and what and where fate and fortune placed you, and
imagining yourself as something or someone or somewhere else is an offense against the All Mighties—'" He
shrugged and smiled. "Whoever and Whatever they
might be. I'm not terribly clear on their religion."

"Which only makes Vered's point," Cade said, "about
theater doing what religion used to do, or is supposed
to do."

"We make people feel, and we're supposed to feel guilty
about it?" Mirko scoffed. "They come to us for exactly
what we give them!"

Again the Elsewhen nagged at him; again he pushed
it away.

"Not all of them want the same thing," Trenal remarked. "Some want to be taken by the hand and led
through the whole thing, with signposts along the way."

Mirko nodded agreement. "Everything explained
on the instant, everybody's background and motiva-
tions given right up front, and when the villain shows
up, they want him to be wearing a great big placard
written in bright red letters—*I'm the frightful nasty
person come to fuck everything up.*"

This was a bit much for Tobalt. "But don't people
trust the playwright to know what he's doing?"

"*You* might," Rauel said glumly.

The slamming of a door to the lobby turned all their heads. "This is a private event!" Tobalt called out.

"But Vered and I have no secrets."

The woman's voice was high and light and what Cade could only describe to himself as pinched, as if each word had been constricted like glass blown into a mold. Vered's dark skin rarely showed a blush, so it was the widening of his eyes that gave him away. He leaped from his chair and down the side steps of the stage, heading into the dimness of the theater aisles. Rauel, for his part, shut his eyes briefly and drew in a controlled breath, then smiled for all he was worth.

"You said nine," she went on, loudly enough for the rest of them to hear. "It's almost ten. I was lonely."

"Bexan?" Mirko whispered to Trenal.

"Bexan," Trenal whispered back.

Before Cade could ask who Bexan was, she and Vered were back. Shaking out her heavy black skirts, she sat in his chair and picked up his brandy glass and turned to Tobalt with a look that expected nothing, revealed nothing. She was little and dark, pretty in a moody sort of way, with plenty of crisp curls and a faint bluish cast to her very white skin that spoke of Piksey in her blood.

Rauel played the well-bred gentleman and fetched the chair that had been set aside when Thierin Knottinger hadn't shown up. He was still smiling a trained masquer's smile. If Vered noticed, he didn't care. He took the seat his partner had brought him, filled Bexan's glass, and only with difficulty took his eyes off her and introduced her all round.

"Umm . . . yes," Tobalt said rather blankly, then finally pulled himself together. "Welcome, Mistress Quickstride. We were just discussing—that is, I hope you won't be bored by—"

"Never," said Vered, fondly, proudly. "Where were we?"

Cade decided to be helpful. "Tregetours and trust."

"Oh. Of course." Tobalt thought for a moment, then said, "I'm not sure if I'm understanding correctly, but it seems to me that tregetours *must* imagine themselves into the minds and lives of a thousand different sorts of people. It's part of the job. You can't write about them if you don't understand them. You have to feel what they feel, and—"

"And think for them," Vered interrupted. "Emoting all over the place is all very well, but a play's naught but rubbish if it doesn't come from the intellect, too."

"How sweet of you," Mirko purred, "to give us all official license to feel!"

Cade hid a smile. This really was turning into quite the entertainment, especially with the addition of an uninvited guest. He said, "By putting ourselves into other people's hearts and minds, and then presenting the results onstage, aren't we providing the experience of other people's lives for the audience? And isn't that ultimately a moral good? To help them understand—"

"To let them see that there are different people in the world with different sorts of thoughts and dreams," Longbranch broke in, then looked embarrassed.

Cade nodded for him to continue.

"I only meant," he said more diffidently, "that you're right about the communal experience, and it even goes beyond that. We're all connected, we can all identify with and understand each other in some fashion. Sorry, Cayden, I didn't mean to barge in."

Vered grinned. "Trenal, old son, if we let Cade talk uninterrupted, we'd be here until Trials. What theater does, showing people different lives and ways of thinking—"

"—and feeling," Rauel threw in.

"—we're also showing them how similar we all are. It's not just the connection made amongst the audience at the play. Nobody in Lilyleaf will ever battle a dragon, but if the thing's worked right, they not only get an idea of what it would be like but they realize that someplace inside them they *understand* what it would be like. And that creates a unity of—"

"Did you just say that *Cayden* talks too much?" Mirko drawled.

Longbranch soldiered on. "I worry sometimes, though, that we impose upon people things they wouldn't ordinarily feel."

"That's where we get to the question of authenticity in imagination," Rauel said. "Cade's 'Doorways' play is a good example. All those different lives behind all those doors—what glover seriously considers the notion of becoming a lawyer arguing a case in court? But when he looks at that portion of the play he sees that what's going on inside that door is a true thing. Cade imagined what it would be like, how it would feel, and pulled the truth out of it to show onstage."

He could hear Mieka's voice then: *You have to do their dreaming for them Quill.*

"And that final door," Longbranch said, "the one he chooses—'This life, and none other'—"

"*There* you have the religious experience!" Vered leaned forward eagerly. "What Chapel is supposed to do, and doesn't, much—it's only words and motions, rituals and mouthings, it doesn't make the connections anymore. *We,* on the other hand, can leave audiences feeling all warm and lovely and pleased with themselves. Oh, stop squirming, Cayden. It isn't only you. We do the same thing with 'Dancing Ground.' Whatever someone most desires, that's what we give them at the end when the Knight tricks the Elf Queen into giving him what he wants."

Cade had squirmed because he hadn't intended the

piece to be seen like that—he'd wanted to make the point that people *did* choose the lives they lead, whether they were aware of the choosing or not. He'd never meant to put people happily in their places, or give them everything they wanted, or make them cease striving—or dreaming—because they left the theater contented with their lives. He wanted them to think about the choices they made, the way he had to think. Had been *forced* to think, because of the Elsewhens. He wanted them to understand that if they didn't like the life they were leading, they could choose to change it. *You've got it wrong,* he wanted to say, *you're not understanding what I meant.*

And this led him a step or two down a different path, one all hung about with questions concerning who decided what a play really meant, and whose fault it was if the author's opinion diverged from the general understanding, and whether a play's purpose was to satisfy the audience or the author—or both. Or, he suddenly thought, mayhap *neither*. Did a work exist because it wanted—no, *needed*—to exist, independent of everyone, including the person who wrote it?

Longbranch, having taken a big enough swig of brandy to renew his pluck, said, "It seems to me that a play shouldn't be so much a new experience as a remembrance. A thing you always knew but perhaps didn't know that you knew. And both of those plays do that."

Cade quoted softly, "'You may look into the water and see deep visions, but in truth, in fact, the pool is naught but a mirror.'" He smiled. "That's not original. I read it someplace."

"Druan Stitchinggrass," said Bexan Quickstride.

"Well—yes," Cade agreed, trying not to appear surprised that she had read the ancient poet. "And here's what I think about 'authenticity,' Rauel. When you put the words onto paper, it's as real as actually having the experience. The thoughts and emotions of imagination are just as real as any other. But there's something more. When you write it down, not only is it as real as having the experience, it's an experience of its own—and the experience *demands* to be written down."

"That," Mistress Quickstride concluded, with a sidelong look for Vered, "is the superiority of a man of imagination and intellect over the man of intellect and feeling."

Mirko's lip curled slightly, indication enough of what he thought of women who put forth opinions. But nobody seemed to have anything to say in reply, though for a few seconds Rauel looked as if he might. The sweetly boyish smile returned to his face and Cade had the impression that even if Vered had noticed its faltering, he wouldn't much care.

The party broke up soon thereafter. Cade was safely alone in a hire-hack on his way back to Redpebble Square when he finally allowed the Elsewhen to claim him.

{Jeschenar walked lithely to the center of the stage, a slim white candle, hair like curls of golden flame. Rafcadion stood at his lectern to the left, just visible beside the lush tapestry curtain, tall and bearded, dressed all in black. Cayden took his position far to the right, clad in subtle shades of gray. And Mieka, scorning as always the glisker's velvet bench, stood behind the arrayed glass baskets, also in white, his hands empty. There was no magic in the air, no shimmer of power. There were only the four men, and the audience was as silent as if every one of the thousand seats had been empty.

Jeska swept his gaze once, arrogantly, through the theater. Then he began to speak the words Cade had written on behalf of them all, as a promise and as a warning.

"We *will* get to you.

"We'll make you feel. That's what you've come here for, that's what you want, isn't it? To feel.

"You may ridicule yourself after, you may accuse us of manipulation, but you knew when you came here that you would feel.

"We're that good.

"And you need us that much.

"We give you an excuse to weep. Within the safety of this theater, you can fall passionately in love. You can hate without reservation, cower without shame—or want desperately to ease someone's suffering. You can laugh at the ludicrous, rage at injustice, pity the afflicted, sneer at folly. You can want and need and desire, without fear. Later you may wince, and tell yourself you were duped, tricked into these emotions and their intensity. But to feel is what you came here for. You know it, we know it.

"You call us Vampires, feeding on other people's feelings so that we may reproduce them onstage. Feeding on our own, so that we may use them, scheme with them. This is true enough. But you feed, too. You lap up the emotions available to you, craving more, devouring the magic that allows you to feel things you're afraid to feel in real life. The dangerous things, the things that are so deep and strong and severe that to give in to them for even an instant would render you utterly helpless. You don't know what to do with such tumult of emotion, do you? You shy away from it, out there in the world.

"But here, you are safe. Here, you can lick at sentimental tears and crunch on the bones of your enemies, sink your teeth into rage, taste the lust, swallow drunken drafts of joy. You can do these things without shame, without remorse, without responsibility. Without retribution.

"You are safe here. We will let you feel all the things that frighten you, elude you, compel you, seduce you. The things you cannot allow yourself to feel in their entirety, in their reality, in their mad intense awful purity.

"But do not pretend that you do not need this. That you do not need us. Do not delude yourself. And do not denigrate us for making you feel. It's what you came here for. It's what you want. What you need. We will accomplish it, you may trust us, and you will be safe.

"But do not say, later, that you were tricked. You were not. You know it, we know it. You want this.

"And we *will* provide."}

Twenty

WHAT TOBALT WOULD do with his notes on all the talking they had done, Cade had no idea. He didn't much care. He was too busy writing down that Elsewhen, tweaking it here and there, trying to guess from the clothes they wore and any changes in their faces exactly when this piece—which wasn't really a play at all—would be presented. It would be within the next few years, for there was no gray in their hair or Rafe's beard, and their faces and frames seemed young, no older than twenty-six or -seven (which seemed far away from the vantage point of not-quite-twenty-two, though much closer than the Elsewhen of that forty-fifth Namingday surprise party). He spent the morning after Tobalt's dinner working on the script and part of the afternoon trying to puzzle out the when of it, before realizing that it simply didn't matter. The words had been written and when the right time presented itself, he would use them.

This was the first time he'd ever Elsewhened a theater piece. "Doorways" had come from a dream he'd had—a real dream, the kind other people had while sleeping—so it didn't count. As for "Treasure"—that hadn't been a play when it appeared to him on thorn.

It had been a combination of speculation and research, dream and fantasy, influenced by thorn and his Fae ancestress and his frustration. But this . . . this statement of purpose and intent and promise and warning, this had appeared inside his head fully formed. It fascinated him to imagine that he might be able to do this again and again, or that, more accurately, it might *happen* to him again and again, with whole plays already written, presented in a private theater inside his own mind, and all he'd need do was remember them and write them down.

It was what he did anyway: collect all sorts of seemingly unrelated things, stir them together with his learning and his imagination, and see what resulted. Still, this was different. It had shown up whole. No randomly occurring bits and pieces to be scrawled out after a frantic search for paper and pen. No glaring in fury at a blank page and wanting to slam his fist into a wall when the words wouldn't come. No writing down and crossing out, writing down and crossing out, over and over until he gave up and got drunk as an antidote for dejection. No finishing a sequence one night and then waking the next morning to find it pointless, senseless, graceless, dead on the page.

It was two afternoons following Tobalt's dinner that it occurred to him, with the impact of a glass basket cracked over his head: What if he really could Elsewhen his work?

What if *all* of his work—even the maddening erratic stops and starts, the discarded pages—was in truth a series of Elsewhens? Wasn't that what imagination was? The ability to visualize things that hadn't happened, project them into a possible future—and to make the vision real?

Further—

"Cayden!"

Mistress Mirdley's bellow from downstairs told him two things. First, it must be the footmen's day off and Derien wasn't yet home from school, or she would have sent one of them up to Cade's room. Second, Lady Jaspiela was not in the house or no bellowing would have taken place at all. Sighing, he went out to the landing and bellowed back.

"What? I'm working!"

There was no response. He trudged down five flights and found a folded note waiting for him, rather pointedly, on the floor at the bottom of the stairs.

"Oh, shit." He'd had an appointment today with a leasing agent. He had his eye on a very nice three-room flat on the third floor of a building one street away from Stillwater. Even though it wasn't strictly within that upper-class ambit, the flat was a bit pricey and wouldn't be available until late summer, when the current occupant returned to Scatterseed to marry his bespoken and run the family firm. For most provincial young men with a business to inherit, a year in Gallantrybanks was considered necessary for establishing contacts, learning how the capital functioned, getting to know the various tradesmen with whom one would be working, and acquiring a little polish to one's manners. And of course no one begrudged a little fun in the meantime, so long as he didn't spend *all* the money his father had provided. The flat's present dweller was the scion of a spice merchant. The place smelled delicious—a definite advantage in a flat with bedroom windows overlooking the local stables. Now, however, having missed his appointment with the agent, he'd probably lost the place. Muttering nonspecific imprecations, he started back up the stairs.

"Cayden!"

Oh, splendid. Mieka frolicked in from the kitchen, waving a broadsheet.

"What?" Cade snapped.

"Temper, temper," the Elf chided. "You don't even know what I've brought you."

The Nayword, of course. It wasn't anything to do with the dinner; Tobalt had said he'd time that issue to coincide with Trials for maximum interest and sales.

"What?" he said again, more calmly this time.

"Pour me a brandy and find out."

"A little early, isn't it?"

"We'll call it 'tea.'"

They went into the parlor, where Cade got out the good brandy from its hiding place in the back of a cupboard. Mieka sulked at the sight of the two small—very small—bell-shaped snifters and the scant finger of liquor Cade poured into each.

"Talk. Or, more to the point, read."

"First tell me about Tobalt's dinner. Though I s'pose it couldn't've been much fun. After all, I wasn't there to keep things lively."

"Not your kind of fun, I think." And then, ashamed of himself, because Mieka had had insights into Cade's work that had often astonished him, he smiled and shrugged. "No girls to flirt with." Bexan was not the sort of woman one flirted with.

"What you mean is that you all sat there being intense and profound for hours on end, and I would've been bored out of me tiny little mind." He shook out the broadsheet with an important rustle and clearing of his throat. "We begin. 'The Shadowshapers are no strangers to controversy—'"

Cade groaned softly. "Couldn't Tobalt think up anything more original?"

"You want to hear this or not?"

"I take it I have no choice?"

Mieka made a face at him to acknowledge the reference to his Elsewhens. "Funny man. Where was I? '—no strangers to controversy, but last night at the Kiral Kellari the contentious turned scandalous when it was discovered a few minutes before their show that there were women in the audience.'"

Cade clasped a hand to his chest. "The shame! The disgrace! The total hypocrisy!"

"'Three unidentified females were hastily and somewhat noisily escorted from the premises. Dressed in men's clothing, they wore voluni—volmin'"—Mieka swore and tried again—"'*vol-u-min-ous* cloaks and concealing hats to disguise themselves, but were found out when one of them sought in her reticule to pay for their drinks.'"

"And just how deliberate was *that* little farce?"

"Oh, very. It goes on—'The Shadowshapers delayed their performance by some minutes while the women were removed, and immediately after the show left the establishment themselves, giving rise to unsubstantiated rumors that the women were in fact known to them personally.'"

"Well, Chirene wasn't there, I'd take oath on that," Cade mused. "Nor Deshananda, neither. They could be muffled to the eyebrows, but one look at them walking across a room and—any ideas who the ladies were?"

"Vered's new friend, for one."

"Can't say I'm surprised. She sort of invaded the dinner the other night."

"Did she?" Mieka laughed. "So that's why you said 'no girls to flirt with'! Vered would have a conniption fit. Anyways, let's see—here it is. 'Constables will be present outside the Kiral Kellari to discourage any further affronts to propriety.' Can't you just see Vered, once he hears the law will be guarding the place at their next show?"

"I'm surprised he didn't use a withie to spell out *Fuck You* on their way out the door."

"There's more. Says in here that it's being nosed about that Persons of Exalted Rank"—his voice gave the words their capitals—"are shocked and dismayed by the incident. And you know who *that* means."

Cade thought for a moment. "Not the Royals. They're always 'sources close to the first rank.'"

"Really? Hmm. I didn't know that. But it says 'a certain gracious lady'—must be Her Grace the Archduchess, don't you think? Anyways, she was overheard to remark that 'the very notion of women attending in a theater is shocking and openly flouting conventions to the furthest degree possible, also.'"

Cade winced. There was no mistaking the sentence structure—or lack of it. He could amost hear her voice. "I wonder who gave him the tip."

"Does it matter?"

"Probably not. Just curious. Easy enough to find out, though. Where she was, who she was with—" He broke off, eyeing Mieka. "You're plotting something."

"Me?"

"No magic."

"Why, Cayden, whatever are you talking about?"

"Clothes. Women's clothes. No skirts, no blouses, no gowns, no dresses. Not with magic. And you can quit with The Eyes. I'm immune."

"You're no fun anymore."

"I mean it, Mieka."

With a groan: "Do you have any idea how uncomfortable a corset is?"

"Tried one on, have you? Already planning your attack on the Shadowshapers' next show?"

"Don't have to try one on to know it looks like one of the more refined torments of one of the worser Hells. And why should I attack the Shadowshapers?"

"Mieka," he warned.

"And you never let *me* have any fun, either!"

"Just because I wouldn't let you take any black powder along on the Royal—"

"You searched me bags! Turned everything inside out, including all the pockets of all the trousers—"

"And I found it, too, didn't I? When I think of what you might've done with it—"

The boy pouted for a moment, then grinned. "There's always this year."

"Mieka!" But it was useless, he knew that well enough. He'd have to inspect even more carefully from now on. Still, that wasn't the main point. "I know you're plotting to sneak some girls into a Shadowshapers show. I saw it a long time ago."

"Did you?"

"Well, it changed a bit," he admitted. "I know there's nothing I can do to stop you, short of trussing you up in your lair at Wistly and letting you out only for our own performances. But you can't use magic like you did in Lilyleaf. You really can't, Mieka. For one thing, I'm not going to give you any. And I'll confiscate all the withies after every show, too, so you won't be able to use any leftovers."

Mieka chewed his lip. "I could dress up as a Good Sister. Nobody would dare touch—"

"Absolutely not!"

"I never knew you had a religion to be blasphemous about!"

"I don't. But it'd get you thrown into jail for crimes

against Chapel. Not only would it cost a small fortune in legal fees to get you out, we've bookings and I need my glisker."

Head cocked to one side, Mieka asked, "Do you?"

What did Mieka want him to say? *"Yes, we need you desperately, we're nothing without you, you can do whatever you please just so long as you show up for performances."* Arrogant little Elf. He ignored the memory of another Elsewhen—*"When Touchstone lost their Elf, they lost their soul"*—and said, "Well, *a* glisker. There are agencies we could consult, with an endless supply of— Mieka, don't you dare throw that glass at me!"

"Give me a reason not to!"

Cade relented and poured more brandy. "No magic. No Good Sister robes."

"And no corset! Mayhap I'll just have a ball gown made to me measure."

Cade grinned. "Now, *that's* a shopping trip I don't want to miss."

Mieka's face was suddenly decorated with his most sweetly, fiendishly, Angelically maniacal grin. "You already did, old son. You already did."

After a confused minute or two, Cade sat down very hard in one of his mother's dainty little chairs. It creaked a feeble protest and he heard a pillow stitch rip.

"Had to get meself somethin' to wear, didn't I? Not often that there's anythin' left in the withies. Got the girls in just fine, with me makin' the distraction. And then Bexan got to feelin' defiant, or so Jinsie told me later, because o' course they wouldn't let me in—"

"Jinsie was there?" Well, he'd known that before. But Megs had been the third girl. Odd that he hadn't had an Elsewhen that corrected the first two, he mused, then realized that his ability to change what happened had been assumed by someone else. Mistress Quickstride, probably.

"Anyways, Bexan pulled out her purse, all silk and beads—Wintering present from Vered—but even *that* would've been all right if she hadn't left her shirt open enough at the neck to make somebody suspicious. A nice pair on her, I'll say that." He finished off his brandy and held out his glass for more.

Cade gulped down his own drink and poured again. "What about Blye? Was she there?"

"You don't think she'd miss the fun, do you?"

"Jed must've been furious."

"Jed helped her get dressed."

Realizing at last that there was nothing about this that he was going to win, Cade gave up—but not on his earlier decree. "You'll try again. I'm fully aware that you'll try something like this again. But no magic. I'm serious, Mieka."

"Yeh, yeh, I'll be arrested for public indecency and you'll have to go to an agency—" All at once he sat up straight and smacked a hand against the arm of his chair. "Agency! We've been looking for that meddling fettler all wrong!"

*   *   *

THREE GROUPS WERE invited to perform at the Downstreet's grand reopening: Crystal Sparks, Touchstone, and the Shadowshapers—and *not* Black fucking Lightning. Cade didn't for an instant believe that this meant his Elsewhen about Thierin Knottinger and that malevolent thorn was now impossible. He'd just have to be on the watch for something else.

Mieka had to be right about an agency. Cade cursed himself for a fool not to have realized it long before.

Before Mieka had come along, he and Rafe and Jeska had not only relied on friends-of-friends to provide a glisker for a few shows, but they had twice hired someone from Clap and Cheer Theatrical Productions. Mayhap he had deliberately forgotten; the experiences had not been pleasant.

Some groups got together after advertising in *The Nayword* or broadsheets like it. Mostly it happened the way it had happened with Touchstone: like-minded friends, somebody who knew somebody, a player dissatisfied with the group he worked with went out looking for another or, as with Mieka, conducted a deliberate stalking. But there were a few small agencies who traded on the hopes and dreams of would-be players by offering to set them up. There were jobs to be had outside Gallantrybanks, and short-term hires for private performances. Very occasionally a member of an established group would become ill—as Chat had on the night when Mieka filled in for him—or be injured or otherwise unable to appear, and if friends couldn't help out, then one of the agencies was contacted. Personally, Cade would rather cancel a performance than risk an inexperienced or incompetent hired player. And what a change that made from the reckless old days.

As it happened, Cade didn't make the rounds of these agencies to ask if someone had hired a fettler to wander about Albeyn during the Royal last year. Just how he would have phrased his questions was a difficulty he didn't have to resolve, though he had made inquiries about where the agencies were located. Two mornings after he and Mieka discussed the possibility, he was in his room at Redpebble Square, about to prime withies for the night's performance and wondering how much brandy it would take to celebrate Jeska's Namingday and how much more to ease his pining over Kazie, when an Elsewhen showed him the truth of the matter.

{"—reliable means of telling who's what," said Thierin, looking quite chuffed with himself. "Took a bit of a while to sort *all* of them out, but—"

"You're that certain of your skills, then?" Cyed Henick stood by the inner doorway of a windowless little chamber, arms folded across his chest.

"Just said so, didn't he?" challenged Kaj Seamark.

"I thought you were having trouble discerning between Piksey and Sprite."

"That was months ago. Now we don't just make them squirm inside, we can tell who's squirming why!"

"Well." The Archduke shifted slightly, fur-lined robes gleaming with silver embroidery in the thin light of a single candle. "And the other matter?"

Thierin stopped looking happy. "It takes some doing, y'know."

"Being neither a glisker nor a fettler, I would not know. Explain it to me."

"Never had trouble with the Humans," Kaj said. "But think how it would seem, with only Humans demanding the goods. We need more practice."

"You'll have the opportunity in Vathis."

"About that," Thierin began.

"It's been arranged. Or are you frightened of sailing across the Flood?"

"Not that. We heard what happened to bloody Touchstone. Windthistle having to hide his ears—"

"Shall I send armed guards to protect you? If the prospect of a few superstitious thugs turns you into puling cravens, then perhaps I ought to reconsider this bargain."

"Oh, fine for you, isn't it?" Kaj burst out. "You in

your castles and palaces, surrounded by swords! It's us who'll be out there amongst the rabble!"

"Enough."

"Not by bloody half! Go here, do this, figure out what magic touches a Gnome but not a Wizard, push this idea or that notion into their heads—but not *all* of them or it'd look dodgy when a whole audience goes out the next day to buy at the same bakery or draper's shop—and now this trip to Vathis—"

Thierin interrupted the spate of complaints. "Ten shows in one city won't be enough to judge how much magic there still might be over there."

"That is my concern," said the Archduke.

Kaj wasn't yet finished. "And as for working out ways of blocking a fettler—"

"That is something else I wish to discuss." Suddenly his eyes were narrow slits of fury. "You hired someone to experiment. On Touchstone."

"Yeh? And what of it? You wanted us to find out how to—"

"And you hate them so much, you thought you'd find out using them. How dare you act without consulting me first? Crystal Sparks, those morons the Nightrunners, Hawk's Claw, even the Shadowshapers would have been better targets. But you had to set your sights on Touchstone. Did it occur to you that once they figured out what was happening, you are the first people they would suspect?"

"So what?" Kaj shrugged.

"Word came to me that Silversun has been asking around various agencies for the past week. Will he discover anything?"

"No. The fettler's just somebody Herris had classes with. Never good enough for a real stage. He won't talk. We paid him enough!"

"Very well. Heed me, little boys. Do not ever — *ever* — initiate such a plan again on your own. Do not interfere with Touchstone again. Or it might happen that I will change my mind. About *everything*."

The resentment in Kaj Seamark's watery blue eyes had told an obvious story. If *"everything"* was not forthcoming, he would react like a child deprived of a promised toy. What shocked Cade was the angry fear in Thierin's face. If the Archduke changed his mind . . . about what? This *"everything"* he spoke of was something Thierin craved so deeply that its threatened loss infuriated him even as it sent him into a panic.

"Everything . . ."

Unknowable, without further information, which might come in additional Elsewhens. What was important right now was that Thierin and Kaj had been behind the meddling fettler. What was more important was that Black Lightning would be forbidden to interfere with Touchstone ever again.

Cade knew why. The Archduke still had hopes of persuading him to his schemes, whatever they might be. Cade was valuable. Cade could see the futures.

He went to the Downstreet on the night of the grand opening as sure as he could be without having actually foreseen it that none of Black Lightning's members would even show up. There would be no grinning, triumphant Thierin Knottinger brandishing a thorn. There would be no need to protect Mieka from him or anyone else. Cade had visited a couple of agencies just to make sure that the Archduke would learn of it and give Black Lightning that little lecture.

The new Downstreet was furbished and frustled and shiny clean. The rows of benches glowed with polishing that had left a faint scent of citrusy wax in the air, soon to be overpowered by the scented clothes of the hundreds of invited guests in the first ten rows of the theater. These smells in turn would be obliterated by whatever fragrances first Crystal Sparks, then Touchstone, then the Shadowshapers cared to bestow upon the audience. Cade peeked out from behind the heavy brocade curtain—all lush flowers and swirling leaves—and grinned to himself as he caught sight of the owner of the Kiral Kellari sitting third-row center, chin sunk sulkily in his neck cloth. Whether Master Warringheath would succumb to temptation and redo the whole of his establishment as a real theater or content himself with a new mural remained to be seen. What he obviously could not resist was the chance to see what the competition had on offer. The rest of the seats were filling with paying customers who had bought tickets weeks in advance of opening night. Cade heard that seats had sold out within two hours.

Vered and Rauel were squared off over in a corner of the tiring room, with Romuald Needler grasping each with a placating hand. The Shadowshapers' manager was Giant-tall but Wizard-thin: towering over both tregetours but without the muscular heft to be any real physical threat. In fact, he looked exhausted, as if he'd been intervening in an argument that had gone on all day.

Cade heard Vered snarl, "Why play it for the toffs at Seekhaven when we can show it to those what's supported us all these years, our *real* audience?"

"Because it's not ready!" Rauel snapped back, and Needler pushed them farther into the corner and told them to keep their voices down.

Someone tugged on Cade's sleeve. He turned to find Jeska fidgeting at his side. "He's not here yet. I *knew* one of us should've gone over to Wistly to fetch him!"

"He'll be here, he'll be here," Cade soothed.

"You don't think Bl—anybody got to him anytime today, do you?"

Black Lightning were engaged to perform at a nobleman's country home. They let it be known that the pay was so colossal, they couldn't possibly refuse, but everybody knew they were hiding their mortification at not being invited to perform here tonight by leaving town entirely. Cade couldn't help but smile every time he thought about it. "They're thirty miles off," he said. "Stop fretting. He'll be here."

"He'll be here or I'll kill him," Rafe muttered.

"Fuck you!" Rauel shouted, and everybody flinched. He stalked off to the drinks table, leaving Needler behind to plead with the equally furious Vered. Sakary and Chat, standing nearby with large beers in their hands, simply looked resigned.

By the time Crystal Sparks had finished "The Glass Glove" to rousing applause—nobody did the old standards better—Mieka still hadn't shown up. Alaen and Briuly Blackpath went out in front of the closed curtains to entertain while the Sparks removed their glass baskets and lecterns and Touchstone set up. Music was its own magic, and the two lutenists wove spells with notes and their voices while Rafe, Jeska, and Cade did what Mieka ought to have been doing.

"I'll kill him," Rafe kept saying under his breath. "I will *kill* him."

"Queue forms on the right," Jeska told him.

Cade was beginning to worry that he'd been mistaken, and that even though Black Lightning wasn't actually present, they had done something in defiance of the Archduke's orders, when Alaen and Briuly broke off in the middle of a song, laughing.

"What the—?" Jeska hurried to the curtain, twitched aside a fold, and half a moment later was doubled over in silent giggles. By now the whole audience was laughing, hooting, whistling, calling out raucous and obscene suggestions. Cade and Rafe joined Jeska at the curtain and peered through the gap.

Flouncing down the aisle was a preposterous vision in bright pink silk ruffles and gold brocade swagged over purple petticoats. Small hands in red lace gloves waved enthusiastic greeting to the audience; a head topped by what looked like a green velvet pancake decorated with an eruption of downy white feathers nodded gracious acknowledgment of the cheers and applause.

"Oh, for fuck's sake," Rafe whispered. "I really *will* kill him!"

Mieka's progress was about to be interrupted by a pair of constables—faithfully posted by the local station because the Shadowshapers were playing tonight—and how he'd got by them in the first place didn't bear contemplation. They were advancing down the aisle after Mieka, who was almost to the front row.

Cade didn't need an Elsewhen to show him what was about to happen. Mieka would be seized by the constables, and yell something like *"Unhand me, you fritlags!"* in the best tradition of Uncle Breedbate, and escape them somehow, and race through the theater, and some people would aid him and some people would try to catch him, and there'd be a bloody riot and not only would Touchstone never work the lovely new theater at the Downstreet but they'd have to pay for the damages, too.

Cade stepped out from behind the curtain. Part of him was cursing the mad little Elf—he had to choose *tonight* to make his point?—and part of him was writhing at the total unprofessionalism of what he was about to do, but most of him was cheering Mieka on and perfectly willing to help. Planting his fists on his hips, he roared, "What's all this, then? Mieka, you're late!"

Mieka came to a halt in a flurry of pink and gold and purple and green, with feathers. "Goodest of good evenings to you, dear old thing! Excessively sorry, sincerely I am!"

Knowing themselves to be superfluous, Alaen and Briuly and their lutes departed for the wings. The audience quieted—more or less—to take in this unscheduled show.

The constables paused, suspicious and confused. One of them said, "See here, now! There's not to be no ladies in no theaters!"

"That's no lady," Cade told him. "That's my glisker."

"But he's not—that's to say, he don't look—"

Cade sighed a long-suffering sigh. "I suppose it's his notion of an educational demonstration."

"A what?"

But his fellow constable had had enough. "There's laws about women bein' in places like this here," he said firmly. "And whatever anyone says, that's women's clothes."

Abruptly Cade saw before him a letter that had not yet been written. *As for the events at the Downstreet, I think you will agree that Silversun's cleverness in outwitting the constables—*"

Not much cleverness needed, come to it. "Ah, but a *man* wearing them!" Cade said. "Are there laws against *that*?"

"If there were," somebody yelled from the upper tier of benches, "there's a noble lord or three would be in quod!"

"As it happens," Cade went on, "there *aren't* any laws about that. And since he really is a man under all that tawdry frippering—"

"Tawdry?" Mieka wailed. "I paid heaps for all this!"

"One can only wonder why!" Rafe yelled from behind the curtains.

Cade went on, "As I was saying, there's no law against a man wearing whatever he pleases—"

"But—" The constable was choking on outrage. "But if that's true—"

Beaming, Mieka finished for him. "Then any man could wear what he likes, and come right on in and sit himself down and watch the show. And it's brilliant we'll be tonight, no mistaking."

"Talking of which," Cade said pointedly, "I really do need my glisker to give this performance, so won't you please excuse us?" To Mieka: "Get your scrawny ass onstage, Windthistle!"

Mieka scampered over to the steps, bounded up onstage, and sank into a deep curtsy. Applause thundered, even from the more straitlaced of the nobility sitting in the front rows. Proof positive, as if any could be necessary, that Mieka was as irresistible as the tide, a thunderstorm, or a brain seizure.

"You can't work in all that lot!" Cade exclaimed, and had an instant of sheer panic. Surely the clothes were real. Surely he wore something beneath them.

"Oh—frightfully sorry, just give me a moment." He peeled off the red lace gloves and smiled brightly at Cade. "Ready!"

"Mieka!" *And if you're dressed in nothing but magic, Rafe can hold my coat while I kill you.*

Next went the hat, sailing to the side of the stage, where Alaen caught it. Cade folded his arms across his chest and glowered.

"Oh, very well. Bloody great bully! You *never* let me have any fun!"

Fingers scrabbled at his waist, strings were untied, and after a suggestive and ultimately undignified wriggle, the gold brocade skirt and purple petticoats dropped to the stage. Revealed—and here Cade paused to be monumentally grateful—were black trousers and boots. The billowing pink blouse stayed.

With a masquer's sense of timing, Jeska reached from behind the curtain and yanked Mieka by an arm. As he vanished with a yelp, Cade bowed to the audience, then slipped between the folds of velvet to find Mieka already halfway to the glisker's bench. Somebody cried out, "Touchstone!" and he and Rafe lunged for their lecterns while Jeska scooted hastily to center stage. With a muttered curse, he nipped back out in front just as the curtains parted, and kicked the abandoned skirts towards the wings. Alaen scurried out to grab them.

"Have a care, mate!" Mieka hollered. "Those go to me mother-in-law tomorrow!"

Rafe shook his head. "Gods pity the poor woman. May we start now, or are *you* the show tonight?"

Mieka stretched elaborately, cracked his knuckles, bounced on his toes a few times, twirled a withie between his fingers, then rapped the withie against a glass basket. "Pray silence for His Fettlership!"

"Enough!" Cayden bellowed. "My Lords and Gentlemen, we present for you tonight 'Feather-head'—"

Mieka wailed a protest.

"—I mean, 'Feather*beds*.'" And praise be to whatever deities watched over theater folk that they'd planned a comedy for this performance. What it might take to settle an audience for something serious after the pre-show farce, he didn't like to think.

Twenty-one

IT HADN'T BEEN in Mieka's plan to get arrested, and he knew full well that Cade would rescue him if things got risky. But he hadn't expected Cade to understand almost instantly what he was about, nor to aid and abet with such enthusiasm and to such excellent effect. The expression on the constables' faces, the reactions of the crowd—he really must stop underestimating the man.

"Featherbeds" (the rude version) was a rollicking success. Mieka clothed Jeska as the Bewildered Bride in gold brocade and purple petticoats to match what he'd worn during his grand entrance into the Downstreet, and even the constables (standing way at the back; the owner had offered them a free show to make up for the trouble) laughed themselves breathless. Mieka was again reminded that wielding his withies was problematic with wrist-ruffles.

Touchstone was called back for two extra bows. Splendid for them; not so great for the Shadowshapers, but not because they now had to follow a triumph. The trouble came because they had additional time to fight over what they'd perform.

When the curtains closed and Alaen and Briuly traded

expert notes that ran each string of their Hadden Windthistle lutes, Touchstone began moving equipment and the Shadowshapers began setting up. Rauel and Vered seemed to be continuing a fight that had started a few minutes ago—or mayhap it was just one more episode in a fight that had started the day they met.

"I keep telling you it's not ready!" Rauel snapped at Vered as he helped Chat carry their glass baskets to the glisker's bench. "The middle part doesn't make any sense, there's no bridge to the final section—"

Vered hurled back, "You're just too stupid to understand them!"

Mieka traded startled looks with Jeska and worked faster at packing baskets into their padded crates. The two tregetours had never been shy about expressing their grievances to each other, but rarely did they take their quarrels public like this. All that separated them from an audience was some velvet and gold fringe, and two lutenists playing old songs.

"What's *stupid* is the whole concept!"

"And how would Your Lordship be writing it, then? All pathetic farewell embraces between childhood friends, and flooding the audience with tears by the fifth line? You never did have a clue about pacing, did you?"

"At least my audiences *feel* something! You're all words, words, words, no real heart to them, never a laugh or a cry or an honest emotion—"

"If you ever put a genuine idea into one of your scribblings, it would die of shock and loneliness! Ask them!" Vered pointed at Mieka and Jeska.

Mieka almost dropped a withie. Quickly shoving it into the velvet pouch, he thrust the whole of it at Jeska and looked round for Rafe and Cade to come help carry the baskets. Kearney Fairwalk had taken charge of

Cade's lectern, staggering a bit beneath the weight of rosewood inlaid with polished dragon bone. The lute music still trilled from the other side of the curtains.

"*Ask* them!" Vered insisted. "C'mon, what d'you think of Rauel's little muddles? Any of them ever manage to make you think a single thought?"

Mieka tried to smile. "Oh, me poor overworked brain's too busy with working out all those deep thoughts of Cade's that I—"

"Deep as a puddle of piss from a parched horse!"

Straightening, Mieka began, "Now, wait just a tick—"

"Partridge," Cade drawled from behind him. "Puddle of piss from a parched partridge. It's not like you, Vered, to miss a word-trick like that."

"Doesn't miss many, does he?" Rauel asked with a silken smile. "When you get right down to it, in spite of what Bexan thinks, they're all he really has."

Vered lunged for him. Romuald Needler appeared out of nowhere and grabbed Vered. "Stop it! Everyone will hear you!"

"I don't fuckin' care!"

Alaen and Briuly seemed to be playing and singing very loudly all of a sudden.

"I know you wanted to introduce the new play tonight," the manager soothed, skeletal hands still holding on like grim death to Vered's shoulders. "But you have to give them something light, something cheerful. You owe them a good, stirring story, a play to have them—"

"To have them sleek and self-satisfied at the end?" Vered interrupted. "You mean like 'Doorways'? Have them go home all cozy-minded and happy with their rotten little lives, and—"

"Vered!"

"Oh, Cade knows what I'm talking of, right enough! Angels forfend that anybody should leave the theater discontented after 'Doorways' shows them their lives are just perfect! Protect them from wanting anything more, anything better—"

"Shut it!" Mieka roared. "You smug sniveler—always moaning about how the greatness of your ideas gets lost in—"

"Boys, please!" begged Fairwalk.

Cade had hold of Mieka's elbow. "Don't, it's all right, he doesn't mean—"

"Yeh, he does! The only one who *really* knows how to do theater, ain't he? That's enough to make a cat laugh! Compared to *you*, he doesn't know which end of the pen to write with!"

Vered laughed a short, sneering bark of a laugh. "Oh, and he's the eminent arbiter now, is he? Tell me, Tinwhistle, do they have to explain the whole story to you every time, or can you actually, y'know, *read*?"

Cade growled, and now it was Mieka holding him back from giving Vered the thrashing he so obviously courted.

"I think that's enough," Chat said mildly. "Unless you have it in mind, Vered old man, for the Shadowshapers to copy Touchstone." As Vered spluttered his outrage, Chat lifted one of his own glass baskets. His eyes were as cold as a wintry sea. "Because if you don't shut up, I'll shatter this right over your head."

With a final snarl, Vered pointed at Rauel. "Here, we do it your way. Your withies, your play. At Trials, we do it *mine*."

Mieka was dragged to the wings by Cade, with Rafe and Jeska carrying baskets and Fairwalk helping out with Rafe's lectern. Safely in the tiring room, they heard the somewhat desperate call of, "The Shadowshapers!" and Rauel saying, "'Piksey Ride,'" but Sakary was much too expert a fettler to allow even a tendril of the magic to go anyplace but out into the audience. So Touch-stone sat, and gratefully drank, and listened to the laughing crowd.

At length, Briuly Blackpath observed, "Well, that was pleasant."

Mieka nodded. "Wasn't it just." Restless, he rose and went looking for his brocade skirt and purple petticoats. Cade joined him after a brief consultation with Alaen.

"He's got the hat," Cade said, "but the rest is over in the wings other side of the stage. Beholden for the defense with Vered, but you were about to clout him a good one, and that wouldn't be nice."

Mieka snagged a wineglass from a passing servant girl and took a few swallows. "I owed you, for the help with the constables."

"When did you and me start keeping score?"

A little snort of laughter escaped him. "We were good, weren't we? Oughta work it up as an opening act!"

"Do you have any idea how ridiculous you look in that blouse?"

Batting his eyelashes, he cooed, "But I thought you liked me in pink!"

Cade pretended to look him over. "Well, at least it's real, and not magic."

"I'm a good boy, I am. I follows me orders."

Cade's turn to snort. "Oh, always. Everybody knows that." His expression changed subtly before he said, "Don't be too hard on Vered. He's been pricking a lot of thorn lately. His wife's sent in the legal papers. She wants a divorce."

"And what does Vered want?"

"His wife and children in one house, his ladylove in another up the road, with him drifting between as the mood takes him. A settled home, *and* the freedom to do as he pleases. An ordinary life, *and* the life of a traveling player." Cade gave a little shrug. "He wants what the rest of us want, I suppose. And, like the rest of us, being denied it makes him angry."

"Vered ought to be growing up a bit, I think."

"This from somebody who frisked in here wearing purple petticoats?"

Mieka refused to take the bait or succumb to the laughter in Cade's eyes. "He didn't have to take his temper out on you."

A second shrug, both shoulders this time. "Doesn't matter." He paused, then said, "I only met her that one time . . . what do *you* think of her?"

Mieka considered. "I can tell you this. Her eyes look right through you, but not because she's looking *into* you, if you get what I mean."

"As if you're not even there?"

"More like she knows you're there but you're of absolutely no importance so why should she waste her time and energy seeing you? I think the only person she bothers to see is Vered."

Alaen approached, the green pancake hat in hand. "Where'd you find this thing, anyways?" he asked, grinning as he arranged it atop Mieka's head. "Your lovely lady wife didn't sew it, that's for certain sure. A woman of taste and discretion—not to mention a sense of color!"

"Bought it off one of the girls on Chaffer Stroll. Had six different sorts of Hell convincing her that was *all* I wanted! How's the lute been treating you? Fa has a couple new ones he'd be pleased to show you and Briuly."

"We meant to come by around Wintering, but we had other things to do—thanks to Cayden, here."

"So you went after the Rights." Cade nodded approval.

"Sought, but didn't find. Skipped a good-paying job

at the Palace to do it, too." He shook his head, reddish-brown curls bobbing. "There we were, right time, right place, freezing our balls off, and not a sliver of sunlight to be had all day long."

"Well, that was the trouble, then," Mieka said. "Next year, mayhap—"

"Next year?" Alaen laughed. "Never again! You're mistaken, Cade, and there's an end to it."

"No, I'm not mistaken," Cade said, voice very soft. All at once Mieka saw the satisfaction of a good performance and the fun of the little farce they'd enacted beforehand vanish from Cade's gray eyes. Mieka knew what the trouble was. Cade wanted Alaen and Briuly, not the staggeringly rich Lord Oakapple, to have the Treasure, but more than that he wanted everyone to know how clever he was to have figured out the truth of it.

"*You* go look for it, then," Alaen muttered. "Haring off to the provinces in the dead of winter, chasing after some delusion—"

Mieka was annoyed, or he wouldn't have said it. "You'd know all about that sort of thing, wouldn't you?"

Alaen turned crimson, then white to the lips. His fist clenched dangerously around the neck of his lute until his thumb slipped and a string thwanged. He realized what he was doing and, with a sharp curse, turned on his heel and stalked off.

Cade nudged Mieka with an elbow. "You're making friends right and left tonight, aren't you? What's got you in a temper?"

"He's got a nerve, talking of delusions. The times he's shown up drunk or thorned to the tips of his ears at Hilldrop, whining over Chirene—it's no great astonishment that his favorite of your plays is 'Doorways.' For that little while at the end, he can believe that she's his."

"And that's what Vered objects to," Cade said softly.

"Give people what they want, if only for a moment. It's not what I meant with that play, not at all."

"I know." All at once it was as if they were alone in Cade's room high over Redpebble Square, or in his own little lair in the tower at Wistly Hall. "It's about choosing. About being aware of the choices as you're making them."

"How much trouble would we be in, I wonder, if we changed it up a bit, and rather than give them the satisfaction of what they most desire, we—"

"—slap them with the exact opposite? 'This life, and none other' as their worst nightmare instead of their sweetest dream?" Mieka shook his head. "Save that for something else, Quill. 'Doorways' makes one point. Use another play to make a different one."

Thin shoulders twisted his discomfort, and before Mieka could say anything more Cade called to Briuly, halfway across the tiring room. Alaen's cousin sauntered over, all spindly limbs and extravagant ears, fingers twiddling idly at his lute strings.

Cade wasted no time. "I hear you looked for the Rights at Wintering."

"Still scraping the mud and cow shit off me boots to prove it!" He laughed the type of loud, strident laugh typical of a little too much greenthorn. And his eyes held something reckless and wild that made even Mieka want to take a step back. Then, voice lowering conspiratorially, he went on, "Been there *twice*, I have. Once with Alaen, and I just got back from a trip on me own."

Cade was frowning his bewilderment. "But it's the wrong time of year—"

"Quarterday." He winked and played a few cascading triplets on his lute. "You think on it a bit of a while, eh? I'm off!"

"Quarterday?" Mieka echoed as he walked away. "What's he mean by that?"

"Damned if I know. Come on, they're finished out there and we'll be asked to join them and the Sparks for some final bows."

* * *

MIEKA WAS STILL trying to think through the puzzle of Quarterdays a week later on the walk over to Redpebble Square. It was a hike from Wistly, but he wanted the fresh air, the exercise, and the chance to hang about the streets of Gallantrybanks. All the months Touchstone spent on the Circuit, the nights onstage, the days going back and forth to Hilldrop, the time he spent there with his wife and daughter (and mother-in-law, *still*), meant that he had few opportunities to wander the city. He missed the noise and the colors, the bustle and the scurry. But he couldn't stroll about the way he used to. He wasn't anonymous anymore, not with Touchstone's placards up all over. Every other block someone called out from loading a wagon or frustling a display of goods.

"Great show t'other night, Mieka!"

"Laughed fit to split me guts at the 'Sweetheart'!"

"I'm takin' the country cousins to the Downstreet next week, special treat. Do the 'Dragon', whyn't ya?"

He spent time with them all, trading quips, delighted to be famous. The walk to Redpebble thus took even longer than usual, and it was almost time for tea when he walked down Criddow Close to the glassworks.

Quarterdays, he kept repeating to himself when not otherwise distracted. There was one in Spring and one in Autumn, with Midsummer precisely in between. Together with Wintering, they marked off the four quarters of the year. Why Briuly would want to visit the place on either Quarterday was a mystery. And none of it could have anything to do with Midsummer, because the setting sun would be in the wrong place to hit the fallen stones hiding the Rights. He couldn't understand it. He was hoping that Quill had worked it all out by now.

He was also hoping that Blye could oblige him with a glasscrafting that was perfectly legal for her to do. Weary of being half-strangled by a neck cloth, frustrated by having to tie the elaborate knots dictated by fashion, and strictly forbidden by his wife to loosen an already tied one just enough to be able to slip it on and off as required, he intended to ask Blye if she could make him a glass ring.

The notion captured her interest at once. "Not plain, of course—knowing you," she chuckled. "A simple glass ring in any color you like—but what if I make it like a real ring for the fingers, with a decoration to set off whatever color you're wearing? I could even make a flat face for it and glue in a gemstone, or something made of glass or porcelain. Would that suit?"

"Down to the ground," he said happily. "You're a darling to indulge me."

"I'm a practical businesswoman," she retorted. "When you're at Trials, every noble in Albeyn will see you wearing something new and bright and stylish. I'll make a small fortune."

"Do I get a cut of the profits?"

"No." She grinned.

"But it was my idea! And me doing the publicity!"

"Half a percent."

"Blye! Who was it gave you the notion for the pottinger? And talking of that, any words of appreciation from the Princess?"

"Not yet. She has better things to do than paw through baby gifts. Two percent, and that's my final offer."

"That's no offer, that's an insult," he groused.

"Two and a half."

"Forty-five."

"Forty-five?" she asked blankly.

Where had that number come from? He covered with a mysterious smile while chasing things in his mind. Forty-five . . . not the number of plays in Touchstone's portfolio, not the address of anyone he knew . . . his mother had just turned forty-six—

An Elsewhen, a good one, about Cade's Namingday surprise party. Not that Cade had ever told him much by way of specifics. Touchstone had just played a show, Cade had forgot that it was his Namingday, Mieka had a diamond earring and gray hair, and they'd had bubbledy wine in a pair of new crystal goblets. Blye's work, Mieka's gift.

So that must be how it all connected, he told himself. Blye, glass, mention of the gift for little Prince Roshlin. With a mental shrug—it was as good an explanation as he ever expected his brain to provide about its own peculiar workings—he smiled wider at Blye.

"Forty-five. Twenty for the idea, twenty for the promoting of it, and five percent because you argued with me!"

"All right," she said at once. "But you realize that whatever I end up charging everyone else for them, I'll have to charge you triple."

"Splendid! I'll collect my forty-five percent of triple the price!"

Blye gave up and laughed. Almost the next instant, though, she made a worried face and said, "But, Mieka— is it legal for me to make them? They'd be hollow, after all."

"When has that ever stopped you?" He pointed to the dinner service she was making for Vered Goldbraider, that lacked only one more platter and a couple of serving bowls.

"If I'm to make this fortune, and give you forty-five percent of it, then I have to be sure it's all right for me to craft them. If not, I'd have to give the idea to someone else, someone with a hallmark."

Mieka chewed his lip. "Not hollow," he stated. "Empty. There's a difference." Then he saw that her dark eyes were laughing at him. "Blye! That's a nasty trick to play on the man who just gave you the fashion idea of the year!"

"My father used to say that the Glasscrafters Guild gave him the authority to make a nothingness for other people to fill. 'I create emptiness,' he called it."

"Withies aren't emptiness or nothingness. They're *possibilities*."

"How poetic of you, Master Windthistle! And talking of withies, let me show you the new ones. I've put a little notch at the crimp end so just a touch will tell you who made them."

"And hide them if the Stewards inspect us. Not that they ever have," he mused. "I wonder why that is?"

"You still have the old ones my father made, and bought a dozen or so from Master Splithook."

"And never use them."

"I s'pose they keep track with the glasscrafters regarding who buys how many. But one of these days somebody's going to figure out that there's a discrepancy in numbers between what you've actually bought and how many you use. If you keep on shattering the poor things—"

"Getting rid of the evidence, just in case. And it shatters me heart as well every time I do it. Blye, I can always tell your withies the instant I touch them. I don't have to check. They feel like *you*."

She regarded him pensively. "Y'know, sometimes I quite like having you for a brother-in-law."

The bell above the shop door rang out. Mieka whisked the illegal glass twigs into a wrapping cloth and stashed them in a drawer while she went through to the shop. Before he could hide more than a few wineglasses and bowls of Vered's new dinnerware, Blye called out in a half-strangled voice, "Mieka!"

He ran into the shop, careful to shut the connecting door firmly behind him. Standing there amidst the bright displays of plates and candleflats was the fettler girl, Megs. At least he thought it was Megs. The messy dark-blond braid had become a pile of intricate plaits atop her head. The well-worn clothing had given way to a black skirt and a smart bottle-green jacket with thin black twists of embroidery on hem and cuffs. The color matched her eyes, and it was by her eyes that he finally knew her for sure.

She was accompanied by an elderly gentleman in Princess Miriuzca's livery of blue coat and brown trousers and lots of little silver buttons. He held a sea-green pillow with brown fringe. On the pillow rested a pair of blue gauntlet gloves, finest cheveril and stitched with silver thread in a pattern of forget-me-nevers.

"Mistress Windthistle," Megs said, and now Mieka was absolutely certain sure it was her, for the voice was the same even if the accents were now those of the Court. "It is my great honor to present you with the first in what Princess Miriuzca hopes will become a tradition in Albeyn as it has been for many long years in her father's country."

"I'm—I'm flattered," Blye managed. "But I'm afraid I don't understand."

Rather than answer, Megs turned to the old man. "The proclamation?"

He looked chagrined. "In the carriage, Your Lady-ship." He departed, leaving the pillow on a counter.

Mieka made astonished eyes at Megs. "'Your Lady-ship'?"

She ignored him. "Mistress Windthistle, if your husband is at home, then perhaps he might want to join us."

"He's—uh, he's upstairs in his office, I think—"

"Go," Mieka advised. She went. He faced Megs again.

"I'll explain, I promise," she said quickly. "It really is me—one 'me,' anyhow."

"How many are there?"

"Several. Just go along with this one, won't you, please?"

He smiled and asked brightly, "I'll go find Cayden, shall I?"

"No! I mean, I'd hoped we could keep this betwixt the two of us." The green eyes narrowed. "You keep my secret—for now, at least—and I'll keep yours."

He had no idea what she was talking of, but decided to go along. For now.

Blye had paused upstairs to tidy her hair and put on a clean shirt. By the time she returned with Jedris—as visibly baffled as she was—the Princess's gentleman had returned with a parchment sporting a big blue wax seal all beribboned with blue and brown and silver. Outside in Criddow Close, a small crowd had gathered, attracted by a Royal carriage, murmuring speculations.

"I think we'll keep this private," Megs said, "but leave the shades up on the windows."

"Witnesses," Mieka said shrewdly.

"Your pardon, m'lady," Jed ventured, "but what's going on?"

She smiled and became almost pretty. "Your wife is

about to become the first crafter in Albeyn to be honored with the Gift of the Gloves."

"Shall I read, Your Ladyship?" the gentleman asked.

She gestured gracious permission and they settled in for what turned out to be a long, long siege.

"Be it hereby and heretofore known to the whole of the Kingdom of Albeyn by these presents and munificences, that the most gentle and skilled Mistress Blye Windthistle, born Cindercliff, who erewhile contrived for Her Royal Highness the Princess Miriuzca, Duchess of Downymede, a fine and loving mathom for which Her Royal Highness the Princess Miriuzca has determined to express her approof in a manner most meet and fitting—"

Mieka blinked. Good Gods—this was worse than listening to Uncle Breedbate. He held up a hand and the flow of words came to a temporary halt. "Sorry. What's a *mathom*?"

"A gift," Megs said. "Say on."

The gentleman cleared his throat, shot Mieka a narrow glance of warning, and said on for a good ten minutes at least. The proclamation roamed about the Kingdom of Albeyn and all its divisions with special emphasis on the larger towns and cities; got lost in Gallantrybanks for a sentence or two; branched off to include all those visitors, merchants, traders, travelers, tourists, immigrants, sojourners, students, guests, and whomsoever else for whatsoever purpose, intention, reason, or function might set foot on the soil of Albeyn ruled over by our most gracious Lord King Meredan; emerged triumphant at the Palace of our most gracious Lord the King; returned to warn each and all and every of these whomsoevers that the protection of the Crown was involved and any treasons, felonies, and or misdemeanors by whomsoever and in whatsoever manner done committed or perpetrated and by whom or to whom or for whom, when, how, and after what manner and circumstances and every one of them and any one of them in any manner whatsoever would be punished to the fullest extent of the law; and finally, magnificently, concluded that the Gifting of the Gloves to the honorable trusty and well-beloved Mistress Blye Windthistle, born Cindercliff, signified that her crafting of any and all items, decorations, objects, articles, and various and sundry other things made of glass was to be viewed as if the hands of Royalty had Themselves performed the necessary work.

Blye was frowning a lingering bewilderment. Jed looked as if he'd acquired a sudden case of the staggers. Mieka wished Cayden were here to translate.

Megs did it for them. "What all that means is that it's even better than a Royal Warrant. When you get one of those, it's because you supply the Palace with cloth or foodstuffs or whatever. But this—"

"It's saying," Mieka interrupted, abruptly enlightened, "that any work Blye does—anything at all!—has to be seen as being done by the Princess's own lovely hands!"

"Exactly," Megs agreed. "It's a very old custom in—" She broke off with a sigh. "I never can pronounce the name of her father's country."

"That's all right," Mieka consoled her. "Nobody else can, either. I've *been* there and I can't pronounce it!"

"It's the symbolism, you see," Megs went on. "From her hands to yours, you wearing her Gloves is as if she were doing the crafting herself. I'm told that the recipients usually have a glass display case made." She smiled again. "Not the slightest bother for you!"

"Say something, Blye," Mieka urged.

"I–I'm—"

"Almost twenty-two years you've known Cayden Sil-versun," Mieka mourned, "and you can't think of a sin-gle word? Don't wait for him to compose something appropriate for putting in a letter. I'm sure that M—that Her Ladyship will be asked for a report when she gets back to the Palace." He'd almost said her name (if "Megs" really was her name), and he didn't want to give away her secret. Not until he knew what secret of his she thought she possessed.

Jed put an arm around his wife. "We're incredibly honored."

Blye nodded, wide-eyed, then found her voice. "Your Ladyship, please tell Her Royal Highness that this is out of all imagining. The gift of the pottinger for the new little Prince was just—"

"Oh, it wasn't *just*," Megs said. "I've seen it, and it's charming. Besides, I'm told there's a little glass box of some kind?"

Mieka nearly whooped with delight. The pottinger was ordinary glasscrafting, but the box Cade had pre-sented her with two summers ago had been imbued with Blye's magic—the same sort that went into the withies, which she could now make without fear and without a hallmark and without having to hide them and make them in secret late at night and—

—and now she could make *anything* she chose. Bowls, basins, jars, teapots, vases, cups, goblets, spoons, all the hollow things that had been forbidden to her before the Giving of the Gloves. The Glasscrafters Guild, he real-ized with glee, would be apoplectic. If they offered her a hallmark now, she could even refuse it as unnecessary.

But there was something else about this, something deeper and more significant. The magic. Blye's magic. *Any* magic. The Princess was signaling her acceptance of it—Hells, she was actively seeking it out in this glass-crafter.

Cade would be inconsolable when he found out he'd missed this.

Jedris had the sense to open a bottle of wine. He poured it into glasses that were the last of those made by Blye's father, a varied collection of samples that would never be sold, because the crafter who made them would never make more. When Megs's eyes noted the miscellany of styles and colors, Jed explained who had made them and why they were still in the shop.

"I think they're perfect for this occasion," he finished. "He'd be even prouder of her than I am right now."

"The pottinger was yours, too," Blye protested, blushing. "The wooden part."

"But it's not my primary trade, woodworking. Mieka, hand these round and let's have a toast to Princess Miriuzca and Prince Roshlin."

Soon thereafter Megs and the old gentleman took their leave. Mieka walked them out. The small, light carriage, drawn by a single horse, had by now attracted quite the crowd. The driver, also in Miriuzca's livery, made friendly shooing motions to his audience and climbed back up to the bench. Megs murmured something to the old man, who glanced at Mieka, then at her, and sighed quietly.

"I've friends on the other side of Redpebble Square," he said to no one in particular.

"You have coin for a hire-hack?"

"I do, Your Ladyship. I give you good afternoon."

"Master Windthistle, may I have the honor of your escort?"

When they were settled in the closed carriage, she opened all the windows. "My father would have a spasm if he heard I'd ridden alone with a young man all the way to Waterknot Circle."

"But riding all the way from the Palace to Criddow Close with an *old* man is fine? Or is it just that I'm a disreputable theater player? How much does he know about your ambition to be a Steward? And how do you know where I live?"

She folded her hands in her lap. "'Twasn't very subtle of me, getting rid of the poor man like that. But we must talk."

"Oh, no." He lolled back in the leather seat, folded his arms, and grinned. "*You* talk. I'll listen."

Twenty-two

SHIFTING POSITION SLIGHTLY so she could look at him, Megs began with her real name. "The original 'me' really is Lady Megueris Mindrising. My father's side is mostly Wizard and Human, and my mother's people are mostly Human and Piksey."

"Piksey?" Mieka asked.

She knew what he meant, and replied tersely, "Yes, I had a twin. He died. So did my mother. May I continue? Beholden to you. As you can guess by the name, we're quite repulsively rich. My father is the last of the Mindrisings, my mother was the last of the Thatchwhites, and I'm the last of both."

"Yet you want to be a fettler. A Steward."

"Tell me, Master Windthistle, do you interrupt everyone so constantly? And if so, how have you escaped bodily harm?"

"It's me winning personality and adorable smile. You're at Court now, with the Princess, yeh?"

"She has an ask of Touchstone, but I'll come to that later."

"Why not now? Because I think I can tell you the rest of it. Your father wants you to make a splendiferous marriage, so he hauled you off to the Palace to become a lady-in-waiting. Everybody knows how rich you are, so you're fending off all sorts of charming young men with their charming proposals, and escape that hothouse whenever you can, so you leaped at the chance to represent the Princess on this errand to Blye. How'm I doin' so far?"

"Fair to middling. The young men and their proposals are the farthest thing from charming, but other than that, you've got it pretty accurately."

He could guess a lot more than was polite to say. For example, as an adored only child, she had been cosseted and indulged until the belief that she could indeed become a Steward was only natural to her. Denied nothing in childhood, grown to be a very wealthy young woman, why should she not do exactly as she pleased? Her father ought to have anticipated her refusal to follow the traditional path of a rich highborn lady. Mieka did admire her, though, for knowing everything wouldn't simply be handed to her on a golden plate. She understood that she would have to work for it, and she was willing to do so.

He said none of that, however. What he did say was, "You were at Coldkettle for the wedding as an invited guest, not extra help."

"How *clever* of you to work that out."

"Another of my endearing qualities. And at Lilyleaf you really were on holiday, but not because you'd saved and scrimped for it." He nodded to her shoes. "A barmaid couldn't pay for those with three months of what she makes in wages and trimmings. And please do forgive me for mentioning it, but those pretty green sparklies hanging from your earlobes aren't cut crystal." With a little shrug of apology, he added, "Knowing a glasscrafter, one notices these things."

"Of course. I'd expect nothing less." She eyed him sidelong. "But you'd still like to know how I know Croodle."

"Hadn't got that far yet," he admitted. "I circled back to that young boy and his sister what you were protecting that night at the Keymarker."

"Children of my father's friends. They were at a Court banquet that night. The children slipped away, just as I told you. If I hadn't gone along with them, they'd only have got into trouble. They've done it before. And working as a barmaid, I wouldn't have to bother with trousers and boy's clothing."

"A Court banquet is *work*?"

"Ever been to one?" she challenged.

"Several," he replied breezily, not adding that all three of them (*three* was the same as *several,* wasn't it?) had been in the Princess's country, and Touchstone had sat with those who couldn't in decency be relegated to the servants hall.

"They're work," Megs said grimly.

"And that night was another chance to escape and have a little fun."

"If you think it's fun to block all that magic you hurl about like a nobleman strewing coins on Beggarly Day—"

"Tell me about Croodle."

Again she smiled, and again he thought that she really ought to do it more often. "She knows who I am, of course. The official me. My father took me to Lilyleaf when I was thirteen, and being a good, dutiful child, I promptly ran off to play and got myself lost. Croodle was out taking the air, and we got to talking, and she brought me back to her inn. She sent to my father and he came himself to fetch me. She refused the purse he wanted to give her as a reward. That impressed him, as you may imagine. So he got her the contract for each of the Circuits. She applied for it, she earned it, and it only took a nudge from my father to secure it."

"If you're the reason we all eat, drink, and sleep at Croodle's, then every one of us is eternally beholden to you."

"It nearly didn't happen," she told him, frowning. "She's from the Islands. There are Dark Elves nearly as black as she is, but from the way some of the commissioners talked . . ." She ended with a shrug. "They put it about that they were concerned because she doesn't have any magic, and they like to place the players with someone who has at least a little, to make them feel at home. Lord and Lady, what twaddle!"

Mieka snorted. "Remind me to tell you sometime about what happened to us on our very first Winterly. The innkeeper had a misliking for Elves. Let's just say I wasn't welcomed with open arms, a flagon of his finest, and the key to his daughter's bedchamber." And he reminded himself to hide the black powder better on this year's Royal, because the road would take them by that inn and Mieka owed the snarge a brief visit. "You go see Croodle whenever you're in town?"

"That I do."

He nodded his approval of her choice in friends. "Now that we've tidied up your past, what of your future? Seems to me you've two choices. Become a Steward and break your father's heart, or wed some flutch of a frustling nobleman and break your own."

"*Flutch*? And I had to explain to you what a mathom is?"

"Y'know," he observed thoughtfully, "you're almost as good at avoiding an issue as Cayden is."

"Very well, then, what did you have in mind for my future?"

He only smiled. "You mentioned the Princess, and an ask."

Megs folded her hands tightly together. "She wants," she said with a barely repressed excitement, "Touchstone to give a private performance. Except that she also wants everybody to know about it."

He mulled that over. "The King gave her a duchy when she got pregnant. He must be in raptures, now that the Prince is born."

"He is. He'll give her anything she wants. Everybody knows he waited years for Ashgar to marry and provide an heir. King Meredan is there in the nursery ten times a day. He's as proud as if he carried the child and gave birth to him himself." She broke off and twisted her fingers together.

"Your father," he said softly, with an insight he felt worthy of Cade, "envies him."

"That's my business, not yours. Well? Would you be willing? Sometime before the Royal Circuit begins, mayhap? You'd come directly to the Palace, right through the front gates, no sneaking about the way they do at Seekhaven—even though everybody knows the so-called secrecy is all pretense."

"You mean some upstanding self-righteous cullion of a guardsman might try to stop us?" He laughed. "I'd purely love to see them try!"

"Then you'll do it?"

"Have to ask me mates first, but I don't see any problem." He hesitated, then said, "What she just did for Blye, that's a huge thing, y'know."

"She wanted to come herself. But once I told her I'd met Touchstone—"

"Does she know you want to be a Steward?"

A slow, sly smile touched her lips. "She wishes she had magic herself."

He whistled soundlessly. That *was* a change from her attitude back on the Continent.

It occurred to him that they now had several good friends at Court. Lady Megueris, Lady Vrennerie and her husband, the Princess herself—Lady Jaspiela would be giddy with the possibilities. And he knew without even thinking about it that it was a thing he wouldn't be mentioning to his mother-in-law.

"Name the night for the show at the Palace," he said. "Though 'tis a pity that any woman who wants to view a play can't do so right out in the open." Turning to look at her, remembering his own triumph at the Downstreet, an idea began to form in his mind. Not just clever, not just mad; a scathingly—nay, *gloriously*—brilliant idea. He fell instantly in love with it, even though he knew Cade would seriously consider killing him.

"It's ridiculous," Megs was saying heatedly. "Everybody knows that women sneak into theaters and taverns dressed as men all the time. All the Circuits play private shows where women are present—the New Halt Charity League, for instance, that's a whole audience of nothing *but* women—it's hypocritical and stupid and—"

"P'rhaps we might do something about that." He paused, glanced out the window, inspected his fingernails, then twisted halfway round in the seat to look directly into her puzzled green eyes. "Tell me, Your Ladyship, have you ever seen the Shadowshapers onstage?"

* * *

THE NEXT WEEK found Touchstone back in their wagon, traveling to and from engagements at country estates outside Gallantrybanks. Mieka was just as glad to be gone from town, where he could let slip to no one else what he and Lady Megs were plotting. Jinsie had been included, because Blye needed somebody to plan

with, and Blye had been the first person he told because
she'd never been caught out yet at one of their shows,
and of course that meant Jedris had to be in on it. Mieka
spoke in private to Jeska, who was apprehensive and
enthusiastic in equal measure—mainly eager, because it
gave him something to think about other than Kazie,
who had returned to Lilyleaf without giving him an answer one way or another. Mieka confidently expected a
marriage; Rafe was of the opinion that Kazie was much
too smart to accept the likes of Jeska; Cade asked that if
that were indeed the case, then why in the world had
Crisiant, who was more than usually intelligent and per-
ceptive, married Rafe? Jeska was simply too depressed
to join in the teasing. So Mieka cheered him up with the
prospect of performing *off* the stage.

He told him about it during a rest stop for the horses,
taking the masquer aside for a little stroll through the
soft spring rain. He didn't want Cade or Rafe knowing
just yet. Jeska had the same sort of objections the other
two would have—the chance of being arrested, the risk
of general outrage from a public that heretofore had
supported them, the possibility that Miriuzca's influence was not what Megs and Mieka thought it was and
the scandalized King would order his Master of Revelries to uninvite Touchstone from Trials and thereby ruin
their career. But Mieka needed him for his skills at por-
traying women, and Jeska's heart wasn't really in his
protests anyways. He was at that stage in a love affair
when anything that provided distraction from his frets
was welcome. Once Kazie accepted him, he would become rational again. But until she did, he was ripe for
any wayward outrageous notion that took his mind off
her.

The rain eased by noon. They arrived under cloudless skies at Whitecrag Castle just in time for tea with

the lord's wife and four doe-eyed daughters. The evening promised to be gorgeous, so rather than cramp themselves into the great hall for the performance, Touchstone played "Dragon" in the courtyard. And if the ladies had to hide behind curtained windows upstairs to witness the show, Mieka vowed it would be the last time any of them would have to do so.

When they got back home to Gallybanks, he had to tell the Shadowshapers. It was, after all, their show Mieka would be disrupting. Vered was all for it, and suggested that Bexan join them. Rauel dithered for a few minutes before saying that he agreed, but leave his wife out of it. Sakary only remarked that if this worked, the Downstreet would have to be rebuilt yet again to accommodate all the new theater patrons. Chat rolled his eyes and said that if clothing in larger sizes was needed, the gowns his wife wore during her pregnancies were at present available.

"But you'll have to stuff the bodices with half a petticoat each side," he added innocently. "She gets a bit chesty when she's in pig."

The Princess's invitation arrived one pleasant spring afternoon, sent to Lord Kearney Fairwalk's Gallantrybanks residence. This brought His Lordship to the Threadchaser bakery off Beekbacks at a gallop (not his horses, which was illegal on city streets, but himself, right out of his carriage and through the front door into the parlor). Touchstone had gathered for a quick run-through for a show that night. That it was not in Fairwalk's power to surprise them with the news of a command performance came as close to annoying His Lordship as Mieka had ever seen. He kept clearing his throat, running his fingers through his limp, sandy hair, and pacing the carpet, despite the kind urgings of Rafe's mother to sit, take his ease, and do please have some tea and muffins.

But a surprise did arrive when they were halfway through "The Princess and the Deep Dark Well." Mieka's sister Jinsie showed up, with Mieka's wife at her side.

"Oh, lovely! I was hoping we weren't too late to see you working!"

"Shh!" Jinsie hissed. "Don't *ever* interrupt!"

Mieka heard this through his self-created haze of magic and Rafe's fine-tuning of it and Jeska's recitation of the dialogue. Even though the strength of it was nowhere near what they'd use onstage, no glisker simply shut it all down without following a procedure learned before he was allowed even to hold a withie. They were professionals; they kept on with the piece, unfaltering. But through that odd connection of his with Cade through these withies, the ones fashioned almost three years ago by Cade's own hand and breath, the ones he almost always used for rehearsals, Mieka sensed a flare of something far more dangerous than annoyance.

It happened sometimes, this spark of Cade's immediate emotions even though the withies had been primed hours earlier. As "Deep Dark Well" drew towards its conclusion, the same thing happened again, only this time Cade was furious.

When the wisps of magic had faded from the Threadchaser parlor, Mieka saw that their audience, originally just Fairwalk, Rafe's mother, and Crisiant, who all knew to stay silently in their chairs, now included not just the two young Windthistle ladies but also Lady Jaspiela.

Mieka busied himself with stashing the spent withies into their velvet bag. He had no ambition in the world to become part of whatever confrontation was about to occur.

He had underestimated Mistress Threadchaser. "Welcome, Your Ladyship. What a delicious gown! That shade of apricot suits you completely. Tea all round, I think," she said heartily. "Mistress Windthistle—both of you!—do come help me choose some dainties from the bakery. Your Ladyship and Your Lordship will excuse us, I hope?" And she hustled the two young women towards the kitchen, with Crisiant following, tall and elegant and wry-faced, behind.

Tea and pastries for ten would take quite a while, Mieka supposed, giving his wife a smile as she went past. She was wide-eyed with sudden nerves and trying not to show it, poor darling. She wasn't shrewd enough in the complexities of social interaction to know that Mistress Threadchaser had just presented Cade with enough time to settle his mother down from whatever high dudgeon she'd come in with.

And lofty it was, indeed. She ignored Fairwalk's stammering civilities and tossed an unfolded, unsealed page of parchment at Cade's feet. "Kindly explain."

He leaned down, plucked it off the floor. It trailed blue and silver ribbons. Mieka realized that it hadn't been just Fairwalk who received the invitation; a duplicate would be waiting for Jeska at his lodgings, and probably a footman was even now trying to find the Threadchaser bakery. Delivery to Wistly Hall had undoubtedly caused the stir that brought his wife and Jinsie. "From the Princess," Cayden said.

"It's an invitation!" Fairwalk burst in. "For a private performance! At the Palace!"

Lady Jaspiela favored him with a flickering glance of pure venom. "*That* is readily discernible from the briefest glimpse at the letter. What I wish to know, Cayden, is how this came about and what you plan to do about it."

Mieka ditched his resolve not to join in. "Well, y'see, Your Ladyship, it was her very own idea. Really truly!" he assured her as her dark eyes widened involuntarily.

"That day a fortnight or so ago, when Blye got the Gift of the Gloves—you'll have heard about that, and isn't it wondrous? The very first in the Kingdom!" His beaming smile invited her to be magnanimous and approve Blye's good fortune; for the first time in his experience, she resisted him. *Oh, shit,* he thought, and during a half-second's pause debated whether reining back the charm would be preferable to urging it to a full gallop. "Anyways, the lady-in-waiting who delivered the Gloves, she asked for my escort back to the Palace"—he was careful not to give this lady a name—"and *she* said the Princess had a mind to a private performance, not like at Seekhaven where the ladies all gather at midnight at the Pavilion—oh, in strictest secrecy, of course, and *we* never say anything about it even though it's impossible not to know we're playing to hundreds of ladies, but you know how some people are at Court, jibbering and jabbering out of turn."

Whatever he was selling, she still wasn't buying. Cade took over. Bless him.

"What Mieka might get to eventually, Mother, is that Princess Miriuzca is of a mind to treat her ladies to a performance by her favorite players, to express her gratitude for their kindness and care of her and Prince Roshlin."

"It's an honor," Fairwalk began.

"She couldn't simply buy them presents?" Lady Jaspiela asked icily. "This is out of the question."

Cade's eyebrows tried to make contact with his hairline. Mieka gulped. Rafe went to hold the door open for Crisiant, who came in with a tray laden with a teapot—the good one, flowery porcelain instead of plain pottery ware—and lots of stacked cups and saucers, none of which matched. Mieka hid an untimely grin, for he knew that for their wedding, Rafe and Crisiant had received a complete tea service for twelve. For all her forthright-ness in almost everything, Crisiant also had means of making her opinion known without saying a single word.

"Your exploit at the Downstreet performance was offensive enough," Lady Jaspiela continued, and now Mieka knew why she had developed an immunity to him. "The Archduchess is in a very delicate condition and she was scandalized beyond words. I heard her say so myself."

"We read about it in the *Court Circular*," Cade said. "We'd been wondering who tipped off the reporters."

The implication that it had been Her Ladyship who had spoken to something so low and vulgar as a re-porter was a thrown gauntlet she refused to pick up. "What Her Grace and the rest of the Court will think of this is past imagining. Of course, the King will not allow it to happen—"

"Then I wonder why Your Ladyship has exercised herself in the matter," Crisiant said smoothly.

Lady Jaspiela was so taken aback that she simply stared at this *nobody* who had the cheek to say such a thing to her.

"Oh, I think it's rather obvious," Cade told Crisiant. "She took the trouble to come all the way over here so she could be seen to order us not to accept, and in front of witnesses. But tell me, Mother, which would be worse? To go along with the Princess's affront to protocol and tradition, or to refuse a Royal command?"

"Refuse—?" Fairwalk somehow managed not to swal-low his own tongue and teeth. "There's surely no ques-tion of—I mean to say, don't you know, it's not *done* to refuse—"

"And why not?" Lady Jaspiela snapped, thoroughly goaded now. "To decline—politely but firmly—would be to show yourselves decent, morally minded young men—"

"In spite of our sordid profession," Rafe murmured.

"—who know better than to overset all propriety—"

"Mother!" Cade exclaimed, gray eyes glinting merrily. "Surely not *all* propriety! We're good, verging on great, but that would be beyond even our talents!"

"—by acceding to the whims of this little nobody—"

"Have a care," Cade said, no longer smiling. "You're speaking of the next Queen of Albeyn, mother of the Heir to the Throne."

Mieka slid a hand into the velvet bag of withies, and even though there was no more of Cade's magic in them, there was enough of magic in their making that he had what he needed. For him, a withie was a focus, a tool, even when emptied of his tregetour's priming. As he had done for Blye after her father's death, gentling her grief and easing her despair, now he worked with exquisite subtlety on Lady Jaspiela to soften her fury and sweeten her temper.

Or he tried to.

She rounded on him in midsentence. "Stop that this instant! How dare you?"

He was so startled that he dropped the velvet bag. Panicking, terrified that even one of the withies might have broken or cracked, he went down on his knees and scrabbled inside the bag. These were of Cade's crafting, the only ones he'd ever made, and if they had been damaged—

"You outrageous creature! You despicable *Elf*! Don't you know who I am?"

"Mother!" Cade shouted.

"Be silent! I will not have that repulsive *Elf* trying to—"

"One more word," Cade snarled, rising to his full height, "just one more, and—"

"And what? You'll leave my house for ever and for good? I've been anticipating that day for almost twenty-two years!"

She left the room in a skirring of silk just as Mistress Threadchaser came in from the kitchen with a heaping platter of pastries. Mieka pushed himself to his feet and went to take another platter from his bewildered wife. Jinsie stood there, a stack of plates in her hands, looking around the shockingly silent room.

"Oh my," she said at length. "One less for tea, I suppose."

Another moment passed, and another. Before anyone could say anything else, Vered Goldbraider poked his head round the doorway.

"The footman at Redpebble said you were here, Cade. But I didn't think I'd be almost colliding with your lady mother!" He came into the parlor, a stack of books in his arms.

Mieka watched Cade's gaze dart towards him—no, towards the trembling girl beside him. She inched closer and he wished he had a hand free to soothe her. Cade's pale eyelids slid closed in an expression of numb submission that Mieka didn't understand at all.

"Well, then!" Mistress Threadchaser suddenly said. "Girls, help me pour out, please?"

* * *

NOBODY ATE MUCH. Mieka wished very sincerely for something stronger than tea. The conversation was stilted at worst and aimless at best. Vered took Cade over into a corner to talk about the books he was returning and those he thought he might still need. Mieka heard bits of their exchange when he helped his wife take the teapot and platter round in a vain attempt to coax them into doing justice to Threadchaser baked goods. *Balau-*

rin and *red dragon shields* surely didn't have enough weighty meaning to have put that expression of weary acceptance into Cade's eyes. Mieka was less concerned with that, however, than with hoping that Jinsie wouldn't let anything slip about their plans for the Shadowshapers' next show at the Downstreet.

Although considering what had just happened, it might be best if he delayed that particular plot for a while.

No. Lady Jaspiela, the Archduchess, and anybody else in Albeyn who didn't approve could go seethe in their own bile. What he planned to do was right. Every instinct told him it was right.

Vered finally betook himself off after compliments to Mistress Threadchaser that were so prettily expressed that she gave him a box of pastries to take with him. Lord Fairwalk charmingly, if somewhat incoherently, begged the ladies from Wistly to allow him the privilege of driving them home. When they had gone, Rafe helped his wife and his mother clear up, then came back into the parlor and said, "Well? What're you all doing sitting about for? We're off to Redpebble Square."

"Why?" Jeska asked.

"To collect Cade's things, of course. Just enough for tonight, I think. We can make up the spare room upstairs. Tomorrow we help him pack and move."

All at once it hit Mieka. Cade would no longer be living with his family. He would have to find a place of his own right quick, and somehow tell Derien, and Mistress Mirdley, and Blye and Jed—

—and it was mostly Mieka's fault.

"Quill, I'm sorry!" he blurted.

Cade shook his head. "You heard her. It's been coming for years."

"But—"

"You weren't listening to the rest of it," Cade told him with a sort of ghastly wryness. "She was there when the Archduchess complained. She's chosen a side, don't you see? Although why the side she'd choose would be in any doubt, considering who her mother was—"

"But at the races—she called the Archduke 'insufferable.'"

Cayden shrugged. "Either she's had a change of heart since, or she likes his wife but not him, or she was shamming for reasons of her own. With my mother, who can tell? Good Gods, I can see it as if I'd written the script. Somehow she got invited to something, it doesn't matter what, and snaked her way to the Archduchess, and made discreet mention of her mother—and don't think Panshilara isn't current with her husband's past! Right and wrong don't matter, nor public disgrace. It's the *power,* Mieka. My mother thought she'd get a share of it when her husband joined Prince Ashgar's household, but it didn't happen. She never really thought any would come through me, but she gave it a try a few times. She sees a path through Dery—but he's still so young, not even come into his magic yet. She's impatient. She isn't old, but she's not young, either. Panshilara is exactly her kind of person. And I've no doubt that my mother suits Panshilara down to the ground."

"It's more than that," Jeska said softly. "It's worse."

Rafe nodded, but it was Crisiant who spoke. "D'you think it's just because they enjoy sitting around sipping tea and commiserating with each other? You talk of 'power,' Cayden, but which of them is likely ever to wield any? Who's the important person in this—the *only* important person?"

Cade was smiling and shaking his head. "I see what you're saying, Crisiant, but the Archduke gave up on

Touchstone almost two years ago. He's got Black Lightning now. He doesn't need us."

"He settled on Black Lightning through lack of any other candidates." Rafe tapped a finger against the arm of his chair. "You've noticed, I'm sure, that this grand new theater he tried to tempt us with hasn't even had a foundation stone laid?"

"But look what they've already done for him," Cade argued. "They can direct specific magic at specific people—they can use it to make a man writhe inside if he's not an Elf or a Wizard, if he's anything Goblin or Gnome or—"

"Why?" Mieka asked. "Why would they want to do that?"

"You mean why would the Archduke want people to *know* exactly what they are," Jeska corrected. "I've no clue, but I'm certain sure it's for more than making those of us with other than Elf or Wizard in us uncomfortable with ourselves."

"The *clean* children," Rafe murmured. "The *blessed* children."

Mistress Threadchaser smacked her hands together and they all jumped. "That's enough of that! I won't have any such talk in my house. You boys have a little more than an hour to get ready for your show. And there'll be no moving out of Redpebble Square, Cayden, much as you might like to and much as I might agree with your reasons."

"I can't stay there."

"You must," she said, firmly but kindly. "For your little brother's sake. And besides, there's only one way to find out if Crisiant is right, even though we all know she is. If your mother says nothing when next she sees you in the house, or if she goes so far as to tell you that you needn't leave, you can be sure she's under orders to keep an eye on you."

"I–I hadn't thought of that," Cade admitted.

"You'll be gone at Trials soon, and then on the Royal Circuit. Leave it until after you return in the autumn. Leave it, Cayden. Derien needs to know that even if you're not in the house with him all those months, you'll be coming back. He'll be ten this summer. You were more resilient at that age, of course, but he's got a sensible head on his shoulders. He'll be better able to accept things in the autumn."

Cade nodded, and excused himself to a quiet chamber to prime the night's withies. Mieka was left to wonder why, if Lady Jaspiela had had a hindering put on her as Cade had said, she had nonetheless sensed his magic. He'd ask his father about it soon; the notion of discussing it with Cade made him cringe.

But on the walk up Beekbacks to find a hire-hack, Cade told Jeska and Rafe to go flag down a driver and took Mieka by the elbow and said, "You tried to use magic on my mother."

"Well . . . umm . . . yeh. How come she felt it?"

"What did you do?"

"Just a little something to calm her down." He shifted nervously and tried to reclaim his arm.

The gray eyes turned falcon-sharp, predator-cold. "And just how often do you perform this charming trick?"

"Never on you!" Mieka protested.

"If you're lying to me—"

"Quill, no! I wouldn't ever do that to you! And why did she feel it?"

"Just because she can't get at her own magic doesn't mean she's insensitive to it in others." He let go of Mieka's arm as the hire-hack neared. "Don't you ever try anything like that on me. Ever."

"I just told you I wouldn't." He rubbed his elbow; Cade's long, thin fingers were brutally strong.

"Well" was played much as usual, but "Dragon" was different that night. The Prince's doubts that he could live up to his forefathers' deeds became defiance of a daunting legacy and a burning need to prove himself better than his ancestors; the speech at the end, about passing along to his own sons the knowledge that it was the striving that counted, and overcoming fear rather than pretending one was never afraid, had particular resonance tonight. Mieka felt the difference in what Cade had used of himself to prime the withies, and played it accordingly. So did Jeska.

Mieka offered Cade a bed at Wistly, knowing in advance that he'd refuse. Rafe's mother had the right of it: Dery wasn't old enough yet not to be grimly hurt by his older brother's permanent departure. Mieka perceived the need to find out if Lady Jaspiela really would either ignore Cade's continued presence in the house or grant him permission to stay (nobody thought she'd apologize or actually *ask* him to remain at Redpebble Square), but he shared Cade's doubts. At best, Her Ladyship paid as little attention to him as she possibly could; how could she be said to keep an eye on him and on Touchstone? After all, as far as the Archduke knew, Cade was naught but a tregetour. They didn't know about the Elsewhens.

The Elsewhens, to ambitious people close to the Throne, would make Cayden Silversun very valuable indeed.

Twenty-three

THE PARTICIPANTS IN Mieka's little spectacle assembled at Wistly Hall at seven by the Minster chimes on Cade's twenty-second Namingday. It would take the better part of an hour to get everyone organized into hire-hacks and over to the Downstreet for the performances (one offstage, one onstage), but Mieka's thinking was that the less time everyone had to be nervous, the better for all concerned. It was always that way, he wisely considered, with any group of amateur players.

Not that there was any specific script for this show. He was trusting to luck and instinct, which had rarely failed him. Of course, none of his previous escapades had had anywhere near the potential this one did for total disaster, but he didn't let that bother him.

The small crowd assembled in the front hall was an impressive one. Chat's wife, Deshenanda, was there, as were several of her gowns. Vered's friend Bexan Quickstride would meet the party at the Downstreet, where Lady Megs would also be waiting. Jinsie and Blye were in their prettiest dresses. Crisiant, lovely in blue almost the same color as the velvet gown Mieka had worn two summers ago, was present at her own insistence and over Rafe's objections. Very stylish, she was, and very tall, but not so tall as some of the other "ladies."

"My hem's too short," complained Briuly Blackpath.

"It's perfectly all right for the petticoat to peek out below it," soothed Mieka's mother. "Most fashionable, in fact."

"I don't know what you're griping about," muttered Jezael. "My ankles are showing!"

"And very well-turned ankles they are, too," his twin assured him sweetly, "almost as attractive as my own."

"What about this bodice?" asked Alaen as he tugged and twitched.

"If you'd stop fidgeting," scolded Jinsie, "you wouldn't come unstuffed. Just stand still!"

Jeska, a poised and accomplished masquer, might have been expected not to squirm. "I'm used to me *own* clothes under *magic*!"

Mieka bounded up to the fifth step of the staircase to survey the gathering. Everyone was arrayed in their—or someone else's—best. Colorful silks and delicate embroideries, cunning hats and lacy gloves, fake jewels, some swan's down here and there, and even a luscious orange velvet cloak that clashed gloriously with Jez's red hair . . . the only difficulty had been shoes, which had been Mieka's despair until his mother suggested that they wear their own carpet slippers.

"Well, Fa?" he asked. "Will they suit?"

Hadden considered for a moment, then said, "I think Tobalt needs more up top. He's a bit saggy. And more than a bit hairy."

"We'll give him a shawl to cover up," Mieka decided. Then, clapping his hands loudly, he called out, "Splendid! You're all gorgeous! Into the hacks now, and try not to get too wrinkled!"

"How I let Mieka talk me into this, I'll never know," said Tobalt.

"I've been wondering that meself for the last twenty or so years," Jez told him.

Mieka gave a snort. "As if you'd miss the chance to write all this up for *The Nayword*!"

"Well, I won't be mentioning my own participation. What would my wife and daughter think?"

"But you look so delectable in yellow!"

Tobalt regarded him sourly. "I'd smack you right in the nose, I would, but you'd bleed onto my gloves."

Outside, they divvied up according to prearranged plan. Jez rode with Blye and Jed; Alaen and Briuly were escorted by Jinsie and Jeska; Rafe had charge of Crisiant and Tobalt. By Chat's specific request Hadden and Mieka accompanied Deshenada. Keen to see her husband perform in a theater, she had, to Chat's astonishment, absolutely insisted on joining in once she found out what her gowns were wanted for, but she was ever so nervous about it as well, poor sweeting.

Missing was Mieka's own wife, who knew nothing about any of it and was at Hilldrop with her mother and the baby. Mieka felt a little guilty about that, but she was just too shy and fragile for such risky mischief. And he could concentrate more fully on the fun if he didn't have to worry about her.

As for Cade . . . Rauel had taken care of that, by telling him that in apology for not attending his twenty-first Namingday celebrations last year—Gods in Glory, had it really been a whole year?—he and Sakary would treat him to a free Shadowshapers show with a party after in the tiring room. Cade, innocent of any knowledge of tonight's festivities, would be waiting at the Downstreet.

Mishia had fretted that the drivers of the hire-hacks

would be scandalized by the appearance of some of their passengers. Mieka had only laughed and said that they were Gallybankers, accustomed to seeing much stranger things. What he didn't tell his mother, because he was still keeping the secret, was that thanks to Lady Megs, the drivers were being extremely well paid.

"Your mother," said Hadden on the way to the Downstreet, "is not at all happy to be left behind."

"But she won't ever have to be again," Deshenanda said softly. "That's the whole point, isn't it, Mieka?"

"Unquestionably," he agreed. "And I must say, Desha, that you coming along is the best possible thing. Everybody will be stunned silent by the most beautiful girl they've ever seen, and that'll give me enough time to talk us all free and clear."

"Mieka!" his father chided. "How dare you tell a woman this lovely that her presence is merely a distraction for your pranking?"

Desha was giggling now, more relaxed. "Oh, nobody will look at me, once they catch sight of Jezael. He looks better in my pink gown than I ever did!"

"It terrifies me," Mieka said, "that you might be right."

"You have the ticket?" his father asked.

"Safely and soundly, Fa." He patted his jacket pocket, then made an alarmed face. "It was here just a minute ago—" But it really *wasn't* there. He felt genuine panic. "I put it there last night, I know I did—"

From an inner pocket of his own plain brown coat Hadden pulled a heavy parchment card. "I beat Jinsie to it this morning. She doesn't trust you, either."

"Me own Fa!" He made a grab for it, but it was held out of his reach. Deshenanda laughed, nerves completely calmed. "Desha," Mieka said solemnly, "I hope you hold your own dear children in higher regard than he holds me. A scandal, it is, the slanders and slurs cast upon me—"

"Mieka," Hadden said, "do shut up. We're here." He paused. "One other thing, my son. If the worst happens, you're sure your friend from the Court has money enough to buy us all out after a few hours?"

"Fa, she has money enough to buy the jail."

Mieka flung open the hack's door and leaped out. The patrons of the Downstreet were tidily queued up, moving slowly inside. The arrival of four more hire-hacks caused no stir until their occupants began to alight. In the gathering dusk with the Elf-light streetlamps not yet glowing, it was difficult to see. But as the hacks moved off and Mieka made a show of himself rallying his players around him, there were gasps and titters, then open guffaws—and at last a ripple of delighted comprehending laughter. Bexan was waiting for them, bravely alone until now—no one could fault the girl for brass— but looked relieved to no longer be the only person in skirts standing outside the Downstreet. It had taken all Mieka's persuasive talents to make Vered and Chat promise to stay in the tiring room backstage rather than come outside to protect their women.

"Everyone here?" Jed asked.

"Not yet," Mieka said, glancing about for Megs.

"This lace is itchy," Tobalt muttered. Then, remembering his role, he cleared his throat and in a high whine repeated, "This lace is *itchy*!"

"Pull your shawl tighter," Jinsie giggled. "You're drooping again."

Mieka felt a tapping finger on his shoulder and turned to find Cayden smiling down at him. "You really do take my Namingday celebrations seriously, don't you?"

"Oh, *very* special this year, not a doubt be about it!"

"Why'd you keep it secret? The girls and . . . the not-exactly-girls, I mean."

"Because I knew you'd have six fits."

"Mmm. One or two, mayhap, but not the full six. Here comes a constable. Start talking."

Mieka turned. "Fine evening, innit?"

"Wot's all this, then?" Seeing and recognizing Mieka—for he was one of the constables from the grand re-opening of the Downstreet—he moaned. "Lord and Lady and all the Angels save me, it's you again!"

"Me my very own self, and properly dressed as a man this time," Mieka replied cheerily. "How've you been keeping, Constable?"

"Look, I know what you're about, and I can't say as I have personal problems with it, like. But it's as much as me place is worth to let you do what I'm mortal certain sure you're scheming to do. Have a heart, won't ya?"

Mieka frowned worriedly. "I don't understand. What could possibly be amiss with a group of gentlemen wishing to attend the theater?"

Cade put in, "As we've already established, what a man wears is his own business—well, except when he has absolutely no taste in clothes and offends the sensibilities, like that big redheaded one over there. Pink, with an orange cloak?" He shuddered.

"It do catch the eye," the constable agreed dryly. "But wot'm I to say to me chief, that's wot I'd like t'know." He cast a despairing eye over the group. "Some of these as is wearing ladies' dresses, it's certain sure to me that they really *are* ladies."

Mieka gave the unfortunate man his most ravishing smile. "Would you really truly care to investigate in order to make sure?"

The constable sighed. "I'm tellin' you again, it's as

much as me place is worth to let this happen. Oughta take every one of you in, I ought."

"Oh, I don't think you'll be doing that," Cade murmured, and nodded over the constable's shoulder to where the queue had come unraveled.

A carriage—not a hire-hack, but a beautifully appointed carriage drawn by a prancing white mare—pulled to a stop. The man driving it wore highly recognizable livery. The boy who leaped down from the back to open the carriage door wore the same blue and brown, with lots and lots of shiny silver buttons.

Out stepped a trim and nimble personage. Gleaming brown boots to the knees, loose black trousers, dazzlingly white silk shirt beneath a dark green jacket that matched green eyes, elaborately tied turquoise neck cloth, green peaked-and-billed velvet cap perched on tightly coiled and pinned blond hair . . .

Mieka was about to alert Megs with a wave when right behind this personage came another: much taller, much blonder, dressed the same but for the color of the jacket and the cap. Both matched the forget-me-never blue of wide, excited eyes.

Mieka almost lost his footing. After a single stunned moment, he glanced up at Cade, who looked about to lose not just his footing but consciousness.

Formal introductions later, Mieka decided crisply. He strolled over to stand between the new arrivals, cupping an elbow in each palm. "Delighted you could join us! Shall we go inside?"

The constable stumbled back. Mieka gave him a look of sincere sympathy. It would be as much as his life was worth to arrest Her Royal Highness Princess Miriuzca of Albeyn.

* * *

"You knew," Cayden accused. "How in all Hells did you know?"

Mieka found himself backed into a wall of the tiring room by his half-drunk and entirely exasperated tregetour. The position and the person were things he had been meticulously avoiding all night.

Ah, such a lovely night it had been! Sweeping past the queue outside, distributing smiles all round. Waving the card, signed by Romuald Needler, that allowed them as many seats as they required. Making their scandalous way down the aisle to the very front row. Seeing the consternation on a few faces and knowing that these men were torn between the expression of their outrage by walking out and the consideration of the money they'd paid to get in. (The money won.) Hearing the muffled laughter from behind the stage curtains that meant the Shadowshapers were watching. Making a polite fuss over the comfort of Jez and Jeska, Briuly and Alaen—and the gobsmacked Tobalt finding himself taken solicitously by the arm and assisted to a seat by the tall, fair-haired young personage in the blue coat. Applauding as the Downstreet owner's wife and her two daughters decided they wanted in on the fun and marched down the center aisle to seats in the second row. Choking on repressed sniggers when he noticed Cade trying not to look at Megs's pert backside.

The Shadowshapers had outdone themselves with one of their silliest plays. Any ill-feeling in the audience was demolished by Vered in his most antic mood, strutting about the stage as Sir Bavin Blatherskite, declaiming his own perfections to a series of admiring beauties (all played by Rauel), until a little girl (also played by Rauel, on his knees in a frilly orange dress) waddled up and socked him right in the crotch.

In a high, lisping voice, as Vered rolled and moaned

on the stage, Rauel said, "Mummy was right. Men aren't much, are they, if you get them right where they live!"

Most of the ladies had left hours ago. Megs and Mir-iuzca had returned to the Palace with Jed and Blye's escort immediately after the performance. Neither noblewoman had entered the tiring room; a theater was one thing, and shocking enough, but at least it was public. No one but players knew what went on in a tiring room, which at times came close to what rumors described. Hadden Windthistle had taken Jinsie and Crisiant home, too. Deshenanda had, daringly, lingered with Chat; so had Bexan, sitting over there on a couch tucked comfortably under Vered's arm.

Mieka had considerately arranged to have men's clothes waiting for Alaen, Jeska, Jez, Briuly, and Tobalt. All of them looked devoutly relieved to be in trousers again (though the carpet slippers rather spoiled their style). The Downstreet's owner, whose shock at hosting not just women dressed as women but a Princess dressed as a man had been beyond his ability to articulate, had revived enough under the ministrations of his gleeful wife to send out for food to go with the many, many bottles of bubbling Frannitch wine he'd laid on for the Shadowshapers. Everyone was well fed, mildly tipsy, and utterly jubilant at the night's triumph.

"Damn it, Mieka, how did you *know*?" Cade demanded again.

"How did I know what?" Mieka parried. Then, hoping without much hope to deflect or at least to postpone Cade's questions, he asked a passing barmaid if bottles had been delivered to the constables outside, to comfort them and possibly their chief when word of this night got round. She simpered and nodded, and glanced him down and up, and he wondered if he mightn't escape using the girl as an excuse.

"A favor, if you would, darlin'," Cade purred. "Bring us a fresh bottle and two glasses over to that corner right there, would you? Much beholden, and here's something for your trouble." He tucked a few coins into her bodice, gave her a wink, and clamped long fingers round Mieka's arm.

"Ow!"

He was dragged to the indicated corner and loomed over.

"How. Did. You. Know. Because I know that you *did* know, I just don't know how you were knowing it."

"You want to untangle that for me?"

"Mieka! Stop stalling!"

"I didn't know about Herself, if that's what you mean. Gods, I thought I'd swallow me own teeth at the sight! Where d'you think she got the cheek to come out on her own to a play?"

"Probably from the person she came to the play with. What the unholy fuck was Megs doing here with her?"

"Now, that's a tale." The arrival of the girl, the bottle, and the glasses gave him a few moments' reprieve. "To the Princess!" he said, and gulped down golden bubbles. "All right, then, here's how it happened. She was the one what gave the Gift of the Gloves to Blye, because she's Lady Megueris Mindrising and a lady-in-waiting, and she really was at Coldkettle for the wedding, only she was a guest and not a servant, and then after the wedding she went to Lilyleaf on holiday because she knows Croodle from a long time ago, and that night at the Keymarker she was with the son and daughter of her father's friends who were at a Court banquet that night, which is a lot of work so she didn't really lie."

Cade's eyes were as wide and round as the rim of his glass. He seemed incapable of saying anything. Mieka knew from experience that this wouldn't last. After draining the glass down his throat and pouring more wine for them both, Cade finally said, "She's Lord Mindrising's daughter?"

"Yeh. But she still wants to be a Steward."

The second glass of wine followed the first. "Please," Cade muttered, "*please* tell me that this will all make sense when I'm sober."

"This will all make sense when you're sober," Mieka repeated obligingly.

Again Cade poured wine. "Do you promise?"

"More or less. The sense, not the promise. I kept me word about the no magic with the clothes, didn't I?" He paused to savor the wine. "How's Dery these days?"

Cade recognized the real question. "She's never said anything directly—she hasn't spoken to me at all, in fact—but I'm still allowed to stay at Redpebble. So I guess Crisiant was right and she really is trying to keep an eye on me for the Archduchess, which of course means the Archduke."

"Of course. Still not clear on what he wants, though." He sipped bubbles and felt them explode delicately on his tongue. A thought struck him and he laughed. "Do you know how much money we're about to make because of him? And him all unknowing!" Then, as another thought struck, and quite a bit harder: "You didn't—I mean, there hasn't been any change, has there? The baby will be born tonight?"

"Tomorrow morning we collect."

They toasted each other gleefully.

"When His Grace approached the Shadowshapers," Mieka said, "Chat thought it was because he wanted to buy his own theater group like they do sometimes on the Continent. For the brag of it. But I don't think that's his reason."

"Nor more do I. Did you see where Black Lightning has returned from their little outing to Vathis?"

"Yeh. I read *The Nayword* yesterday mornin'. Rousing success and suchlike rubbish. Tobalt will have something *much* more interesting to write about in the next issue."

"He did look a fright, didn't he?" Then he frowned and said, "She's *really* Lord Mindrising's daughter?"

* * *

HE WAS STILL muttering much the same thing a fortnight later at Trials.

"For fuck's sake, Quill, give it a rest!" Mieka exclaimed on their second night in Seekhaven. "Yes, she's Lord Mindrising's daughter! Yes, she's unspeakably rich! Yes, she's a lady-in-waiting to the Princess! Yes, she wants to be a Steward! And yes, she stayed in Gallybanks with the Princess because the Prince is too young to travel." He'd learned this last only that afternoon, when the invitation to perform at the Pavilion came from Lady Torren, who complained comically that the recent uproar caused by the Shadowshapers and Touchstone had taken all the fun out of pretending to sneak about at midnight.

Cade seemed embarrassed. "I only wanted—I mean, I haven't seen her to talk to since that night, and didn't even have the chance to be introduced then, and—and I've never seen her all frustled up in Court clothes, so I guess I can't really believe it, y'know?".

They started downstairs, where dinner was waiting for them out in the back garden. The inn had renamed itself this year—not that Mieka remembered what its previous name had been—partly for their favorite group and partly for the group who had got round the nominally random voucher system and demanded to stay there from now on. Touchstone and the Shadowshapers had taken over the whole of the Shadowstone Inn for Trials. Mistress Luta had made gruff apology that her boys hadn't got first place in the naming, but Jeska had assured her that *Touchshapers* made no sense, *Stoneshapers* sounded like a school for sculptors, *Stoneshadow* was a bit creepy, as if something might fall over on you, and *Touchshadow* would simply look weird on a sign. But Shadowstone, he soothed, was something to sit beside on a hot sunny day with a cold beer; a nice, sheltering name.

Vered had brought Bexan Quickstride along on the trip. His partners were studiously neutral about this development. Less convivial than usual, he'd so far kept to his bedchamber. Mieka thought it was for the usual reasons when one's woman was readily available, especially after the journey from Gallantrybanks in their wagon—which must have been an ordeal for all concerned. Cade considered it a result of nerves over the new play.

The second night in Seekhaven, right after the obligatory appearance at High Chapel, Vered displayed no discernible nervousness.

"Bit of a bore, innit?" he was saying when Mieka and Cade walked into the taproom. "Trials."

"For you, mayhap," Jeska observed wryly. "You know where you'll end up. Us, we've got the Sparks and Black fucking Lightning to worry about."

"Sparks, possibly," Rauel told him. "Black Lightning—oy, here you are, Mieka, Cade. Mistress Luta has a rack of lamb going for us tonight. Sit down and snap your napkins so we can eat."

Mieka settled at the table next to Chat and whispered, "Where's Bexan, then?"

"Dining alone upstairs."

The careful lack of inflection in his voice confirmed Mieka's opinion: the Shadowshapers were not markedly fond of Vered's new love, but didn't like to say so where he might be listening. It must have been a fun trip to Seekhaven, he didn't think.

At least Vered and Rauel weren't at each other's throats anymore. Mieka took this to mean that the new play was done and dusted, and everyone was happy. Well, as happy as Vered ever was, and as happy as Rauel could be when the play wasn't strictly his own. Two tregetour-masquers in one group; madness, simply madness.

"What's Black Lightning got this year?" Rafe wanted to know.

Rauel smirked. "A fettler still seasick from the trip to Vathis, and a masquer who caught some sort of pox."

"Not at their best," Vered confirmed.

Mieka waved this away. "As if we couldn't beat them on the best day they ever had!"

"Modest," Sakary commented.

"It's what we all love about him," Rafe confided.

"Among the thousands of other things," Mieka shot back. "I'd made note that Black Lightning didn't do much gigging before Trials."

"Do much what?" Rauel asked.

"*G-i-g-g*—'Get in, get gone,'" Jeska translated. "Thinks he's clever, he does."

Dinner arrived. Talk meandered away from Black Lightning to speculation about the differences between theater on the Continent and theater with magic.

"Wish we'd gone to see one of their plays while we were over there," Mieka said. "It's one thing to know we're better than anything they've got, but it'd be nice to know what they've got that we're so much better than."

Cade eyed him askance. "Y'know, I worry when you

say things like that and I understand them. I think I've a few scripts someplace, or at least the old versions that came over here and got changed up when somebody had the bright idea of using magic for the masks and suchlike."

"What was his name?" Mieka asked. When Cade blinked at him, he grinned. "There'll be a person and a name behind the changes, count on it."

"Well, yeh. Naught but a basic education, which in those days wasn't much. He either went traveling on the Continent or read every book he could get his hands on, nobody's really sure. But he was the first to use magic onstage. His name was Shuddershaft. No, seriously!" He smiled as they hooted at the name. "What's worse, he came from a village called Snitterfield. Is it any wonder that in all the official histories of theater they give Lord Bullbeck all the credit?"

Mistress Luta came in with the sweet—gorgeous mounds of brandy-soaked cake layered with fresh berries, heavy cream, and four sorts of drizzles, including burned-sugar and mocah. They were in the midst of ecstatic devouring when she returned with a sealed and beribboned parchment on a silver plate.

"That'll be for us, then," Vered said complacently.

And it was: the coveted invitation to perform on the last night of Trials for the lords and gentlemen of the Court at Fliting Hall. Mieka knew it had to go to the Shadowshapers and not Touchstone. There were too many rumors about what Vered had been working on, and Romuald Needler had been promoting the mysterious piece with placards all over Gallantrybanks for more than a month. He also had his suspicions that the more conservative Stewards were taking the opportunity to spank Touchstone's collective bottoms for the stunt Mieka had pulled at the Downstreet. It couldn't actually be laid to the Shadowshapers' account, and somebody had to be reprimanded somehow. Still, at least the summons hadn't gone to Black fucking Lightning.

Cade, of course, had already had all these thoughts and more. It was a right pain, Mieka told himself glumly, being friends with someone whose brain not only kept nattering to itself pretty much constantly but never even paused for breath.

"It wouldn't've been us anyway," Cade said as they settled into bed for the night. "Though it ought to've been the Sparks this year. We had the invitation three years ago, and then the Shadowshapers, last year Black Lightning—" He gestured and the little blue Wizardfire winked out from the candle. "And they're not really punishing us because of what happened at the Downstreet, if that's what you're thinking. If it was, then it wouldn't've been the Shadowshapers on the last night, either. Needler's good at bigging up his group, but Kearney has more connections."

"Then why—?"

"Because somebody's caught wind of Vered's disgust with Trials and they want to keep him happy. Or at least performing in the regular way."

"What's he thinking of? I mean, I know he hates having to come here and play one of the poxy old Thirteen just to get on the Royal when everybody knows it's just going through the motions."

"What I think he's moving towards is playing whatever the Shadowshapers feel like playing at Trials. And after that . . ."

Mieka waited.

"He's hinted once or twice that they won't be coming to Trials at all."

"But—but how would they get onto the Royal?"

"That's the whole idea."

"*What* idea?"

"No Trials, no Royal Circuit. So then what? Go out on their own, of course. They have the stature, the following. They have their own wagon. They've played every town and city in Albeyn for years, and for most of the nobility at their country houses and in Gallybanks as well."

Mieka thought this over. "Sounds like Vered," he admitted. "A lot of work for Rommy Needler, though. Not just the winter giggings, but all summer to organize as well. And what if they turn up at the same place and at the same time we do when we're First Flight?"

"We finally go into head-to-head competition with them for money instead of a place on the Royal. And we probably lose."

"No, we don't! Damn it, Quill, we're *Touchstone*!"

"Yeh, and they're the Shadowshapers. But they're good enough friends of ours that it won't come to that. I hope." There was a rustling of covers from the other bed, and after a moment Cade said, "You haven't asked why I didn't have an Elsewhen about what you did at the Downstreet."

Mieka shrugged in the darkness. "No decisions for you to make, were there?"

"And I have no influence on *your* decisions at all, Gods help me." But there was a smile in his voice as he said it. "Dream sweet, Mieka."

Twenty-four

LEAVING THEIR INN just in time to hurry over to the castle for the Shadowshapers' last-night performance, Touchstone arrived to find they had been assigned excellent seats—so good, in fact, that they earned nasty glances. Cade wasn't as amazed as his partners were to find Thierin Knottinger installed a few rows back and to the side. If Cade was right about the direction this play would be taking, Vered would want Black Lightning's tregetour right where Chat could aim the withies directly at him.

"Smug bastard," Rafe muttered.

"Let it go," Cade advised quietly. "We won. They lost. We're Second Flight, they're Third."

"By one point," Mieka reminded him sullenly. "One, when it ought to've been a thousand!"

That one point was Cade's fault, and he felt guilty about it. He hadn't mentioned to the others his Elsewhen about the Archduke's reprimand of Black Lightning. But how was he to know they'd still be nervous about that nameless fettler? Neither Rafe nor Jeska nor Mieka had said anything to him about anticipating yet another interference. They'd gone into their performance of "Dragon" (another rigged draw, he was certain) cautious and on edge. Everyone had noted the difference. Black Lightning had gone immediately before them, doing a violent—and violently reworked—version of the Eighth Peril, which involved the treacherous murder of an heir to the throne. The standard text called for the death to happen offstage, or at the very most in the shadows, to spare the feelings of any Royals who might be watching. Knottinger had rewritten it to show not just the quick knifing by an unknown assailant described in historical sources but also a crowd of spectral figures swarming around the Prince, all of them armed with gleaming steel—and all of them very much shorter than Humans or Wizards. Not so blatant as "The Lost Ones," still it clearly implied that the killers were Goblins and Sprites, Pikseys and Gnomes. As Cayden watched the audience from the wings, he saw disgust on some faces, dread on others, and was sure that the same specificity of magic was being directed to pick out those of "unclean" blood and make them uncomfortable. Thierin had said in that Elsewhen that they knew how to do it now, how to identify who was what. But to what ultimate end, Cayden couldn't begin to guess.

The piece had been good enough to earn Third Flight on the Royal for Black Lightning, displacing the Crystal Sparks—who were so furious that they departed Seekhaven before the next dawn, their manager lingering to give some excuse about family emergencies that no one believed.

Cade had to admit that the Eighth had been good, if bloody. It wasn't his fault Black Lightning had done well, but it was partially his fault that Touchstone hadn't done their best. He was beginning to agree with Vered, that Trials were a pain in the ass and it would be better to have done with them altogether. This was easier than admitting to himself that he'd failed in his resolve to share his Elsewhens with his partners.

It would be a relief to go home tomorrow. They'd play at the usual venues in Gallantrybanks, perform for the Princess, pack up the wagon, and set off a few days before the official start of the Royal for a private show—*gigging,* as he was learning to call an engagement—this one at Shellery House, the seaside manor belonging to Lord Mindrising. Kearney had been startled by the request, unaware that they knew Megs in circumstances other than Her Ladyship self. Nobody enlightened him. Equally amazing was that Lord Mindrising had requested Touchstone to visit his two other summer residences—he had seven major properties in total, which he regularly visited on a kind of circuit of his own—during the Royal to entertain his guests and his villagers. Women included. This made Kearney nervous; it made Mieka laugh.

But Romuald Needler had been right, years ago: now that women were beginning to dare attendance at theaters, swollen audiences would bring swollen profits. And it began to seem to Cade that this was what Vered had been waiting for. With twice the number of tickets to be sold, a group could afford to go out on its own and thumb its collective noses at Trials and the Circuits. Cade wasn't sure he was quite that brave. And besides, he wanted First Flight on the Royal at least once in his career.

The audience in Fliting Hall settled. There were no women present. Too soon, Cade thought, just a little too soon for the Stewards to unbend. He hid a smile, thinking how flummoxed they'd be when the daughter of one of the oldest noble houses in Albeyn voiced her intention to become one of them. Not that he could quite believe it himself. Her ambitions, those he understood perfectly. That Megs really was the daughter of Lord Mindrising was something he still couldn't quite work into a comfortable place in his brain.

There was no announcement from the stage of the name of the group or the title of the piece. Curtains parted on a swirl of pale gray haze. The Shadowshapers were already onstage as the mists of their own making cleared. Chat was seated at the glisker's bench, dressed all in black that emphasized his starkly pale face and the streak of white in his hair. To Cayden's eye, he looked apprehensive. Sakary stood behind his lectern, also in black, more solemn and aloof than ever. Rauel was near but not standing at the tregetour's lectern, his tumble of dark hair a boyish contrast to the grim determination of his expression. Vered, whose play this was but who would be performing as masquer, with Rauel seconding, occupied the center of the stage, looking defiant. From what Cade knew of what the audience was about to see, all four Shadowshapers were hiding that they were just plain scared.

Between Vered and Chattim a scene appeared: a score of knights in antiquated armor that was little more than thickly padded tunics and metal breastplates limped frantically towards a castle gate. They staggered and stumbled, dragging each other along, swords used as crutches encrusted with blood.

"Another battle lost. The taste of bloody defeat bittering their mouths. The heartbeat thunder of terror thudding in their ears. The tremors of exhaustion shaking their limbs. The swords besmirched with enemy blood trailing enemy guts behind them—and yet the enemy was undefeated. Another battle lost, another of dozens that ravaged their numbers, and mayhap next time battle raged, the whole war would be lost. Skill and valor counted for naught. Love of homes and families and rich green fields and towering mountains meant nothing. For they were not fighting mortal beings. They were fighting the *balaurin*."

The knights staggered through the castle gates and vanished into mist that swept across the stage. As it faded, Vered was now seen to be a tall, blue-robed Wizard, wearing his own compelling face and long white-blond hair. Around him in a stone chamber, an incomparable display of skilled and powerful magic coalesced the score of exhausted knights and a gathering of their leaders, one of each: Goblin and Fae, Elf and Giant, Gnome and Piksey and Human. Their voices rang out, first one side of the stage and then the other, startling in their speed and volume.

"They are wounded unto death but do not die!"

"Killing even one is the work of half a day!"

"Such spells and strengths as each of our kinds possess and use against them—"

"—they pause for only moments and then attack again!"

"They hang from our swords and laugh—"

"—unless their heads be lopped from their necks and even then they laugh with their last breath—I can hear their laughter even now—"

The Wizard held up a hand and all was silence. "The very first battle taught us their only weakness. How many battles have we fought since then, against warriors of speed and strength and skill and shrewdness, who kill ten of ours for every one of theirs whose head we claim? I tell you that we fight as cripples. Unless we fight as one, we all will die. Our separate powers must be as one power, our individual gifts one gift."

Mutterings there were, and gestures of dismissal. The Wizard strode back and forth before them, the representatives of each race.

"I will hear neither argument nor opposition. We must forget petty jealousies. We must set aside the instinct to hoard to ourselves what we can do and what we know. We must become one strength. We must do away with contention amongst us, and give of ourselves without stinting or withholding. Gnome and Elf, Wizard and Goblin, Piksey and Giant and Fae, we must become as one to defeat our common enemy. Or all is lost."

Slowly, reluctantly, between each elder's cupped hands appeared a glow of light: Goblin green, Wizard blue, Elfen yellow-gold. Hovering between the gnarled palms of the Giant was reddish-brown fire. The Piksey's fingertips sparked dancing blue and green. The Gnome held a red-orange gout of flame. The long, elegant hands of the Fae grasped a sphere of blazing silver. Of them all, only the Human held no fire. The audience murmured softly.

"Strength beyond the normal strength," the Wizard said. "Flashing quickness of sword and limb. Hearing that hears the flicker of an eyelash. Cunning to discern not just an enemy's next move but the moves three moves beyond it. Might and speed, sight and feeling, what was given to each of us must be shared by all."

The distinct glowing fires rose and met in midair and combined into a huge white sphere of flame. This spread, paler and more transparent by the moment, moving with quick ragged flashes of lightning over all the knights and flowing back through the castle walls—and out over the theater. And the confidence that came of strength and speed and craft and magic touched every man there.

Shadows reclaimed the stage, leaving only Vered as the tall, blue-robed Wizard. He paced a few steps in one direction and then the other, irresolute, fretful. Another figure moved into the light: Rauel, clad in a plain green cloak and carrying a knight's sword. He wore his own boyishly handsome face, big brown eyes worried as he gazed at the Wizard.

"That which troubles you, my old friend, also troubles me," he said. "How long have we known each other? How well do I know you, and you me? For all that you chose the Wizardly path and I the training of a Knight, still we are known, one to the other, even after all these years. So tell me, my old friend, tell me your thoughts and fears. Share them with me."

"With you and no one else," the Wizard admitted. "We have given you, our knights, all that we can give. Yet I fear it is not enough. I *know* it is not enough."

The Knight strode forward and clasped the Wizard's arm. "What must we do?" he asked quietly.

"It is a thing I must do alone. Wait for me here, my friend. I swear to you I will come back unharmed. But I must know. I must be certain sure."

And with that he flung off his blue cloak and reversed it, and it became a cloak of shimmering black all shot with rainbows, and he vanished.

The Knight was the one who paced now: up and down, boot heels clicking on stone. He rubbed at a spot on his breastplate, trying to polish it back to silvery gleam. He raked both hands through his sweat-damp hair. At length he spoke. "I *do* wish he wouldn't do that," he muttered to no one. "Why, I recall once, when we were children, his parents spent a whole day looking for him. Couldn't find him, of course. Invisible! First spell he ever perfected, and still the one he's best at. He's never seen unless he wishes to be seen. And he never *would* lend me that cloak, not even when we were older and there were so many interesting things to see in the neighbors' bedroom windows!"

There was humor in his voice, and threading through the audience, but it was the sort of humor provoked by nerves and fear, and those things touched the audience as well. Cade knew what Vered was doing: taking up a bit of time, not much but just enough to indicate time had passed, and using the droll little speech to ease the tension a trifle. But only a trifle.

The Wizard reappeared, flinging off his cloak, shaking. The Knight ran to his side, steadying him.

"What is it? What did you see?"

"I saw—oh gentle Gods and blessed Angels, I saw—"

The Knight released him, went to a table, plucked up a goblet, and gave it to his friend. The wine was too sweet, gaggingly sweet.

"I saw such things as made me certain," said the Wizard, recovering himself somewhat. "I saw the skulls of our dead that had been made into cups from which these creatures drank. The braided hair of our warriors hung from the golden handles affixed to stark white bone and—and I recognized the bright red hair of your brother, whom we lost three battles ago." His head raised slowly, and he grasped his friend's arm. "What they drank—it was not wine. It was blood. And it is blood from which they receive their strength."

The horror of it atop the cloying sweetness of the wine was nearly overwhelming. All through the theater men made soft retching noises, or coughed, or covered their mouths with trembling hands.

"Go to your chambers, my friend," said the Knight, guiding the Wizard to a doorway. "Close your eyes. Rest. Think no more upon it. Close your eyes and your mind to it for now, and rest."

Shadows of sleep swirled gently around the Wizard and he faded from view once more. The Knight turned, and went to stand beside the discarded cloak, a puddle of black rainbows. Softly he murmured, "My only brother . . . his wife, his sons and his daughters . . . this I cannot endure."

And so he gathered up the cloak, swirled it around himself, and new shadows swallowed him.

Instantly the Wizard became visible again, standing at a castle window on the far left, anxiety and anger gushing from him in almost visible waves. Just as he came into view, so did the Knight, on the opposite side of the stage, wrapped in the black glistening cloak, kneeling before a campfire, a cup made from a skull cradled between his hands. From the golden handles swung two plaits of fine red hair.

Gasps and outcries swept the audience as the Knight upended the cup over his own mouth and a few shining crimson drops of blood trickled onto his lips.

Then the Wizard stood alone again. He whirled round from the window as the Knight came reeling, stumbling into the castle chamber, the shimmering cloak dragging from one hand.

"What have you done?" the Wizard rasped. "By all the Old Gods—*what have you done?*"

"You said—you said that their strength comes from this—"

"From blood—so you have made yourself as strong as they by drinking as they do of blood—" He took a step forward as if to grab the Knight by the shoulders, then flinched back. "Do you know what you have become?"

"If it saves our lands, our homes, our families, I care not what I have become." Straightening, he faced the Wizard defiantly. "I can feel the power in my bones and sinews. It is beyond what was given before. I can hear the falling of a feather from a preening bird in the dovecote high in the castle tower." His expression crumpled slightly. "But it takes no special magic to see the pain in your eyes. You know what I have become: a creature like them. And you know that I cannot stand alone against them. There must be others of our Knights willing to do what I have done."

"No," the Wizard breathed. "No. Please. Nothing is worth—"

"Thousands upon thousands of lives are worth this." He glanced to the windows. "Morning and battle will soon be upon us. I have brought the cup made from my own dead brother's skull. There linger yet some drops of blood within."

"Then give it to me."

"No! A warrior you have never been. And—and I need you to remain as you are. For once the *balaurin* are defeated by those who join with me of their own free will—we must not be allowed to return to our homes. You know this is true. The risk is too great."

"No—there must be a way—"

"I feel the craving of blood," he continued quietly. "I taste compulsion on my tongue and dripping into my belly. I am become like them."

"No. It cannot be, there must be some spell, some solution—"

"I tell you there is not!" And the Knight's eyes glowed suddenly the midnight black of death and the blood red of fury, and there was a feral stench in the air.

The Wizard stumbled back, pressing his hands and his spine against the stone walls. "No!"

The hideous burning eyes became the Knight's own once more. "There is no other way. We swore the severest vows that we would be rid of the *balaurin*—and that means *all* of the *balaurin*. All of us who will become as they are. All of us." He paused, gazing with compassion at his friend. "Even me. When this is finished, I must die. If I am not killed in battle, then you must kill me. You must promise this. Please."

The black shadows were so abrupt and appalling that the audience cried out. A flicker of a moment later, the Wizard stood alone at the castle battlements, wind whipping at his blue cloak and his white-blond hair. The clamor of battle changed slowly to tumultuous shouts of victory.

"And thus we prevail," the Wizard murmured. "Their heads tumble from their shoulders, and they die. The *balaurin* threat repulsed, our lands and peoples saved. Yet—ah, Gods, the cost!"

Slow, dragging footfalls echoed on stone steps. The Wizard turned. His friend, come to make sure he kept his promise?

Gray churning shadows swept the stage in silence. Six hundred men sat there in the empty darkness, shattered more surely than any glass Touchstone had ever broken.

* * *

"I MADE UP a good bit of it, y'know."

The eight of them were lounging in the back garden of the Shadowstone Inn. Tonight Cade conceded without resentment that this was the order those names would be spoken for as long as theater existed. What Touchstone did, they did superlatively well. But the Shadowshapers were matchless.

Vered went on, "The Wizard and his friend the Knight, f'r instance. No book had a specific tale about how it all happened. But it did happen, and the friendship gives it emotional impact—"

Rauel chuckled a bit uneasily. The effects of the performance were still very much with him. "It's a wonder and a marveling, isn't it, that the man who scorns emotion in his work avows that emotion is essential to this one."

"Fuck off." The tregetour spoke amiably, raising his glass to his partner. All the animosity of that night at the Downstreet was gone. The play was brilliant and Vered knew it; he could afford to be generous. "You were right about not showing the blood-guzzle the Wizard sees at the camp. Much better saving it for when the Knight does it himself, with the taste and smell of it in the audience's mouths and nostrils."

Rafe made an inarticulate noise. Sakary gave a snort.

"Got you, did it?"

Another grunt, which evidently didn't quite satisfy his fellow fettler.

"The glowy red eyes were a nice touch, don't you think?" Sakary persisted.

Mieka broke in with, "They were perfectly ghastly."

"But effective," Vered said, sleek and complacent. "And that's what counts." He paused for a sip of wine. "Wasn't sure about the colors, either—I mean, we all know Wizardfire is blue, but I'm not sure that Giants can even make magical fire. Never seen one do it—must remember to ask Rist one of these days. But the effect was too good to pass up."

"We saw someone do a sort of purply-gold once," Mieka said.

Cade kicked him under the table and spoke up for the first time since ordering their drinks. "The play ends up saying the opposite of Black Lightning's piece of last year, yeh?"

"Glad somebody noticed," drawled Vered, but in the next instant, unsmiling, he went on, "Not that I started out to do that. But the forrarder I went, the more it seemed to me that it was something that ought to be said. All that tripe and twaddle about whose blood is pure and clean and whose isn't—" He snorted, and finished a bit gloomily, "Though how many people will understand that part of it, I don't know."

Considering that Vered had willfully misunderstood "Doorways," Cade was remarkably unruffled. "Could've done a whole play based just on the arguments about sharing their powers."

"Oh, and what fun *that* would've been!" he jeered. "Right up Black Lightning's road! Jealous Elves and secretive Pikseys, the whole lot of 'em guarding their rights—" He paused. "And talking of Rights, you didn't do 'Treasure' this year."

"No, back to the good old reliable 'Dragon,'" Cade said. "I wasn't looking to see how Thierin Knottinger reacted to your work, but I hope he was writhing. Just a bit. Do him good."

Chat wore a smug little grin. "Oh, he writhed. Squirmed and squiggled like a worm on a hook."

"Well done, old thing," Mieka said, toasting him.

"The problem," Rauel mused, "is that the legends are all agreed, and the Knights couldn't win with just the magic given to them. They had to become like the *balaurin*."

"Not just knowing your enemy in order to defeat him," said Vered. "But *becoming* him."

"Not completely," Chat argued. "The Knights know they have to die. There's self-sacrifice in that."

"Same as any warrior," Jeska observed, from long experience playing warriors onstage. Or mayhap it was because he was the grandson of a soldier. "Doing his duty no matter what the cost."

Rauel shook his head. "But this is a choice they made. It wasn't an order from a commander. They chose to become what they became. And they knew they'd become too dangerous and too different to live amongst their fellows anymore."

Remembering the whipsaw between the horror and grief of the Wizard and the burgeoning savagery of the Knight, Cade repressed a shiver. He signaled to Mistress Luta, standing in readiness at the back door, who nodded back and disappeared to fetch more liquor.

Mieka turned to Vered, smiling that sweetly endearing smile that always meant mischief. "And what happens next?" When Vered narrowed suspicious eyes at him, Mieka laughed. "There's more. I'd know there's more even if I didn't know from hearing the legends that there's more. I'm knowing you tregetours, I am. Never leave anything well enough alone, do you?"

"The next part," said Vered, conceding the point, "begins with the Wizard standing at the battlements and reciting his little speech—and then the Knight comes upstairs."

"And then?" Jeska asked eagerly. Cade wondered if he was seeing himself playing the Wizard or the Knight. "What happens then?"

Vered grinned. "Twenty kinds of Hell break loose!"

"Both plays on the same night," Rauel explained happily. "Never been done before!"

"Exhausts me to my bones just thinking about it," Sakary growled.

Chat nodded glumly. "Tonight was weariness enough. Two plays like that in one evening—none of us will be any use for a week after."

"Well," Mieka said musingly, "none of you is as young as once he was, Gran'fa."

Chat cuffed him playfully upside the head. "I'm still trying to get used to two masquers onstage," he admitted. "Bit tricky, keeping the two sets of withies separate and remembering which is used for whom. I can't imagine putting in a third masquer."

"A second glisker?" Rafe asked, smiling. "And a second fettler to keep his magic organized—Gods know just the one gives me trouble enough."

Mieka laughed and blew him a smacking kiss.

"Why not a dozen of each?" Vered asked with cheerful malice. "One for each masquer onstage!"

"Oh, you'd like that, you would," Sakary said. "Lolling about at your lectern, giggling at the collisions!"

"And collide they all would," Rauel stated with an exaggerated shudder. "Them, the sounds, the scenery, the feelings—all that magic scurrying across the stage and out into the audience and all the way to the rafters! Doesn't bear thinking of."

"I quite agree," Cade said. "Have a care what you start with your two masquers onstage, and your two-plays-a-night," he went on, smiling. "Soon enough you'll have us in chaos, like Rauel says—or we'll have to abandon magic onstage altogether and work the plays like they do on the Continent. Lots of masquers, bad lighting, and scenery painted on wood."

A short time later everyone began to amble up to bed. Cade hung back with Vered, making what he knew to be a futile attempt to caution him.

Scornfully, as Cade knew he deserved, Vered told him, "Don't you be daring to tell me what to write or how to write it. So somebody might not appreciate what I have to say? Who the fuck cares? What can anybody do to us? We're the Shadowshapers!"

"Vered—all I mean is that you need to be careful."

"What was it Mieka was saying about *us* being doddering old grandsirs? Take your worries and frets and drown 'em in the garderobe!" Vered laughed through his nose and strolled along after his partners.

Cade watched him go, wishing he hadn't said, *"What can anybody do to us? We're the Shadowshapers!"* It felt wrong to him, but he couldn't have said why.

Mieka fell into step with him across the lawn. "Oy," he said suddenly, "wasn't it this table I'm s'posed to've danced on last year?"

"What?"

"Starkers, you said."

A smile began to curve his lips. Mieka could always do that for him. Mad little Elf. "Why, yes, I believe it was."

"With a lace cloth as a veil, and a rose betwixt me teeth."

"I had you convinced for a minute, there."

"But *only* one. That's because you just don't have any idea at all how to finish off a prank, Quill," he scolded. "Now, if it'd been *me* authoring that particular jest, I'd see to it that the table was in splinters next morning as proof."

"And you'd've paid for the table, too!"

"Of course! But you—" He shook his head sadly. "Your imagination, though prolific and terrific, runs inwards and not outwards."

"In other words, my imagination makes us money, and yours costs you a fortune."

Abruptly serious, Mieka said softly, "If it banishes that look from your eyes, I'll gladly give over every pennypiece in my bank account."

Moved, Cade slung an arm around slight shoulders and hugged. Mieka settled comfortably against his side on the walk upstairs. The usual routine of washing and changing into nightshirts was accomplished in silence. Cade was waiting for it, and soon enough the question came.

"You've had Elsewhens about this play of Vered's,

haven't you? It's not about me, so you can tell me with a clear conscience."

Cade sat wearily on his bed, then stretched out, hugging a pillow to his chest, and stared at the ceiling. "No, it's naught to do with you."

"What, then?"

"I saw the Archduke receiving information from somebody who'd heard Vered was reading up at the Archives and in my grandsir's library for this play. His Grace . . . shall we say he wasn't thrilled, and leave it at that?"

Cade was fully aware that Mieka knew him well enough by now to know that by leaving it at that, whatever *that* might be, he was leaving something out. He wasn't exactly lying. He knew Mieka well enough by now to know that he would never be able to get away with lying. He was grateful that tonight Mieka didn't seem to be inclined to plague him about it, and only nodded.

Cade was quiet a moment, then said, "All this business of the Knights and so forth supposedly happened in the Archduke's ancestral lands, or near to. You know what Vered will write about next."

"How the Knights didn't all die, and some of them went back to their homes, and the common folk brought them offerings of newly dead animals, like Lady Vrennerie said."

"For the blood."

Mieka paused to wash his face, then climbed into his bed. After a while Cade did the same, and closed the lamp, and the two of them lay there in the darkness on opposite sides of the room.

All at once, unable to help himself, Cade murmured, "Mieka? What if it's not just legends? What if it's true?"

Twenty-five

EVERYONE KNEW SOMETHING had happened at Mieka's Hilldrop Crescent house before Touchstone left on the Royal Circuit. No one, not even Cade, had the temerity to ask about it. The lingering purple-green bruise on Mieka's jaw wasn't something anybody cared to bring up in conversation. Cade did sneak a few glances at Mieka's hands. The reddened knuckles of a thrown punch sickened him. And he hoped with all his might that Jindra was still too young to remember any of it.

The Elf was surly the first day out, keeping himself to himself with a mutter and a snarl. By noon of the following day, as their route to the coast took them through Gowerion, he livened up during a brief stop for lunching at Brishen Staindrop's distillery. Brishen was gone to the Pennynines, hunting for rare flowers that bloomed but briefly and only once a year, and herbs said to be exceptionally potent when gathered at Midsummer. Mieka led them on a tour of the facilities and they all got tipsy just on the fumes from the huge oaken barrels of whiskey. There was a separate building, squat and thatched atop gray fieldstone walls, where Brishen concocted various types of thorn. This, in the absence of its proprietor, was sternly and magically locked.

A whole barrel of whiskey was loaded into the wagon. They made a stop at Yazz's parents' house to drop off Robel, who would be staying there until the birth of their child. The Giant looked so forlorn when someone mentioned that it was time to get back on the road that Cade decided they could just as easily leave early tomorrow morning. It was a small thing, and only a few additional hours to spend with his wife, but Yazz was almost tearfully grateful.

This made Cayden feel a bit of a shit, because he'd suggested it for his own convenience. Had they stayed with the original schedule, they would have passed Sagemaster Emmot's Academy in the late afternoon, and someone—probably Mieka—would have suggested they call round for tea. By spending the night many miles from their intended stop, there was no time to linger anywhere. He lazed in his hammock, staring out the window, glad to avoid the awkwardness of a visit, wondering in spite of himself where the old man was these days. Cade hadn't seen him since leaving this place of tall brick towers and heavy slate roofs years ago; he'd heard Master Emmot resigned from his post, but had no idea why or what he might be doing with himself. He supposed he could have found out by stopping in and asking, but he had no desire to be pointed out to young scholars as a famous former pupil, a shining example of the advantages of an education at the Academy.

Ten miles beyond the Academy, the skies churned up great gray mountains as if every weathering witch in Albeyn had coaxed every cloud to this one particular place. The rain was beyond torrential. It didn't fall in individual drops, but as if a million colossal buckets had overturned all at once. Though it lasted only ten minutes or so, it turned the road into a river. The drenched horses—four of them, not of Romuald Needler's stock—struggled to haul the wagon up a hill, fetlock-deep in mud, as water flooded down. At last Yazz reined in and simply waited it out.

Had they not lingered in place last night, they would have been nearly to Lord Mindrising's estate by now. It was an interesting little lesson on the consequences of one's choices, Cade thought, and resigned himself to having to get out and push.

He consoled himself with the memory of their latest Gallybanks triumph: the command performance before the Princess and her ladies in the garden of the Keeps. Miriuzca had developed a liking for the tower on one side of the river, and the King had ordered its apartments redone for her. Touchstone, the Shadowshapers, and Crystal Sparks had been invited not just to play but to stay the night as well. A look at little Prince Roshlin wasn't part of the schedule, but a tour of all the presents sent from around the Kingdom and across the Continent was. There were hundreds, divided into three groupings: those that would be used, those that were too expensive to use, and those that were duplicates (sometimes quadruplicates) and would be sent with the Princess's compliments to young mothers who might not be able to afford such luxuries. Cade took the opportunity to move, quite unnoticed, a certain embroidered velvet pillow from the "use" tables to the "send" tables. The card identifying the crafter as one Mistress Windthistle of Hilldrop he pocketed for later disposal in a garderobe.

Rafe pointed out the place of honor given to Blye and Jed's pottinger and spoon, and Chat joked that if he was ever given the Gift of the Gloves, it would make handling the withies rather difficult, and Mirko Challender told them he'd hold out for a knighthood, beholden all the same.

The Elsewhen that ensued had left Cade smiling then, and brought a smile to his lips now, even in the rain and mud.

{In the antechamber, all sea-green velvet and gilt, a small commotion was centered round a tall, good-looking blond boy who was talking with shy eagerness to Jeska and Rafe and Mieka. Cade approached in time to hear Jeska startle everyone in earshot by saying, "You're more than welcome to come along tonight to our celebration at Wistly Hall, Your Highness."

The boy, after a glance over his shoulder at his grandfather in the next room, as if wondering whether he mightn't get away with it, mumbled, "Supper and King lessons tonight with Gran'fa."

Cade told him, "All well and good, Your Highness. But I hope you pay attention to what your mother can teach you, too."

"Every day," the boy said with a smile that knew more than his years could account for. "I hope His Majesty kept a good grip on the sword. Sometimes, when he's knighting somebody wearing a uniform, there's shreds of shoulder fringe all over the carpet after."

Mieka snapped his fingers and exclaimed, "Damn! I forgot to ask when I'm gettin' the sword!"

"You're *not*," Cade said firmly.

The Prince was grinning. "I'm sure we've a few spares round here someplace."

Before Mieka could yelp his delight, Cade clapped a hand over his mouth and said, "Please, Your Highness, don't encourage him. He's behaving himself for now, but it won't last. And the thought of a real sword in these destructive hands—it just doesn't bear contemplating."

"That's a pity," the Prince replied, flashing his mother's smile. "I was hoping for some practical advice. There's a perfectly terrifying old wardrobe in my rooms, about ten feet high and ten feet wide, and it's just begging to be redesigned. From everything I've ever heard, Sir Mieka is just the man for the work!"

"What're you all grinagog about?" Rafe muttered as they freed the wagon's left rear wheel from the muck.

"The prospect," Cade told him, "of getting back in the wagon and getting warm."

Arriving many hours beyond the expected time, they were welcomed to Shellery House with glad exclamations and a dinner made up fresh at ten in the evening by a Trollwife who, far from grumbling and grumping about the trouble they'd made for her, greeted them with the news that her great-aunt Mirdley had warned her to treat these boys right or else.

"Our Mistress Mirdley is your great-aunt?" Cade couldn't help but say.

"More or less," Mistress Gesha said with a shrug. "It's been a bit of a tangled while. Most Trolls are related to each other, or claim to be." She pointed to the small mountain of mussels set before each man. "Eat!"

They woke the next morning in a comfortable room overlooking the sea. Almost all the rooms, Cade found, overlooked the sea and the small fleet of fishing boats that plied the ocean and smaller craft that tended the lobster pots. Many generations ago, a previous Lord Mindrising had used the fallen stones of a very old castle to build a rambling house that undulated along the cliffs. Facing the courtyard was a long, narrow two-storied hall with a set of stairs at each end and one set in the middle. These led up to a gallery set with a dozen or more doors into the bedchambers and private rooms of the house. Only this upper floor was all of a level; the lower, more public rooms featured a few steps either up or down as the original foundations dictated. It was odd and rather charming, but not one member of Touchstone could figure out exactly where they would be performing.

Lady Megs showed them. Her presence was a surprise to Cade; he'd expected she'd stay in Gallantrybanks with the Princess and the new little Prince, as she had during Trials. But here she was, dirty-blond braid and all, dressed in a simple brown skirt and tan shirt, a turquoise scarf tied loosely around her throat. Cade finally knew why she kept wearing a color that so obviously did not become her: the family arms featured a black arrow on a turquoise background.

"You'll have to decide for yourselves, of course," she told them as they walked outside, past the courtyard and along a pathway paved in a chevron pattern of gray and brown bricks. "But it's the only place that will accommodate everyone in comfort and provide you with a backdrop."

Cade was just itching to say, *In your professional opinion, of course,* but wisely held his tongue.

Their destination was a lighthouse atop an outcropping of rock. The base of it had obviously once been part of the earlier castle; a hundred feet of solid stone, a hundred feet wide, with only one entrance set halfway up the wall. Back then, wooden stairs would have led up to the door, easy to burn down once everyone was shut up tight in the tower during an enemy attack. Now there were brick steps—steep ones—and a wooden platform with a balustrade outside the door. Rising another hundred or so feet was a more modern tower made of the same gray and brown bricks. The top was open for twenty feet beneath the roof to let the light shine out.

"Like a gigantic candle in a stone holder," Jeska said, tilting his head back to look. "How often is it lighted?"

"Every night in winter," Megs replied. "And other times, when it's foggy or stormy. We use Wizardfire."

"Not Elf-light? Not like in streetlamps?"

"It's yellowy gold. Wizardfire is blue."

As if that explained anything.

But then Cade remembered the purplish-gold light conjured by the old man that called up the *vodabeists* in the Vathis River, and wondered if the gold of Elf-light attracted them as well, and if they were indifferent to the blue fire of a Wizard. What had the old man said to Mieka? Looking at his ears, saying, *"Kin"*—was there something about the nature of light created by an Elf that differed in more than color from Wizardfire? Yet hadn't it been Cade's use of magic, Wizard's magic, that had disturbed the monsters, unsettling them so much that final night on the river?

Passing by the Academy had put Master Emmot back into his thoughts, where the old man hadn't been in months. Would Emmot have known about such things? And if he had, would he have told Cayden about them?

Rafe paced off the dimensions of the paved forecourt and pronounced it acceptable. Mieka decided to set up the glass baskets to one side, and use the stone wall as his backdrop, just as Megs had suggested. Workmen were already setting up benches and chairs, and standing torches here and there, for they would be doing the show at night. This was a rarity for Touchstone. They'd played outdoor venues before, but not often in the dark.

On the walk back to the house, Cade asked Megs about the Princess.

"Blooming, glowing, and quite pleased with herself," said Her Ladyship, grinning. "She had so much fun that night at the Downstreet!"

"I would imagine that Prince Ashgar is beginning to wonder what happened to his meek and charming little golden mouse."

"Oh, he is, that. There's a look in his eyes these days, for certes. He put a good face on it, attending that night when you and the Shadowshapers and Crystal Sparks played for her and the ladies at the Keeps, but he could play the proud husband much better if she were somebody else's wife!"

"Tell me, my lady," he said with a delicate emphasis on the title, "how can one be so forthright about other people—" His hesitation was right out of one of Jeska's performances, and created the same effect. Her smile was gone by the time he finished. "—And yet so evasive about oneself?"

"I didn't lie!"

"Not that I recall."

"If I'd told you who I really am, would you have believed it?"

"You might have said something, y'know."

"And been laughed at, even more than you laughed at me for wanting to be a Steward?"

"Laughter at my ambition to become a tregetour was the least of the reactions I got." He paused, then said with a sidelong smile, "Knolltender isn't bad as a punning alias."

She seemed relieved to be discussing something other than herself. "Mindrising is an old Gnomish name, truth to tell. Anciently, Gnomes were given lands all round the country, marking the limits of the Kingdom. Your Lord Fairwalk's ancestor, for instance. His name is one of the oldest, because his holding is so close to Gallantrybanks. As Albeyn expanded, Gnomish families were sent farther and farther out. Sometimes Gnomish names are mistaken for those that describe a particular place, but they're really *gnomons,* markers, indicators of the Royal lands."

"And you're a scholar as well. Tell me, how did you come to be so good at serving drinks?"

Any other highborn girl would have blushed with embarrassment that he knew she'd demeaned herself to become a barmaid, or with fury that he dared mention it at all. Megs looked him in the eyes and said, "I can be at a tavern without having to dress up in men's clothing. I can watch the fettlers at work. And," she finished, "my father owns a half interest in the Keymarker, so I can go there anytime I like." With that, she walked off.

He was watching her, musing idly on the difference between the charm of a woman's rustling skirts and the interest of a woman's legs in trousers, when Rafe came up beside him.

"Learn anything from the Elf about that blossom on his jaw? It's fading, but it must've been a sight to see when fresh." When Cade only shrugged in reply, Rafe persisted, "After the garden show at the Keeps he went back to Hilldrop. One might assume they said their farewells rather less than tenderly."

"Not our business."

"True," Rafe admitted. "But she's got a fist on her wrist, that's for certain sure."

They played "Hidden Cottage" that night, the silly version complete with Mieka's beloved pig. The residents of the estate and the inhabitants of the three nearby villages were still howling with laughter as they made their torchlit way home. Cade was feeling pleased with himself in particular and the world in general. There had been dozens and dozens of women at the performance, a little scared at first and looking to their young Lady Megueris for reassurance. Before Touchstone came on, she and her father circulated amongst the crowd, greeting everyone by name. They made sure people were comfortable on the benches and called occasionally for a pillow to be brought out from the house for this or that elderly person. The Mindrisings, Cade gathered, were universally adored.

Touchstone was served a late supper upstairs in a private parlor, just the four of them after the maids had brought platters of local shellfish and bread still warm from the oven. Mistress Gesha came in to collect empty plates and leave another two bottles of wine, mentioned that Yazz was already tucked up in bed, and recommended an early start tomorrow for Shollop. When the door closed behind her, Cade refilled his wineglass and settled back to relax and enjoy the rest of the evening.

Mieka, who had accounted for two of the bottles all by himself, suddenly turned to Jeska and asked, "Tell me, old thing, how would you like to fuck my wife?"

Cade stopped breathing.

"She's the most beautiful thing you've ever seen, yeh?" Mieka persisted. "Doesn't everybody say so? The most beautiful thing they've ever seen." He waited for an answer, then challenged, "What man wouldn't want to fuck her?"

If the masquer said yes, he'd be admitting lust for Mieka's wife. If he said no, Mieka would demand to know why in all Hells not, or go into some sneering rant about Jeska's manhood. Cade froze, expecting an explosion that was as certain as striking flint to a pile of black powder.

But Jeska had been trained to nimbleness of wit, and just as he sometimes had to do within a play, he found a way out of it.

"It's not question of *like* or *want* or *would*," he said calmly, "but of *could*. As Rafe has said a good few times, I can't get it up without the smell of hay and horseshit, and your lady wife is certainly not the class of woman a man takes to a barn."

Mieka roared with laughter and the moment passed and everybody relaxed. Yet it nagged at Cade, the reason for the outrageous question. And then he remembered the business card from the Finchery, and it occurred to him that Mieka must still be wondering just why she would have such a thing in the first place. Cade thought that the issue had been settled, that he'd accepted the explanation that she wanted something to use when he was drunk or thorned and lost his temper— and Cade had seen enough in Elsewhens to know that violence was indeed more than possible in the futures. He hadn't been all that surprised, truly, when Mieka showed up with that bruise. But he hadn't realized that Mieka would keep mulling over the why of that folded Finchery card as Cade had done. He'd been hoping that the visit to the Ginnel House shelter had served its purpose, and shocked Mieka enough that he would never raise a hand to his wife again. But the contemplative bitterness, accentuated by thorn, in those changeable eyes when he'd asked Jeska, *What man wouldn't want to fuck her?* frightened Cade. There was never any telling what Mieka might do when drunk or thornlost.

Talk started up again on uncomplicated topics: the long drive to Shollop over the next few days and whether it was more or less tedious than the even longer trip to Dolven Wold Road; relief that this year they'd refused the invitation to play at the sinister mansion outside New Halt; whose turn it would be tomorrow night to empty the wagon's slops. Cade didn't join in. He was thinking about what a contrast Shellery House was to Castle Eyot. Lord Mindrising was not an indiscriminate collector, like Lord Rolon Piercehand, but a discerning selector of fine, fascinating, beautiful objects. The floor of this very room was demonstration of his taste. At Castle Eyot, one walked on intricate tiled mosaics and costly marbles inlaid in dizzying patterns. Here, where storms would blow in all winter and half the spring off the Flood and the North Deeps, the floorboards had been painted as if sunlight were perpetually shining in through the windows. It was as much fool-the-eye as Mieka's riotous gaiety that evening.

Jeska and then Rafe departed for their rooms. Cade lingered because Mieka lingered, and because somebody had to make sure he actually made it to his assigned bed.

"I didn't hit her."

Cade sat up straighter in his chair.

"I know you've been wonderin'. And she's not the one as gave me this." He gestured to his jaw, where the bruise was by now almost gone. "Not that she didn't want to. Not that *I* didn't want to." He stared into his nearly empty glass and said softly, "She sewed me a yellow shirt."

When he glanced up, Cade said, "And you reacted . . . badly."

"She couldn't've known. But it set me all wrong, y'see, and then that wretched foxling of hers damned near bit me, and after *that* she was all in a mistemper that there'd been no invitation for her to our show at the Keeps."

"Oh."

"Met the Princess, she has," he went on in a nasty whine. "Talked with Her Royal Highness, she has. Sent her a pretty little pillow for the baby's head, she did. As much right as anybody and more than most." He finished his drink and reached for the bottle. It was empty. He sat there gripping it by the neck as he said, "That was when the third party showed up."

"And he was the one who hit you."

"Only because I hit him first." Mieka snorted. "Don't tell me it was stupid. I know it was stupid. Big strapping young muscly rustic, come by to check on what her mother wants by way of gardening done to pay for their secret, he says. A dress for his sister's wedding, to surprise her."

"But you thought it was something different."

"Fuckin' right I did! So would you, after half an hour of 'I don't mean anything to you anymore' and 'I have to go to Gallantrybanks to see you' and 'even when you're home, you're never really here' and 'so bored I could scream' and 'you think more about your next show than you do about me' and—" He finally paused for breath. "And 'Touchstone means more to you than I do.'"

Cade knew instantly what Mieka's real problem was: His wife had spoken the truth.

"So when he winked at her and said to keep their secret, I had a swing at him. I'm tellin' you, Cade, he was a head taller than me, all bulges in his arms from shoveling shit, and as purely and boringly Human as any Human ever born. I knew it was stupid even when I was doin' it. But you know what really did it for me? The look in his eyes. Like he was doin' me a favor because if we really got to slugging, he'd have to hurt me or I'd hurt meself. Like he felt sorry for me." He shook the empty bottle as if it might have magically refilled in the last few minutes. Then he hurled it against the wall. "*Me!*"

Cade thought it likely that Mieka had mistaken the reason for the young farmer's pity. Not because a slight-boned little Elf was no match for a hefty Human in a brawl, but because he had everything a man could want and still wasn't happy.

As if Mieka had heard a partial echo of the thought, he said, "I give her everything she wants! I married her and gave her a child and a house and clothes and jewelry and her silly blue tassels on the curtains and everything she asks for and a shitload of things she doesn't and I give them to her because I love her! I even let her Gods-damned mother live at the house! What more does she want?"

Cade had no answer for him. Or, rather, he had too many answers that Mieka wouldn't want to hear. He settled for the obvious. "Fidelity, perhaps?"

"She's the only girl I've ever loved and the only girl I will ever love. What's it matter if I fuck half the girls in Albeyn, as long as I come home to her and love her and—"

"Women tend to see these things a bit differently than men do," he ventured. And it was odd, but in a way he agreed with Mieka. The betrayals of the flesh meant little compared to the betrayals of the heart, the mind, the soul.

"All I know is that seeing her with another man—"

"She wasn't *with* another man. You know that. But if you keep on as you're going, she might start to think about it, just to make you take notice. Like with that card from the Finchery."

"She put her hand up to her cheek, y'know. Just like I thought she would. To remind me what I did. But I didn't, Quill. I swear I didn't. I never will again."

"I know," he said softly. But Mieka didn't hear him, for he had succumbed to three—or was it four?—bottles of wine and slumped down in his chair, loose-limbed and senseless.

Cade sat there contemplating him in silence until a gentle scratching at the door made him glance round. A maidservant tiptoed in, glancing about her, and nodded to herself when she saw the green glass shards over by the wall.

"I'm sorry," Cade said, and heard the thickness of his voice, and decided it was time he went to bed, too.

"You're *Touchstone,* ain't you?" the girl said with a quick smile, and went out again, presumably to fetch a broom.

Yes, they were Touchstone. They shattered glass for a living. It was probably time that they stopped.

Mieka revived enough to take a few steps on his own as Cade helped him to his room. He saw the Elf safely on his bed, if not actually in it, and went down the hall to his own bedchamber.

But he couldn't sleep. Waiting for him on a low table was a large, flat package. Imagings of Touchstone collectively and each of them individually, sent by Kearney Fairwalk for their approval before being printed up on placards. There were several of them all together, two each of Rafe and Jeska, four of Mieka. Only one of Cade himself had been deemed fit for public viewing. This didn't surprise him. What was a trifle astonishing was that he looked rather good, with his longish hair and high-necked white shirt, Derien's little silver falcon pinned at his throat.

He spread the imagings of Mieka out across the table. *I know what you will look like,* he thought. *I know that there are doors you might choose where youth and whimsical beauty will decay and the misery will weigh on you like whole mountains of wrong. I know that inside other doorways, your hair will turn gray and your face will be lined but you'll be wearing a diamond in your ear and you'll be happy. I know what you will look like and what you will become. What I don't know is how any of it will happen.*

It wasn't the usual thing, he supposed, to look at an

imaging and see future damage, future pain marring that beautiful Elfen face and haunting those incredible eyes. He tried to see that other Elsewhen, the night of his forty-fifth Namingday with the wineglasses and the friends coming to celebrate, but this night he could see nothing but sorrow. It was a twisting of time, that he should see the future in these imagings, as if the Mieka of right now, today, did not belong there on the page. But then he realized: the one who didn't belong was the Mieka he'd seen in the Elsewhens. That Mieka wasn't real. He didn't exist.

Not yet.

Not ever, he vowed silently. Not if things kept on as they were at Hilldrop Crescent. Hateful as the present and those futures were, he didn't hate her. Why bother? Sooner or later, one way or another, she would be gone. What he felt for her was contempt, which had begun when she groped him at the races. He still wondered what she had been after. To attract him? To mock him? To assert silently but graphically that her beauty could get any man to want her? To make it impossible for him to meet Mieka's gaze? He could just imagine that conversation—Mieka asking what was wrong, nagging and pestering until Cade lost his temper and told him, Mieka furiously accusing him of being a liar. Was that what she'd wanted?

In truth, Cade still didn't understand why she'd wanted Mieka in the first place. Oh, he was beautiful, and he had an ancient Elfen name, and she was obviously in love with him, but why go to all that effort for some traveling player who at that time didn't make much money and didn't have great prospects? The conquest of it? Getting to Gallybanks to conquer further? What did she *want*?

Or mayhap the better question would be, what did her mother want?

He didn't know. Perhaps an Elsewhen would show him. Something about the Archduke, and power, and secrets. What part did her daughter play in it? And Mieka—what about him?

Well, it was beginning, he told himself, the slow, agonizing process of their untangling, one from the other. All he could hope was to spare Jindra as much as possible, defend and protect her as he'd promised himself he'd do that night of his twenty-first Namingday. She was just a baby, too little to understand anything of what might happen between her parents, but as she grew older and the doubts and questions inevitably came, he would have to work hard to prevent her from becoming that cold, bitter woman who refused a Royal invitation to a ceremony honoring her long-dead father.

As for Mieka's marriage . . . that it would end he had no doubting. Mieka's was the dilemma of the traveling player, and solving it had defeated men older and smarter than he. Boredom threatened during the months at home; longing for family could taint the months on the road. The only certainties were onstage.

An ordinary home life . . . Cayden finally accepted the warning of that Elsewhen, the one where he'd been married to a woman who had no interest in his work except for the fact that it paid the bills. *Ordinary*—that was the word he'd used with Blye, the word that had her scoffing and scorning. Oh, she'd been right about him. She always was. He couldn't be ordinary; no player could. Crisiant understood and accepted Rafe's absences, but they all knew that she suffered when he was gone. Whether or not Kazie would adapt was as yet an unanswerable question; she was probably still trying to decide. Mieka's wife did not understand and could not accept, and whereas Cade regretted her anguish just as he did Crisiant's, it seemed to him that the nature of their unhappiness differed. Simply put, Crisiant knew that Rafe would not be the man he was, the man she loved, if he stopped being what he was meant to be. As far as Cade could tell, Mieka's wife had never tried very hard to figure out who her husband truly was. How many times had Mieka described her as being *"the most beautiful thing I've ever seen"*? How many times had Cade reviewed that Elsewhen where she cried out to her mother, *"I want him!"* Blye had been right about that, too: that they didn't really know each other at all.

As he wearily undressed and made ready for bed, a memory came to him—a real memory, not an Elsewhen. Alaen, just before Touchstone performed "Treasure" for the first time, and Cade had tried to tell him to watch carefully—but Alaen cared for nothing but Chirene.

"I don't see her that often, and never alone, but I love her, I want her—oh Gods, she's the most beautiful thing I've ever seen—"

"Is that the criterion, then?"

"Wh-what d'you mean?"

"The most beautiful thing, you said. Like she's a tapestry or a lute you can possess—"

The words stuck in his head, repeating over and over. That was what Mieka had said about *her,* too. The most beautiful *thing.* An item to be admired, adored. A fine carriage, gold embroidery on a velvet tunic, a thick carpet on the polished floor of an elegant house. A thing to be proudly possessed. The way she wanted to possess Mieka, down to his soul. Take him, tame him, break him, own him.

"When Touchstone lost their Elf, they lost their soul."

Ownership, he mused as he lay in the darkness, implied

purchase. What was the price of a heart? Even if an amount could be set and paid, it must be paid again and again—for the heart changed, the price went up—

—or plummeted, like the price of grain or venison, depending on supply and demand.

It wasn't his problem, he told himself again and again. It wasn't his to decide.

Except for Jindra.

And Mieka.

"My glisker you are, and mine you stay."

And didn't that mean that he was just as bad, wanting to own someone who couldn't be bought?

Twenty-six

WAITING FOR THEM in Shollop were Jinsie and Jezael Windthistle. The latter had come to investigate the chances of bidding on some new buildings the University was planning to construct, and the former had decided to meet with her scholarly contacts about ideas for theater for the deaf. She would be taking Cayden to these discussions for his professional perspective.

The trip from Shellery House had been gloomy. Another summer squall had washed out sections of the coastal road, so rather than follow it for a bit and then turn due west for Shollop, Yazz had been compelled to backtrack for a good forty miles to another connecting road. They were almost a whole day late in arriving and their first show was the following afternoon. And it turned out a very good thing that Jez had come along, for Yazz muttered the whole journey to Shollop about his poor wagon having to slog through all that mud. He and Jez went to work on the wagon, and Touchstone took the only two rooms left at the inn where Jez and Jinsie were staying.

"Ridiculous," Jinsie announced at lunching the day after Touchstone arrived. "Fa insisted on Jez coming as escort—at my age!"

"That would be almost twenty-one, wouldn't it?" Rafe asked mildly, from the exalted perspective of almost twenty-three.

"I'm perfectly capable of sitting on a public coach by myself—"

"For two days and nights?" Jez said with a weariness that meant they'd had this conversation many, many times. "With who knows who as your fellow passengers?"

"And with who knows what intimidating little spells that Mum taught me?" she countered. "All right, all right, I know you and Jed finished the wooden stands for their precious glass baskets and had to deliver them. Enough said on the subject? Good." She turned to Cade. "How was Shellery? Did you see Megs?"

They told her all about the estate and the performance, and how pretty it was to watch the boats sailing out to sea and back each day, and exactly nothing about Mieka's appalling question to Jeska. Mieka, it seemed, had forgotten all about it. He might not even remember saying it. Cade worried that he was actually becoming used to that. It was convenient at times—for all of them—but who could tell what he'd forget next?

Jinsie was looking especially lovely, excited by the talk she'd had yesterday with one of her correspondents, looking forward to a larger gathering with Cade in attendance for expert opinions. When lunching was over at the inn she and Jez had chosen, and Touchstone walked to Players Hall, where they would perform in a few hours, Mieka told Cade to keep an eye on which of the young men she favored most.

"Have to get a look at me first brother-in-law," he said.

Amused, Cade said, "I take it that in your world, men and women can't possibly have conversations and be friends without that sort of thing entering into it." Too late he realized he probably shouldn't have said that, remembering Mieka's quick irrational jealousy of the young farmer and the resulting bruise on his jaw.

But Mieka only laughed and replied, "In any world, Quill. In *any* world!"

For the first time in their experience of Shollop, women were openly in the audience that night. The few females who attended the University—not officially, of course, but allowed to sit in on classes—had usually shown up in male clothing. Now they were here in skirts and summery dresses. So were quite a few faculty wives and daughters. The next night at least a third of the audience was composed of women. And for this reason all the groups on all the circuits from now on would be playing at least one and sometimes two additional shows at each stop to accommodate the increased demand for tickets. It was part of Vered's resentment against the system that none of the players would have a share of the money. The contracts for Royal, Ducal, and Winterly had been signed before the schedules were altered, and the Master of the King's Revelries would be raking in the coin for the Royal coffers. Cade wasn't pleased, either, but he had every faith that by next year, Kearney Fairwalk, Romuald Needler, and other managers would have righted the situation—with a bit extra, he hoped, to compensate for the swindle of this year.

On their third day in Shollop, Rafe headed out before lunching to meet with some art students regarding his idea of a children's play and ancillary book. Mieka and Jeska tagged along. Jinsie dragged Cade round to a tavern where six young men awaited with huge pitchers of beer and dozens of bright ideas. Though all of them admired Jinsie's looks, Jinsie didn't particularly look back at any of them. Mieka, Cade thought with amusement, was wrong. His future brother-in-law wasn't among this group.

Theater for the deaf. Theater for the blind. Cade realized that in a way, Touchstone had already done the former. The plays performed on the Continent had relied perforce on the conjurings of the withies and Jeska's physical presentations, for their audiences had understood perhaps one word in ten of the scripts. But to work a play without any sounds at all . . . that intrigued him.

About excising all the visuals he was less convinced. One of the young scholars suggested that they surprise the audience by giving it a try at the performance for the Marching Society in what had been the old greenhouse, yet Cade resisted this as unprofessional. These men were roughly his own age, but suddenly they all seemed very young—which was absurd because his first time in Shollop he'd been intimidated by everyone he'd met, and what was the difference except for two Winterly Circuits, one Royal, a trip to the Continent, friendship with a Princess, artistic acclaim and financial success, and now their second Royal . . . well, all right, he'd done quite a lot. But at twenty-two, had so many experiences crowded his life that he should feel so much older?

"We'll try it," he said impulsively. "Only you'll have to let everybody know beforetime. And if they want a refund after, we'll be glad to oblige them."

"Oh, good Gods, Cade!" Jinsie exclaimed, laughing. "Don't say that! Poverty-stricken students? They could love it up one side and down the other and *still* ask for their money back!"

Now all he had to do was convince his partners. And what fun *that* would be, he reflected gloomily, wondering why he hadn't just kept his mouth shut.

"What you and the Shadowshapers did at the Down-street," one of the young men said suddenly. "That was brilliant. The first step in the revolution."

"And we've all read that article about you in *The Nayword*," another said. "The one where you talked about theater changing the world."

"There's no more articulate spokesman for innovation and transformation," confirmed another.

"Oh," he said, inadequately, flummoxed that they were treating him as if he actually knew things. As if he had become Somebody.

Well, he rather supposed he had.

Walking back to the inn, he asked Jinsie, "What revolution?"

"In theater, in the crafts, in society," Jinsie said firmly. "There's nothing men can do that women can't."

"Fathering a child might be a little beyond a woman's capabilities," he responded dryly.

"I don't see you becoming a mother anytime soon," she retorted. "And who's more important to a child's raising, the mother or the father?"

"Whoever's there the most," he said at once.

"Which is always the mother."

"Why couldn't it be the father? There are plenty of men who lose their wives and are left with children to raise—"

"And a whole family to provide for, and how many of them stay at home to take care of the children? They just marry another woman to manage the household."

"What a romantic you are!"

She ignored the teasing. "My father works in our home. He's always there. He was at least as important as Mum when it came to the raising of us."

"It sounds," he said gently, "as if you might be criticizing your brother."

She looked up at him sidelong. "Where," she inquired acidly, "shall I start?"

"He's learning, Jinsie. He really is. It's just taking him awhile to grow up."

"Wish Mum had a spell for it," she muttered.

He wanted very much to ask what form Jinsie's own magic took, but didn't. He'd never seen her work any spellcrafting, never heard Mieka or anyone else mention what her talents were. Elfen though her looks were, it didn't necessarily follow that she had Elfen sorts of magic in her—or indeed much magic at all. It would be rude of him to ask.

They paused to browse in a bookshop, but there wasn't a lot besides secondhand texts—nothing for him and nothing for Jorie's new passion for books. They kept looking, though, and in the quiet and relative privacy of the back shelves, Jinsie said, "He does send money and sometimes supplies to Ginnel House, when he remembers. Usually when he's just back from Hilldrop. Right before the Royal started he left an envelope and directions, and asked me to take it for him."

"But not because he—because anything happened."

"No. It's because he feels guilty, as well he might! Mum and Fa keep wanting to tell you somehow that they're grateful, but they can't think up anything that wouldn't embarrass everybody." She smiled up at him. "You see? Just me mentioning it has made you uncomfortable."

He stopped trying to pretend interest in a hefty text on the history of the King's Council. "It had to be done," he said flatly. For Mieka's sake, and for Jindra's. He knew what he'd seen in those Elsewhens.

"Nobody else could have managed it. You're the only one he ever listens to."

"Not that often."

"More than anybody else." She started for the shop

door and he followed. When they were outside on the street again, she went on, "Years ago, Jed and Jez would take him along to a tavern to watch a show, and he'd come back and talk about it for hours—what he'd do different, mistakes the group made. But one night they went to see you and Rafe and Jeska and whoever your glisker was at the time, and never said a word after. Oh, except to disparage the glisker as a talentless fribbler who didn't know a glass withie from a wooden spoon and couldn't use either if he thought about it with both hands for a fortnight. I went with them a few nights later, dressed as a boy, of course."

"And found out for yourself how dreadful we really were!"

"You were pretty rotten," she agreed. "But Mieka was right. The glisker had no idea what to do with the magic you gave him. Jeska and Rafe always made the most of it, because they're brilliant. But even I could sense the potential. And *that* was due to you."

"I'm embarrassed again, had you noticed?"

She laughed at him. "I don't care—had you noticed? What's important is that Mieka respected you first as a tregetour, and now as a man, as a friend. He couldn't be everything he is without your magic to work with, and he knows it." Suddenly she whirled round on her toes with the exuberance Cade associated with her brother. "The lovely part is that now I get to see all of you at the theater any night I choose, and so can any other woman in Gallybanks!"

"Pleased to have been of service," he told her with a bow. "I've been trying to work out exactly why he did what he did at the Shadowshapers' show. Just for the fun of breaking the rules?"

"Oh, Cayden! D'you think he doesn't pay attention when you talk? It was partly for the excitement, of course.

This is Mieka, after all! But you made him think about something he never thought about before—and there's not many people can make him think at all. What's he always saying? That thinking only gets in the way? He doesn't believe that anymore, not really. And that's due to you."

Now he really *was* uncomfortable.

"As for where his own thinking will take him," she went on as they left the bookshop, "Fa just rolls his eyes and says we'll all have to wait and see."

"I've heard Sakary Grainer say that if you don't know where you're going, any old road will get you there."

"And that's why Mieka's lucky to have you giving him a nudge now and then. We really are beholden to you, Cade. All of us." She paused, and then with a twist of her lips as if tasting something sour, finished, "Even *her*. Even though she'll never know it."

He shrugged a reply. He could tell himself that his concern was for Mieka, or for Jindra, but at bottom it was really for himself. So that he didn't have to live through in reality what those Elsewhens had shown him reality could be.

He considered enlisting Jinsie's help in convincing the others that they ought to perform for the Marching Society without visual effects. Upon further consideration, though, he thought it best to broach the subject in private. Not for the first time, his partners surprised him. Rafe merely shrugged, but seemed willing. Jeska was intrigued. Mieka couldn't wait to give it a try. They spent a fascinating afternoon discussing the adaptation of a play so as to perform it without visual effects. Sound, sensation, taste, scent, emotion—but the backdrop and physical action would all have to be conveyed with words. After their show that evening at Players Hall, Cade sat up very late writing and rewriting. He hadn't felt this frustrated and provoked by work in a long time. It made him very happy.

They'd decided on "The Silver Mine." Nothing much happened in it to look at anyway, just the back-and-forth from the lamplit cavern with its dully sparkling veins of ore to the torchlit hillside where the sons kept vigil. Cade had rewritten it so that there were only four characters instead of six. Jeska had to provide really distinctive voices for each. He was nervous about conveying the changes and personalities without costume or facial expression, although during the run-through he managed it so well that Jinsie, watching from the back of the converted greenhouse, leaped to her feet and began to applaud.

"I haven't even started using any magic yet," Mieka complained loudly. "Do you need me at all for this?"

"Probably not!" she called back, grinning as he scowled.

"No bullying the glisker!" Cade exclaimed. "Even if he is your twin brother and an annoying little git!"

Mieka stuck out his tongue at him, and flourished a withie. "May we continue? Ever so beholden to you, O Great Master Tregetour! Jeska, we follow the usual script for the first part. Cade got rid of or condensed the other speeches. I want a hand signal from you as to when *exactly* you want the changes, right?"

"Won't the audience see any gestures I make?"

"Not with what I've got planned." He bounced excitedly on his toes behind the new polished oaken frames that snuggled the glass baskets. "We don't want total darkness. That would only send them looking at the side-lights over the doors. But there won't be anything *definite* to look at, either. Just swirls of black on blacker, some dark grays, bits and flashes of silver." He twirled a glass twig between his fingers, then pointed it at the masquer. "You're used to being all alone out there, but

with supporting scenery and the like to look at. This
will be just your voice. Are you game, old son?"

"One other thing," Rafe warned. "Just because there'll
be nothing to look at, don't overcompensate with sensations and emotions."

"We know our jobs," Cade felt compelled to say, and
Mieka grinned at him.

Black Lightning was known for slamming an audience with everything and then some. Touchstone's performance that night was a marvel of delicacy and control.
They had come a great distance, Cade told himself with
pride, from the flash and flamboyance of the "Dragon"
that first Trials.

Only one thing troubled him. Just as the words—
new words for this playlet, *his* words—described the
slow rising of the sun on the hillside, he felt the sudden
sting of an Elsewhen, like the fine pricking of a glass
thorn. Resisting it was surprisingly easy. *I haven't time
for this now!* he'd thought, and concentrated on Jeska's
voice and the ebb and flow of magic, and the Elsewhen
faded. But upstairs in his room that night, with Mieka
quietly snoring in the bed nearby, he couldn't bring it
back. He couldn't coax it or command it. This might
have been because during the time since that muted nee-
dling, he had done or said or thought something that
made it change, so that it simply disappeared.

Or it might mean that by resisting it, he'd lost it forever. Pleasant vision, urgent warning, baffling foreseeing, or even a theater piece as had happened after Tobalt's
dinner party—he had no way of knowing. Smaller than
a mote of shattered glass it had been, nothing to see,
just a feeling of eager expectancy. He tried to re-create
the anticipation, like a call into the future, but nothing
answered.

Mayhap the Elsewhens really were changing as his

brain reached maturity. There was no difference in their length—anything from a quick flash to a minutes-long scene—nor in the amount of time between the here and now and the where- and whenever. He'd seen things mere instants or twenty or more years into the future. What was different was his new ability to postpone the visions, and the distinct sensation that warned him of their approach.

Must he succumb to an Elsewhen as it happened? He'd only just got the knack of postponing them. The sense of control over this thing he'd never even dreamed he could control had been exhilarating. To suspect that if he refused it at the exact moment of its occurrence was to lose it entirely—

—and what if the Elsewhens simply stopped?

"Quill."

Soft though it was, Mieka's voice startled him so much that he struggled to sit straight up in bed, tangling himself in the sheet. "What? What is it?"

"Go to sleep."

Cade fell back onto the pillows. "Can't."

"The show was great. Nobody will ask for his money back. Or *her* money, either!" he added with a chuckle. "Stop anguishing yourself."

He barely heard what Mieka said, for the turn took him violently, as if it knew not to give him even an instant to refuse it.

{**Dolven Wold; its outdoor theater, the Rose Court, where they'd played for the first time last summer; the strange iron grate in the middle of the stage in the shape of a full-blown rose; the blood flowing down into it, fresh blood, thick bright red blood, spilling through the grate—**}

"There's something down there!" he cried.

"What? Where?" Mieka demanded.

"Something—I don't know, I didn't see—"

"Quill!" Mieka's hands were on his shoulders, not shaking him, just supporting him. "Quill, it's all right. You're back. You're safe."

He shook his head. "Nobody's safe." He had no idea where that thought had come from, but he knew it was true. Or would be true. Or might be true.

"You are. We are. I promise, Quill."

Mieka sat on the bed, squirming around so his back was against the wall. He coaxed Cade nearer and wrapped his arms around him, tugging the sheet up to cover them both. Cade rested his head on Mieka's shoulder, his spine to the Elf's chest.

"It's all right. Close your eyes and sleep, Quill. You're safe."

No, not *safe,* not exactly. His own mind would never permit it. But what he did feel was . . . *protected.* Although a less likely protector than this wild, mad, clever little Elf could not be imagined—perhaps it was because even if the world and the Elsewhens turned his life curly as a corkscrew, Mieka was just that much crazier. He found both comfort and amusement in that idea, and was smiling slightly as he fell asleep.

Which sweet and mellow feeling did not interfere with a powerful desire to strangle Mieka two nights later.

Cade had glimpsed the new thorn-roll when Mieka unpacked his satchels. The wagon being across town at a blacksmith's for repairs, they'd had to remove almost all their clothing and other gear from its tidy shelving and carry it with them to the inn. Before leaving Gallantrybanks Cade had inspected Mieka's bags— not really caring about the thorn, because he had his own supply of blockweed and such in the wyvern-hide wallet Mieka had given him years ago. No, what he was searching for was black powder and, sure enough, five little parchment twists of it had been tucked inside a presumably secret pocket in one satchel. Mieka had protested that he wanted it for teaching Master Pricksur up north not to deny Elves room at his inn. Cade sternly quashed temptation to aid and abet, and got rid of the black powder. Mieka pouted elaborately. Not elaborately enough, Cade discovered that night at Players Hall, not with his heart really in it, and for good reason.

Scorning as always the glisker's bench, which he pushed off to one side now that he had the wooden support frames, Mieka danced and chortled his way through "Troll and Trull." At the very end, when usually he jumped over the glass baskets to join his partners onstage for their bows, he paused, reached into a jacket pocket, struck a flint-rasp, and blew up the glisker's bench.

"It was naught but the padding," he said backstage. "And Cade keeps saying we ought to give over shattering glass."

Rounding on him, Rafe growled, "You could've killed us all!"

"That measly little bang? 'Twasn't much more than a damp baby-fart."

Jeska was still picking bits of upholstery and feather stuffing off his shirt. "You put the baskets and withies in danger, too."

"Not for an instant," Mieka scoffed.

Keeping his arms tightly folded across his chest, Cade asked softly, "What's in the thorn-roll? The purple one Brishen left for you at her place."

Mieka shrugged.

"You never would have done this if you were only drunk." He heard his voice getting louder. "So it has to be some new sort of thorn that makes you *completely insane*!"

When he saw in those thorn-blurred eyes that Mieka

was calculating whether or not he'd get away with a lie, he made a grab for the Elf's left wrist. He felt the gallop and stutter of the pulse beneath his fingers. Rafe closed powerful hands around slight shoulders to hold Mieka steady as Cade ripped the seam of his shirtsleeve to expose the marks. There were old ones, long since healed, and newer ones still faintly reddened, and one inside his elbow that was so recent that Cade's roughness tore off the tiny scab. A drop of blood welled up. Rafe let him go as if to hold on an instant more would scar his hands.

"What's it to you?" Mieka snarled. "We gave them a great show!"

"And you think that's all that matters?"

"I think that's all that matters to *you*!"

Cade pushed him back, and he stumbled against a support pillar, barely keeping his feet.

"Sleep in the wagon tonight," Cade told him. "Don't come anywhere near me until our next performance."

Just then the supervisor of Players Hall pushed through the curtain to the tiring room. He was in perfect raptures about the show, not a bit concerned with the partial obliteration of his glisker's bench. They were *Touchstone,* after all. Something of the sort was only to be expected. And it was better than losing the expensive glass shades on the doorway lamps, or a row of windows. Mieka threw Cade a look of pure venom behind an enchanting smile. Cade turned on his heel and walked out.

Twenty-seven

HE WENT TO bed early that night—before the Minster chimes struck midnight, anyway—unwilling to listen to any more of the argument going on inside his own head. One voice kept ranting about how foolish, how reckless, how malicious, how just plain stupid Mieka Windthistle could be. Another voice nattered on about how close Cade had come to what he feared most: losing his temper for good and all, and using his thin, strong Wizard's hands to take that fucking little Elf apart, piece by bleeding, broken piece.

A third voice suggested that tonight would be a good time for the combination of blockweed and greenthorn that could calm him. Usually he avoided it, for the hangover could be annoying, but tonight he was just angry enough, and there were enough hours ahead of him to sleep it all off, that he got out the wallet Mieka had given him years ago. Scarcely had he pricked a delicate hole in his arm when he sensed the Elsewhen approaching. It was almost a relief. He didn't even consider trying to reject it. If he did that too often, they might stop altogether.

Nearly sunrise. The scene of the finding of the Rights appeared, lit by the full moon that outlined the tumble-down wall. And then he realized that there was no snow.

It wasn't winter, or Wintering sunset. Neither was he inhabiting the tall form with what he'd thought were Elfen ears but he now knew to be Fae. He was bodiless. He didn't really exist.

{"If the sun strikes the stones from behind at Wintering, then it must strike the stones front-on at Midsummer dawn. I figured it out when I was here at Spring Quarterday—did the measurements and everything. Simple!"

"Clever, clever you," Alaen snapped. "I don't see any evidence of it yet."

"Sun's not up," Briuly pointed out.

Alaen turned to the east and a sudden shaft of light struck him right in the face. The next moment he was on the ground, shoved aside by his cousin, who was laughing with delighted vindication.

The shine of gold and silver threaded through spun glass: a chain of a hundred perfect links and a crown that was a circle of sunbursts and crescent moons and diamond-studded stars. The Rights rested on a flat rock that formed the seat of the throne, its back the stone wall. Whole, immaculate, glowing like rough-carved chunks of moonlight sparkling in the new morning sunshine at his back.

To take up the carkanet and crown, to sit upon the throne, to cause the suns and moons and stars to ignite and proclaim a True King—how dazzling bright it would be, no paltry yellowish Elf-light nor sickly blue Wizardfire nor red-gold glower of a Caitiff's spellcasting, but the pure silver and gold radiance of the Rights.

Briuly seized the crown with his long, thin hands and put it on his head, still laughing, his thorn-sharp eyes wild with joy. "The Fae King!"

Yet there was naught but sunglow on the crown. No inner fire, no eldritch shimmer. Briuly's eyes lost their exultant sheen and his smile wavered and died. "I don't—I don't understand—"

"Idiot. What did you think would happen? And look, you've dropped the necklace." For in his taking, the carkanet had been dislodged, dangling on a jag of stone just above the mud of last night's rain. Alaen bent, reaching for it, saying, "For Chirene—I couldn't bear to see any other woman wear it."

Yet before his fingers touched it, there came the yowling of the hounds.

Alaen scrambled to his feet and ran like all Hells were after him—which a goodly number of them were. They rode out of the Westerlands, Sentinels charged with the safekeeping of the Rights until the crown encircled the brow of a True King and the carkanet clasped the throat of a True Queen. These were not the Fae of mortals' pretty imaginings, portrayed in stone and glass and paint as winged, exquisite, elegant. These were the other sort of Fae. Fanged, hideous, filthy, huge, riding gigantic black horses with clawed feet, horses that screamed enraged reply to the belling royal hounds.

The dogs were skeletal and hideously swift, with bony bodies and narrow muzzles and a ridge of tufting fur along their spines. They formed a boundary of bared teeth and shrill growls round Nackerty Close, the field with many corners. The Sentinels drew rein, most of them at the broken wall. Two of them on their gruesome mounts continued on, halting when they loomed over Alaen where he had stumbled to the ground. They paused, glancing coldly at his twisted limbs and bloodied forehead.

"Carkanet?" one of the Fae yelled over a massive shoulder, and the rocks littering the ground quivered. The second Fae raised his sword.

"Untouched!" the cry came back.

"Unsullied, then." A nod, reluctant; the sword dipping back down, deprived of a kill. "Leave him. We'll take the other."}

Cade opened his eyes to the darkness of his bedchamber, gasping, covered in clammy sweat. *I did this*, he thought helplessly. *I did this. My fault. I told them to search. I told them where to look. But not on Midsummer dawn!*

"Cayden?"

An opening door, a bit of Elf-light—no fear in it, a willing conjuring. He saw her only in outline, the slight and slender shape, the pale hair glowing.

Why couldn't it have been Mieka coming through the door? Mieka would have understood. Would not be staring at him like this, shocked and frightened. Mieka—

{Cade gripped the tregetour's lectern in both hands, watching in horror as Mieka's dance became a flailing stagger. The magic surged, faltered, swept the audience with a ferocity that took all Rafe's skill and strength to control. The images and sensations of *Bewilderland* were even more bizarre than usual, and that was what people came for, returning again and again to be assaulted by Cayden Silversun's nightmares. But whatever he had put into the withies, Mieka was enhancing with drunken, thorn-roused horrors of his own. People began to scream.

Cade lunged for the glisker's bench, shoved Mieka out of the way, grabbed the withies. The Elf didn't even protest, so completely thornlost that he merely sat down on the floor and began counting his fingers like a toddling child.

They finished the performance, Lord and Lady alone knew how. The only thing Cade could think of was how much he would enjoy kicking the living shit out of Mieka Windthistle. Two thousand people were out

there, gasping, shaking, trying to recover from an on-
slaught more brutal and undisciplined than anything
Black Lightning had ever dared to do.

He turned, fists clenched. Those eyes were looking
up at him, but they were no longer Mieka's eyes. Parts
of him were gone, lost to whiskey and thorn and despair. The memories stored in muscle and bone took
him through the work, but none of it was guided by his
conscious mind. Where before, instinct and intellect
had combined with physical grace to produce an un-
matched brilliance, now the muscles remembered the
basics of the movements, but didn't really know what to
do without that inspired mind's direction.

Cade felt no compassion. He would never forgive
Mieka for this, never.

"Quill—"

Those big, pathetic eyes; that once-beautiful face;
this drunken, thorn-thralled stranger who used to be
Mieka Windthistle—

"Get out!" he roared, and kicked over the wooden
frames, and all the glass baskets made by Blye so long
ago shattered onto the stage.}

"Cade? What's wrong?" The little yellow-gold Elf-light
trembled. "You look like you've seen—"

Something that might have been laughter scraped out
of his throat. What had he *seen*? What *hadn't* he seen?
What more would his "gift" from the Fae show him?

A challenge. A dare. A taunting to his own mind. He
had no illusions that he'd seen the worst that the futures could offer. If there were more horrors in store, he
wanted to know them.

And so they came, one after another: Elsewhens, all of
them possible, all of them because of his choices, his decisions, crowding into his dazed mind, silent glimpses and
sudden visions and long scenes like in a play, weaving

in and out of each other as if in competition to find out which could stun him the most. But these were no stage productions, no excursions of imagination and ideas. These were the futures. His futures.

{Mieka looked up, those eyes bewildered, hurt, the eyes of a child betrayed by everyone he had ever trusted.

"How did this happen?" he whispered. "I don't—I can't understand how this happened."

Cade felt his lips move, the vibration of air in his lungs, his throat, heard his own voice say with flawless coldness, "*You* made it happen."}

He struggled uselessly against those words. *No, it wasn't you—it was me. My choices. My decisions. My fault—*

{Mieka plucked the spectacles off Jeska's nose and peered through them. "Lord and Lady save us! Why not just strap a pair of bottle bottoms to your face?"

Jeska tossed aside the broadsheet he'd been flipping through. "It may come to that." He took back the spectacles and tucked them in his pocket. "Please tell me the snow has stopped. Stuck here for two days, and us not on the Winterly these twenty years and more!"

"Up to the eaves by morning, Yazz said." He sat at the table across from Jeska, casting a quick glance over his shoulder. At a far table in the taproom, Cade and Rafe were playing cards with Yazz, who as usual was winning.

The masquer waited patiently for a few moments, then frowned. "Something wrong?"

"D'you ever—does it worry you? I mean, we been doing this for more'n twenty years now, and—"

"We're still selling out every show, ain't we? We still have a good time onstage, Cade's writing is better than ever—" He broke off. "What's worrying *you*?"

"Nothin'. Everything's fine, nothin' to worry ab—"

"C'mon. What's really wrong?" Then, with a frown: "Twenty years—" A tiny smile curved his lips. "Oh, Mieka! You think we're finally too old to work the stage, don't you?"

"*You* ain't. Nor Cade nor Rafe, neither." He gulped, then admitted, "It's me. I'm still quick enough, but what happens when I'm not? If I'm not everything I've always been, Cade's work suffers. And I won't have that. I just fuckin' *won't*."

Amusement faded from the beautiful face framed in curls touched here and there with silver. "You really mean it. Have you talked with Cade?"

"Oh, right. That'll happen." He hesitated, then rushed on, "Never occurs to him, does it—two hours a night, three if it's *Bewilderland*, five nights of eight on a tour like this one—how do I give the audiences everything they came for if I'm not quick like I was at twenty? That's when we worked out some of these pieces, Jeska—and I ain't seen 'twenty' for over twenty years! The minute I slow down, the minute I'm tired in the middle instead of at the end—that's the night I'm finished as glisker for Touchstone."

"Mieka—"

"I don't give a shit if they start sayin' the Elf's gettin' pudgy, getting' gray, lookin' his age. I—"

"You don't. That's the best part of Elfenblood."

Mieka brushed that aside. "What I never want to hear 'em say is that I'm not livin' up to the work anymore."

"Talk to Cade," Jeska urged. "He'll understand."

Mieka laughed without humor. "He'll understand that he can't write what he needs to write, because his glisker's too old and feeble to perform it."}

"Shh," Jinsie was whispering, "calm down, Cayden, it's all right, everything's all right—"

Mieka, he tried to say. All that emerged from his throat was a muffled groan. *Where's Mieka—?*

{"Where is he?"

The woman shrugged. Then she looked up into his face, his eyes. She took an involuntary step back, made an involuntary glance towards the stairs.

He pushed past her, up the dark stairs, through a double door discreetly labeled *diversions*. The room within was littered with little girls. Little girls in school-girl skirts and deep red lip rouge and makeup thick and heavy and black on their eyes. Little girls in miniature silk gowns cut low over flat chests. Little girls in boys' trousers, corkscrew curls cascading down neatly tailored jackets as they moved about the room with silver trays of prepared thorn. Little girls draped across velvet couches, posing with glasses of wine in one hand and skinny knees poking from between the folds of silken chamber robes.

A burst of raucous laughter directed him to a hall, and a muffled giggling shriek took him to the third door down. Inside, Mieka sprawled naked and fleshy on the bright blue coverlet of a bed hung about with shimmering crystal ropes, as if someone had captured rainbows to drape around the bed. Within reach were bottles, glasses, and three girls. Not little girls, praise all the Angels; these girls were sixteen or seventeen, with breasts and hips.

Those eyes, bleary and hazy, caught sight of him. "Cayden! Do join us, dear boy! These three are mine, but I'm sure we can find a few for you!"}

The horror of it was that in the Elsewhen he was neither sickened nor shocked. This was usual, this evening in a whorehouse, even normal—not just for Mieka, but for him.

He turned his head feebly, saw the penstrokes of silver light from the full moon along the wall. Like a moonglade through the gaps in the shutters, and he grasped desperately at the image, remembering a moonglade Elsewhen where Mieka had been gentle and whimsical and happy, and oh Gods how he wanted that Mieka here beside him now—*I'll make your moonglade for you, just as I promised, I'll do it, Mieka, I swear I will—*

{"You daft little cullion," Jeska said, reaching across the table to hold tight to Mieka's shaking hands. "You think you're the only one scared? I'll be forty-five next spring, and you needn't think it's any easier for me than it is for you. What if my knees crack in the middle of a speech—that'd be good for a laugh, right in the middle of *Window-wall*! And that's not even considering my voice. The shouts aren't as loud, and the whispers get gravelly by the fifth show out of five, and as for everything in between—how do I make Cade's work everything it should be if I lose the shadings?"

Mieka looked thoroughly ashamed of himself. "Gods, Jeska—I'm sorry. I shoulda realized."

"None of it's gonna last forever," he said softly. "We're lucky it's gone on as long as it has. We're still the greatest players in Albeyn."

The Elf was silent, staring at his hands, and then said, "I always knew it'd get harder as I got older. I just—I can't just *sit* there, that's not how glisking works. Not mine, anyways. One day I really will be too old, I won't be quick enough anymore, I won't be able to last through the whole show—and now here's Cade talking about adding another sequence to *Window-wall* and what if I don't have it in me anymore?"}

"Cade, please! Tell me what's wrong! Tell me what to do—"

Nothing to be done. Nothing. He had opened himself

to the Elsewhens and they were taking him, claiming him, possessing him. And he had invited this. He had dared his own mind to do its worst.

["Beholden for the invitation," said Tobalt, bowing the exact degree required by her rank. "Though it wasn't unexpected."

"Wasn't it?" She gestured for the maid to leave them alone in the pretty little parlor, an elegantly feminine room that was obviously hers alone from the flowered carpet on the floor—irises, the purple-blue matching her eyes—to the painted plaster foxes chasing each other above windows looking out onto the gardens.

"I've been waiting to hear from you, in fact. Ever since I announced that we'd be doing chapbooks on Touchstone, one for each of the founding members."

She smiled. It was a charming smile in a face hardly touched by time and certainly not by trouble. Her second husband had kept her well. "I read the chapbooks about the Shadowshapers. Impressive."

"Much beholden, Your Ladyship. Of course, I'm intensely interested in anything you want to tell me. May I take notes?" A mere formality, a conventional politeness; she was obviously eager to have her side of the story chronicled.

"Shall I begin at the beginning?" she asked when he was seated.

"Anywhere you like."

"Then I'd like to start at the end."

Tobalt glanced up, surprised.

"The night he died, all my fingernails turned black and split down to the quick, and by the next day had fallen off. I don't know how he managed it, but there was some sort of spiteful spellcasting put upon me, his last bit of cruelty. He always said I had the most beautiful hands. . . ." She held them out so he could admire them: lovely indeed, slender and graceful, the nails pink and shining. "I wore gloves to the Chapel service, of course. Over the bandages. The bleeding hadn't stopped."

"It was surprising," he said carefully, "your making such a long journey so swiftly to attend. A forgiving gesture."

"I owed it to my daughter. And to his poor dear mother and twin sister, who always adored me." She leaned forward and spoke in a low, confiding tone. "Mishia told me later that it broke her heart to see him—her beautiful boy, and he really had been beautiful, you know—covered in thorn-marks, reeking of whiskey, with a pouch of dragon tears almost empty—"

Tobalt said flatly, "He never touched dragon tears."

"Is that what everyone's saying?" The suggestion of a smirk twitched her lips. "It was one of those gold velvet bags so familiar to everyone from Alaen Blackpath's tragedy. The ones people bought at the Finchery."

"But Mieka knew he was too much Elf, that dragon tears would kill him."

"I don't suppose it mattered to him anymore." A tiny shrug. "They'd been threatening him. Especially Cayden. That if he didn't stop all the thorn and the alcohol, they'd throw him out and find another glisker. Have you spoken with the others yet? The rest of Touchstone, I mean, and all the other wives?" She gave a little glittering trill of laughter. "I know what that sounds like—as if I still consider myself one of the wives. It's a thing you never escape. Ask Jeschenar's first, and second, and third—I've forgotten, is he on his fourth or his fifth by now?"

"Fourth," Tobalt said.

"Well, as I say, ask all the others. *And* the 'lightly loved,' as Cayden so delicately put it in *Stolen Torches*.

One thing I'll give him, he can be very eloquent about other people's suffering."

"You never liked him much, did you?"

"I never really knew him. I only know what my husband was like when he was around Cayden—that's how the thorn started. He never would have become thornlost if it hadn't been for Cayden Silversun."

"I've heard it was the other way round. That Mieka introduced Cade to various things. At Cade's request," he added.

"And see who's the only one still here to tell the tale of it!" she replied sharply. Then, recovering herself, she gave a one-shouldered shrug. "I'm sure you'll be hearing a different version from everyone." She held out her hands again. "All my fingernails," she murmured. "I can still remember how much it hurt."}

"Stop," he breathed. "No more . . . no more . . ."

"I don't understand. Cade, tell me how to help you!"

There was a sudden rush of cool air into the room as the door opened. Mieka's voice—oh praise be to all the Old Gods, Mieka's voice—

"Quill, I'm sorry, you were right, it was stupid—" An abrupt gasp. "Jinsie! What in all Hells—?"

"I don't know! I heard him from the hall—like a wounded animal—"

Cade watched, wide-eyed and not daring to blink, as Mieka crouched beside the bed. He felt thin, warm fingers holding on to his hand.

{He held gently on to thin, cold fingers, smoothed thick silver hair, tucked it behind delicately pointed ears. "You feel up to it? You're sure?"

A nod. A suggestion of a smile tugging his lips; a familiar brightness shining in those tired eyes. Still beautiful; still Mieka's beautiful eyes.

Within a few minutes the chamber was crowded.

Jindra nearest the bed, her husband directly behind her—}

"Oh Gods," Mieka whispered. "How long has he been like this?"

"What's happening to him? Mieka—"

{Scant weeks after Cade's Namingday—his fortieth, Gods help him—Mieka escorted Jindra across the sun-soaked river lawn of Wistly Hall and gave her in marriage to her bashfully ecstatic Master Imager. Cade watched, smiling, remembering another wedding long ago in this very spot. Almost everyone who had seen Blye marry Jedris was here today, and dozens more besides. Still, despite constant and dedicated circling amongst the huge crowd of family and friends, Cade was unable to avoid Jindra's mother.

"Cayden," she said, and he turned, and there she was. "I don't need to ask how you've been—you look very fine."

"So do you." He smiled as sincerely as he could. In her summery green silk gown with a spray of roses pinned to the bodice, she was almost as beautiful as she'd been at sixteen. "I'm glad you could be here. I know it means a lot to Jindra."

"So do you."

He cast about for something else to say, something neutral, innocuous, polite, impersonal—

"Years ago," she said, "I told myself that if I ever saw you again, I'd thank you for letting him go long enough for us to have Jindra—but you never really let him go for an instant, did you?"

"No."

"And you never will." Her words were measured, calm. "We would've been all right, you know, the two of us. We would've gone along in our way. But we never would've been happy." She looked up at him again. "Take care of each other, Cade. I don't suppose we'll ever meet again, so I wanted to be sure to say that."

All he could do was nod. She had been far more generous than he ever could have been—which he knew was quite small-minded of him. After all, he'd won.]

"Quill, look at me. Please. Just look at me."

"Is he thornlost? Is that what—?"

"Quill, please!"

[The office was familiar: wood furniture and books and framed first pages and various trinkets given by friends. The girl behind the desk was perhaps eighteen, plainly dressed, with ink-stained fingers that tapped the stack of scrawled notes before her.

"How much of it was true, Da?" she asked.

Tobalt paced the cramped office. "There are things I believe—Mieka's threats to her second husband, for instance, because I've seen the constable's reports and there were quite a few witnesses. But not the dragon tears. I know that for a stone cold fact. He never went anywhere near the stuff. As for her fingernails falling out? Nonsense. A stupid and clumsy lie."

"How do you know?"

He smiled grimly. "Because it's an appalling insult, if not actual sacrilege, to wear gloves when the Good Brother or Good Sister clasps hands during a service. I was seated one row back from her, and I saw her take off her black gloves and I didn't notice a damned thing wrong with her hands. No bleeding, no bruising, no bandages."

The girl shook her head. "By now she probably thinks she can say anything about him and be believed."

"She can tell herself she won," he agreed with a nod. Then, bitterly: "The legend of Mieka Windthistle. There are so many stories, why not add one or two more?"

"This came today from Cayden," she said, reaching

for a folded sheet of paper. "He'll talk about his work in an interview, if you like, but not about his glisker. Here—" She read aloud. "'My emotions for and about Mieka Windthistle were too complex and too personal to be put on display.'"

"That's Cade," Tobalt said with decades of resignation. "The only feelings that matter are his, you see."

"What I can *see* are the icicles dripping off the page!"

"You noticed the past tense, didn't you? His emotions for Mieka *were*. Not *are*. His mind's cold, but his heart's colder."

"He wasn't always like that. I remember when I was little, and he'd come round to the house for dinner—Da, he wasn't *always* like that."

"No." He hesitated, then said, "About ten years ago, when he was still pricking dragon tears, he told me that sometimes in the morning just before he opens his eyes, for just a moment Mieka Windthistle is alive and the world is wonderful."

"And then he wakes."

"Yeh. When Touchstone lost their Elf, they lost their soul."}

Warm fingers stroked his hair. He couldn't see Mieka's face but he could hear terror shaking his voice as he said, "Quill, it's all right, I'm here. You're safe."

Don't leave me, he wanted to say. *Please, Mieka, please don't ever leave me*—

{—Jindra and her husband, their girls, their husbands. Blye and Jed and all the brothers and sisters, Rafe and Crisiant, Jeska and Kazie. Mistress Mirdley was outside in the garden, taking care of the great-grandchildren. Cade could hear their games through the window open to the warm summer air, and the sounds of life and laughter were the best sounds in the world, especially today.

He knew it would be today. In the scant fortnight since Mieka's Namingday, there had been unmistakable changes. It would be today. He needed no Elsewhen to tell him it would be today.

He felt thin little fingers move restlessly in his palm. "What is it, Mieka?"

"How . . ." He tried to sit a little higher against the pillows, but there was no strength left in him. Those eyes looked in bewilderment at all the people gathered in the room. "How'd all *this* happen?"

Cade smiled. "Oh, Elfling, didn't you know? *You* made it happen."

"Go away, Jinsie. Go *away*!"

"Not until you tell me—"

"Tell me, Cayden," said his mother, "are you truly so blind?"

He waited her out.

"It's only that I don't want to see you hurt."

When had she ever worried about his hurts? "What do you mean?"

"When he moves on. And he will, you know. Elves are notoriously capricious. He's worse than most. Everything you've built in the last few years, your career, your ambitions, your art—" She bit off the word as if it had a rancid taste in her mouth. "You've come to depend on him and I'm only saying—we've had our differences, you and I, but I never thought you could be such a fool as to depend on that vile little Elf!"

Although he was aware that Mieka had forfeited all Lady Jaspiela's goodwill, he hadn't expected this intensity of venom.

She had control of herself again. "You're of age, and how you live your life is beyond my influence. But no matter how little you care what I think, I don't want to see you break your heart over this Elf when he leaves Touchstone. And he will leave. Mark me on this."

"He has a name. Mieka Windthistle. Even if you won't say it anymore, you'd best get used to hearing it said in the same breath with my name for the rest of your life."

"His name is rather the point. You'll no more be able to hold on to him than you could the wind."}

"No," Cade breathed. "No more . . . please . . ."

"Quill, I'm here, it's all right—you're safe—"

{Jeska looked up at him with weary compassion, and even wearier sorrow. "You just threw him away with both hands."

Nonsense. Mieka had been throwing his own life away for years. Cade had given up trying to hold on to him. He didn't want to feel this much. He couldn't feel this much; it would kill him. Mieka had always made him feel too much. Care too much. It wasn't wise, it wasn't safe, that sort of feeling.

He'd tried for so long to hold on with one hand and let go with the other. Mieka's life wasn't his to live. The decisions, the choices—they weren't his to make. If Mieka had made all the wrong ones, that wasn't Cade's fault. He refused to be responsible. He refused to hang on with both hands. It would hurt too much.

Could that be any worse than the pain that stalked him now, waiting for an unguarded moment?

Well, it was simple enough. There would be no unguarded moments. He would feel nothing. He would keep himself to himself, and to Hells with everything and everybody else.

He still had his work. The work was all that mattered.

The work was all he had.}

"Mieka, *what's happening to him*?"

"Nothing," her brother retorted in a voice that shook. "Bad dreams."

How noble of him to keep the secret of the Elsewhens. A little late, but perhaps it was churlish of Cayden to make note of that. Obviously Mieka wasn't drunk or thorned enough to blither on without caution.

That would change. "You *made it happen.*" Nothing anyone else did would make a difference.

Cade opened his eyes. His heart was slowing from its frantic pounding. He felt cold with more than the sweat drying chill on his skin. "Oh, come on, Mieka," he said quite clearly. "Why not tell her?"

"Quill!" He smiled, relief shining from those eyes. "You're back. It's all right, it's gone now—" But he faltered to a stop, confused.

Cade twisted his fingers away from Mieka's. "You told your wife. Why not your sister? Tell everyone. What does it matter?"

Mieka recoiled, caught his breath, lost his balance. "No—I didn't—" he breathed. "I *couldn't* have—"

"But you did." He curved his lips into something resembling a smile. "I didn't see you do it, but I saw what resulted. He knows, Mieka. The Archduke knows. You were drunk and you told her, she told her mother, and her mother told him."

"Cade—*no*—"

"Yes. You told her. He knows." He supposed he ought to feel sorry for the Elf, sitting there on the rug with his jaw hanging open and horror in those eyes. Gods, those eyes: muddy-dark with fear, glancing this way and that as if searching for an escape. Cade looked at Jinsie, standing now beside the bed. He didn't remember when she'd let go of him. It didn't matter. Not much mattered, he found, except one thing. "Find Rafe and Jeska. Tell them Briuly and Alaen are going after the Rights at dawn on Midsummer. I saw them. They have to be warned off."

Jinsie scowled. "What d'you mean, you *saw* them?"

"Nothing," Mieka said swiftly. "He didn't mean anything."

Cade almost laughed. "Oh, c'mon! How do you think your brother and I made all that money off a bet on the Archduke's daughter? I *knew*, Jinsie."

Mieka was staring at him, horrified.

"I watch the futures happen inside my own head, like a play," he went on, relentless, brutal. "There are dozens of them. I watched the Archduke write a letter the night his daughter was born, a letter about how he plans for her to marry Prince Roshlin, so I knew Miriuzca would have a son. But it's not legal to bet on the Royals, so—"

"Cade," Mieka whispered. "No. Stop."

"Well, mayhap you're right. She's got quite a lot to be thinking about, hasn't she? My dangerous secret that you blabbed to your wife. The point is, Alaen and Briuly are about to go after the Rights of the Fae, and they have to be stopped."

Mieka—trusting Cade's Elsewhen, desperate to run away, or both—said, "I'll do it," in a voice like death, and scrambled to his feet. As he hurried to the door, yelling for Rafe and Jeska, Jinsie turned to Cade with more irrelevant questions.

It really was a pity, he told himself, that life was not a play where the only words spoken were those necessary to advance the plot.

Epilogue

ONLY MIEKA STILL clung to the hope that they could get a message to Alaen and Briuly at Nackerty Close. It was too far. It couldn't be done. Mieka knew that. But as he stood with Rafe and Jeska in the lamplit upstairs hall, conferring in low tones, every time he told himself it was hopeless, he thought of the staring gray eyes and the stricken, almost contorted face of the man on the other side of that closed bedchamber door.

A door, he told himself, into a life Cade had no choice but to live. *This life, and none other*—complete with Else-whens that this time had tormented him near to madness.

"It can be done," he said again, stubbornly.

Rafe shook his head. Jeska said the same thing he'd been saying for the last ten minutes in the same soft, reasonable voice.

"Midsummer is the day after tomorrow. Nobody could get there in time. It's too far, even changing horses every fifty miles or so, and that's assuming we can find enough money to convince the stable-masters along the way to part with their best horses."

"Or find somebody we can trust with the message," Rafe added. "Mieka, it's two hundred miles from here, maybe more."

"But if somebody rode crossland," Mieka said stubbornly, "taking shortcuts and not sticking to the roads, it won't be as far or take as much time."

"And how would you like to gallop a succession of horses across open country in the dark?"

"It's a full moon—" Abruptly, absurdly, he wished for a river and Quill beside him to watch the moonglade.

"Listen to me," Jeska said tiredly. "Even if the impossible happened and a rider got there, there's no telling whether he'd be able to find Alaen and Briuly."

"Or that they'd listen," Rafe said.

And that, Mieka knew, was unanswerable. He wanted so desperately to be able to tell Cade that they'd give it a try, at the very least. But he knew it was impossible. This was an Elsewhen that would haunt Cade all his days. This one would happen for real. Cade had solved the mystery of the Treasure, and chosen to pester Alaen about it—and now there was nothing Cade or anyone else could do.

As for that other Elsewhen, the one that made him writhe inside . . . what had Cade seen? It couldn't have been Mieka's fault. There were any number of ways the Archduke could have found out that Cade was—was—

There was no other way. No one else who knew would be so careless with this crucial truth. So it had to have been him. Just as Cade had said: telling his wife, who'd told her mother, who'd got word to the Archduke and been believed.

Mieka had discovered this winter that he didn't like having to feel guilty. Or ashamed. No, he did not like either of those feelings at all. They hurt too much, and he was afraid of them. But it was nothing compared to this terror that sent rivers of sickness through his body in place of blood.

He tried to tell himself that Cade must have only just

seen it. He couldn't possibly have known all these months. But the Elsewhens didn't work like that. He saw *futures*, not pasts. It had been weeks since they left Gallantrybanks, and longer than that since Mieka was forget-everything drunk around his wife. Not since the night he'd slapped her. He didn't trust himself.

Cade had been so patient about what had happened that night, neither lecturing him nor railing at him nor going all cold and superior in that spiteful way Mieka hated. Cade had taken him to Ginnel House—a pathway from one life into another, he saw that now—and let him realize for himself. Helped him to do that painful bit of growing up. He hadn't drunk more than a glass or two of ale when he was with his wife since that night. He didn't trust himself. Why in the name of anything holy did Cade still trust him? After such a betrayal, how could Cade stand to be in the same room with him?

Either Cade had forgiven him—a thing he knew he didn't deserve—or Cade had been playing a part better than Jeska ever could do onstage.

Cade wasn't that good an actor.

"Mieka!"

At Jinsie's call, he lunged for the bedchamber door, panicking at the thought that Cayden had slipped back into the Elsewhens.

"Quill? Are you all right?" Quite probably the stupidest thing he'd ever said in his life.

Cade was sitting up in bed, perfectly calm, perfectly cold. "I've just realized," he said, "that it's impossible. Nobody could reach them in time."

"We can try."

"No. It's all quite useless. Even if they were found, it wouldn't change anything. They wouldn't believe it." A twitch of a smile. "The people who ought to believe almost always don't, and the people who shouldn't know at all are the ones who believe right off. That's called *irony*, Jinsie."

"That's called 'I have no idea what in all Hells you're talking about,'" she returned angrily, and betook herself out of the room.

"Quill . . ." Mieka approached the bed slowly. "I'm sorry. For all of it."

"You always are."

"And you always forgive me," he said without thinking—which after all was most of his problem, wasn't it?—and was immediately scared by his boldness.

"It would seem so."

"Quill—" *Get mad at me*, he wanted to beg. *Yell at me, call me every name you can think of—I deserve them all—just please don't sit there like you're made of ice!*

Cade shrugged it all away. "Never mind, Mieka. I've learned something. People will do what they'll do, and there's no stopping them. Things happen and there's no changing them. Nothing anybody does or says makes any difference—because how can anybody know what's going to come of any single action, or even a single word?" He raked his hands back through his sweat-damp hair. "So I'll give up anguishing myself about it. There's nothing to be done. None of it matters, anyway. Nothing matters at all."

There was so much that Mieka ought to be saying. He was certain sure there must be words somewhere to bring Cade out of this frightening indifference. When the wintry gray eyes finally met his again, he took an instinctive step back.

Cade noted it with a grim little smile. "You wrote to me once," he said, "that you'd always come find me if I got too lost. How do you like what you've found?"

"Quill—!"

"Don't worry, Mieka. You needn't ever come looking again." He shifted in bed. "I'm tired. I need sleep."

But not dreams. Mieka silently begged the Gods to send Cayden no more dreams.

* * *

"And so the excursion to Vathis was a success, and trade is picking up?"

"Of course. They're all greedy little thorn-thralls, but they know their work. Thought it beneath them until I explained the advantages of encouraging customers to favor one sort of rumbullion over another. Rolon Piercehand is overjoyed."

"He'll make yet another fortune to spend on inanities for his castle. Pity Your Grace couldn't persuade him to part with his library."

"Knottinger tells me there isn't much of interest."

"He has only a sketchy idea of what would be . . . interesting."

"True, for now. But the books are safely in a tangle at Castle Eyot. I'll send that imbecile Wordturner to sort them out. And to take what I might want, even if no one but his family can read them anymore."

"An excellent thought, Your Grace. Now, what of Goldbraider? If that play of his is anything to judge by, he has more than a suspicion about things that are interesting to us. And he'll wish to satisfy his curiosity, as well as produce something even more shattering to amaze the world and gratify his own exalted opinion of himself."

"He doesn't concern me as much as Silversun does."

"I have told Your Grace again and again that the way to him is clear enough."

"The Elf. Yes, I know. But if he could be persuaded, rather than owned—"

"Delicacy is required—oh, not regarding the Elf. He's no more subtle than a flash flood in Weltering Gorge. But with Cayden . . . if he ever suspects your involvement in Windthistle's ruin . . . and that remembers me, Your Grace. How does the Caitiffer woman?"

"Sullen. Unwilling to honor the ancient pact except as it benefits herself. Fortunately, her current desires are monetary, and easy to satisfy."

"That will change. Touchstone is vastly successful . . . forgive me for mentioning it, but I don't understand why you're laughing."

"As long as Kearney Fairwalk has control of their finances, her wants will remain easy to satisfy. Oh, it's none of my doing. Entirely his. I give it another year, two at the most. Although I wish I'd known before I attempted to entice him with the Wordturner boy."

"There are times when the path is already prepared for us, and all we need do is walk down it. On a pleasanter matter—I trust your lady wife is well?"

"How kind of you to ask. She and my daughter are thriving. Did you believe the rumor that Panshilara was so shocked by the events at the Downstreet that she went into labor?"

"Of course I didn't believe it. Though I do believe the talk of her efforts to have Touchstone and the Shadowshapers arrested for inciting public indecency, and if not all of them, then at the very least Mieka Windthistle."

"A show of indignation seemed appropriate. Ah, Emmot, now I have made *you* laugh! I admit that she is not subtle, either. But she is useful."

"Yes. She establishes both of you as pillars of tradition while winning sympathy for herself. At the same time, more and more women are now attending theaters, exactly the outcome you desired."

"And none of my doing at all! I believe it's now time to get started on my own theater in earnest."

"So you have thoroughly abandoned Touchstone for Black Lightning."

"There seemed no other choice. Regrettable, of course. But it will take some years to prepare them."

"And the theater. But why go to all the trouble and expense yourself, when you can get Princess Miriuzca to do it for you?"

"I'm afraid I don't follow."

"The girl is theater-mad. Just as you were at that age, although she is not pretending."

"I've learned to value the art."

"Doubtless. Build your theater in Gallantrybanks for Black Lightning to caper about in if it amuses you. But what I have in mind, now that the Princess has shown herself so cooperatively unconventional, is something rather more . . . interesting."

THE PLAYERS

(most of them, anyway)

BELLGLOSS, MASTER   purveyor of thorn
BLACKPATH
  ALAEN   lutenist
  BRIULY   Alaen's cousin; lutenist
BOWBENDER
  AIRILIE   Jeska's daughter
  JESCHENAR   masquer, Touchstone
CHALLENDER, MIRKO   tregetour, Crystal Sparks
COLDKETTLE, LORD   Prince Ashgar's private
  secretary
CROWKEEPER, HERRIS   fettler, Black Lightning
CZILLAG
  CHATTIM   glisker, the Shadowshapers
  DESHENANDA   his wife
DAGGERING, LEDERRIS   masquer, Crystal Sparks
EASTKEEPING
  LORD KELINN   Vrennerie's husband
  LADY VRENNERIE   lady-in-waiting to Princess
    Miriuzca
EMMOT   Sagemaster; Cade's teacher, now retired
FAIRWALK, LORD KEARNEY   Touchstone's manager

FLUTER, TOBALT reporter, *The Nayword*

GOLDBRAIDER, VERED tregetour and masquer,
the Shadowshapers

GRAINER
  CHIRENE Sakary's wife
  SAKARY fettler, the Shadowshapers

HENICK, CYED Archduke
  PANSHILARA his wife, the Archduchess

HIGHCOLLAR
  LORD ISSHAK Lady Jaspiela's father
  LADY KIRITIN Lady Jaspiela's mother; born
    Blackswan

KEVELOCK, RAUEL tregetour and masquer, the
Shadowshapers

KNOTTINGER, THIERIN tregetour, Black Lightning

LONGBRANCH, TRENAL tregetour, Hawk's Claw

MISTRESS CAITIFFER Mieka's mother-in-law

MISTRESS GESHA Trollwife at Shellery House

MISTRESS LUTA Trollwife in Seekhaven

MISTRESS MIRDLEY Trollwife at Redpebble Square

MISTRESS TOLA Trollwife; friend of Mistress
Mirdley's

MISTRESS WINGDOVE innkeeper in Lilyleaf;
"Croodle"

NEEDLER, ROMUALD the Shadowshapers' manager

OAKAPPLE, LORD distant cousin of the Blackpaths

PIERCEHAND, LORD ROLON owner of Castle Eyot;
compulsive collector

ROBEL Yazz's wife; part Giant

SEAMARK, KAJ masquer, Black Lightning

SILVERSUN
  CADRIEL Zekien's father; Master Fettler
  CAYDEN tregetour, Touchstone
  DERIEN Cade's younger brother

LADY JASPIELA   Cade and Dery's mother; born Highcollar

ZEKIEN   their father

SPANGLER, PIRRO   glisker, Black Lightning

STAINDROP, BRISHEN   Mishia's sister

TAWNYMOOR, LORD   Princess Iamina's husband

THREADCHASER

CRISIANT   Rafe's wife; born Bramblecotte

RAFCADION   fettler, Touchstone

MISTRESS   Rafe's mother

MASTER   Rafe's father; baker

WARRINGHEATH, MASTER   owner of the Kiral Kellari

WINDTHISTLE

BARSABIAS   Hadden's great-uncle; "Uncle Breedbate"

BLYE   Jed's wife; born Cindercliff; glasscrafter

CILKA   Mieka's sister

HADDEN   Mieka's father

JEDRIS   Jez's twin brother

JEZAEL   Mieka's brother

JINSIE   Mieka's twin sister

JINDRA   Mieka's daughter

JORIE   Tavier's twin sister

MIEKA   glisker, Touchstone

MISHIA   Mieka's mother; born Staindrop

MISTRESS WINDTHISTLE   Mieka's wife; born Caitiffer

PETRINKA   Cilka's twin sister

SHARADEL   Hadden's great-grandmother; born Snowminder

TAVIER   Mieka's youngest brother

YAZZ   Touchstone's coachman; part Giant

The Royals

ASHGAR   Prince; heir to the throne
IAMINA   Princess; King Meredan's younger sister
MEREDAN   King of Albeyn
MIRIUZCA   Princess; Ashgar's wife
ROSHIEN   Queen of Albeyn

GLOSSARY

approof approbation; approval
backspang a tricky evasion
bantling infant
bemoil daubed with dirt
blatherskite obnoxious, loudmothed braggart
blatteroon person who won't shut up
breedbate someone who likes to start arguments or stir
  up quarrels
caitiff witch
carkanet necklace
chankings food you spit out
chavish the sound of many birds chirping or singing
  at once; the sound of many people chattering at once
cheveril kid leather
clinquant glittering
clumperton clownish, clumsy lout
The Consecreations *consecrate* collided with *creation*;
  the local holy book
coof simpleton
crambazzle worn-out, dissipated old man
cullion rude, disagreeable, mean-spirited person
dizzard numbskull
dwarmy unhealthful weather

fliting an exchange of invective, abuse, or mockery, especially one in verse set forth between two poets

flutch world-class couch potato

fortyer forty days of quarantine imposed on ships to guard against plague

fribbler foolish, fussy man; also *a fribble*; *to fribble* as a verb

fritlag worthless good-for-nothing

frustling shaking out and exhibiting feathers or plumage

giddiot "giddy" and "idiot"

ginnel a narrow passage between buildings

glunsh to devour food in hasty, noisy gulps; by extension, a glutton

grinagog a stupid, gaping grin

hindering a warding put on an individual's magic so it cannot be used

kagged mutilated Elfen ears

luffed drunk

mathom gift

quat a pimple; used in contempt of a person

rumbullion an old term for rum

smatchet impudent, contemptible child

snarge a person no one likes; a total jerk

staggers a disease in horses characterized by giddiness; hence any bewildering distress

swizz swindle; con

tiring room from *retire*; a private chamber

twee just too absolutely cute for words

yark vomit

*The paramount obligation of a college is to develop in
its students the ability to think clearly and independently, and the ability to live confidently, courageously,
and hopefully.*

—Ellen Browning Scripps

These words are displayed at the Honnold Gate of
Scripps College, my alma mater (and that of the friends
to whom this book is dedicated), and I am personally
convinced that this is the last time the word *hopefully*
was used correctly in an English sentence.

For the history and literature geeks out there—the de
Vere Earls of Oxford (original creation, not the Earls of
Oxford and Asquith) had no subsidiary titles, and so the
invented courtesy title of Lord Bolebec (sometimes
spelled "Bulbeck") was given to the heir. And if a certain
man had not moved his family to a certain town before a
certain son was born, that son might have been known
as the Bard of Snitterfield these four hundred years.

Much beholden for:

 my parents, Bob and Alma Rawn

 my sister, Laurie Rawn

James J. W. Taylor, whose (definitely *not*
    tumbling-down) wall gave me an idea
Tracy, Derek, and Tiffany Taylor
John and Gena Lang
Mary Anne Ford and Phil Dion
the Busbys and the Johnsons
Russell Galen and Danny Baror
Beth Meacham
Amy Saxon

Turn the page for a sneak peek
at the fourth book in Melanie Rawn's superb
Glass Thorns series

Window Wall

MELANIE RAWN

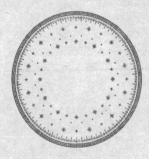

*Available from Tom Doherty Associates
in April 2015*

 A TOR BOOK

Chapter 1

MIEKA WINDTHISTLE ARRIVED at the kitchen door of Number Eight, Redpebble Square, with a frown on his face. It was not an expression that suited him. Yet with the exception of the hours he spent onstage, these days it seemed all his face could do was frown.

He conjured up a smile for Mistress Mirdley and for Derien Silversun, but the frown returned when the Trollwife, busily slicing carrot bread, told him why a huge basket was being filled with baked goods.

"Tea. It's his Namingday. He won't come here, so Derien's taking it to him."

Cayden's Namingday. Thoroughly ashamed of himself, Mieka didn't bother to pretend that he hadn't forgotten. Dery, seeing the expression on his face, only shrugged and said, "I don't think he wants to remember, himself. Which is stupid, of course. It's not as if he's turning fifty or sixty—he's only twenty-four. But I'm sure he has nothing planned."

Mieka slouched on a stool by the worktable and felt his frown grow even deeper as he regarded his tregetour's little brother—who admittedly wasn't so little anymore. Not that Mieka had been around to notice. Redpebble Square hadn't seen much of him these last two years. He was no longer welcome when Lady Jaspiela was at home; indeed, she hadn't spoken to him or even acknowledged his continuing existence since he'd attempted a bit of softening magic on her. How she'd been able to sense it, what with the hindering put on her long ago, he'd no idea. But sense it she had.

Today Mieka had arrived just after lunching, confident that he wouldn't be running into Lady Jaspiela. This was her day, every fortnight, for visiting the Archduchess whenever the latter was in Gallantrybanks. Mieka made it his day for visiting his brother and sister-in-law at the glassworks. Sometimes—well, rarely—he called in at the kitchen door of Redpebble Square, where Mistress Mirdley provided tea and Derien provided conversation. Cade no longer lived there. He had taken his own flat just after Touchstone's third Royal Circuit. And even though Mieka saw him every single day when they were traveling and at least twice a week for performances in Gallantrybanks during winter, he had to go to other people to find out what Cade was thinking.

Not that either Mistress Mirdley or Derien knew. That was made clear when the boy slumped down in a chair beside Mieka and said, "He hasn't been round to see us in almost a month. And it's not that long until Trials, and then he'll be gone on the Royal again, and—and I miss him."

So do I, Mieka thought glumly.

"There's an item about him in the latest *Nayword*— did you see it?" Dery made a long arm to snag the broadsheet from a pile by the kitchen fire. "Not that he talked to Tobalt Fluter, either."

Mieka had read the piece, just a few lines about how Cade would doubtless have new and startling plays to be performed in Gallantrybanks and at Trials. The tone of it had been just slightly sardonic, as if Tobalt was annoyed that he could no longer get an interview from the eminently quotable Cayden Silversun.

Mistress Mirdley had finished wrapping the carrot bread. "Here, and take some of this honeycomb along with you. He always liked it when he was a little boy."

Mieka was appalled to see sudden fierce tears in her eyes. He leaped to his feet and threw his arms around her. "I'll bring him back here soon, I promise I will—and with three pages of apologies in rhymed couplets set to music for being so horrid to you!"

She shook her head and extricated herself from his hug. "He'll come round when he comes round. And it's a few dozen more turnings he'll be doing before that happens. Is that basket full? Tuck a cloth in, then, and get along with you."

"Did you put in something for Rumble?" Dery asked.

"Of course. A nice bit of fish. Go!"

Cayden's only companion in his flat—well, his only steady companion; there were plenty of girls, all of them transitory—was a ginger-striped cat named Rumble, inexplicably brought home as a kitten by Blye's cat, Bompstable. It was as if, Jedris had remarked, Bompstable knew Cade required some sort of company, and went out to find a suitable candidate.

In the hire-hack, with a hamper of food between them, Mieka looked at Dery and asked, "Could we stop off someplace maybe? I really ought to bring a gift."

"Well ... can you make it quick? Mistress Mirdley will be furious if I'm out after dark. And I want to spend some time with my brother," he finished in a voice much too grim for someone not quite twelve years old.

Mieka directed the driver to take them through a convenient shopping district. For a full quarter of an hour, he turned from side to side in the hack, peering through the windows, desperate for a shop that caught his imagination.

"You're giving me a neck ache," Dery complained. "He won't mind if you don't bring him anything. I'm sure he'd rather nobody remembered at all."

Especially after what happened last year, hung unspoken between them.

When Cayden turned nineteen, Dery had given him a silver hawk pin and Mieka had taken him to see the

Shadowshapers at the Kiral Kellari. On his twentieth Namingday, he'd been at Fairwalk Manor, giving Mieka no opportunity to celebrate. To make up for that, Mieka had thrown a lavish party at Hilldrop Crescent for Cade's twenty-first. His twenty-second had been another Shadowshapers show—the one where Princess Miriuzca had shown up with Lady Megueris Mindrising, both of them dressed as young men. And a grand lark that had been, an exploit Mieka wasn't sure he'd ever be able to surpass . . . though Cade had once had an Elsewhen about his forty-fifth, something about bubbly wine and a surprise party and a diamond in Mieka's ear. Forty-five; Mieka couldn't imagine it. But Cade had seen it, and by his scant telling, it had been a wonderful evening.

Last year they'd all gathered at Blye's glassworks, ostensibly to watch her make their new withies but in reality to present Cade with the complete table service for eight she had spent weeks making. She had forbidden them to transport the plates, bowls, cups, goblets, and platters to Cade's flat that evening, relenting only when Mieka promised a doubling and tripling of the cushioning spell his mother had taught him. Problem was, he'd had quite a lot to drink—although so had everyone else, raising the new wine goblets again and again, then deciding that the brandy snifters also deserved a try-out, and of course there were those bottles of Auntie Brishen's whiskey that needed sampling in the cut-crystal glasses, and . . . the conclusion being that Blye had had to spend another week replacing the broken items. Mieka still winced with the memory of the crashing and splintering of two inadequately cushioned crates down four flights of stairs. And one couldn't mend glass with an Affinity spell, not and have it hold water ever again.

There were plenty of things that needed mending after these last two years. Nothing that was permanently broken, or at least so Mieka told himself with grim resolve—well, except in Alaen Blackpath's case. The loss of his cousin Briuly two years ago this Midsummer dawn had shattered him. A month later, he'd shown up at Sakary Grainer's house in Gallantrybanks with a glass thorn in one hand and a little gold velvet pouch of dragon tears in the other, and announced to Chirene, Sakary's wife, that if she didn't run away with him that very night, he'd begin using and wouldn't stop until she was his or he was dead. Romuald Needler, the Shadowshapers' manager, had succeeded in hushing up most of the scandal. But the fact remained that Chirene had taken her children and gone to live with Chattim Czillag's wife, Deshenanda, until the Shadowshapers returned that autumn from the Royal Circuit. Alaen wasn't dead. Yet.

"Here, stop," Mieka said suddenly, and hopped out of the hire-hack before it had come to a full stop. "Won't be a tick-tock!" he called over his shoulder to Derien, and hurried inside.

The shop featured all manner of decorative collectibles. Mirrors, figurines, clocks, imagings, paintings, exotic flowers from faraway lands preserved under glass or with magic. But Mieka knew exactly what he wanted, having seen it displayed in the window, and a few moments later emerged with a wrapped package almost as tall as Derien.

"What is it?" the boy wanted to know as the hack started up again.

"Not *it*," Mieka said. "*Them*." He teased a corner of the paper wrapping to show a glint of iridescent blue.

"Peacock feathers?"

"A round dozen of 'em."

"But, Mieka, aren't they horrid bad luck for theater folk?" An instant later, he understood. "Whistling past the urn-plot?"

"Exactly. Because if what we've been having is good luck in the theater, I'll risk it. Me Mum calls it *un*sympathetic magic."

"Do the opposite of what you really want to happen? That's a little crazy, y'know."

"My specialty."

Not that anything truly awful had happened onstage—unless one counted Cade's last new play. That had been over a year ago now, and the reactions had been ... regrettable. Nobody, including the rest of Touchstone, really understood what he'd meant to do. Mieka's analysis was that whereas theater patrons didn't mind thinking a bit, both during and after a play, they didn't much enjoy thinking as a grim hour-long slog through far too many ideas.

"Turn Aback" was in Cade's hands an exercise in stupefying boredom. Boy and girl in love. Girl dies in tragic accident. Boy tries to broker a deal with the Lady to go get her; Lady is moved by True True Love and says fine, but on your way out, you mustn't look back. Boy girds himself to travel into whichever Hell girl inhabits (though why she deserves any of them is left unclear), journeys through various unsavory provinces of punishment, increasingly nasty but not gruesome or bloody or even scary. At least Mieka could have had some good old gory fun with that sort of thing, been creative with the dragons that feasted on flesh that healed in an hour, or that poor stupid pillicock forever putting sand into a leaky hourglass, or the one about somebody standing lip-deep in a lake of shit.

Cade's Hells were all intellectual (which didn't surprise Mieka one bit, but made for a colossally dull play). Boy is distracted from search for girl by philosophical conversations with the tenants of each Hell, blither blather blether. Boy finally remembers what he's there for, finds girl, fingers burned and bleeding as she spins molten gold into straw. Boy leads girl back to the entrance gates. She trips on a rock (silly cow). He looks back to make sure she's all right, and just as their Eyes Meet with Longing and then with Sudden Horror, she vanishes. The End.

Tobalt had tried to put an interesting interpretation on it—something about how Cayden Silversun had woven scholarly moral speculation into a heartbreaking love story—but even he knew it was a bad play. Touchstone had performed it exactly three times. Then Mieka, Rafe, and Jeska all rebelled, and the script was mercifully scrapped.

But the fact remained: Cayden Silversun had failed. He hadn't liked it much.

Derien subsided into a corner of the hack, and Mieka read *The Nayword* during the rest of the drive to Cade's place. The broadsheet had grown in recent years from one very large page folded in half to three very large pages folded in quarters—more the size of a book, really, than the standard broadsheet. It wasn't the same old *Nayword* anymore, as its front page trumpeted.

THE NAYWORD
What to read—What to see—What to wear—
What to avoid!

In this issue:
Special reports from our correspondents
at Court, throughout the Kingdom, and on the Continent
PRINCE ASHGAR and PRINCESS MIRIUZCA
welcome a daughter
Exclusive interview with VERED GOLDBRAIDER
Complete coverage of this year's Trials hopefuls
Student unrest at Stiddolfe after a rise in fees

With: ideas and advice from our regular columnists on all the latest in theater, books, dress, food, wine, gardening, and interior design

Mieka felt rather smug about the theater and fashion sections, considering that Touchstone (with the Shadowshapers) constantly innovated in the former and were known (with the Shadowshapers) as exemplars of the latter. He was even more smug about the gardening, because one of the regular columnists was his sister, Cilka.

Just fourteen, still in school, and already an authority (under a pseudonym, of course) in her field. Their mother, Mishia, wasn't terribly surprised; her own sister, Brishen, had started up a little herb shop at the age of fifteen. The Greenseed Elfen line obviously dominated in them both. Cilka and Petrinka were already doing a brisk business in sculpted hedges, as prompted by Mieka's description of such at Princess Miriuzca's home castle on the Continent, and would someday take over Grandfather Staindrop's gardening business.

As for "design"—for certes, Cade never paid any attention to advice columns about interior design, or exterior either. Rather than the grand town house Mieka had once envisioned for him, he had taken a corner room on the top floor of a building near the Keymarker, one of the old abandoned manufactories refitted as blocks of flats. The view was spectacular—from his windows, one could see the Keeps in one direction and the Plume in the other, with the rooftops of Gallantrybanks spreading between, though these rather blocked any sight of the Gally River—but the hike up four flights kept most people from visiting very often. Mieka knew that was precisely why Cade had chosen it.

The staircase was stone to the second floor, then wood—nice and sturdy, according to Jed and Jez, who had insisted on examining the place before Cade signed the lease. Originally the top floor had been fitted out as a dormitory for the workers. Mieka shuddered, as he did every time he visited, at the idea of waking before dawn, working all day, and trudging back upstairs for food and sleep without ever once having breathed fresh air or seen the sun. A great many manufactories had moved out of the main sections of Gallantrybanks as the city expanded and the demand for urban housing increased, and there was no reason to believe that conditions were any better for workers even if the places were now in the countryside.

A knock on Cade's door elicited an annoyed, "What?"

Derien grimaced, tried the handle, found it unlocked, and traded scowls with Mieka.

"On the other hand," the boy murmured as he opened the door, "except for the books, what's he got worth stealing?"

"I heard that," Cade said from the depths of his big, soft, overstuffed chair. "The brass is bespelled to recognize you. I've forgotten her name, but she was rather good at useful little tricks."

Mieka resisted the urge to roll his eyes. There were lots of girls whose names Cade had forgotten. That there wasn't one at the moment was obvious; the place was a mess. Clothes, glassware, paper, books, broadsheets, spent candles, towels, pillows, empty bags that must have contained food at some point because there was nowhere to cook—all manner of clutter was spread about the room.

Jez had built Cade a platform bed that was seven feet long, four feet wide, and six feet off the floor. The little cavern beneath was where he huddled at a desk to write. In the winter there was a firepocket to keep his feet warm, and in summer all the windows were left open to cooling breezes, but it was dark under there when the lamps weren't lighted and there was nothing to look at but bricks and the bed's wooden scaffolding. The other features of the flat were Cade's big black upholstered chair, some uncushioned wooden chairs that did not encourage visitors to linger, a huge standing wardrobe to hold Cade's vast collection of clothes (nearly as impressive as Mieka's), a massive carpet given him by Lord Kearney Fairwalk, a small table that seated four, a cabinet for the glass dinner service made for him by Blye, another cabinet behind a latticework willow screen for the pisspot, and bookshelves—also built by Jez—almost to the twelve-foot ceiling.

Of decoration there was very little. No placards advertising Touchstone, no tapestries, no paintings, no imagings. His Trials medals—two Winterly, three Royal—were in glass boxes on the bookshelves, and Mieka had the feeling whenever he saw them that the only reason they weren't stashed in a drawer somewhere was that Blye had made the boxes. The counterpane made by Mieka's wife and mother-in-law was crumpled at the foot of the bed. The only color in the room was the rug, its greens and blues like a forest pond in the middle of the city. The peacock feathers, fanning out in a jar or vase, would be an improvement.

Derien ignored Cade's mood, putting on a smile and wishing his brother a happy Namingday. Cade expressed his gratitude indifferently. Mieka busied himself clearing off the table and setting out Mistress Mirdley's tea. The search for a kettle took some time, and he kept his expression carefully neutral as Dery tried to engage Cade in conversation. Mieka went out to the landing where the spigot was, and encountered Rumble coming up the stairs.

"Anything to report?" he asked the cat, who curled around his ankles a few times before stepping lightly into the flat. "Big help you are," he muttered, and hoped that Dery could coax Cade into some semblance of good manners.

No such luck.

When he got back, Dery was reading bits from *The Nayword*. "There's something in here about Briuly, too." Before Cade could say he didn't care, Dery read out, "'Still no word on the whereabouts of Master Lutenist Briuly Blackpath. His family is initiating legal proceedings to have him declared dead so that his estate can be sold to pay his debts.'"

"You'd think," Cade mused, one finger scratching idly at his pathetic excuse for a beard, "that Lord Oakapple, his esteemed cousin or whatever he is, would pay up Briuly's debts just to keep the family out of the law courts. But I never did get exactly how they were related, so perhaps it doesn't signify." He turned to Mieka. "How was Lilyleaf?"

"Fine. Croodle sends her best."

Nodding to the new silver bracelet on Mieka's wrist, he said, "Very nice. What did you give your lovely lady?"

"She saw a pink pearl in a shop. I had it made into a pendant." It had cost a bloody fortune, too, but that was a small price for peace in his household.

Derien was the one who conjured up Wizardfire to heat the water. There was an iron ring for the kettle above a small iron cauldron, and the glances the boy gave his brother told Mieka that this was a new skill. Cade didn't comment on it at all. In fact, nobody said anything while the water had boiled and the tea was brewed. The three of them sat there like polite strangers who have exhausted every topic of conversation and could find no reason to keep up any pretense of being interested in one other. As Cayden bestirred himself to pour out, Mieka considered various methods of shocking a reaction out of him—any reaction at all. But he'd been trying that, hadn't he, for going on two years now, and with what results? Rarely, a response, of the *Do that again, and I'll feed you your own balls marinated in plum sauce* variety. Mostly, a look of mild contempt for his childishness. It was infuriating.

"Uncle Dennet died."

Cade looked up from pouring out. "I hadn't realized he was still alive."

"Well, he was," Derien went on. "And now he's not. First we learned of it was when the Shelter sent his ashes to Redpebble."

Mieka searched his knowledge of Cade's family tree, and came up with Dennet Silversun, elder brother of Cade's father Zekien, mad as a sack of snakes.

"Wasn't he the one wounded in the war?" Mieka asked.

"What a refined way of phrasing it," Cade observed. "He was seventeen and got in the path of somebody's spell. He's been in a puzzle house ever since."

"Almost forty years," Derien added. "It's called the Shelter and it's supposed to be very nice, very clean and kindly—"

"—as insane asylums go," Cade interrupted. Then, with a nasty little smile, he said, "That's our fate in the theater, Mieka. Forty years surrounded by madmen."

Mieka eyed him thoughtfully. "Y'know," he said at last, "you're being a right pain in the ass. You've *been* being a right pain in the ass for a long time, and everybody's tired of it. Write yourself some new lines, why don't you?"

Cade's smile spread fractionally. "I prefer to improvise."

Mieka paid no heed to the pleading look on Derien's face. He'd had enough. Long ago, he'd had enough. Setting down his cup, he snatched up a slice of carrot bread and made for the door. "Rehearsal tomorrow at the Kiral Kellari," he said by way of farewell, and took the stairs three at a time.

Emerging into the thin spring sunshine, he found himself in luck at last: a hire-hack was just pulling up at the building's front door, which meant he wouldn't have to go searching. He signaled the driver with a raised hand, but the man shook his head.

"Hired to return," he said, just as a boy of about ten jumped out and, on seeing Mieka, demanded, "Cayden Silversun?"

"Top floor. What's the worry?"

"There's been an accident. Mistress Windthistle sent me to fetch him at once." He yanked open the front door.

"Wait—*which* Mistress Windthistle?"

But the boy had vanished.

Mieka's mother, his sisters, his wife, Blye—all of them and plenty of others besides were Mistress Windthistle. He dithered in place for a moment, then asked the hack driver, "Where'd you come from?"

"Originally? Ambage Road. In this case, Lord Piercehand's new gallery."

"The woman who hired you—was she little and blond?"

"That she was. Bit of the Goblin about her, mayhap, but nothing to notice outright."

Blye. Something had happened to Jed or Jez. "Cayden!" he shouted. *"Cayden!"*

It took forever before he and Cade and Dery were in the hire-hack driving towards the river. The traffic leading to the bridge was maddening. Even if a gallop had been legal, carts and riders and other hacks were so thick that only a walk was possible—and even so, their progress was in fits and starts. The boy Blye had sent was up top with the driver, yelling, "Make way! Make way!" every so often, which had no effect except to infuriate everyone else, all of them going nowhere in a hurry.

The interior of the hack was silent with the tension of ignorance. Cade had explained tersely that on the walk downstairs he questioned the lad, who knew nothing except that there had been an accident and Mistress Windthistle had sent him with orders to bring Master Silversun.

Finally, with the Gally River in sight, Mieka could stand no more. "Get out," he ordered Cade and Dery. "We'll hire a boat. It can't help but be faster."

Scrambling down the embankment, they ran for a dock. Mieka dug in his pockets for coin, cursing himself for spending so much on those damned peacock feathers, coming up with enough to hire a craft that looked more or less able to hold the three of them plus the boatman. He forestalled the man's attempt to haggle the price by saying, "Double when we get there. Just hurry!"

"Double? Easy enough to say, young sir!" Then he took a closer look at tall, Wizardly Cade and short, Elfen Mieka. "I know your faces from someplace, don't I?"

"They're half of Touchstone," Dery put in. "They're famous and they're rich—please, I promise we'll pay you double if you just get us there quickly!"

"Touchstone." After further scrutiny, during which Mieka strove to look as much like their placards as possible (though, truth be told, there was never any mistaking Cade's nose), the man gestured them into the boat.

Mieka hated boats. By the time they reached the site—a nice plot of land beside the river, nothing but the finest for Lord Rolon Piercehand—he had chewed his lower lip almost raw. Dery leaned forward in the prow, the way a rider leaned into his horse's neck to urge speed. Cade squeezed in beside the boatman, took one of the oars, and rowed white-knuckled. By the time they reached the site, Cade's hair and shirt were damp with the sweat of effort.

A gift to the Kingdom of Albeyn, it was, this new gallery to display a selection of Piercehand's foreign plunder. Castle Eyot wasn't big enough to hold the jumble of wonders and oddities and some genuinely beautiful things collected by His Lordship. On progress a year ago, Princess Miriuzca had professed herself enchanted with the place and very prettily persuaded him to share his haul with the public. The Palace would be lending certain of the Royals' own hoard of paintings and statuary. Whether or not the Princess had also managed to steer some of the contracts for building the place to Windthistle Brothers was a matter of conjecture, but it remained that Jedris and Jezael were doing the wooden parts of the building and Blye would eventually be making the windows.

The foundation and exterior stones were golden yellow, with two curving grand staircases leading up from the street to the main entrance. Scaffolding laced the stone shell together: a few walls, unfinished interior columns, steel support beams. Arches and balconies abounded, some completed and most not. But the most notable feature was a tower, tall and spindly, made of stone and rising two hundred feet into the air. Word had it that when the gallery was finished, the tower would be topped with a solid gold statue brought back from some remote land by one of Piercehand's many ships.

Currently the only decorations were clouds of dust.

"Right," said the boatman. "So where's my double the fare?"

Mieka and Cade scrambled up a few stone steps to
the embankment as Dery snapped, "What you already
have is all you get! My brother did half the work!"

Mieka blinked; for just an instant, the boy sounded
like Lady Jaspiela. In the best possible way, of course.

"Rich!" the boatman sneered. "Famous! Rich and famous coggers is what you are! Come back here and
honor your word!"

They left the boatman cursing unoriginally behind
them. The crowd was all streetside: a mass of craned
necks, like astonished cats peering out a window. Mieka
got a good grip on Cade's elbow and an even better one
on Dery's, and forced a route through the tangle. As he
pushed and shoved, Mieka heard snatches of conversation, none of it pleasant. Speculation about how the
scaffolding collapsed; contention that the scaffolding
was intact but the stonework had crumbled; assurances
that both wood and stone were to blame; estimates of
how many had died. He wished he had Cade's height,
because then he might have seen the two red heads that
were his only concern.

Suddenly they were at the Human barrier that kept the
crowd from pressing forward. Not constables, but Lord
Piercehand's own liveried guards, dozens of them link-
ing arms and looking grim. Mieka confronted the one
directly in his path.

"I'm Mieka Windthistle—"

"Good for you."

"But my brothers are—"

"Nobody gets in. Not until the physickers arrive."

"They're not here yet?" Cade demanded. "All these
people, and not a single—?"

"Some ugly old Trollwife is tending the injured,
that's all. Stand back."

"Cayden!"

It was Blye, dusty and frantic, running through the
maze of stacked stone and cut boards. Cade tried to
push through. The guardsman snarled. Cade snarled

right back. A brief tussle ensued, during which Derien ducked down and darted between guards. Mieka tried to follow, and got a knee in the ribs. As he doubled over, Cade's snarl turned to a roar.

"Stop it!" Blye shouted. "I'm Mistress Windthistle and these are my brothers! Let them by! Damn it, let them by!"

In the end, it was not a raised voice or angry words that got them through. It was Hadden Windthistle, in a calm, soft tone, saying, "Gentlemen, would you allow these young men through? Much beholden to you."

A sliver of space was made. They slipped through. Mieka looked in wonderment at his father and asked, "How'd you do that?"

Hadden only shook his head. But as they jogged towards the building, Cade leaned down and whispered, "Didn't you see that guard's face? Your father magicked him!"